THE POISON PEN LETTERS

FIONA WALKER

Boldwood

First published in Great Britain in 2024 by Boldwood Books Ltd.

Copyright © Fiona Walker, 2024

Cover Design by Rachel Lawston

Cover Images: Rachel Lawston

Map Design by Fiona Walker

The moral right of Fiona Walker to be identified as the author of this work has been asserted in accordance with the Copyright, Designs and Patents Act 1988.

Every effort has been made to obtain the necessary permissions with reference to copyright material, both illustrative and quoted. We apologise for any omissions in this respect and will be pleased to make the appropriate acknowledgements in any future edition.

A CIP catalogue record for this book is available from the British Library.

Paperback ISBN 978-1-83561-935-3

Large Print ISBN 978-1-83561-936-0

Hardback ISBN 978-1-83561-934-6

Ebook ISBN 978-1-83561-937-7

Kindle ISBN 978-1-83561-938-4

Audio CD ISBN 978-1-83561-929-2

MP3 CD ISBN 978-1-83561-930-8

Digital audio download ISBN 978-1-83561-931-5

This book is printed on certified sustainable paper. Boldwood Books is dedicated to putting sustainability at the heart of our business. For more information please visit https://www.boldwoodbooks.com/about-us/sustainability/

Boldwood Books Ltd, 23 Bowerdean Street, London, SW6 3TN
www.boldwoodbooks.com

For my fairy godmother, Harriet, with much love.

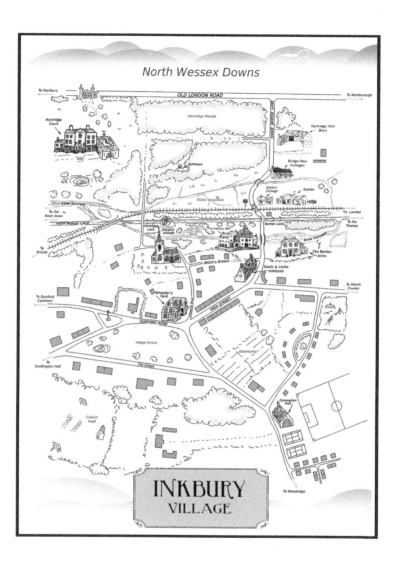

North Wessex Downs

To Marlbury

OLD LONDON ROAD

To Newborough

THREE BRIDGE LANE

Hartridge Woods

Hartridge Court

Hartridge Holt Barn

Bridge Pew Cottages

Icehouse

Station Cottage

Station

Water meadows

River Dunnell

To the River Avon

NORTH WESSEX CANAL

To London

To the Thames

Barton Locks

Inkbury Mill

River Dunnell

To Bristol

Hartridge Lock

Derelict Cottage

The Barton Arms

Witch's Broom

Davis & Locke Antiques

To Marsh Combe

Wheeler's Yard

To Dunford Common

HIGH STREET

CLIFFORD ROAD

Village Green

Allotments

To Godlington Hall

The Green

Coronation Hall

Cricket Field

INKBURY
VILLAGE

To Woodridge

1

JUNO

'It's seven fifteen and you're listening to Smiley Face Radio, for happy people who love happy tunes. And heeeeeeeeeeeeeeere's the Boo Radleys!'

Juno opened her eyes to find Kevin Bacon snuggling into the nape of her neck. Low golden light was pouring through the casement windows of her little attic apartment onto them both.

'Beautiful morning!' she agreed with the Boos.

Spilling sleepily out of bed, Juno and Kevin padded into the reception room together and through to the open-plan kitchen, where she filled the kettle while he stretched extravagantly, handsome head low and pert bottom high in the air. He then settled neatly by his bowl to crunch his specialist dry food for veteran cats.

Black and white epicurean mouser Kevin had come with the accommodation Juno was renting, while she searched for somewhere to buy locally. In a cobbled courtyard tucked off Inkbury's Church Lane, it formed part of a cluster of converted buildings housing artisan village-centre businesses. Her little flat was above a vintage bric-a-brac shop, currently closed while its owner took a sabbatical.

Outside in Wheeler's Yard, the neighbouring florist was taking her morning delivery; boxes of roses, lilies and zinnias for brides to carry, coffins to bear and old romantics to thrust into the arms of lovers.

Sighing wistfully at the idea, Juno perched at the breakfast bar with her mug of tea and phone to check messages, many arriving late last night from New York where she'd previously lived for over twenty years, familiar names striping her screen. Old friends, colleagues from the comedy scene, her late husband's family, all eager to know how she was settling in: *Have you found a job; have you found a man; have you found any more dead bodies, Miss Marple?*

She scrolled on. Grown-up son Eric – up all night competing in a Pacific time eSports gaming tournament from his Oxfordshire houseboat – had shared an early-hours screenshot of his high score. In the past few minutes, Juno's elderly mother Judy had sent a selfie to the family chat group of her and fiancé Dennis enjoying a champagne breakfast in their penthouse balcony hot tub in nearby retirement village, Godlington.

Juno loved living closer to family, but she did sometimes question the need given they all communicated online.

As did the village. There was a different group reminder about that afternoon's Clubbercise class in the Church Hall, and a voice note from landlord Mil about the pub quiz, his lovely Wexshire accent at its deepest and creamiest: 'Need you tonight, gorgeous!'

She replied to him first:

Try to stop me!

Juno adored being needed. Being needed was her *raison d'etre*.

Competitive as her son, she also loved quizzes, grateful for her team.

The Merde Squad were reuniting!

The others didn't like her calling it that, she reminded herself. They were the Village Detectives, they had agreed. When poor handsome Si Locke had died in her arms before he could finish gasping the word 'murder', it had brought the four of them together, united in finding his killer. Cool, clever Phoebe 'Freddy' Fredericks and her jet-setting filmmaker husband Felix Sylvian came as a double act, the *Hart to Hart* of Wexshire; nobly battered ex-rugby pro landlord Mil Winterbourne, who knew everyone locally, provided the brawn and banter; Juno liked to think of herself as the bubbly, Britpop-loving action girl, with a knack for uncovering secrets and a photographic memory for *Seinfeld* episodes.

She checked whether writer Phoebe had read any of the three reminders she'd sent so far about The Barton Arms Brainteaser. The grey ticks suggested she was on airplane mode as usual. Juno sent another just in case, before starting to compose emoji-loaded replies to far-flung friends.

> Still looking for my metier and my man, but loving village life…

Juno did indeed love busy, pretty Inkbury, which spanned a chalk stream, canal and railway in a picturesque dip of the North Wessex Downs. Yet moving back to England after two sociable decades in New York had come as a huge culture shock, overlaid by widowhood's long shadow. The news that Eric would soon make her a grandmother added another shockwave. Then there was the very real prospect of Juno being orphaned by her mother and Dennis's wild partying at Godlington Hall. Both Eric and

Judy needed Juno less than she'd hoped. She missed her Brooklyn friends, husband's family and many interlinking social circles in New York.

Nor was the job hunt going well. A natural socialiser, Juno had been working hard on building up local contacts since arriving in the village. The trouble was she wasn't qualified for much. Being a woman over fifty whose on-off career in comedy had died onstage years ago didn't offer up many transferable skills.

In her fantasies, Juno really would set up her own detective agency; herself as its wise-cracking, glamour-puss chief sleuth with a gut instinct for rooting out fraudsters, conmen and thieves. Pulling a corpse out of the pretty River Dunnett a few days after she'd arrived had given her unrealistic work expectations, she suspected. No matter that she and clever Phoebe had tracked down the killer with intrepid tenacity, a vocational degree or business experience would serve her far better. And no more dead bodies, she reminded herself, swigging her tea. A stolen diamond maybe, or a dognapping.

She looked up as Kevin sprang up on the windowsill to watch the pied wagtails on the opposite roof, black tail flicking, a low chirrup in his throat. His was a murderer's impulse, devoid of self-doubt.

Juno was more of a dog person, waggy-tailed and good at following her nose. She also worried that for middle-aged single women in a small, old-fashioned English village, there was an uncomfortably thin line between cougar and crazy cat lady. She needed positive, proactive PR.

After showering and dressing in her customary bright colours, she tucked her laptop under her arm and let herself out through the shuttered shop below, intent on occupying a table at Inkbury's overpriced deli with a coffee, pastries and LinkedIn.

In Wheeler's Yard, the village's stout, round-faced postman Craig was standing outside the closed beautician's salon, ringing the doorbell to the flat above.

'She's away,' Juno told him, aware the owner was on a midweek birthday minibreak with her perfectly waxed boyfriend. 'She'll be back at lunchtime. Do you need me to sign for something for her?'

'That won't be necessary, madam!' he beamed over his shoulder.

Talkative, over-eager Craig the postie had been delivering her mail for weeks, but Juno was still struggling to make an impression, his jobsworth manner a rolling morning roadshow of self-interest in shorts and a red van.

'It's honestly no trouble,' she said, reminding him, 'I'm Juno from next door.'

'Between you and me, it's not related to my Royal Mail operational duties.' He stepped closer, voice lowered. 'I need to change the time of an appointment for a facial pamper package.'

'No wonder you have such lovely smooth skin!'

'It's for my mum.' He looked perplexed. 'I gave her a voucher for her birthday a year ago and can you believe she still hasn't got around to using it yet? It's about to expire. I mean, would you do that to your loving son?'

'Especially not with these pores!' Juno exclaimed, secretly longing for the day Eric gave her a beauty treatment voucher.

Craig was explaining that he'd booked his mum the pamper package appointment himself in the end. 'I said to her: "Mother, if you love me then you *must* have a hydra-facial and a peel on the 30th, no excuses!" Only now I have to change it to 11 a.m. because she's having the patio pressure-washed first thing. I have your post, Mrs Mulligan,' he beamed at her, fishing into his bag.

'Just call me Juno, please!' She loved the chatty companionability of village life, where friendly oddballs like Craig – and herself – thrived.

'Lots more stuff here forwarded from the USA.' He was handing envelopes over one at a time. 'Also Custom and Excise, HMRC, something from Plus Size Shapewear. And this looks like a mammogram screening invitation, if I'm not mistaken. Mum got hers through this week. They do it in a mobile trailer in Morrison's car park. Very convenient for you ladies. And this last one is from your solicitors. Not in trouble with the law, I hope?'

'Thanks.' Juno plucked it from his fingers, feeling less chatty.

She took it all to open in the deli, her forwarded mail belonging to a past life: seasonal Broadway theatre schedules, show invitations, newsletters and circulars.

Waiting for her laptop to boot up, Juno watched a group of dog walkers pass the windows in the direction of the church.

She recognised a few of them: the patron of the village book club with her yellow Labrador, a pub regular with a Staffy, the elderly couple at the back whose smiling spaniel kept stopping to sniff and mark everything.

Yes, Juno was definitely a dog person, she decided. She might ask Phoebe if she could borrow her terriers to join the Inkbury Dog Walkers some days. They seldom cocked a leg beyond the Hartridge boundary, poor things. Then again, it helped to have several hundred rolling acres of your own in which to play.

She messaged again, glaring at the one grey tick:

> We need you tonight!

Phoebe rarely ventured online since being publicly 'cancelled' and losing her weekly newspaper column four years earlier. She didn't like talking about the events surrounding it, which had happened when Juno was living in the States. All she knew was that it had involved a relentless hate campaign on social media.

Not for the first time, she gave in to temptation and googled the story. A *Yorkshire Post* headline caught her eye in the results.

Columnist Questioned by Police About Suspected Suicide

She quickly closed the tab, feeling horribly guilty and slightly sick.

Bolstering herself with a mouthful of cinnamon swirl, Juno opened the solicitor's envelope instead, reading a long – and no doubt expensive – letter about paternal rights.

Phoebe

'I say, you're a frightful bore, Annie. Wearing pearls down one's back is de rigueur at the Café de Paris these days, so why not at the Dingledale Ladies' Reading Circle?'

'But, Lady Dee, what about the Library Steps Ripper?'

'Isn't that the point? They're all back-stabbers and we need to flush the murderer out. Be a poppet and knot mine at the end.'

'As you wish, milady.'

A noise from outside made Phoebe look up from her laptop, but it was just a magpie chattering on the coach house roof, not wheels crossing the cobbles below.

She had been avoiding Craig the postie since he'd elected himself her literary advisor. He was more of a fantasy fiction fan, he'd explained, but he'd made an exception for her crime capers

seeing as she was a local author. Also because he'd bought a job
lot of her Dorothy De'Ath murder mysteries at the fete for 'a quid
the lot!'

Her doorstep critic was now always eager to impart his well-
meaning opinions – 'guessed the killer from page one!' – and
nitpick errors – 'I think you'll find a two-four-zero locomotive,
not a two-six-two, pulled the Orient Express circa 1924.'

She'd started dreading the sound of his van, listening out for
it like a dog from mid-morning, which was more than her terriers
were doing, both flat out in a blade of sunlight cast from the high
window, an inadvertent kitchen sundial warning Phoebe that
Craig's arrival was imminent.

Theirs was a long drive with a secure letter box at the road
end, but he'd waved away any suggestion that there was no need
to bring the post to the house. He insisted on 'going above and
beyond!' like a pink-cheeked Buzz Lightyear in black cargo
shorts and Royal Mail gilet. And he was as reliable as
clockwork.

Nevertheless, today Phoebe jumped at the sound of a fist
hammering cheerily against the door. The dogs leapt into
delayed action, skittering and snarling along the back corridor,
claws against flagstones, fighting to be the one to thrust their
head through the cat flap.

'Please desist from opening this until the dogs are safely
contained!' Craig ordered from the far side, having last week
recounted – at length – how a recent incident with a miniature
schnauzer at Meadowview Cottage had escalated his cynophobia.

Shutting the yapping pair in the boot room, Phoebe reluctantly went to open the door. Why hadn't she heard his van?

Craig's eager face greeted her, so perfectly shaven and egg-
like it resembled a balloon with features drawn in marker pen.
'Good morrow, Mrs Sylvian, or is it Ms Fredericks, or should I say

Miss De'Ath?' He pronounced the final nom de plume with relish.

'Do please call me Phoebe,' she reminded him. 'I didn't hear your van.'

'Been issued with an electric vehicle!' He indicated it proudly, shiny and red as a new toy.

'Lovely. Very... quiet.'

'Indeed!' He stepped closer, fleece crackling with static as he pulled out her post from behind his back. 'Now brace yourself, lucky madam, because I have a stiffy for you!'

'I'm sorry?'

'That's what Lady Penelope calls them,' he beamed, brandishing a luxurious woven cream envelope. 'Gets a *lot* of stiffies, does Lady P.'

'So I've heard.' Phoebe smiled back, silently impressed he could say it without innuendo, while her gutter-press mind was already nudge-nudge wink-winking.

Phoebe's socialite near-neighbour Penelope Fermoy – who, despite Craig's *Thunderbirds* reference, was no lady – was an old-school party animal. Nicknamed Bad Penny in her It Girl heyday when she'd always turned up late and rarely behaved, her barn conversion's mantel was still tomb-stoned with ultra-thick embossed invitations. By contrast, Phoebe and husband Felix used the rare 'stiffies' they received to prop up wonky chair legs. Antisocial Phoebe, who dreaded premieres, private views, sports fixtures and weddings with equal measure, hoped today's would be easily turned down.

But when she reached out for the envelope, Craig whipped it away, pulling out a small, familiar paperback from behind it. 'First, I've got some more corrections for you, Dorothy De'Ath.'

Her heart sank. 'You really shouldn't have gone to all the trouble.'

'It's the least I can do to spare you disappointed readers!'

Craig's 'edits' had started with Dorothy De'Ath's debut, *Blood in the Village Pond*. Written in haste while Phoebe had still been learning the ropes as an indie author, she'd paid an agency to proofread it, badly as it turned out. Although nobody bar Craig had ever complained about the number of typos, she'd been shocked and grateful when he'd presented her with a helpfully marked-up copy. Ignoring Felix's advice to do nothing – he cheerfully claimed the extensive IMDB 'goofs' list for each of his movies simply added to their charm – she'd uploaded the corrections and added Craig's name to the acknowledgements by way of thanks. After that, there was no going back.

Now Craig thought they were a 'team'. He was already up to Book Four in the series, *Blood at the Altar*.

'If you could let me have this back in a week, I'll pass it on to Mum to read while she's waiting for the mobile library to get more cowboy romances.' He thrust the book towards her. 'I took the liberty of colour coding my corrections – green for spelling, red for repetition, blue for grammar; there's a key at the front, see?'

'How helpful.' Phoebe opened it obligingly, spotting her handwritten dedication on the title page opposite Craig's colourful guide. Like the others he'd already corrected, this copy was from a signed set she'd been asked to contribute as a raffle prize to the Inkbury Book Group. A week later, the postie had found the lot in a box of assorted paperbacks at the fete's book jumble stall.

It had done nothing to improve Phoebe's unsociable view of the village.

'New novel coming on well?' he asked, still withholding her 'stiffy'.

'Gloriously.'

She was in the early plotting stages of a Dorothy De'Ath mystery in which the members of a ladies' reading circle were murdered one by one in the style of famous crime novels, she told him.

'Just let me know when you want me to cast my eye over it.' He finally relinquished the thick cream envelope.

Expecting it to be addressed to Mr and Mrs Felix Sylvian, Phoebe was surprised to find hers the only name written in blue fountain pen above the embarrassingly grand *Hartridge Court, Inkbury, Wexshire.*

'Are you going to see what it's for?' Craig was hovering, pink balloon face quivering, anticipating at least a royal wedding invitation.

'I am. That's my phone ringing, excuse me.' Phoebe turned inside and shut the door behind her before returning to the kitchen to liberate the yapping dogs. She glanced at her silent mobile, muted on 'do not disturb'. Abandoning the envelope and book on the table, she picked it up guiltily.

Predictably, there were several messages from Juno, eager to recruit her friend to her pub quiz team:

> I'm determined to get you out more, Freddy!
> You're way too much fun to hide at home. And
> too good at History and Literature. Also at
> making me laugh. Drinking. Encouraging Felix to
> introduce me to eligible menfolk. Being you.

Phoebe sent a heart emoji, grateful for the boost. Juno was right; she must make the effort to finally let down the social drawbridge. It was over two years since she'd moved here, after all, gratefully retreating behind Hartridge Court's high walls after a tough period that she and the family called the Stormy Cs; one of those her humiliating cancellation. The fast-moving media circus that had fired her from its cannon had already forgotten, if not forgiven, her. By Inkbury standards, meanwhile, she remained a newcomer, the elusive crime writer in the big house, inventing stiffs and receiving stiffies.

Picking up the envelope, she went in search of a knife to slice it open.

Inside – thick as a hardback cover and edged in gold and black – was a funeral notice, she realised sadly. The service was in a fortnight's time.

Then her sigh turned into a sharp intake of breath as she read:

The Fredericks family regrets to announce the death of Phoebe...

It was *her own* funeral notice.

The date of her death was tomorrow.

2

JUNO

'See you next week, ladies!' Juno hurried out of Inkbury Baptist Hall, ignoring her sweaty pits, aching muscles and chub rub as she belted along the village High Street.

The Clubbercise class had been a frankly sadistic hour and a half long. She'd been a fool for imagining she'd have time to go home, shower and knock back a bolstering wine before meeting the others for the quiz in The Barton Arms. She was already late, breathless and less than alluring in damp Lycra.

But Juno wouldn't miss this for the world. The Merde Squad would be united again!

'Village Detectives,' she reminded herself under her breath as she panted around the corner onto Three Bridge Lane.

Tonight, they'd need all their wits about them.

'Where have you been?' Mil pounced on her as soon as she came through the door. 'We've all been waiting for you. Loving the Olivia Newton John drip, by the way.'

Ex-international flanker Mil was so broad and burly, he always looked as though he was wearing a suit of armour under his clothes, but his battered and dimpled smile was the warmest in Wexshire. Although he was at least a decade too young for her, Juno had a secret crush.

'Getting match fit,' she panted, striking a pose, never happier than when fantasising herself Scully to his Mulder. 'Mine's a large dry white. Where are we sitting?'

'Change of plan, gorgeous. You're compèring.'

'But what about the Village Detectives?' She looked around, spotting Felix's silver-streaked blond pelt amid a rowdy gang of village sportsmen. 'Where's Freddy?' She remembered that Phoebe wasn't keen on being called that either, at least not in public. 'We're a team!'

'She's not here. You're the only one I can ask to be quiz host, Juno,' Mil pleaded, putting a big, muscle-bouldered arm around her shoulders. 'You're such a pro behind a mic, and I'm needed at the bar. Please? Free wine and snacks all night, and a sticky toffee pudding at half time.'

Staring up into his cheeky gaze, Juno found herself momentarily mesmerised by it – he'd lost an eye in a rugby accident and she could never remember which was the prosthetic one – wishing she had the willpower to say no. 'With extra sticky toffee sauce?'

'I'll announce you!'

Before she could protest more, Juno was clutching a mic in one hand and a *Big Book of Pub Quiz Questions* in the other, beaming at tables crammed with competitive villagers. 'Good evening, friends and neighbours! I'm Juno Mulligan.' Adept at emcee patter from her years struggling to make it as a stand-up and comedy songstress, Juno clicked into auto mode: 'Last time I was at a bar quiz, it was back in Brooklyn. Question One was: "You lookin' at me?"'

Polite titters greeted her de Niro impression. They weren't big on ballsy women in conservative Inkbury. Or misquotes.

'You talkin' to me!' a voice shouted back.

'I am!' Juno agreed, then realised her mistake. That was what Travis had repeatedly asked his own reflection in *Taxi Driver*. She raised her glass. 'Right answer!'

She'd been corrected by village postie, Craig, who was nursing a pint of Coke at a back table. Gone was the ingratiating camaraderie that had greeted her this morning. Unsmiling, shiny faced and pen poised, he was flanked by two older female team-mates, the trio all sporting matching T-shirts emblazoned *First-Class Minds*. They clearly took their quizzing seriously.

Juno hurried on: 'And let me assure everyone here that we offer the warmest of welcomes to The Barton Arms Brainteaser, where we don't take "no" for an answer... unless it's to name the first Bond movie villain...'

Grateful for the good-natured groans, she asked each table in turn for their quiz team name, perking up to realise how many participants she knew personally. Juno might have lived in Inkbury less than two months, but she was a joiner and a befriender. Her stage banter still owed more to frenzied stints in New York comedy clubs than her dry-witted British upbringing, but they forgave her chutzpah when they were on first-name terms, as with the village GP:

'The Wise Quacks? I dated a quack once, Phil, but he billed me for feeling down.'

With each punchline, she made a beatbox cymbals sound. Beyond the local medics, the Dawn Till Dusk team were all village shopkeepers: Juno's neighbouring florist, deli owner and beautician fresh from her midweek minibreak, along with the antiques dealer whose partner's mysterious death the Village Detectives had helped solve. Beyond them, the Burn Nerds were made up of elderly male members of the Model Railway Club, one of whom – unsurprisingly called Bernard – she'd spoken to

recently about renting an allotment. It was Bernard and his wife
she'd seen pass with their smiling spaniel among the village dog
walkers that morning, typical of the many Inkbury old timers
who seemed to belong to everything.

To Juno's left was a quintet of women from the Inkbury Book
Group, reigned over by academic glamour-puss Gigi and her
posh, boozy sidekick Penny. The long-established literary group's
reputation was fearsome, although when Juno had joined last
month, she'd found copies of the novel under discussion merely
served as drinks coasters, the evening a thinly veiled excuse for
wine-fuelled character assassination. Tonight, they were
competing under the name 'Well-Thumbed Elite', which she
worried might be open to interpretation.

Flame-haired Gigi was casting covert looks at Felix Sylvian,
she noticed. Dreamily boho-politan in board shorts and a faded
blue sweater that matched his naughty eyes, Phoebe's husband's
occasional appearance at village events between making movies
inevitably triggered girlish delight amongst women old enough
to know better. To her shame, Juno was one of them. He was with
the Overs and Outs quiz team, mostly Inkbury Cricket Club
veterans, alongside whom Felix appeared positively youthful, his
hair still more blond than grey and sun-bleached from yet
another exotic film shoot.

'You can come over and take me out anytime, honey.' She
made him laugh with her Mae West schtick, earning a black look
from Gigi's Elite.

'Okay, let's get on with the quiz!' she hurried on. 'Answer
sheets at the ready? Round One, General Knowledge! What
number is a baker's dozen?'

The *Big Book of Pub Quiz Questions* set a low bar. Reading out
the questions with as much Clive Myrie brio as she could muster
through the opening two rounds, Juno let her mind wander back

to the Village Detectives and how valued being a part of uncovering Si's killer had made her feel, particularly by Phoebe.

Juno hoped her friend was okay. They'd barely spoken all week, which wasn't unusual because Phoebe was often incommunicado when writing. But Juno had an ongoing, mildly paranoid worry that she'd over-egged their friendship since arriving in the village. She felt bad about snooping online. She'd also stored a *lot* of stuff in Phoebe's and Felix's barns.

She needed a bigger, more permanent home, but her heart was unrealistically fixed on a cliché thatched cottage with roses around the door, in the same way it was set on a sexy dreamboat with whom to share it, an unfashionably alpha stud with ruffly hair, furled brows and a hint of ageing New Romantic meets Marlboro Man.

'Here you go, gorgeous.'

'Thank you, handsome.' She blew a kiss at Mil as he brought her another big glass of white, and then announced, 'Round Three: Arts and Culture!'

The quizzers greeted the next question – a ridiculously easy literary poser – with amused confusion.

'I'll repeat that.' Juno glanced down at the *Big Book of Pub Quiz Questions* to read it out again. 'The hero of which gothic romance by Daphne du Maurier is the wealthy and charismatic Maximilian Winterbourne?' She fanned herself with the book and added a 'phwoar!' for comic effect.

Honks of laughter went up from the Well-Thumbed Elite.

Delighted that her audience appreciated this, Juno added an aside: 'Spoiler alert, ladies – he killed his first wife. Still, I wouldn't say no, would you?'

One of the Overs and Outs called, 'You're in there, Mil, mate!'

Then Juno spotted her mistake. '*De Winter*! Maximilian de Winter.'

The menopause brain fog had struck again.

She didn't dare look at their landlord, and her secret crush, whose name above the door read *Mr Maximilian Winterbourne, Licensed to Sell Ales, Wine and Spirits.* Easy mistake, she told herself, swigging more wine. Not remotely Freudian.

Some regulars were still guffawing.

'Very poor judge of housekeeper. Also needed better home insurance,' she deflected, finding herself again picturing Phoebe alone in the big, isolated house beyond the woods and hoping she was okay.

* * *

Phoebe

Which two cities provide the setting for Dickens' A Tale of Two Cities?

Given Phoebe's reluctance to tell her husband about the creepy invitation she'd received to her own funeral, it came as little surprise that Felix's plea for her to switch her phone off airplane mode that evening had nothing to do with her personal safety.

In which century did Leonardo da Vinci paint The Last Supper?

She replied:

Stop cheating.

He surely knew that answer; he'd once made a film about da Vinci's wily, seductive assistant Salai. Perhaps Felix *was* checking up on her after all, she realised. He always knew when something was up.

How many lines are there in a sonnet?

They'd exchanged more than fourteen lines of cross words about her not joining him tonight, but she couldn't face a crowd, preferring to stay home with the terriers and her black dog. Felix could always sense her mood darkening, like a cat anticipating a storm. She'd been so much better lately, he'd pointed out. And she had, massively. But that could be undermined in an instant.

'When in disgrace with fortune and men's eyes,' she quoted to the terriers, 'I all alone beweep my outcast state.'

Whereas Shakespeare had just needed to think of his lover to be liberated from his gloom, hers was trying to lift her with trivia.

How many time zones are there in Russia?

Phoebe ignored him. Then she googled it because she didn't know. Eleven.

What country has the most islands in the world?

'Sweden,' she told the terriers.

Where is the lowest place on earth?

'The Dead Sea.'
The terriers cocked their heads with interest.

Who wrote To the Lighthouse?

Phoebe flinched.

A moment later he must have remembered the answer:

Sorry!

Just as she was about to switch her phone to airplane mode after all, another message arrived:

Bloody love you. Shall I come back?

Phoebe typed *Bloody love you too*, then deleted it and sent:

Stay and win. And stop bloody cheating.

Now she turned on airplane mode.

Would he read the double meaning, she wondered?

Probably not. Felix was mercurial and instinctive, not remotely reflective. It was what she'd always loved about him. She did enough over-thinking for them both. Her depressive episodes always made her paranoid.

She got up and paced around the big kitchen. Unable to settle, she found herself wishing she'd gone to The Barton Arms Brainteaser after all, her brain currently in dire need of teasing out of its vicious circles.

She returned to the table to pull out the funeral invitation, then stopped herself, slamming the drawer shut so quickly that she caught her ring finger painfully, snagging the setting of her engagement diamond.

Phoebe had no intention of dying tomorrow, but for insurance she wasn't about to spend her last night on earth naming capital cities, eighties hits and US presidents whose surnames began with C. She would, however, like to spend some of it with the one she loved most.

She turned her phone off airplane mode.

> Bloody love you too. Don't be late.

Switching on the TV, she surfed her way up to a channel screening old movie repeats, grateful to sink into *Sherlock Holmes and the Deadly Necklace*.

* * *

Juno

'Right, folks, please pass your quiz answer sheets onto the neighbouring table ready for marking when I read out the answers! Before that, there will be a very short break for you to refill your glasses and empty your bladders, although the management politely requests that you don't do both at the same time!'

Juno smiled self-consciously at Mil, who gave a thumbs up from the bar, to which the pub quizzers were already flocking.

She was still mortified about her Maximilian de Winter gaffe. Having focused hard on reading out each question accurately for the remainder of the rounds, she needed something sweet and sinful, and fast.

While the teams swapped sheets, she refuelled with sticky toffee as gratefully as a tennis pro scoffing a banana between sets, waiting for all The Barton Arms Brainteaser participants to retake their seats. She then read out the answers in a sugar rush, getting ever faster because she also now needed the loo quite badly herself.

'Please double check the scores and I'll be right back to announce the winners after this break!' she told them, galloping to the ladies' loo.

While she was peeing, she heard others coming in behind her. One low voice muttered furiously about the standard of the questions, then was hushed by another, the door to the adjacent cubicle swinging closed and locking, a cloud of Georgio Armani Sí drifting across to Juno.

When she emerged, Penny Fermoy from the Well-Thumbed Elite was reapplying her lipstick by the mirror, cool gaze flicking up to catch Juno's, her big-toothed humourless smile fixed like a gumshield. 'That took jolly big balls.'

'Thanks.' Juno was grateful for any praise, however faint.

'Is that outfit a stage costume, like Victoria Wood?'

'I came straight from an exercise class.'

Penny shrieked with laughter as though this was a punchline. '*Hilaire*! I gather you used to perform for a living. Tell me, do you have a manager or agent?'

'I'm not looking for representation.'

'But I am, you see. Reality TV, personal appearances, chat shows, that sort of thing. I was rather well known once myself.' Stepping closer, Penny lurched slideways slightly, and Juno realised that she was quite drunk. 'Thought you might recommend somebody? Mine's a leech.'

'I'm afraid I've been out of the business too long, especially here in the UK.'

'Told you she'd be no help!' boomed the voice behind the cloud of Sí in the second cubicle. 'Just like that stuck-up cow from Hartridge Court.'

'Phoebe's lovely!' Juno bristled, uncertain who the voice belonged to. It surely couldn't be Penny's book club crony Gigi? She'd thought better of an academic.

But the woman who bustled out was wearing a *First-Class Minds* T-shirt, shooting Juno a withering look from beneath a burgundy perm as she elbowed her aside to get at a hand basin. 'That's your opinion, love. She's stuck up, if you ask me. When Penny here lived up at the big house, there were always parties, and the village was welcomed along, ain't that right, Penny?'

'Happy days!' With a gumshield grimace, Penny headed into a cubicle.

'Some of us prefer the questions without the back chat, by the way.' Burgundy Perm caught Juno's eye in the mirror. 'Just so's you know. That last fella was way better.'

'Thanks for the feedback!' Juno hurriedly returned to announce the Brainteaser victors, feeling quashed.

Mil was too flat out at the bar to adjudicate, so the marked answer sheets had been gathered up by one of the elderly Burn Nerds, a stooped figure in checked shirt and cords who carried them across to her as she returned to her quiz-master corner: 'Close-run match.'

'Who won?' she asked, gratefully falling on the third glass of wine that was ready waiting for her. Or was it her fourth?

'You're supposed to tell *us* that, my dear.' He lowered his voice, leaning closer. 'We're all frightful cheats. Most of these will be mismarked.' As he offered her the quiz sheets, he raised two bushy white eyebrows sagely.

'Would you mind double-checking them with me?' Juno pleaded.

The eyebrows tilted in amusement. 'Do you trust me to?'

The fact he was carrying a beer tankard in his other hand told Juno this man had gravitas – only well-respected elders of the village were granted the right to hook their pewterware above the taps in The Barton Arms – and she needed authority onside.

'Please.'

'I don't think we've met.' Placing the answer sheets and tankard on the table, he shook her hand: 'Alan Bickerstaff. Veg grower, railway modeller and astronomer. Here with the Burn Nerds. My old friends Bernie and Ree said you'd bring some fun to the occasion, and you have.' Alan sat down at the table to beam at her over the quiz sheets. 'Happy to help.'

Settling opposite him gratefully, Juno knew you could always trust a man of self-effacing charm and expressively hirsute eyebrows. 'Have you lived in the village long?'

'You're the detective, you tell me.' He plucked a set of wire-rimmed reading glasses from his chest pocket to start double-checking answers.

'Word's got out, then.' She was happier still.

'Very few secrets in this village amongst the widowed, especially ones recently bereaved.' Alan looked up over his spectacle rims, then glanced pointedly across to the antique dealer's table. 'Your merriness is most welcome in our ranks. I gather you lost your husband a few years ago?'

Juno stopped herself cracking a joke about widowhood and her merry men, aware that she often over-egged her jollity to compensate for her discomfort when the subject was raised. Losing Jay was something she struggled to talk about with her closest friends, let alone kindly strangers in pubs.

'Yes.' She forced a smile. Swigging more wine, she let him check the sheets uninterrupted, wishing again that Phoebe was here, making her feel young, edgy and eligible again, not an ageing Widow Twankey comedy turn in bright Lycra.

'Here you go.' Alan handed her the scores, adding in an undertone, 'The book coven over there had predictably under-marked their rivals.' He indicated Gigi and her Well-Thumbed Elite with a discreet nod. 'But I've corrected that.'

Waving away her profuse thanks, he took his tankard to be

refilled while Juno turned on her mic to announce the leader-board in reverse order. First-Class Minds and Wise Quacks shared fifth place; the Burn Nerds came in third, with Well-Thumbed runners up.

The winners were shopkeepers Dawn Till Dusk, their victory down to Oscar, the village antique dealer, and his encyclopaedic knowledge of everything from eighties ska music to Crufts winners, ancient Greek philosophers to the volume of the Great Lakes. Juno marvelled at clever people like him and Phoebe; both were fact squirrels, whereas she still couldn't remember her new postcode.

Gigi, clearly miffed that her waspish elite had lost out on top honours by just one point, paused by Juno's table on her way out, one thin red brow aloft, grumbling that the Arts and Literature section had been too populist. 'Your para-praxis during the *Rebecca* question was utter genius, by the way.'

'*Geni*oush, darling!' horse-toothed Penny parroted, words slurring. Icy blue eyes half-focused, her sneer was even more fixed, although Juno suspected the clamorous blonde had no more idea what a parapraxis was than Juno herself.

'How are you finding *Possession*, Juno?' asked Gigi.

Juno took a beat to realise she was talking about the Inkbury Book Group's next title.

'Marvellous!' She made a mental note to download it to her Kindle and look at an online study guide before next week's meeting.

'I loved it,' Penny drawled, eyeing Felix as he loped past to the bar.

'Watching the film doesn't count,' snapped Gigi, eyeing him too. 'Byatt's classic is a literary exploration of desire, sexual iden-tity and narrative voracity.'

'No plot spoilers,' Juno warned, adding, 'I've told Phoebe that this time she *must* come.'

'Really?' asked Gigi coolly.

'Must she?' drawled Penny.

'Oh, she must!' cried an eager voice, and Juno turned to find the book group's patron Beth Trascott panting up eagerly, a sturdy ash blonde in a Sea Salt tunic. Kind-hearted Agatha Christie fan Beth had also been on the Well-Thumbed Elite team. 'Won't that be a treat, ladies, a proper author!'

The others forced sickly smiles.

As soon as Juno had waved them off, she sought out Felix. 'Why wasn't Freddy here? Is she okay?'

'You know what she's like when she's working.' His easy blue-eyed smile was as belly-melting as ever.

Like many women of her generation, Juno's burgeoning teenage hormones, sexual awakening and Athena poster habit had coincided with Felix's brief modelling and acting career. He'd long since moved behind the camera to produce and direct, but she couldn't shake the awkward memory of him gazing down from her bedroom wall, a sulking monochrome archangel. He remained somehow strangely immortal.

This was in direct contrast to his hot-blooded wife, whose brush with mortality made Juno perpetually anxious. The cancer that had once threatened to leave Phoebe and Felix's daughters without a mother was firmly in the family's rearview mirrors, but it didn't stop Juno fretting that workaholic Phoebe needed to put her wellbeing before writing. 'She should eat more, sleep more and take more breaks, don't you think?'

A flinty glint in Felix's smile told her she wasn't alone in worrying. 'Please can you come and tell her that in person?'

'I'll get my coat.' She felt a guilty flutter of pride at the thought of walking back with him to grand Hartridge Court for a nightcap, hoping Gigi and Penny might still be outside to witness it.

'Tomorrow, maybe?' he added with a polite grimace. 'I'm in London all day. She'd love to see you.'

'Yes, of course! Tomorrow! I'm there!'

She recognised another hidden message in his polite smile, the amused bewilderment men reserved for their wives' friends. Jay had been an expert at it. He'd never found hers easy.

'Bloody brilliant, Juno!' Cheering noisily, Mil joined them, carrying a trio of rum shots.

Even more self-consciously blabby, Juno was soon digging herself into another fast-talking hole to explain away her not-at-all-Freudian slip. 'I can't believe I never noticed how similar your name is to Maxim de Winter's. Was your dad a du Maurier fan?'

'Which team were they on? Sounds Belgian, yes?'

To her relief, the gaffe had totally bypassed Mil, but he did have something to say about her score-checking, his voice dropping. 'Stroke of genius penalising Well-Thumbed for undermarking. Cheered our deserving winner up no end.' He nodded towards the Dawn Till Dusk table noisily toasting their victory with a bottle of Pinot, the antique dealer hailed a hero.

'But I didn't—' Juno stopped, looking around for Alan Bickerstaff and his tankard, but he'd gone. 'Yes, I thought that was only fair.'

She caught Felix giving her another bemused look before he glanced at his watch, smiled to himself, muttered, 'Must get back!' and vanished like smoke.

Juno longed for a man who smiled like that at the prospect of rushing home to her. But she knew his and Phoebe's history was as chequered as a chessboard, their marriage a battle of wits, and more challenging than most. She was also aware Felix asked Mil to look out for his wife when he went away.

Unable to stop herself, she asked, 'What do you know about
Phoebe being cancelled, Mil?'

'None of my business,' he told her firmly.

'Absolutely,' she agreed, feeling abashed, quietly vowing not
to google it again.

* * *

Phoebe

Phoebe was grateful when Felix bounded home to Hartridge just
the right side of squiffy – funny, affectionate, cheeringly full of
news and gossip from the pub. His innate capacity for happiness
was always infectious, his prize her laughter.

'Please don't get sad again,' he pleaded, cupping her face and
kissing her cheeks, then her throat, then lips, smiling into her
eyes. 'I can't bear it when you're sad.'

'I won't be sad,' she promised, kissing him back, then quoted:

> *'Haply I think on thee and then my state,*
> *(Like to the lark at break of day arising*
> *from sullen earth) sings hymns at heaven's gate.'*

'You're so sexy when you quote Shakespeare.' Felix leaned
back, all smiles. '*Romeo and Juliet*?'

'Sonnet 29,' she told him. 'Fourteen lines long. But you knew
that.'

'Let's go to bed.' He reached for her hand. 'One line.'

'Spoken by my favourite poet.' She took it and led the way.

Lying in bed later, her middle and little fingers worried at a
new sharp snag on the setting holding her engagement diamond
like a chipped tooth.

Felix folded around her, warm and protective, murmuring, 'I love your larks.'

Phoebe was doubly determined to keep the invitation secret.

* * *

Juno

Home in her temporary new digs, sitting on the reclaimed timber bed left behind by the owner of the closed-down vintage shop, Juno cued her most melancholy Britpop playlist, kicking off with Ash's cover of 'Coming Around Again', reminding her to believe in love, no matter how sad and mundane life got.

It sometimes seemed the more people and places she crammed into hers, the more acutely Juno felt her loneliness now that her grumpy, protective, friend-averse Jay was no longer here.

She felt very alone right now.

Even Kevin Bacon was out on the tiles.

In need of succour, she messaged Eric. Self-contained and idealistic like his father, their only son was currently floating on a canal somewhere near Banbury where he'd taken his tatty house-boat after losing his Oxford moorings. Although Eric viewed his suspension from intelligence training at GCHQ as a minor blip in his James Bond career trajectory, Juno worried his wishful thinking was even more naïve than her own. She also sensed his own unborn child remained an abstract concept to him, the pregnancy a result of an affair with his boss. Eric and the mother weren't together, and most of his focus seemed to be on his stop-gap side-hustle as a rookie international gamer. He sent back a cheerful emoji, no doubt still embroiled in his eSports tournament.

Not yet feeling sufficiently loved, Juno messaged her mother, then worried she might be already tucked up in bed with Dennis and a Philippa Gregory. Calling straight back with the Rolling Stones blaring in the background, Judy apologised for not being able to 'use the confounded little keyboard on the phone screen! Did you get my piccy of the hot tub this morning? We watched the dawn rise. Thank heaven for afternoon siestas!' She was clearly at the lower end of a wine bottle, possibly not their first. 'Are you coming to see us this week, Pusscat? Bring your cossie. Have some brunch in the bistro! They've started to do skinny salads. You can use the exercise suite! Please say yes!'

'I did a fitness class tonight.' Juno found Godlington Hall's luxury spa and high-tech gym intimidating, almost blacking out on the treadmill last time because she'd mis-set its speed to sprint. 'But I'll pop in at the weekend.'

'We'd love that! Just ring ahead first – we might be in bed again. Need to make sure we have our clothes on this time, eh, Doobee?'

Hearing Dennis growling close to the receiver and making 'mwa mwa' kissing noises, Juno hurriedly rang off.

If she found her son's lack of connection with the real world disorienting, Juno found her mother's sexy octogenarian lovefest even more so.

She opened her dating app and listlessly contemplated the most recent identity parade of chunky, greying fifty-something men deemed yin enough for her voluptuous, optimistic yang. Why did they all look like they were auditioning to run the Albert Square car lot? Where were her ageing pirates?

Then she spotted a face that stood out – swarthy, direct-eyed, and sexy. Lots of lovely hair, still dark. She swiped right. It was a match!

Hi, she messaged scintillatingly.

Hey, you, he messaged her straight back.

Oh wow!

What's your answer?

Which was when Juno realised that she hadn't even bothered to read his profile. How shallow was she?

She checked it quickly, her heart sinking a little:

Kendall, 44

Hired assassin by day, by night an aficionado of fine wine, laughter and dancing.

Passport and tuxedo always packed, scuba gear ready.

Tell me your lethal weapon then guess mine?

Oh, dear.

Still, Eric might approve of him given he sounded quite spy-like.

Determined to stay positive, Juno replied:

Me: killer dance moves. You: squirty bow tie.

He sent a row of dots. Not a good sign. In her opinion, men had to be able to laugh at themselves. Then, just as she was about to log off, he messaged:

Wanna meet up?

Juno sat up in surprise. Maybe the dots had been masking a period of celebration whilst Kendall was dancing for joy and toasting his luck. She looked at his handsome pic again.

When?

Now.

Just for a moment, she was drenched with the naughtiness of temptation, deliciously unfamiliar. Game on!

This is pure fantasy, she reminded herself as she glanced down at her yoga leggings then around the bombsite mess surrounding her.

Where?

Book your favourite hotel, I'll bring the wine and laughter...

Juno reread this with one eye closed, fantasising him rolling into a luxury suite at The Vineyard with a 2015 Côte de Beaune and more one-liners than *The Office*. If he genuinely made her laugh, she might even forgive him bringing something German from Aldi's bottom shelf.

But then he added:

It's two hundred for a night. You won't regret it. Ken.

For a moment she thought he was just suggesting she pay for the room. Then the truth dawned on her.

She logged off without replying.

3

PHOEBE

'He wanted me to *pay* him, can you imagine?'

'You passed on the offer, I take it?' Phoebe watched Juno unpacking deli treats onto the scrubbed oak table in the Hartridge Court kitchen.

'I'm not *that* desperate!' Two dove-grey eyes saucered at her in shock over a bag of Rocky Roads. She closed one and tilted her head to reconsider this for a moment before confirming 'nah'. Then she turned away to fill the kettle. 'Coffee?'

Ambushed, Phoebe couldn't help admiring the way Juno made herself at home, beaming in at high contrast like daytime television, all bright separates and bonhomie, both addictively distracting and strangely cheering.

'This kitchen is three times the size of my entire flat!' She recrossed the flagstones to fetch milk. 'And this fridge is bigger than my bathroom!'

Hartridge Court was a vast mausoleum of a country house designed for an aristocratic family, guests and staff. Phoebe and Felix operated out of just one room, now more boho studio apartment than kitchen. They were acting as custodians to the stately pile that had belonged to Felix's late uncle, its ownership much contested. Just a temporary solution to their cashflow problem, Felix had assured her two years ago; like so many of their unconventional life choices, it had been his idea to move here.

Now it seemed Felix had been the one to encourage Juno to call round unannounced this morning: 'He says you need cheering up. You should join my Clubbercise class for an endorphin hit. Or yoga, maybe? Are you getting enough Vitamin D?'

Phoebe's depressive spells were unfamiliar to Juno, who had known her in their misspent youth when she'd masked it more and self-medicated with blood-orange Hooch, warehouse raves and small tablets with smiles on them.

'You even sound like Felix,' she grumbled. 'He's been badgering me to try ashwagandha.'

'Is that like Tantric sex?' Juno looked thrilled.

This made her laugh. 'It's a wellness supplement for better sleep and renewed energy. He bulk-ordered me gummies from America that one of his leading actresses swears by.' Phoebe was reluctant to admit just how impatient she was to test ashwagandha's magic claims since receiving an invitation to her own funeral. 'They still haven't arrived.'

'Felix worries about you,' Juno sighed. 'We both do. He thinks you're hiding something; I can tell. I'm not leaving until I find out what it is.'

The new collaboration intrigued Phoebe. This smacked of husbandly interference. Or concern. Either way, Felix knew something was up. They hadn't spent twenty-five years hiding truths from one another for the sake of the marriage to let one slide.

Unleashing Juno on her was a no ball. The bubbly, brightly dressed interloper might be a crack interrogator who had a way of getting information out of people – as she'd proven when they'd found themselves in pursuit of Si Locke's killer – but Felix had underestimated how much more Juno liked talking about herself.

'I've deleted my profile on that dating app!' she went on breathlessly, fishing a cafetière out of a cupboard. 'I might have guessed any matchmaking service specifically targeting over-forties would attract wannabe escorts. I'm going back to Bumble, or maybe I should ask my friends to matchmake? Surely Felix has a lovely single chum he can set me up with?'

'Strike "lovely" and possibly.' Phoebe watched her spooning barely enough coffee into the cafetière to cover its base. 'I thought you and Mil were getting on rather well?'

'He's far too young!'

'He's almost forty and he likes older women. Plus he wouldn't charge you.'

Turning pinker, Juno told her off for not coming to the pub quiz. 'I didn't believe Felix when he said you were working last night. You're an early bird.'

'Research.' She pointed at a big pile of leather-bound hard-backs on the table beside her. 'I'm murdering off Lady Dee's reading circle a classic detective story at a time, starting with Sherlock Holmes.'

'Tell me more.' Juno was a big fan of the Roaring Twenties crime capers, which featured sleuthing aristo Dee Jekyll and her trusty lady's maid Annie Logg.

'One of the first to die is Oxford don's wife Georgiana Gilmore,' Phoebe explained, 'who is poisoned by an adder whilst reading *The Adventure of the Speckled Band*.'

Juno gave her a wise look. 'Is "Georgiana" Gigi from the Inkbury Book Group?'

'I couldn't possibly comment.' They both knew Phoebe based murder victims on people against whom she had a grudge.

'Gigi's really not that bad,' Juno countered. 'You must come to the next meeting, for research. They're *such* village scandalmongers. I've already promised you'll be there.'

Phoebe narrowed her eyes. It had been Juno who had persuaded her to donate Dorothy De'Ath's signed canon to Gigi as a raffle prize. Phoebe had yet to uncover who had won it, immediately donating the lot to the fete's bargain book stall. Juno claimed not to remember.

'That group is toxic,' she pointed out. 'Bad Penny's a member for a start. She's been trying to have us evicted from this house since we got here.'

'I still don't get that.' Juno broke off from coffee making to come closer, perplexed. 'It's not like she ever married the guy who owned this place, is it? Aren't there ex-wives, children and grandchildren already fighting over it?'

'But none are trustees, whereas Penny is. The family want it sold. The trust claims Boozy's legacy was to turn it into an art gallery, museum and cultural hub.'

When media magnate Bob 'Boozy' Faulkland had been alive, he'd delighted in his material wealth, collecting fine art and beautiful houses as well as a succession of decorative blonde wives, all of whom were now fighting for a share of his substantial estate.

'Now the dispute's going to court, which could take years and cost them all this place's value in legal fees. Meanwhile, it's falling apart.'

'Some legacy. Did they call him Boozy because he was a lush?'

'One of the few things he and Penny had in common if so,' muttered Phoebe, although she had a feeling the nickname dated back to his humble upbringing, long before he made his fortune in newsprint and broadcasting.

'Where did those two even meet?'

'She dated one of his sons and Boozy stole her.'

'Ew.'

A notorious roue, Felix's media mogul Uncle Boozy had been two generations older than high-born brattish It Girl Penny, their much-publicised relationship short-lived. Yet unlike his many ex-wives, the pair had parted on amicable terms; Penny still lived rent-free in a barn conversion on the estate and remained on the board of several of his companies as well as a trustee of the Hartridge Foundation. After his death, she'd astonished the family by setting her sights on overseeing the house's reinvention.

'Penny thinks the family asked us to look after this place to spy on her,' Phoebe told Juno. 'The trust's been extremely threatening.'

'Hardly great spies when Felix is always abroad or in London and you're completely unsociable.'

'I am very sociable. I'm just not a village person.'

'How do you know if you never try?'

'I've been there before; one minute you're judging the Best Scarecrow, the next you're being burnt at the stake as a witch.'

'You have to start a revolution from within, Freddy.' Juno carried the cafetière across to the table, lingering to eat a Danish pastry.

'What have I told you about quoting Britpop lyrics at me?' Phoebe got up to fetch the milk and selected two cups from the draining board.

'You're thinking it's Oasis, which it isn't. Liam started a revolution from his bed.' Mouth full of pastry, Juno started humming 'Don't Look Back in Anger'.

'I don't want to start one in this village or anywhere else,' Phoebe told her firmly.

'Go on, Inkbury needs revolutionaries like you, Freddy.'

Only Juno called her Freddy, a throwback nickname from her

twenties. She secretly cherished the way it transported her back to those easy, breezy days.

'You'll be running that book club in a year,' Juno predicted.

'My handbags-at-dawn days are over.'

'Bad Penny never gets up before midday, so you can start hand-bagging at lunchtime.'

Juno and Phoebe shared a laughter sweet spot, often offbeat and unfunny to others, which could reduce them to silent, cramping tears without warning, or loud, delighted hoots as now. Soon they were weeping with giggles, stitches taking hold.

'You *must* come to the book group with me, Freddy!' Juno pleaded. 'Call it research.'

'Absolutely not.' Phoebe refused to subscribe to Juno's desire for social self-enrichment. 'I blame them entirely for inflicting Craig the pedant on me. Our jolly village postie goes *above and—*'

'—*beyoooond.*' Juno did the Buzz Lightyear impersonation, sitting back down on a sofa. 'Is Craig still "correcting" your books then?'

Phoebe cocked her head to listen out for him, a cup in each hand, then remembered the electric stealth van. 'Daily.'

'I don't know why you can't tell him to get lost.' Juno poured coffee as Phoebe joined her on the sofa. 'You do it to everybody else. Me, for example.'

'I never tell you to get lost,' Phoebe protested.

'You so do! I'm starting to think Craig has a mysterious, hypnotic hold over you, Dorothy De'Ath. Why else d'you always do his bidding?'

'I can't let readers down by ignoring mistakes,' she said seriously.

'There are loads of mistakes in my Mother Love blogs.'

'You don't charge for it.'

Juno was munching her way through a Danish pastry, cheeks

bulging. 'I think it's the imperfections that make art magical and human.'

'You sound like Felix.'

Phoebe was too proud to explain the Achilles' heel she now bore professionally. Riding a rollercoaster marriage and facing off mortality at close quarters were blows that she had taken in her stride by comparison, losing their family home even. But the mortification of no publisher wanting to touch her work after she'd lost her newspaper column often left her doubting every word. Writing was her force-shield; every mistake felt like a crack in it.

'Are you sure you're okay, Freddy? You're very pale.'

Phoebe looked into those hypnotic blue-grey eyes, brimming with kindness, pastry flakes flecked on the concerned smile.

'I'm worried about you,' Juno pushed. 'You can tell me to get lost, but are you ill again?'

'Get lost, and no,' she scoffed, forcing a smile.

'You *do* need to get out of this place more.'

'I ran four miles this morning,' she said truthfully, then admitted, 'and that put me in a worse mood. Some man putting his bins out shouted at me for having the dogs off the lead along Three Bridge Lane. Said it would be my fault if one of them got run over. It was half past six, and there was no traffic.'

'Where was Felix?'

'Early train. Breakfast meeting with Betsy.' Betsy was her husband's constantly chirpy, people-pleasing young assistant.

'Has Felix been misbehaving?' Juno was shrewd enough to guess Phoebe's marriage was complicated.

'No more than usual.' But we weaponise our secrets, she added silently, even those problems that sharing would halve.

She pulled out the drawer beneath the table and felt for the thick creamy envelope hidden beneath the linen napkins there, dropping the funeral notice 'stiffy' in front of Juno, whose mouth opened into a perfect shocked O as she read it.

'You must go to the police! This says you're being buried in a fortnight!'

'It also says that I "died" today,' she pointed out.

'Who could have sent it? What does Felix say?'

Phoebe shrugged. Sharing this with him would mean restarting the timer on a bomb they'd never fully defused. He was already telling her off for being sad. She'd received multiple death threats when the Twitter storm that had ultimately ended her media career was raging. At the time, Felix had been beside himself; he'd wanted to hire her twenty-four-hour security, to move her into to a safe house, to annihilate her enemies with his own hands. Some of the trolls had been relentless, with one particularly toxic double act the most vicious and career-destroying of them all. She'd ultimately blocked and banned every one of them, but the threats kept coming back, even years later.

She explained a little of this to Juno now. 'The funeral invitation must be from one of those original trolls. All the press coverage about Si Locke's murder mentioned my name more than once. My whereabouts is public knowledge for those who wanted to root around online and find it.'

'So they still bother you, the trolls?' asked Juno, shocked.

'Occasionally.' Girding her loins, she reached for her laptop and clicked it out of hibernation to show Juno the most recent abusive messages sent to her author websites and social feeds for Dorothy De'Ath and P. F. Sylvian, her other pseudonym. 'These are standard issue. I have very little social media any more, but what is out there for my book PR gets targeted too, especially recently.'

Just looking at it made her palms sweaty, her heart sledge-hammer in her chest.

'We must investigate!' Juno insisted, as enthralled as she was appalled. 'This is surely a case for the Village Detectives. I'll get Eric straight onto it, shall I?' Her son was a whiz at cyber-sleuthing. 'Can you forward those to me?'

'See if he has time first,' said Phoebe, reluctant to make a fuss, and aware Eric had a lot on his plate. She spam-junked a new message screaming at her in caps lock. 'I'm sure they'll get bored eventually. There are refreshingly long periods of respite these days.'

'What exactly did you do to upset these people?'

'You must have looked it up?'

'Can't bring myself to.' Juno went very pink. 'I'd rather hear it from you first.'

Phoebe closed her laptop, both humbled and quietly relieved that she still didn't know. 'I'll tell you another time, I promise. Soon. Needs a bit of a run up.'

She could see Juno was about to press her further, but then she clearly thought the better of it, the big, kind smile mugging her frown. 'Eat something. You're wasting away.'

Overwhelmed with a wave of exhaustion, Phoebe took a swig of coffee and shuddered. 'You make it too weak, like American diners.'

'It's not soup. You need solid food.'

Phoebe reluctantly helped herself to the smallest of the deli treats Juno had brought. It immediately stuck her teeth together.

'Baklava.' Juno nodded sympathetically. 'It did the same to me last time I ate some. Couldn't open my mouth for twenty minutes. Had to gargle with cider vinegar afterwards to get the sticky lumps off. I'll get that, shall I?' she offered as a familiar excited knocking started against the back door.

Still unable to speak, Phoebe grabbed the dogs before they could follow.

Out of sight, Craig sounded surprised to see Juno there. 'Is the lady of the house in?'

'She's a bit busy.'

'I have a signed-for delivery here. Looks *very* special.'

'Shall I take it?'

'My portable barcode scanner has malfunctioned. It's my contractual duty in such instances to seek the addressee, and I'm afraid I don't know you, so...'

Crouching out of sight in the kitchen, her jaws still glued together with baklava, Phoebe groaned quietly, tempted to let the terriers loose. Craig was bound to demand feedback on his colour-coded corrections to *Blood at the Altar* and she hadn't so much as glanced at them yet.

'You do know me – Juno Mulligan – you deliver to me in the village.' Juno sounded affronted. 'I moved into the flat above Mr Benn's Favourite Emporium last month. We've talked lots. And I hosted the quiz last night: "Are you lookin' at me?"'

'I *am* looking at you, madam, yes. Are you feeling quite all right?'

'Are you twarkin' to me?' came an even more pronounced Bronx drawl.

In the kitchen, still sucking her glued-together teeth, Phoebe wondered whether Juno suffered the same unpredictable midlife anger explosions she herself did.

'Do you have ID?' their postie was demanding.

'Not on me, no.'

'Then I'll have to take this back to the sorting office.'

'Wait there.' Juno's footsteps came trotting back. Marching into the kitchen, she pulled the door closed behind her and whispered: 'He's very persistent! It must be your Tantric sex supplement – you'll need to sign.'

Phoebe stood up reluctantly, still trying to suck enough sticky treat from her teeth to ask her to hang onto the dogs, both of whom now launched into a frenzy of barking as they heard a muffled bang coming from the back door like a moped backfiring.

It was followed by a brief, ear-piercing scream.

Shutting the terriers in the kitchen to hurry along the corridor, Phoebe saw Craig framed in the open doorway, his pink balloon face and neck peppered with what looked like dart tips, his expression a horror-mask of shock as he slowly fell backwards off the step.

4

JUNO

MOTHER LOVES BLIGHTY

Followers, Mother Love is once again embroiled in a homicide! The quiet English country life I envisaged when leaving Brooklyn is not panning out at all. Somebody has murdered our mailman! It happened three days ago. I'm bound to secrecy while the police make their enquiries, so my lips are sealed. More soon, I promise. But as all of you who have experienced trauma will understand, right now I need my mum. I also need to borrow her car.

So until next time, here's another picture of Kevin Bacon…

(Catnapping.jpg)

'*Pusscat!*' Judy Glenn threw open the door to her Godlington Hall penthouse in welcome, arms wide, bracelets rattling. 'My poor darling, come *in*! We're going to cheer you up. Have a drink. *Champagne*, Doobee!'

'Is that really quite appropriate in the circ—' Juno found

herself dragged briefly into her mother's deep, musk-scented bosom '—umstances?'

'Heidsieck's already open,' Judy explained, hushing her voice to add, 'Some chums are joining us for lunch; the Campbells arrived early. We've had to shut Dally in the utility because Sandra's allergic.' There were whines and yelps from behind a nearby door as the elderly shih tzu registered Juno's presence.

'You said it would be just the three of us?' Juno felt panic rising. She needed soothing. Also, she was wearing her least flattering cycling shorts and an oversized ironic Barbie T-shirt.

Now she noticed her mother was resplendent in yellow layered linen, her wild curls freshly crazy-coloured pink and pinned up in a messy bun, an oversized pearl statement necklace propping up her several chins.

'Don't worry, they're jolly discreet. The Campbells are our downstairs neighbours, a retired circuit judge and GP. Both keen local historians. *Very* eager to hear about your murdered postman.'

'That's in the hands of the police, Mum.'

'But you and Freddy are bound to investigate, yes, along with those hunky chaps of yours?' Not waiting for an answer, Judy led the way through the thickly carpeted hallway, its freshly painted walls mosaiced with framed covers of her once-popular recipe books, publicity shots and encounters with famous celebrities. Interspersed were vintage photographs of Dennis with his arms around daytime television's movers and shakers, ad men and antiques experts, his toothpaste smile and concrete quiff identical in each.

Judy and Dennis – who called one another Boppa and Doobee – had been introduced by a mutual friend a year earlier, and their whirlwind engagement had led them to downsize together at Godlington retirement village, if its largest penthouse counted as downsizing. There they had rapidly become party central, reliving their best lives. As well as enjoying a romantic renaissance, the two old TV pros had come out of retirement, director Dennis persuading erstwhile celebrity cook Judy to make one-off specials.

Dennis was a Teflon-coated, non-stick charmer. The same concrete quiff and toothpaste smile combo on show in the hallway photos – both now glacier white – greeted Juno in the reception room as he thrust a champagne flute in her hand, air-kissing extravagantly through a cloud of Acqua de Parma.

'Looking radiant as always, dear girl! Or should I say dear Barbie Girl, ha!' Gesturing at her T-shirt, he beckoned her through to the open-plan reception, past a table set for eight, Juno counted in alarm. 'Meet the Campbells!'

Beyond the dining area lay a wicket-long coffee table laden with platters of Judy's hors d'oeuvres, surrounded by a herd of fat sofas, one of which engulfed a smartly dressed couple who Dennis introduced as 'Eugene and Sandra – you must tell them all about your dice with death, Juno!'

The huge, smiling husband creaked upright to shake her hand while his thin, bright-eyed wife remained seated, quite possibly because she was trapped in the squishy depths of uphol-stery and scatter cushions.

'The postman blew up on your doorstep, we hear?' Eugene asked in a canyon-deep voice, a hint of Caribbean lilting the vowels.

'I, um, that is...'

'Give the girl a chance to say hello, Eugene,' his wife muttered, violin sharp to his double bass. She raised a bony, manicured hand in greeting, her gaze lingering on the Barbie T-shirt. 'You're lucky to be alive, we hear?'

'Crudité?' Dennis plucked up an oval platter, which Juno felt somewhat diminished the impact of her dramatic near miss.

There followed a polite round of vegetable stick selection before Eugene again urged Juno to tell them more: 'It must have been one hell of a crime scene. My interest is professional, you understand; I was a defence barrister for forty years. Never heard of anything like this.'

'Ruthless.' Sandra shuddered.

'You witnessed the death?' asked Eugene eagerly.

'I didn't actually see anything.' Juno plunged a heritage carrot baton into artichoke dip. 'It wasn't my doorstep. It was my friend Freddy's – that is, Phoebe Fredericks's – and I was in her kitchen when the device went off. By the time we reached Craig, he'd stopped breathing.' She took a moment to hold down a sudden wellspring of high emotion. 'He had all these darts in his face and neck – pen nibs that went everywhere – which must have been poisoned.'

'No poison works that fast.' Sandra flicked her celery matchstick dismissively.

'My wife has a medical background,' explained Eugene.

'What does the forensic pathologist say?' demanded Sandra.

'Who is the Senior Investigating Officer?' Eugene overlapped her.

'Cucumber canapé with whipped feta?' Dennis thrust out another platter.

Juno ate two to buy time, disconcerted to find herself under cross-examination. Phoebe insisted it should be left to the police, but her detective urges were pricked by their interest, along with unwelcome tears. She'd thought of little else but poor Craig's doorstep demise in recent days.

'Well, I didn't speak to anyone in forensics personally,' she told them, helping herself to another comforting clutch of carrot sticks. 'There were all sorts of police and people in hazmat suits wandering round afterwards; Phoebe's back door is still cordoned off. The guy in charge is a DI Mason. He hasn't told us anything, although Mil Winterbourne – he's the landlord at The Barton Arms – has a cousin who is a local bobbie and a mate on the CID team. Word is, it was a burst meningitis artery.'

'Meningeal,' corrected Sandra, still wagging her tiny celery baton towards Juno for emphasis, like a conductor.

'That's it. Mil's cousin's friend told him one of the poison darts was driven into Craig's skull when he fell. Severed the artery. Huge brain bleed. Pretty much instant.' Juno scooped beetroot and mint dip onto her carrot, then stared at its red tip, appetite evaporating.

'Unlucky.' Sandra sounded sceptical.

'Murder often is, dear heart,' Eugene sighed.

As they fell silent to consider this profundity, the door buzzer rang in the hallway.

Sandra's face lit up. 'Could that be Kenneth? He used to be in the military police,' she told Juno proudly.

'Super.' She smiled, starting to suspect that her mother and Dennis might be assembling Godlington's own Thursday Murder Club.

As Judy opened the front door out of sight, they heard a bright squawk of 'cooees!' from the hall, followed by a demand for 'Two more shampoos for Pam and Spike, *Doobee!*'

'Coming right up, Boppa.' Dennis jumped up, pausing by Juno's ear. 'Wait until you meet Pam's friend, Juno. *Quite* the card.'

Sandra relaxed back into the sofa. 'You know Pam, I take it?'

'Since childhood.' Pam was her mother's closest friend from her schooldays, a regular feature in Juno's life, and one of the reasons Judy had chosen to downsize to Godlington, where sociable Pam was already resident.

'The talk of the village, these two,' murmured Eugene, licking his finger and pressing it against his other hand with a hiss. 'Fy-er!'

Juno was intrigued. Bright eyed, bouncy heeled and elegant, Pam had many admirers at Godlington, but the sprightly ex-games mistress, who had remained defiantly single into her eighties, was rarely ever seen with a plus one.

When Pam marched in, her stooped, grey-haired companion was matching her pace with a wheeled walking frame. But before introductions could be made, they executed a swift U-turn and wheeled back out, calling back in a theatrical tenor, 'Must pee!'

'Who's in the frame?' Pam demanded, hurrying to sit beside Juno.

For a moment, Juno was nonplussed, thinking she meant the walking frame that had just wheeled out of sight at speed. 'I think I heard the name Spike?'

'Who's in the frame for Craig's death, silly!' Pam perched on the edge of one of the sofas. 'Terrible waste. Very well liked here, that boy. He was always happy to stop and chat. Budge up, shrimp.' She sat beside Juno, straight spined and nimble. 'Spill the beans.'

'The police are telling us nothing,' Juno sighed, 'but my money is on one of Freddy's trolls making a letter bomb.'

'Why would anyone try to kill Freddy?' asked Judy, coming in to plonk a big bowl of green salad leaves on the table.

'She's still got a lot of enemies online.'

'From public cancellation that time, you mean?' Judy made it sound like being voted off a talent show.

'Horrid being singled out,' said Pam. 'I was thrown out of the local tennis league once. They never let me back in. I was furious. Some of the members wouldn't speak to me for years.'

'What did you do?' asked Sandra.

'Wore shorts. Did your friend get thrown out of some sort of club, Juno?'

Juno's loyalty to Phoebe – as well as her own ignorance on the matter – made her reluctant to say too much. 'She used to have a regular Sunday column, Undomestic Goddess. It ran for years, hugely popular.'

'Oh, yes, I remember it. Rather fun.'

'Then the paper pulled it after internet trolls tore her reputation to shreds. She lost her income.'

'These things are usually triggered by saying something highly controversial, am I right?' asked Sandra beadily. 'Extreme views, ideologies.'

'Or being misinterpreted,' Juno evaded the question because she still didn't know the full story.

'Alarming to be targeted like that,' Pam said chippily, 'even if one's views are controversial. A letter bomb!'

'She came to Inkbury to get away from all that,' Juno agreed.

'And because that husband of hers gambled their house on a movie,' Dennis chuckled, picking up the champagne bottle with an insider swagger to refill their glasses, adding in an undertone, 'One hears these things in the industry. Huge budget. He blew the lot.'

Juno gaped at her soon-to-be-stepfather, whose past career making daytime television was a far cry from Felix's international film one, but who table-hopped shamelessly around media-heavy private members' clubs whenever he was in London. 'Who told you that?'

'I forget,' Dennis said vaguely, flashing the toothpaste smile, which made her suspect he'd simply done a lot more googling than she had. 'No wonder she needs to write those clever books non-stop and never gets out. Crying shame. Gorgeous-looking girl. I've promised I'll try and find her a television deal,' he boasted to the Campbells. 'Channel 5 are already nibbling.'

Juno was still in shock. It was true Phoebe had confided that the Sylvians' beloved Dales farm had been sold to cover family debts, part of a turbulent phase during which she'd lost more than just her job and reputation. But Juno hadn't realised Felix was personally to blame.

'Freddy's lovely,' Judy assured them, giving Dennis a stern look as she offered more canapes around, 'and married to the most heart-melting man you can imagine.'

'He was probably behind it,' Eugene said with a sleepy smile, palming several gougères. 'It usually is the husband.'

'Absolutely,' agreed Sandra, demanding, 'Have the police interviewed the husband yet?'

'I don't know,' Juno said in a tight voice, even more alarmed at the suggestion Felix might be a suspect. 'We're all meeting up in The Barton Arms this afternoon to share the latest.'

'Oh, how thrilling!' Judy offered round asparagus spears wrapped in prosciutto. 'Did you hear that, Dennis? The Merde Squad is investigating!'

'The others prefer Village Detectives,' Juno corrected, taking one, 'and we're really not.'

'Phoebe is a terribly clever crime writer,' Dennis told their new friends, topping up their glasses from a freshly popped bottle of Piper Heidsieck. 'So this is life imitating art. Going undercover, stilettos at the ready, eh, Juno?'

'That sounds dangerous,' said Sandra, glancing at her husband.

'Phoebe doesn't want us to investigate,' Juno said quickly.

'Very wise,' Eugene nodded, telling Juno, 'Our oldest boy has done a lot of close surveillance work and it's a very unreliable business.'

'Our son's a highly trained professional,' Sandra added tightly. 'It's man's work.'

'Then again, a woman's intuition is her super-power,' said Pam, giving Juno a Miss Marple wink.

'Juno, Phoebe and their chaps are *such* good sleuths,' Judy took over. 'An awesome foursome.'

'I thought you said Juno was single?' Sandra asked sharply.

'I am.' Juno gave her mother a questioning look.

'Oh, she is.' Judy cocked her head as the door buzzer went off. 'And that must be Kenneth. Could *you* go, Pusscat?'

Juno eyed her more suspiciously, sensing subterfuge.

'Must check on Spike.' Pam accompanied her to the hallway at a companionable jog.

'Tell me, Pam,' Juno whispered once they were there, 'are Mum and Dennis assembling an expert team to find Craig's killer? Am I about to open the door to Wexshire's answer to Cormoran Strike?'

'Nothing gets past you!' Pam elbowed her fondly. 'We're all in on it. Entre nous, Spike's ex-bomb squad, shit hot on incendiaries.'

Juno turned to her in amazement. 'You're pulling my leg?'

'Of course I am.' Pam chuckled. 'Spike was a librarian. Dicky bladder, but sharp as a tack. Nobody better at crosswords.'

There was another buzz from the door intercom, longer and more impatient this time.

'You'd better get that,' Pam urged. 'Can't keep love waiting.'

'Love?' Juno asked, confused.

'Judy's fixed you up, haven't you guessed?' Pam whispered. 'That'll be the Campbells' son. Quite the catch, they tell us.'

Juno hurried to the little high-tech screen by the door and pressed the camera intercom icon.

A huge figure seemed to fill the entire screen, the top of his head out of shot, at least six feet four with shoulders as broad as an armchair, a piratic smile playing on his handsome features.

It was a face Juno recognised straight away; she'd first set eyes on it just last week. She'd swiped it right, then zoomed in on it, then flirted with its miniaturised avatar.

'Hi there.' His voice was as dive-in deep as his father's. 'Am I at the right apartment? Judy Glenn, yeah?'

It was Kendall, forty-four.

'Yes! I mean, Judy's my mother. I'm Juno! Come up!' She buzzed him in, mind racing as she waited.

She must have read their dating app exchange all wrong, she realised joyfully. This man was a military-trained gun for hire, not a gigolo. The £200 line had been a joke she'd failed to spot. Hook-up messages were such a minefield for misinterpretation. She could even understand him tweaking his name; Kenneth was a bit dated. If he really was looking for love, she had a second chance. It was kismet.

And he was *gorgeous*.

Given all the awfulness of the past few days in the aftermath of Craig's death, with the police asking questions and Phoebe being so uptight and chippy, this was the perfect antidote. Her mother was a genius setting her up.

By the time Juno opened the door to the penthouse, she had Wet Wet Wet playing in her head, feeling the tingle in her fingers and her toes.

'Well, hello, Kendall!' It came out as 'Ken doll', she realised as soon as she said it, but no matter.

On closer inspection, Kenneth/Kendall was at least ten years older than he advertised online and wearing leather trousers last seen in the eighties, ruffly hair bleach-streaked like a barcode. As retro cliches went, he was just Juno's furrow-browed, ageing New Romantic meets Marlboro Man type.

He looked her up and down dispassionately, the smile freezing as he spotted the Barbie T-shirt. Then he muttered in an undertone, 'It's Kenneth. And I am only here to keep my parents happy, understood?'

5

PHOEBE

'Would there be reason to believe, in your opinion, Ms Fredericks, that Craig Jackman may have, on balance, harboured a grudge against you, at the end of the day?'

DI Ross Mason was nothing like Carrick Lowe, the fictional Wexshire CID detective in Phoebe's gritty eighties crime series. Her sexy ex-Met renegade fired out questions in short, direct bursts.

Ross Mason peppered his professional opinions with endless fillers. 'If push came to shove, say, would he, so to speak, want to harm you?'

'I don't see why,' she replied, 'although he did complain more than once about the lack of alien abductions in Dingledale.'

'What is Dingle...?'

'Dale? It's the setting of my Dorothy De'Ath mystery series.'

'Ah.' DI Mason smiled politely. 'Alsop's a bookworm, aren't you, Sergeant?'

Behind him, his round-faced deputy looked up from patting the dogs, nodding eagerly. '*Big* Stephen King fan.'

'Me too,' Phoebe agreed, catching the younger woman's eye.

'I mostly read manga, myself,' the detective mused.

Phoebe, who remembered her father complaining, 'You know you're getting old when the policemen start looking younger,' had been trying to ignore how startlingly youthful she found Ross Mason. With his trope-filled expositions and his surfer dude asides, he was a boyish enigma to her.

Felix was finding it hard to hide his irritation.

'Is this going to take much longer?' he muttered now, glancing at his watch. 'You've asked all this before, and we're supposed to be meeting friends.'

The police inspector cast him a serene, patient look across the generational divide. 'Cool.'

Not something Carrick Lowe would ever say.

Unlike quick-thinking, explosive Carrick – and indeed Felix – Mason was a measured and phlegmatic young man. He'd visited Hartridge Court several times in the days since Craig's death, and he always called ahead, parked considerately, brought his own thermos flask of decaffeinated coffee with almond milk, and occasionally shared his wordy, circumlocutory train of thought without revealing much at all.

'In my professional opinion, on balance, based on our search of the victim's residence, along with the clear line of connection, speaking candidly, it may not be necessary to look much further when all's said and done.' He tipped his head, soft brown eyes placid as he offered Phoebe a brief smile, revealing front teeth covered in metal tram-wires.

That was another reason she found him unfeasibly young; DI Mason still had a brace.

'Are you telling me you know who did it?' asked Phoebe, relieved.

'I'm not at liberty to say yet given the results are still being gathered, but at this moment in time, all things considered' – he looked from Phoebe to Felix – 'I don't believe we need to take this investigation any wider.'

'What about the names I gave you?' Felix demanded. 'All those people who might have a grudge against my wife—'

'Not that many,' Phoebe muttered.

'—Have you interviewed any of them?'

'I don't think that will be necessary.'

'That's a relief,' said Phoebe, who hadn't wanted him to dredge all that up.

But Felix wouldn't let it rest. 'Someone has just tried to do her serious harm! You've seen the funeral invitation she got sent, the historic death threats, the years of targeted abuse. It's still ongoing.'

'With all due respect, I suggest you chill out, Mr Sylvian.'

Felix glared at him, too angry to speak.

'Sergeant Alsop will accompany you outside now, if you don't mind.'

At this, Mason's deputy straightened up from petting the terriers again to stand protectively alongside her boss, arms crossed over her broad chest. She was at least a decade his senior and several inches taller and wider, and only her gummy smile stopped her being faint-makingly intimidating. 'Please come with me, sir.'

'You're not arresting *Felix*, are you?' Phoebe gulped.

'Of course they're not!' Felix snapped.

'I'd just like a quick look around outside again, if you don't mind accompanying me,' said Sergeant Alsop, giving her boss a nod before leading Felix out, pursued by eager terriers.

Mason waited until he heard the outside door close.

'Ms Fredericks, I need to ask you something alone.' He stepped closer. 'It's rather delicate, which is why I thought it best to suggest your husband step outside.'

'We have—' About to say *no secrets*, Phoebe stopped herself, casting a wise look to the space Felix had just occupied. They had too many to count.

Mason tapped his fingertips together, running his tongue over his brace. 'I won't beat about the bush if you'll forgive my frankness, but cutting to the chase, to put no finer point on it, were you and Craig ever in what is popularly termed... ahem, a situationship? A sexual one, shall we say?'

Phoebe took a moment to unravel this. 'An affair, you mean?'

'In a manner of speaking.'

'Absolutely not. What on earth makes you think that?'

'Craig left some rather, shall we say, compromising material.'

'Involving *me*? Photographs, video, what?' She racked her brains for what might be in circulation. She posted nothing on the internet, but friends might have: sunbathing holiday snaps, a few ill-judged fancy dress excursions, no more.

DI Mason cleared his throat. 'I don't want to alarm you, but he filled an entire CMU wall.'

'Is a CMU wall some sort of dark web cloud storage?' She'd never had Craig down as a techie despite being at least a generation her junior. He read old-fashioned paper books and made handwritten colour-coded keys in the front.

'Concrete Masonry Units are breeze blocks, Ms Fredericks. We found a notice board on his garage wall, a mind map if you like. And it's our belief that Craig had a very disturbed mind. He was an obsessive and a fantasist.'

'Can I see it?'

'At this stage, I see no advantage in exposing you to the sordid details. Craig Jackman also kept a very well-equipped workshop in his garage, with model-making tools and machinery as well as the board. Conclusions can, so to speak, be drawn on that.'

'You're saying he had the means to make a letter bomb?' Phoebe drew them for him.

'An IED – that is, an improvised explosive device – could be made anywhere, Ms Fredericks, even in this magnificent kitchen.'

'And it would probably taste better than my cooking,' she joked distractedly.

'It may reassure you to know that our forensic psychologist's early conclusion is that, to all intents and purposes, the killer's intention may not have been murder so much as, let's call it maiming.'

'What makes them think that?'

'I wish I were in a position to reveal more, but as things stand, putting everything into perspective, I do believe you are quite safe, in the grand scheme of things. Now if you'll excuse us, Ms Fredericks, Sergeant Alsop and I must press on with our enquiries.'

'Who are you interviewing next?' she asked, eager for closure.

He checked his note pad. 'A garden centre in Dunford about the theft of five ride-on lawn mowers.'

'How is that connected?'

'It's not. The Wexshire Constabulary is a busy force, Ms Fredericks. Keep plodding on is our motto!'

'And don't let the grass grow,' she smiled.

'I can assure you we won't,' DI Mason assured her earnestly, not getting the joke.

By contrast, Felix saw a darkly funny side after they'd gone and Phoebe told him about Craig's notice board, his expression turning from outrage to bewildered amusement when she added that the police thought his intention might not have been murder. 'That's ridiculous! Why would he want to maim you? Why not finish you off?'

Feeling peeved, Phoebe pointed out that Craig might have

had twisted sexual Pinhead designs on her. 'Doesn't it bother you that there's a whole garage wall devoted to me?'

'Of course it does! I'm appalled. But I'm also certain that device was intended to kill. It's too clever, too targeted. Literal poison pens. Quite brilliant when you think about it.'

Phoebe glanced around the kitchen, remembering what DI Mason had said about it being possible to manufacture an IED anywhere. She looked at him suspiciously. 'You'll be saying you made it next.'

'Well, I don't think our funny little postman did. He couldn't even work a barcode scanner.'

Phoebe knew he was talking sense, yet she craved the simplicity of Craig being behind the sick funeral notice and the exploding package that had killed him. Their strange, pedantic postie had to be a secret monster.

But Felix refused to buy into the idea that Craig was to blame for his own death, convinced there was more to it: 'I won't believe you're safe until I know for certain who sent that parcel, and why. Were you expecting any packages?'

'That consignment of high-grade ashwagandha, for a start.'

'What?' he scoffed, having clearly forgotten.

'You were the one who ordered it,' she reminded him. 'Or was that Betsy? Something to cheer up the wife?'

'I don't recall.' He had the grace to look awkward. The subject of eager, devoted Betsy was a grenade Phoebe occasionally picked up to test the pin when she felt under threat. Maybe Betsy sent the package, she wondered idly. She was more than a little in love with Felix.

She watched his face, so familiar that she knew when it was hiding something big and bad. A film going bust; a friend in a mess; an affair?

'Reminds me, I must call her back,' Felix said now. 'I've let three incoming calls go to voicemail already. She'll be worried.'

Click! The pin was pulled. Phoebe's illogical jealousy was about to detonate.

She whistled the dogs and headed towards the back lobby to tug on her trainers. 'I'm going for a run.'

'We're meeting the others at the pub!'

'That's where I'm running to.'

Phoebe had reached the grassy bridge over the River Dunnett by the time Felix caught her up, his trainers unlaced and his gilet inside out.

'This is ridiculous!' he panted. 'What did I even *say*?'

She kept running, aware it was usually something he hadn't said that made her feel like this.

Dropping down the track to the canal, they jogged along its north bank for half a mile without talking, the tow path so narrow they had to take it single file, jumping out of the way for afternoon cyclists and runners coming in the opposite direction, the terriers plunging in and out of reeds in search of moorhens and ducks.

It was a glorious afternoon, the canal a green-fringed, sun-streaked, grass-seed-flecked watery go-slow on which narrow-boats glinted and puttered, and wildfowl called and splashed. Ahead of them, the village's picturesque old stone bridge – once made famous as the backdrop for the closing kiss in a Richard Curtis movie – looked ready to star in another close-up celluloid clinch. Not that Phoebe was volunteering to pucker up. Her head was too busy, her irritation with Felix still fierce.

She finally pulled up by Barton Lock where a narrowboat was

ascending from the Newborough side, the rush of water through the gates so loud they had to shout breathlessly over it to be heard, which seemed to suit the mood.

'I'm sorry, okay?' both bellowed at the same time, not sounding it.

'Forgiven!' Phoebe said it first, not feeling it.

'I just want to protect you!' Felix took off her baseball cap, the other hand reaching up to tuck the stray hairs behind her ears.

Jerking back, she crossed her arms, regarding him sceptically. She didn't need to say anything. He knew this expression too well. But she said it anyway. 'What have you done, Felix?'

He looked away. 'Okay, yes. I've done something dumb I'm not proud of.'

Phoebe guessed this was to do with Betsy. It was bound to happen sooner or later. The more she imagined it, the more likely it was to become a self-fulfilling prophecy.

Her chest already hurt.

'What dumb thing?' If it was seducing his PA, she'd push him in the lock, she decided. Then she'd fish him out and push him in again.

Crushing the baseball cap in his hand, he kicked at the ground beneath them. 'I think what happened might be my fault. The letter bomb.'

The sluice was being fully opened with a winding key now, the ratcheting sound and the whooshing of water deafening.

They moved further away.

'Your fault, how?' she asked.

He looked away again, screwing his face up. 'I got riled by something on Twitter.'

Phoebe took a beat, not seeing the problem. 'It's X, and so what?'

'It was about you.'

'We agreed not to feed the—'

'It was OhFeelYa,' Felix interrupted urgently. For a moment, she couldn't hide her fear, as kneejerk instant as flinching from a punch.

Phoebe's social media detractors had been marshalled by two ringleaders, @OhFeelYa and @OhManiacNymph, anonymous accounts that drew a huge following by posting defamatory rants about her. She and Felix had been convinced they were the same person, one who was allergic to capitals, punctuation and spellcheckers. The two accounts had fed off each other, a clever tactic for gaining traction and visibility.

Both accounts had been inactive for years. Until now.

'What did they say?'

'I'll show you.' He reached in his pocket for his phone.

Phoebe felt the kick in her throat.

'No!' She stepped away, instinctively looking for an escape route, eyes running along the tow path at the steps up to the Three Bridge Lane and the safety of the pub. 'Just tell me, it's quicker.'

He sucked his teeth. 'They said that you deserved to die for what you did. They tagged me in. I replied that that I'd see them in hell first.'

'When was this?'

'A couple of weeks ago. They've been getting themselves wound up ever since, tagging me into everything. Most of the posts get taken down within hours for violating Twitter rules. I haven't blocked them yet. I figure they're safer where I can see them.'

'Why didn't you tell me sooner?'

He bit his lower lip, eyes softening, not needing to say it.

She nodded in acknowledgement, grateful he hadn't. She'd said it herself enough times in the past: don't tell me; let them say what they like; I can't bear to read any of it; please, Felix, I'm begging you, just don't repeat it!

'Do the police know?'

'I've passed it on, but they didn't seem to think much of it.'

'Neither do I.' She sounded more dismissive than she felt.

'I think we should tell Juno and Mil about this.'

'No!' Fear's steel toecap was kicking at her throat again. 'Don't tell them. And don't mention those names you gave to the police either.'

'Phoebe, be sensible. Juno's son can find out if one of them is OhFeelYa, surely?'

She shook her head. 'I don't believe OhFeelYa would physically target me. Why now? It all blew over years ago. It's got to be a coincidence. This has to do with Craig.'

His phone was ringing. 'It's Betsy again.'

'Take it.' She called the dogs, willing him to dismiss the call.

He took it.

Walking away, Phoebe put Betsy's name alongside Craig's on her shortlist of suspects. Internet troll OhFeelYa didn't even make the cut.

6

JUNO

Juno had promised herself never to discuss her love life with Mil. She longed to maintain an air of mystery, feminine mystique and lady detective chutzpah.

But Phoebe and Felix were late, and they'd agreed not to talk any more about poor Craig's demise until the Village Detectives were all present. Thus far their summary had been:

Juno: 'Any idea who could have done it?'

Mil: 'Your guess is as good as mine.'

In The Barton Arms' oak-panelled private dining room, Mil had been spouting about premiership rugby for half an hour, which was fifteen minutes longer than Juno's concentration threshold.

Now he was telling her about a match he planned to watch in the pub that evening with a bunch of local mates. 'There'll be a few birds watching, if you want to stick around?'

Phoebe always told him off for saying 'birds', but Juno was prepared to forgive it this time because Phoebe had also revealed that Mil got nervously boorish and blokey when he was around women he found attractive.

His ears were unusually red, Juno noticed as he went on. 'Alan and Bernard are big Wexshire Warriors fans, and Felix always loves a match so there'll be some oldies there too.'

Juno was less forgiving of 'oldie', especially in connection with a man the same age as her.

He resumed describing his years playing for Wexshire Warriors, which he seemed keen to approach game by game, starting with the Under-18s squad.

'Shall we have another cup of tea?' she interrupted. 'Take it outside maybe? The sun's gorgeous. I'll tell you about Mum trying to fix me up. It's honestly hilarious.'

Juno needed a change of subject, breaking her promise before she had time to mull it over. She'd had a bad day, and Mil already knew about her dating app gigolo. What had just happened at her mother's lunch party was a comic pay-off waiting to be gifted. And Juno craved laughter.

Mil's reaction was gratifyingly raucous when he heard about her being set up with Kenneth/Kendall. 'That's just sick, that is!'

'It was awful,' she complained as they shared mugs of tea on The Barton Arms decking. 'He couldn't wait to get away. His mother obviously hated me; his father fell asleep twice; Pam's date spent more time in the loo than at the table. Doobee and Boppa got squiffy and flirted non-stop. They were dancing to "Brown Sugar" when I left.'

'They crack me up, your mum and Dennis.'

'They're certainly not into cracking murder cases. At first, I thought Mum had gathered everyone there to help us solve Craig's murder, especially when the Campbells started grilling me about it, but I think they were just establishing that I wasn't the murderer before their precious son arrived. They claim he used to be in the military police, but he looks more like a lawless gangster. Rugged and ruthless, rude and brooding,' she sighed, not adding that there was something about Kenneth's sheer alpha, silverback maleness she was finding hard to shake from her head. Instead she joked, 'He has what you kids call rizz.'

Mil looked gratifyingly perplexed. 'What's rizz?'

'Charisma.'

'Sounds a right prat.'

'Takes a loyal son to let his mum and dad set him up on a blind date at a retirement village, though, doesn't it?'

'Only after trying your mum's famous cooking, I reckon.'

'You could be right. He had thirds of everything. He's certainly not after me.' Despite herself, this hurt rather a lot.

Mil's big, battered face widened into a slow smile that creased his crow's feet handsomely. 'So you and fake Ken didn't arrange to meet again?'

'No.'

'That's good, because you're marrying me, remember?' He made a big show of going down on one knee, groaning as his old hamstring injury reminded him why his rugby career ended. 'Will you do me the honour?'

Mil's jokey flirtation usually cheered Juno up, but she was feeling too downcast. 'I'm not ready for that sort of commitment,' she told him flatly. 'I just want mindless sex.'

'I can do mindless sex.'

'Preferably with somebody not born *after* I lost my virginity.'

'Harsh.' Mil clambered upright again, glancing over his shoulder into the pub for signs of Felix and Phoebe. 'They're an hour late now.'

'You don't think something's happened?' Juno fretted. 'I knew I should have driven round there to pick them up.'

'Still borrowing your mum's car, I see.' Mil nodded towards the garish orange Honda Jazz in the pub's car park with its many scrapes and dents. 'Mini not fixed yet?'

Juno felt even grumpier. She'd bought her dream car online when she first arrived back from the States, only for Dennis to slam his big Range Rover into the back of it on a driveway. The garage had been holding it hostage for weeks demanding ridiculous money, the insurance company was refusing to pay up, and until the dispute was resolved, she was reduced to borrowing Judy's small, battered runaround that seemed to provoke inexplicable road rage from even the mildest-mannered motorists.

She complained to Mil that her neighbours in Wheeler's Yard no longer let her park on the courtyard cobbles because they claimed she kept blocking them in.

'You can leave it here if you like.'

'People will think I'm staying overnight.'

'Having mindless sex,' he nodded cheerfully. 'I won't charge you.'

'For parking or sex?' she sighed, certain she'd feel far sassier if she was cruising round the Wexshire Downs in a Mini Cooper with a Union Jack roof. Also if men she found attractive shared the spark. 'The thing is, Mil, Kenneth Ken Doll was *just* my type.'

'Five feet ten, built like a brick proverbial, massive guns, one eye, dodgy hamstring?'

'Tall, dark, piratical.' She was about to add *with ruffly hair*, but decided that was thoughtless given Mil's receding crew cut.

'Was your husband like that?'

Juno stiffened. She was never comfortable talking about Jay, her lithe, red-blond lynx.

'Not like that, no,' she said carefully, glancing at her watch. 'Where *are* they?' Then she gasped as a thought occurred to her. 'You don't think Felix has been arrested, do you?'

'Why would they arrest Felix?'

'At Mum's lunch, Eugene Campbell – who was a criminal barrister once – told me it's almost always the husband.'

'No way! Those two are solid.'

'C'mon, Mil, Felix is always swanning off to burn cash and chat up his PAs. It drives Phoebe mad.'

'I've never once heard her diss him.' Mil was staunchly loyal.

Remembering what Dennis had said about Felix's costly movie gamble, Juno felt a flash of outrage. 'Well, she should diss him because he's incorrigible. He's the reason they lost their house in Yorkshire, and the flat in Notting Hill too I bet, and he—'

'Hello, both!'

Juno clapped her hand over her mouth as Phoebe slid into a chair beside them. She was wearing running gear, her terriers bounding out through the pub's open doors behind them.

Then she spotted the headphone buds Phoebe was pulling from her ears, and felt a wash of relief.

'Felix sends his apologies,' Phoebe told them, 'but he's swanned off to burn money again.'

At this, Juno's cheeks flamed red as two freshly ignited fifty-pound notes.

Phoebe shot her a darkly amused look over her sunglasses. 'He's just taking a call. We would have got here sooner, but underage police officer DI Mason turned up wanting to ask yet more questions while his sergeant poked around in the topiary.'

'Are they still doing scene-of-crime stuff at your place?' asked Mil, surprised.

'Thankfully not, although we still can't use the back door until they say so. We have to go out through the main house. We're swaggering in and out of the columned portico and up and down the balustraded steps like Evelyn Waugh characters.' She got her vape out to puff, eyes narrowing against the first plume, every inch the willowy Waugh heroine. 'Not for much longer, hooray.' She spoke with it clutched between her teeth. 'The case is as good as closed according to Ross Mason.'

'How come?'

'He's not giving away much detail, but it's clear they think Craig made the device himself.'

'No way?' Juno scoffed, then stopped when she realised Phoebe was serious.

'Keen model railway hobbyist who had a workshop at his place worthy of *Doctor Who's* Davros, apparently. Maybe he had everything needed to craft together that poison pen letter bomb. Except that it detonated before he could hand it across. Self-inflicted.'

'Why would Craig want to kill you?'

'He was jolly annoyed by my typos.' She tilted her head thoughtfully, looking across the river to the canal, where a group of kayakers were carrying their crafts along the towpath to bypass the lock. 'Besides, the police seem to think the device wasn't intended to kill – just wound and scar.'

'That's ridiculous! The nibs were poisoned! One punctured his artery.'

'Only as a result of Craig falling. The poison was hemlock according to Mason, who says trace amounts suggest the pen tips were dipped in it, no more. Not a fatal dose. So if I had opened the package, chances are I'd be sick, scarred and scared, not dead.'

'But still...' Juno hated the idea of anybody targeting Phoebe's beautiful, aquiline face, although it was admittedly preferable to murder. With a shudder, she remembered the date of her death on the funeral invitation. 'He must have sent the funeral notice too!'

'Have they traced the package to Craig, then?' asked Mil.

'Mason told us that Royal Mail is trying to track it through the computer system, but the address label was largely destroyed when it went off, and Craig's barcode scanner was malfunctioning, so it's not straightforward. But if it *was* him, it's hardly going to be traceable, is it?'

'What about the funeral notice? Stamps have barcodes they can trace now, don't they?'

'Mason's team have it.' Phoebe shrugged, helping herself to a swig of Juno's cold tea and wincing. 'Ugh, no sugar. But I do remember Craig was super keen to hand the envelope with it in over to me personally, so it makes sense. Let's face it, he was obsessive, insular, quite possibly an incel. The police say a wall of his workshop was covered in stuff about me. Frankly, it's a huge relief if there's nobody else involved.'

'I still don't see why he'd want to hurt you.' Juno was struggling to make sense of it.

'Maybe he was a hired assassin?' Mil suggested ardently.

'For whom?' Phoebe asked doubtfully.

'It doesn't sound to me like DI Mason is doing his job properly,' Juno huffed. 'What does your cousin have to say about him, Mil?'

'Just says Mason's old school, whatever that means.' His mouth turned down uncertainly.

'Sexist and easily bribed?' Juno suggested.

'Still young enough to be taking A levels at Mil's *old school*.' Phoebe caught her eye over her sunglasses again, and they were both forced to look in different directions to stop the shared giggles bubbling up.

'I think he meant thorough, like DI Lowe,' offered Mil, who was a big fan of tough man's man Carrick in Phoebe's eighties crime thrillers.

'Or lazy,' drawled a voice behind them, and Felix's shadow fell across the table, a *Marlbury Gazette* landing on it. 'I just picked this up from the shop. Look at the Death Notices section.'

Juno leafed through to them, running her finger past much-loved grandparents to a familiar name that made her heart jolt in her chest.

Phoebe Fredericks, suddenly, aged 54.

There followed the same funeral details Phoebe had received through the post.

'I'm fifty-three!' Phoebe protested indignantly.

* * *

Juno knew Phoebe well enough to realise that the more flippantly she reacted to something, the more rattled she was by it, like the heroine of her Dorothy De'Ath books, an aristocratic 1920s flapper with a penchant for nonchalant epigrams.

By contrast, Juno was a flapper in the modern sense, reacting to shock by waving her arms a lot, her voice climbing scales.

'This is awful!' she cried. 'Who would do this?'

'It proves we have to look into it,' said Felix.

'The Village Detectives have a case!' bellowed Mil.

'This proves nothing,' Phoebe argued. 'Craig could have placed it before he died. We are *not* investigating his death; the police are.'

'Oh, we are.' Felix sat down, a dog springing on his lap. He pressed his lips into its domed white head and looked up. 'Tell her we're doing this, Juno.'

Faced with those heart-stopping blue eyes, Juno was power-less to do anything but assent. 'We must.'

'Agreed!' Mil was right behind them.

'I've already renamed the WhatsApp group chat,' Juno revealed proudly. 'If you check it, you'll see our new branding. Also I've posted an invite to my housewarming party!'

Mil looked it up on his phone. 'This is fire – you've done a logo and everything. Look, guys.' He held the screen up for the Sylvians to see.

'I'm having postcards printed,' Juno boasted, 'and we can have other merch – bags, pens, baseball caps.' Best not mention she'd already ordered mugs, a cushion cover and coasters for her flat.

Phoebe regarded Mil's phone screen with her brows creased. 'Juno, did it occur to you that VD might not be the best abbreviation to use?'

Juno was indignant. 'It has plenty of positive associations: Valentine's Day, Victory Day, Virtual Desktop, Vampire Diaries – I was a big fan and er...'

'And VD.' Phoebe took off her shades and folded them on the table, her expression hard to read. 'What does it make you think of, Felix darling?'

'*Vir Devotus*?' he suggested, not taking his eyes from her face.

'That too!' Juno enthused, wishing she had a man who looked at her like that, and wondering vaguely if *Vir Devotus* was a plant name.

'I don't get what's wrong with it?' said Mil, claiming his phone back to admire it. 'This looks great, Juno! I love it! The Village Detectives are back in business!'

Juno was discreetly googling *Vir Devotus* on her phone – it stood for Devoted Man – when Phoebe asked her husband, 'How did you know to buy the local paper?'

'I always buy it when I'm home.'

'No, you don't. And why go straight to the Death Notices? It's as though you knew it would be there.'

'Are you accusing me of placing the announcement myself?' Felix laughed. 'C'mon, Phoebes, it's obviously OhFeelYa!'

Juno guessed Ophelia had to be another of his comely PAs. She'd thought the most recent one was called Betsy, but he had a frightening turnover rate and a knack of hiring overly devoted ones.

'Well, it's not OhManiacNymph,' Phoebe was murmuring.

'We don't know that for certain,' said Felix.

Feeling lost, Juno looked to Mil for reassurance, only to find him deep in the sports pages of the *Marlbury Gazette*.

Phoebe and Felix were still exchanging cross words, both *sotto voce* and stiff jawed, a strangely sexy tango of a domestic scrap.

'OhFeelYa is not behind what happened, Felix,' Phoebe growled. 'Craig is! Mason as good as said so.'

'What if the police are jumping to conclusions to get this off their caseload? It's not enough me telling them about OhFeelYa and OhManiacNymph. You need to back me up.'

'Am I missing something?' Juno asked them.

'They were Twitter trolls,' Phoebe muttered, playing with her sunglasses on the table, not looking up.

'One still is,' Felix countered.

'What did they troll about?'

'You must know about the hate campaign against Phoebe?' He turned to her, blue gaze intense.

'We've never actually talked about it.'

'But you've googled it, surely?' he asked matter-of-factly.

'I have not!' She looked to Phoebe for back-up, but she was still focusing on her sunglasses.

'Seriously?'

'Not once!' Juno protested, although that wasn't entirely true.

'I think we need to tell them everything, Phoebe darling.' Felix plucked the paper out of Mil's hands and folded it to the

Births, Marriages and Deaths section again. 'Because this isn't your first death notice, is it?'

'It's not?' Mil looked up in surprise.

'Died a thousand deaths, me.' Phoebe reached for her vape and sat back to give it a femme fatale puff, trying to look insouciant. She'd gone very pale, Juno noticed.

'Back when Phoebe was being trolled on Twitter, we discovered somebody was placing a recurring announcement in the local paper,' Felix told them. 'That's why I bought this one. This is just the same. It's happening all over again.'

'Why would anyone want to do that?' gasped Juno, appalled.

Phoebe hugged herself, glancing away, the most discomfited Juno had seen her. 'I might need a drink.'

'I have the perfect Japanese malt whisky set aside.' Mil bounded off through the terrace doors.

'I meant coffee...' Phoebe turned too late to catch him, her eyes meeting Juno's, and summoned a rushed reassuring smile. 'I really don't like talking about it.'

'Tell me, Freddy!'

* * *

Phoebe talked quickly, playing events down as though recounting a tiresome day at the office. Juno could tell it was her coping mechanism, in the same way she herself peppered everything with jokes and overdid the funny voices and accents.

'It's not as though I'm the first female journalist targeted by cranks.' Her tone was swift and unemotional. 'Not the first cancelled by social media mudslinging either. When you write opinion pieces, you grow accustomed to robust criticism; the comments section beneath my column was always a minefield.'

'Some were vindictive bastards,' Felix defended her. 'Mostly unjustified.'

'Mostly,' Phoebe echoed wryly, shooting him a grateful, if sceptical, smile. 'They got worse as time went on. I'd also noticed my socials become increasingly toxic over the years, which just went with the times, also with being an outspoken woman over forty. There were a few names that kept repeatedly popping up, a couple of them particularly vicious and personal, but it wasn't until a Twitter storm broke over a comment made on a news story that they launched a character assassination.'

'What had you commented on?' asked Juno worriedly. Whilst generous and liberal to a fault, her friend had a very sharp tongue. She was terrified Phoebe had been cancelled over something truly terrible – a racist or homophobic rant, say.

'A bench.'

'Is that slang for something?' Juno's on-off affair with dating apps meant she knew ghost, breadcrumb and bench were all verbs, although she wasn't certain what they stood for.

'Long outdoor seat in a public space,' Felix murmured helpfully.

'A literal bench? You were cancelled over a *bench*?'

'Yup.'

'There must be more to it than that.'

'Virginia Woolf.'

'Virginia Woolf?' Juno parroted, struggling to follow the logic.

'The last female British tennis player to win Wimbledon, yes?' Mil sauntered back outside with a bottle and four shot glasses.

'Twentieth-century modernist writer,' Phoebe corrected. 'One of the Bloomsbury Set who lived in squares and loved in triangles.'

'Famously fluid,' added Juno, an unpleasant thought striking her. 'You didn't say something TERFy about identity politics, did you, Freddy? Please tell me you didn't. Was it about the character of *Orlando* changing gender?'

'Of course not.' Phoebe gave a piqued eyeroll. 'I've always loved *Orlando*. No, it was just about where to put a commemorative bench.'

'A *bench*, did you say?' Mil laid out four brimming shot glasses in front of them.

'Long outdoor seat in a public space,' Felix repeated, picking his up.

Phoebe pushed hers away. 'A London publisher raised money for a sculpture of Virginia Woolf sitting on a bench that they wanted to put in Richmond Park to recognise the decade she'd lived and worked nearby. They found a lovely spot overlooking the Thames, but the good bergères of the Richmond Society objected that it might be "triggering" to suicidal passersby.'

'Of course, Woolf drowned herself,' Juno gasped, immediately seeing their point.

'In Sussex, decades later, yes.' Phoebe rolled her eyes again. 'I mentioned the news story in my column, asking why her likeness shouldn't look out across the river she drew inspiration from in *Mrs Dalloway*. That's when things took a dark turn on my Twitter feed. My trolls – and there were already plenty – accused me of inciting depressed Woolf-inspired teenagers into suicide.'

'Some would say they had a point, though...' Juno ventured.

'I wasn't denying how tragically Woolf died; I was just putting a different point of view about honouring her life and legacy. Some of the pushback was engaged and informed, but two of my most persistent detractors posted non-stop about my "weaponised words", branding me a self-harm enabler. They called themselves OhFeelYa – three words, Oh Feel Ya – and OhManiacNymph. It seemed almost laughable at first.'

'You made fun of them, didn't you?' Juno covered her mouth, imagining Phoebe's blasé, incendiary wit pouring gasoline on their fire.

'They'd spent all year slagging off my column, my lifestyle, my opinions on everything, so I thought this was just another personal attack and I gave as good as I got, suggesting they read *To the Lighthouse* to better understand art and perception. And water. I also recommended *The Waves*. "I am rooted but I flow." I had a terrific army of supporters. Hashtag "GoWithTheFlow" trended for ages. But the two trolls got a lot more vicious after that. Don't think they read either book, mind you, or indeed anything by Woolf.'

'You didn't block them?'

'I never blocked anyone in those days; I advocate free speech, and I always tried to be fair minded and good natured about it. But soon their posts got really disturbing, blaming me for personally impacting their mental health. They somehow managed to twist everything I said, retweeting out of context, no matter how hard I tried to soothe the situation or firefight.' She rubbed her face then took another slug of Juno's cold, sugarless tea rather than the brimming shot glass in front of her.

'Soon OhManiacNymph was accusing me of making them personally want to commit suicide. I should have blocked them at that point, I realise, but my editor was stoked by all the attention and told me not to. Paywall views of my column were going through the roof, physical paper sales rocketing. He told me to push it further. I refused, but it turns out I'd already crossed the Rubicon; *iacta aliea est*. The die was cast.'

Juno, who had binged-watched *Roman Empire* on Netflix, recognised this as the point of no return when Julius Caesar had crossed the river with his army, triggering civil war.

Mil was more confused, asking, 'Was this Di another troll?'

He and Felix were already on their second whisky shots. Juno took a swig of her own then regretted it, the peaty heat making her eyeballs burn, her own jaw going slack in appalled shock as Phoebe went on.

'A day later, OhManiacNymph and OhFeelYa announced on social media that they were going to kill themselves, driven to it by me. They made a public pact naming a date and a time, which the site took down as soon as I reported it, but followers had screen-shotted it and kept retweeting. It refused to go away. The pact was trending everywhere within hours, a countdown hashtag shared and reshared for days.'

She looked down at her vape, twirling it round in her fingers like a pen. 'The moment the deadline passed, OhManiacNymph's account went inactive.'

'She *actually* killed herself?'

Phoebe looked away, vape twirling faster and faster.

'Definitely not,' Felix jumped in. 'OhFeelYa was still very much online, and they're the same person as OhManiacNymph, remember.'

'We think they are,' Phoebe cautioned. 'OhFeelYa went berserk, posting fifteen-part threads night and day accusing me of murdering their friend, calling for the police to arrest me. I was questioned more than once.'

'Did they ever find a body?'

'Well, nobody left a note on a pier end saying I drove them to it.' She raked her fingers through her short dark hair, leaving its prominent white streak poking up punkily. 'On average eleven people drown each week in the UK, four by taking their own lives.' She looked out towards the River Dunnett, where they had found poor Si Locke gasping his last waterlogged breaths just weeks earlier. 'We couldn't know for certain.'

'Did you ever find out who they were?' Juno asked, noticing

Felix had already drained his second whisky, a muscle fluctuating in his handsome cheek.

Phoebe shook her head. 'We tried, but both accounts were untraceable, buried behind a VPN and fake email. Not uncommon, apparently. People held a vigil for OhManiacNymph by the Thames. A few also came to our house, shouting insults and painting "murderer" on the walls. I got multiple death threats online, mostly wanting to drown me. It was an awful time. The girls were in the middle of taking their A levels. Felix had to come back from filming in Hungary halfway through a shoot.'

'It was clearly a precision strike.' Felix stood up, moving to stand behind his wife's chair. 'As soon as Phoebe got booted off the paper, OhFeelYa came off Twitter too. Their job was done.'

'Officially, my contract wasn't renewed.' She put her dark glasses back on, reaching back to cover Felix's hand on her shoulder. 'The senior editorial team gave out a lot of groupthink media babble about refreshing the brand, as in getting someone younger. Once I'd come off social media, the oxygen was all one way. It didn't help that a lot of the paper's staff believed the hype.'

'None of those bastards stood up for you,' Felix pointed out angrily. 'One of them petitioned the others against you. If you'd just let me go in and—'

'I was glad to leave in the end,' Phoebe insisted quickly, withdrawing her hand. 'Although then I found all my other work drying up too – freelance writing, talks, panels, a book deal I was at the point of signing fell through. Old friends stopped returning my calls. But it wasn't until my agent suggested I find alternative representation that I finally realised I'd been cancelled.'

'You didn't fight it?' Juno looked at Phoebe wide-eyed, astonished by her sangfroid.

'I planned to. After a brief period of naval gazing, maybe. But other stuff got in the way. It was a tricky year.'

Juno remembered too late that what Phoebe had once described to her as her 'Stormy Cs' had all occurred within twelve months: Cancellation, Cash Crisis and Cancer.

Her diagnosis had coincided with the media storm that ended her career. Sudden, brutal and life-changing, it had turned the Sylvians' worlds upside down, an urgent hysterectomy followed by chemotherapy.

It was also while Phoebe was still undergoing treatment that a movie Felix was heavily invested in went bust halfway through filming. From what Dennis had said earlier, Juno now knew who was primarily to blame for the cash crisis C. Dorothy De'Ath's invention had staved off the creditors for a while, and helped Phoebe recover body and mind, but they'd eventually been forced to sell their house to recover his debts.

She watched as Felix's thumb stroked his wife's shoulder before he moved back to his seat, picking up the *Marlbury Gazette* again.

The folded paper snapped against his open palm, making Juno jump. 'Our local paper in Yorkshire ran a death notice for Phoebe every week for two months until we found out and put a stop to it. Now OhFeelYa is back on Twitter.' The *Marlbury Gazette* was slapped angrily back down on the table, making them all jump this time, shot glasses included. 'Phoebe isn't on social media, so they're taking swipes at me. They've also worked out she writes fiction under pen names, so Dorothy De'Ath and P. F. Sylvian are also taking a fresh hammering.'

'It's nothing new.' Phoebe's eyes flashed a warning at Felix. Then she forced a smile, turning to the others. 'When you've burned your bridges, you don't worry about the trolls hiding underneath.'

'But what if OhFeelYa is the same person who sent the device that killed Craig?' asked Juno.

'Exactly!' Felix accepted another brimming shot glass from Mil.

'Craig made it himself,' Phoebe said firmly.

'That doesn't really make sense with all this death threat business.' Mil scratched his head, closing his good eye. 'More likely this nympho Ophelia character.'

'We all think differently to you, Phoebe,' Felix murmured, leaning closer to his wife, blue gaze on her face. 'You have to trust us on this.'

Phoebe glared back at him. They stared at each other for so long, Juno started to feel seriously awkward. She looked to Mil, but he still had his face tilted up to the sun, good eye still closed.

'It surely merits investigating?' she ventured.

'I'm in!' Mil opened both eyes and helped himself to Phoebe's untouched whisky.

'Well, I'm *not*.' Phoebe stood up and marched into the pub.

'Aren't you going to follow her?' Juno asked Felix.

'To the loo?'

* * *

Feeling stupid, Juno decided to answer the call of nature too and hurried to the Ladies', tracking Phoebe down to the basins where she was splashing water on her face.

'That was intense!' Juno checked her reflection, horrified to see her mascara had run and she had a red blob on her chin which dated back to the beetroot hors d'oeuvre at Godlington. That lunch felt like a lifetime ago, not a few hours. Phoebe's revelations had thrown her, sweeping Juno up into the Stormy Cs, which she feared were still circling.

Phoebe regarded her own reflection alongside, pulling up her wet cheeks in a facelift that made her look incredible, her nineties ghost in the room. 'Christ, I look like I've not slept in days.'

'That's because you hardly sleep.'

'I need to try those ashwagandha gummies, even if Betsy did order them for Felix with extra poison pens.'

'To de-stress, you'd be better off trying mindful—' Juno did a double take, realising what Phoebe was saying. 'You think Felix's assistant could be a suspect?'

'Ignore me,' Phoebe insisted, letting her face drop back to its customary, age-appropriate beauty. 'I'm pathologically jealous of all my husband's assistants by default. Infuriatingly shallow habit. It's not her. She's just a kid with a daddy crush.'

Juno nonetheless added Betsy to her reasons for Phoebe to diss Felix.

'You two seem seriously tense?' she ventured.

'He's driving me mad,' Phoebe confessed, starting the hand dryer and performing an impressive body swerve to dry her face beneath it, shouting over the blown air noise. 'I'm going home. He can stay here to get drunk and watch rugby with you and Mil.'

'I'll walk with you. Not a rugby fan.'

Straightening up, Phoebe looked like she was going to say no, then she shrugged. 'Just don't talk to me about trolls.'

'I loved that movie. Singing, dancing and hugging is the answer, Freddy.'

'Stop it, Lady Glitter Sparkles.'

Juno started humming 'Can't Stop the Feeling', desperate to lift Phoebe's black mood.

From nowhere, they had another laughter-stitch moment, the giggles brief and intense as a sneeze, which cheered them both up immensely.

Outside on the sunny decked terrace, Felix and Mil were working their way through the Japanese whisky like two sleazy gumshoes, talking about nothing but trolls and how to lay online traps by which they'd reveal their identity.

Felix didn't protest when Phoebe said she was leaving, which Juno suspected might have been because she added, 'Juno and I want to have a long chat about her love life. We need to find her a man she can trust.'

'Good plan,' he said softly.

Mil protested that *he* was Juno's trustworthy man, reassuring her with a cheering wink of his good eye. 'Me and Felix here will come up with a plan to catch this poison pen bomber. You look after Phoebe, while we give the Village Detectives our full attention. That and Wexshire Warriors. Bring it on!'

Unconvinced anything would distract his attention once the rugby was on and the pub full of evening punters, Juno hurriedly followed Phoebe, who was already out front with her vape and the terriers, looking distinctly Greta Garbo.

'Come on.' She whistled for the dogs and, Juno half suspected, her too.

Phoebe always walked ridiculously fast on her long legs, meaning that within moments of crossing the lane to the alleyway known as Witch's Broom, Juno was far too out of breath to say anything much.

Arriving at Inkbury's flint Norman church at the opposite end of the path, Phoebe paused to squint up at the squat bell tower. 'It *had* to be Craig targeting me, Juno.'

'What if it wasn't?'

'I need it to be him.'

'But Felix thinks—'

'Felix doesn't think before he acts, that's the point. He charges straight in without a plan, unless it's making a movie, which is the *only* thing he always plans down to the finest detail. He's a haphazard parent, hopeless flirt, high-risk provider. Good job I love him to death.'

Juno would have liked to select at least one of these things for more detailed examination, but Phoebe carried on angrily: '*He's* the one who keeps poking the Twitter hornet's nest. He wants to settle old scores. But why look back?'

'I thought we agreed not to talk about trolls?'

'We're not.'

Juno glanced across at her in profile, that androgynous beauty with its sharp chin and beaky nose, the big fierce green eyes still glaring up at the church tower as though seeking a sign from above.

Since moving to Inkbury, she'd witnessed the tension between Phoebe and Felix just a few times, but already sensed theirs was a rare dance of combative long-term love, on the back foot one moment and head over heels the next, yet rarely out of step. It was a relationship Juno struggled to understand, her envy of its passion tinged with disquiet. The couple seemed so high-octane glamorous, and yet their lives had ricocheted between boom and bust.

'You must have old scores to settle too, Freddy,' she said cautiously, and before she could stop herself, she added, 'With Felix, even?'

Shaking her head, Phoebe turned to glance around the gravestones in the churchyard. 'And you were wrong earlier; I have no reason to diss Felix.'

'You have literally just dissed him,' Juno pointed out.

The shrewd green eyes glinted as they caught hers. 'Okay, maybe a couple of reasons.'

Juno knew it. 'He gambled your family's home on a movie that went bust. He's the reason you lost your farm in Yorkshire.'

'Not that.' Phoebe shook her head more fervently.

'Betsy?'

'God, not that either. Let's not say her name again.'

'Understood,' Juno nodded. She didn't, but Phoebe had a scarily intense look.

'When I was ill and we all thought I might die,' Phoebe said quietly, green gaze phosphorus bright, 'Felix laid everything on the line to get me through it. There was nothing he wouldn't do. He was my guardian angel.'

'Wow,' Juno said in a small voice, vicariously a tiny bit in love with Felix once more.

'Then I got better and reality struck. He couldn't direct real life like one of his movies. We couldn't simply go back to how it had been before. He was brokenheartedly angry. Angriest of all with my black dog.'

Juno's love wavered. She wanted to ask if this was a real black dog – a Labrador perhaps – or a black dog in the depressed Churchillian sense, but Phoebe was talking again, crossly blinking away a rare rising tide of tears.

'This needs to be over,' she repeated, looking up at the church tower once more. 'It *was* Craig, Juno.'

'Absolutely.'

'Now I'm going home. Change that bloody group chat logo.' She swept away, dogs at her heels, moving far too fast for Juno to make chase.

'I thought we were going to talk about my love life?' she called hopefully, but Phoebe was already out of earshot.

It was only as she was wandering back along Church Lane to her little flat, eyeing Inkbury's handsomest houses behind their high brick walls and longing for a man as sexy and brooding and fiercely loyal as Felix, that Juno remembered again what Eugene Campbell had said about the husbands usually being behind murderous attacks.

Could Phoebe secretly suspect so too?

7

PHOEBE

'Are you saying that the Library Steps Ripper might be a woman, Lady Dee?'

'This murderer kills in cold blood, with imagination and panache, Annie. So far, they've crushed one victim with a shelf of first editions, stabbed another with a jewelled letter opener and now poor Mrs Gilmore's just been bitten by an adder.'

'Could that not be an unfortunate accident, milady? The underbutler had a nasty nip on his ankle out beating for Lord Marsham last week.'

'This adder is from India, Annie. It's not native. And the murderer left the same calling card, a torn page of a pocket diary marked with a B in a feminine hand.'

'Didn't Professor Gilmore visit India recently, milady?'

'So he did! But our killer is a woman, mark my words, and not one of us is safe until she's caught.'

Phoebe looked up from the glowing laptop screen to glance across at her husband's lifeless body, a thought occurring to her.

She made a quick note in the Moleskine book beside her before resuming typing.

She worked best in the early morning, often starting before dawn, whereas Felix was a night owl. Watching him sleep wasn't a new distraction for her, but it was one she never tired of. Living in their glorified bedsit for the past two years had shifted her perspective, lending her continued exile from the media circus an intimacy that almost compensated for the seclusion. When Felix was in situ, working from home felt magical and other-worldly, Titania with Oberon in their enchanted forest.

And even though Oberon had been out carousing late – spilling back in to fall over the dogs after she'd gone to bed, his kisses smelling of expensive Japanese whisky as he tiredly apolo-gised for getting drunk and watching rugby – his magic remained undimmed. It had always been a magnetically dark art, inventive and imaginative.

Her own creativity fed off his. She typed quickly and quietly, developing the difference of opinion between headstrong Dee and her trusty maid, culminating in the discovery that Professor Gilmore had been murdered, suffocated by a pillow on which lingered the scent of Molinard Habanita, a cologne that neither he nor his wife wore.

Movement from the bed made her glance up.

Felix had rolled over onto his belly, arm dangling over the side, smartwatch glowing for a moment like a tiny unwatched TV screen before darkening as he slept on. The two terriers re-curled themselves rebelliously on his far side, Velcro-ed to his warmth.

Phoebe envied them all their oblivion.

This morning she needed the logic of plotting to take her mind off things, eager to lay a path of clues that drew her sleuths ever closer towards the killer, and to reassure her readers that the baddies were always apprehended at the end rather than blowing themselves up before anybody knew what was going on.

As the words flowed, so her mood lifted, happiest in this golden hour. She only broke off to message both daughters good morning in their far-flung time zones, where it was the previous evening for one and the coming afternoon for the other. They were safe, far from her chaos, she reassured herself. Their father, meanwhile, captive and unconscious, was just where she wanted him.

When Phoebe looked up again, dawn was in full swing, its birdsong chorus trumpeted from the branches and wires around Hartridge, cool light stealing in through the high windows, gilding the tufts of Felix's silvered blond hair poking from beneath the bedsheets.

His phone alarm was going off. He'd changed the music again, although it rarely had the desired effect of rousing his subconscious. Phoebe vaguely recognised the song, trying to place it while it rang on unheeded. It sounded vintage and Brit-poppy; he shared Juno's retro taste, whereas Phoebe's own fickle playlist veered from Bach to Trap via Mitski on a whim.

The alarm stopped of its own accord and she glanced up at the windows, the sky already faded from dark to light denim, its blades of sunlight shifting across the flagstones towards the big rug, the tufted threshold of which had so recently marked her cue to listen out warily for Craig.

Phoebe pulled the Moleskine notebook closer and reread the single word she'd written earlier, her fingers tapping the page.

HANDWRITING.

The envelope containing her funeral notice was with the police, but she could still picture the big, looping hand it had been addressed with. Somewhere in the recesses of her mind, she was sure she'd seen the handwriting before. It was certainly nothing like Craig's small, neat writing in the copies of the Dorothy De'Ath books he'd corrected.

Like an old-fashioned rolodex, her mind whirred backwards through invitations and Christmas cards, trying to place the looping handwriting.

Felix's alarm went off again, the song playing through once more without waking him. She recognised it this time: 'Mr Brightside', that sexy, breathless anthem for cheated-on hearts.

Picking up her own phone, Phoebe switched off airplane mode and checked the notifications from the Village Detectives WhatsApp group chat that had pinged in when she'd messaged her daughters.

Juno had changed its profile picture the previous evening from her VD letter logo to a dubious Scooby Doo silhouette. She had also posted:

> Who killed Craig Jackman? Let's put together a forensic character profile – can you ask around the pub regulars, Mil? Background. Hobbies. Sex life. And if not Craig, then who? Suspects? MMO?

Multiple incomprehensible voice notes followed from Mil and Felix, sent whilst still at the pub. Almost drowned out by a loud background rugby commentary, they seemed to be proposing the need for high-tech spyware. For this, a pair of locals called Alan and Bernard had offered to help.

Later still, Mil had sent another voice note after last orders, now apparently alone and sleepily slurred, but eager to relay his omnipresent landlord nous: 'So Craig lived with his mum Denise on the edge of Dunford Common, Nightingale Avenue. Used to

be a rough estate when I was a kid, but now there's a lot of
camera doorbells and less ABH. Denise is a single mum, bit of an
oddball, not an easy character. Abrasive. Worked up at Hartridge
for a bit when Boozy was there. A guy who drinks here was in the
same year as Craig at school, says he was a lonely swot who went
to Reading uni for a bit, but he dropped out then got a job with
the Post Office. Bit of an old woman by all accounts. Never saw
him with a bird, or bloke come to that. Not on any social media I
know about. Liked his model making, quizzing, pub grub. Very
fond of N Scale Graham Farish locomotives with manual points,
according to Alan and Bernard. I wrote that down. He also
bought a lot of second-hand precision equipment off them for his
workshop. Remind me, what's MMO again?'

Juno had replied at midnight with a monocle emoji:

> Motive, means, opportunity.

There followed a lot of bedtime emoji flirting between her
and Mil involving monocles, winks and X-Files GIFs captioned
The Truth Is Out There.

Scrolling past them, Phoebe read another summarising
message from Juno.

> We know Craig could have potentially made the
> device in his workshop, and he certainly brought
> it to Freddy's door, but why target her? Could
> *he* have been the intended victim all along? Or
> did somebody else send that parcel and our
> postie was a mule who got in the way? If so, and
> Freddy was the real target, who would want to
> hurt her? And is it connected with @OhFeelYa?
> More importantly, *who* is @OhFeelYa?

Phoebe flinched at this, annoyed at Juno for bringing it up.

Then she spotted her husband's avatar alongside a message sent at 1 a.m. He'd shared a familiar trio of names.

Growling under her breath, she crossed the room to clamber onto the bed and sit on him, holding the phone to his face as he woke with a groan. 'Couldn't you have run this past me first? I was literally lying beside you when you sent this message.'

Felix opened his eyes groggily, crossing them as he tried to focus on the screen. 'You were asleep.'

'I don't believe these three names have anything to do with what happened to Craig.'

He lifted his head, rubbing his eyes with the balls of his palms before tapping at his watch face. 'This seems to have stopped at 6 a.m.?'

'It is six.'

Groaning, Felix pulled a pillow over his head. 'Then I'm pressing snooze on this row.'

'Well, I'm not. Why on earth would Otis New try to target me after all this time? We were using fax machines and plastic cups for the water cooler when he and I first locked horns.'

'And he was still gunning for you from his iPhone 12 four years ago,' the pillow couldn't resist fact-correcting.

'Well, Gail Lamb has moved on,' she argued. 'She and I fell out when our kids were in primary school. It only rumbled on so long because we were living in the same village. And as for Seraphine, do we really need to drag her into this? Isn't it painful enough?'

'Please let me sleep,' came the groan beneath the pillow. 'My train's not until after nine. My head is killing me.'

'Good, that saves me the trouble.'

'You wouldn't kill me. Torture's more your style.'

'Let's not test it. I feel jolly murderous right now.'

'Who will tweak your meta-tags for you?' came the indignant

protest. 'Upload your brilliant novels?' He shifted beneath her, tipping her forwards so she was forced to grab the headboard to balance. 'Make mad passionate love to you?'

'All at the same time?' she muttered, struggling to stay cross when he was warm, hungover and rumpled beneath her. 'Is that a promise?'

He laughed, a sleepy hand reaching out and feeling its way towards hers only to be intercepted by an eager terrier flopping over to offer a speckled belly to rub.

'I can stay here today if you like,' Felix offered, yawning croakily beneath the covers, 'do my meetings remotely?'

'Don't use me as a hangover sicknote. You'll only distract me.' She dropped a kiss on the pillow that was obscuring his face, half-imagining the bergamot tang of Molinard Habanita lingering there.

'I'm not happy leaving you alone here.'

'You were happy enough last night.'

'I'm easily corrupted,' he mumbled drowsily. Then, sounding more awake after a pause, he said, 'Didn't Juno come back here with you?'

'I put her off.' Phoebe watched the second terrier crawling jealously beneath his arm to be stroked too. 'I have these guys here to protect me.'

She was starting to get cramp, adjusting her weight off him and onto the bed. 'Besides which, no one is going to try to do me harm, Felix, because it was Craig who made that device, and it literally backfired on him.'

The pillow slid sideways; his blue eyes were sharply focused now. 'I don't think you believe the postman was targeting you any more than I do.'

She pictured the handwriting on the envelope of the funeral

notice, wondering if was the same as the package label, destroyed when it detonated.

'Well, I certainly don't think it was any of these three.' She brandished her phone again. 'You can't just share the names of everyone I've ever picked a fight with, Felix.'

'That list would be much longer, with me at the top.' He propped himself up on his elbows, looking handsomely piqued. 'You realise the police insinuated they thought I might be behind it? They even questioned me about that health supplement I ordered for you.'

'Which never arrived,' she pointed out. 'You're an obvious suspect. If I didn't know you better, I'd think you might be trying to kill me.'

They locked gazes, both refusing to drop eye contact, a familiar ritual after three decades of pillow-talk and pillow-fights.

Then a slow, seductive smile slowly stole across Felix's face. 'I'm awake now; I can think of far better things to do than confess my crimes. Come here.'

The terriers were promptly ejected.

But after one brief kiss, Phoebe was on her feet again, mind too busy for sex, beckoning him to follow her back to her laptop. 'Now that you're fully conscious, you can come and tell me why this isn't evidence of malicious intent.' Cracking her knuckles over the keyboard to steel herself, she turned off airplane mode and logged into Outlook.

'Have the police finally sent details of Craig's workshop notice board?' Felix scrabbled out of bed to follow, wrapped in a throw.

'They're hardly going to email that. The Wexshire Constabulary has a code of conduct, unlike the Village Detectives,' she huffed, opening their joint email. 'Can you please explain why you gave those three names to Mil and Juno—'

'They want to help.'

'—and left out Penelope Fermoy's?'

Felix let out an amused snort as Phoebe navigated to the folder crammed with their neighbour's hyper-aggressive emails, some sent directly, others through the Hartridge Foundation and its solicitors. 'If anybody wishes us ill, Penny does.'

'It's not Bad Penny,' he said emphatically, slumping into the chair beside hers.

'She wants us out of here. She's made threats.'

'She's not OhFeelYa.'

'How do you know?'

'Pen wasn't part of all that; it's way before her time.'

It irritated Phoebe that Felix defended Penny no matter how aggressive she got, always simply repeating how fond Uncle Boozy was of her. Penny was three or four years his junior, but they'd grown up in overlapping social circles, sharing the same Gatecrasher Balls, regattas and ski resorts, privileges Penny lapped up as much as Felix played them down. And now they were connected by the same squabbling, dysfunctional family, both satellite socialites relying upon it for the roofs over their heads.

'She threatens our lives right here in black and white.' She pointed to one of many late-night rants. 'Dead between the lines, I'll evict you... and here... Take it as dead, you're not staying there!'

'Don't you think she maybe meant to type "read"?'

Phoebe ran her eyes over it again, feeling a bit silly as she conceded the point. Penny's typing was atrocious. Then it occurred to her. 'OhFeelYa also spells badly!'

'It's not Penny.'

They locked gazes in another unblinking face-off, longer this time.

'Whoever it is, I *will* find them,' he promised.

Realising he wasn't going to blink or look away until she believed him, which she already did, she broke eye contact first. 'Let's go back to bed.'

He let out a soft huff of frustration. 'Don't try seducing me just because you don't want to talk about it. I will resist.'

'You won't' – she stretched across to kiss him – 'because we both know it cheers us up enormously. It also just happens to be the only way to shut you up.'

'I resent that!' he protested. 'I often talk a lot during sex.'

'Not about murder.'

'I'm romantic like that.' He kissed her back.

'Always.' She stood up, pulling him with her, a familiar thrill quickening her senses.

Ignoring caffeine cravings, too familiar for the self-conscious need to scrub up first, they kissed and tripped their way through the angled sunlight towards the bed. Before they could climb in, a knock at the back door sent the dogs into a flurry of yaps.

'Ignore it,' Felix insisted, lifting her up onto the mattress. 'It's way too early for house calls.'

'What if it's the police?'

'Come to arrest me?' He dropped the throw he was wrapped in.

The fist pounded again.

'That's Mil's special knock,' Phoebe recognised.

'Mil has a special knock?' Felix's lips were working their way at speed along the shelf of her breastbone.

'You know he does.'

The kiss moved up her throat. 'That back door's out of bounds.'

'You've been using it.'

A third knock rang out.

Momentum lost, Felix smiled into the hollow beneath her jaw

before turning away, pulling on a pair of board shorts to go to open it.

'They're back to front!' Phoebe pointed out.

* * *

Mil's voice was loud and cheery in the rear lobby. 'I know you're early birds and Alan and Bernard are off to a railway modellers' convention in Bristol, so I wanted to pick up the kit they were talking about last night before they set off. Thought I might as well bring it straight round.'

Hurriedly redressing, Phoebe found she too had tugged on her jeans back to front in her haste.

Mil looked far less hungover than Felix. Despite always being far quicker to get loud, dance and slur his words, the ex-rugby pro's wide flanker legs were famously hollow. 'That was some great hooch last night, hey, mate? And what a match! Couldn't sleep afterwards, I was buzzing so much. Here's the spyware.'

As a gadget-loving petrolhead, Mil relished manning the Q Branch of their operation, opening a briefcase on the table. 'Two solar-powered CCTV cameras – Alan's just put in hard-wired ones like Bernard's on account of these running out of charge so often, but they're fine if you bring the batteries inside every few days to plug in for a quick boost. And here's that GPS SOS they mentioned, see? You wear it like a watch, the charge lasts over a week and it works off its own mini-SIM card, so as soon as you raise the alarm, it opens a line to your emergency contact, plus they'll have a map trace on you.'

'Superb.' Felix put it on Phoebe's wrist.

She eyed it in horror. 'You seriously expect me to wear this like an electronic tag?'

'When I'm not here, yes.'

'What if I don't want you to track my every move?'

'It only locates you when you press this,' Mil assured her, pointing to a big red SOS button in the centre of its face. 'That sends an alert call and text to your main emergency contact number. I'll programme it to be Felix's mobile. You have two back-up numbers using these buttons, see, that'll be me and Juno, and this big button with the green microphone on it is the—'

'Forget it.' She slid it off her wrist. 'I have a perfectly adequate phone.'

'That you always keep on airplane mode,' Felix muttered.

'I'm not wearing something designed for vulnerable elderly people,' she huffed.

'Extreme orienteering,' Mil corrected. 'Alan and Bernard used to compete all over the world. This saved their arses more than once. It's shockproof and waterproof, works on any network.'

'If I orient anywhere extreme, I'll pop it on,' she promised grudgingly.

Apparently in no hurry to leave, Mil stayed for coffee, eager to enlighten them with the finer aspects of extreme sports: 'I'm more of an Ironman fan myself. I've done all the big ones. The secret's in the training programme.'

Phoebe adored Mil's gregarious loyalty and generosity, but today he was a mansplaining, GPS-tagging passion killer, oblivious to her polite hints that he should push off. Eager to feed his hangover, Felix was soon making them all toast, casting occasional hot, regretful looks in her direction.

Phoebe felt one of her dark moods descending like rain clouds, wishing they'd ignored the knock on the door after all. Life with her husband sometimes felt like an endless spell in student digs: fascinating conversations, wild parties, crazy deadlines, daytime sex, beautiful strangers coming and going, painful mistrust, reconciliation – and toast with his boorish friends.

After twenty minutes regaling his hosts with his Ironman competition highlights, Mil moved on to the Village Detectives' case, demanding details on the names Felix had shared on WhatsApp. 'Them three *all* might want Phoebe dead?'

'I'm a very disagreeable woman,' Phoebe pointed out, adding quickly, 'But we've discounted them for now. We're focusing on Craig's motives.'

'You listened to my in-depth character profile, then?' Mil asked proudly.

'Insightful.' Phoebe tried to catch Felix's eye, but he was loading his fifth toast slice with peanut butter.

'Reminds me, I got a message from my cousin while I was driving here. Not looked at it yet.' He fished his phone from his pocket, his battered face contorting from surprise to shock as he read.

'What does it say?' Felix demanded. 'Any new information?'

'He's away on a Sensitivity Awareness course,' Mil explained. 'A load of the Dunford squad got in trouble for sharing a WhatsApp photo of something they found in Craig's shed, apparently. It was well kinky, he says. Could be useful intel?'

Skin prickling, Phoebe looked at Felix. This time, he wasn't amused. Expression darkening, he dropped his toast on the plate and leant back in his chair. For a sickening moment she thought he was going to tell Mil that she might be the subject of those pictures, but he just sucked his lips with a vague, 'Maybe.'

Impervious to undercurrents, Mil pulled a goofy face and pointed out, 'You do know you've both got your trousers on back to front?'

'It's the latest fashion,' Phoebe told him.

'Right you are.' He nodded cheerfully, then caught himself and laughed. 'That was a joke, wasn't it?'

'Yup.'

'So was extreme orienteering, wasn't it?' she asked.

'Yeah,' he admitted, reaching for another slice of toast, looking surprised. 'How d'you know that?'

'You might have the gadgets, Mil, but I have this.' She tapped her nose.

'Alan's wife Norma had a dicky heart,' he explained. 'She wore the SOS wrist tag when she took their dog out. Loved that little dog, she did. Went for miles. After Norma died, the local dog-walking group kept finding it out on its own, retracing routes it had taken with its mistress. Alan keeps making the fence higher to try to stop him getting out.'

'That's heartbreaking.' Felix's eyes met Phoebe's, catching her blinking too fast, a lump rising in her throat at the thought of Norma's small, grieving dog.

She looked quickly away, glancing down at the two terriers begging for toast crusts at their master's feet and tried to imagine them retracing her favourite walks after she pegged it, but suspected they'd be straight down a rabbit hole.

Felix was examining the CCTV cameras again. 'Mil, did you say Alan has new surveillance equipment?'

'Yeah, Bernard recommended it. They're very competitive, those two. He's now got every angle covered round his model rail-waying shed, and one of them doorbell cameras out front. He was showing it off to me – 360-degree view of the drive and the lane, all 4K. Says he can talk to people through it and watch the road even if he's miles away, like today.'

'Do you think he might have footage of the day Craig died? His cottage is just a few drops before Hartridge, isn't it? It might throw some light.'

'We can ask.'

'Penny Fermoy's barn is the post drop immediately before us,' Phoebe pointed out, noticing Felix roll his eyes. 'That's worth checking out too.'

'Beautiful place, she's got,' Mil enthused, turning instantly red. 'Fridge full of champagne and a swimming pool out the back. High hedges, very private. You ever been there?'

'No,' Phoebe told him, already suspecting Mil had intimate knowledge of it. 'But I remember Craig was very wowed by her. He told me she always got a lot of stiffies there.'

Mil choked on his toast.

* * *

Juno

From the moment Smiley Face Radio woke her up with Queen's 'Don't Stop Me Now', Juno knew she was destined to have a good day.

Today's message on her motivational desk calendar was:

Opportunities don't happen, you create them.

The sky outside was pure azure, Kevin Bacon was draped becomingly on a chair, and her little flat was bright and sunny. Filled with furniture and framed posters she'd grown up with, her surroundings made her feel like she'd rolled back to a happy time stamp. Last night, whilst eating mezze then later enjoying some fabulously flirtatious WhatsApp emoji interaction with Mil, she'd binge-watched three Richard Curtis movies on the trot, including the one featuring the kiss on Inkbury's famous bridge.

Juno refused to dwell on death. Instead, she was dwelling

quite a lot on thoughts of Mil making declarations of love in The Savoy and, rather shamefully, on daydreams involving a tall, piratic man who looked a little like Kenneth Ken Doll – but who worshipped her and wanted to heroically protect her – sweeping her into clinches on river bridges. These were severely stress tested when her mother phoned to say that the Campbells had *adored* her, and wasn't Kenneth gorgeous, '*obviously* smitten with you.'

'Were you at the same lunch as me, Mum?'

'Eugene says he always takes a bit of warming up, like his mother.' Loud bubbling noises in the background suggested that Judy was either in the hot tub or cooking. 'But we agree you're a perfect match, didn't we, Doobee?'

Juno heard Dennis's approving tenor.

'He hardly spoke to me.'

'You like them quiet, and isn't he *dishy*? I'll arrange another liaison, shall I? Shy men deserve a second chance at a first impression. *Please* say yes!'

'I do like a strong and silent type,' she admitted, as much to placate her mother as anything, but then thought about Kenneth Ken Doll's bored indifference again. 'No, I want someone to sweep me off my feet and—'

'I'll see what I can do!' Her mother already had the bit between her teeth. 'Leave it with me, Pusscat. And bring my car back!'

Ringing off, Juno sensed she needed to spread her romantic net wider, and fast.

She threw open the windows overlooking Wheeler's Yard, spotting her beautician neighbour signing for a parcel from the temporary postwoman, who arrived far earlier than Craig had because she didn't stop to chat to everybody.

'Beautiful day!' Juno called down, soaking in the sun's warmth on her face, fantasising herself starring in her own romcom. One with a tall, dark stranger and just a sprinkling of danger and intrigue.

Then she jumped with a lightning strike of déjà vu, glancing back at her desk calendar again to confirm it was the 30th before shouting to her neighbour: 'Can you fit me in for a facial this morning?'

Opportunities don't happen, you create them.

Before he'd died, Craig had told her his mother had a pamper package booked in today.

Steve Winwood had taken over from Freddie Mercury, yowling rockily for a 'Higher Love', and she couldn't agree more, dancing around the flat, the mood music on song.

She was ready for love. And detective work.

Checking WhatsApp and finding Felix had shared three names with the group who he suspected of trolling Phoebe further bolstered Juno's positivity. How could she imagine he might wish his wife harm? Felix loved Phoebe. He was desperate to find who was targeting her. He was one of the Village Detectives.

Ignoring the little ticking noise in the back of her head that still sensed danger, she forwarded the names from Felix's message to Eric, asking him to put them through his mysterious dark web X-ray searches.

She then messaged Phoebe to see if she was up for a coffee before her facial, quietly hoping they could have that postponed conversation about Juno's love life. She had a lot to say on the matter and was bursting to share it all.

Typically, Phoebe remained on one grey tick as Juno treated herself to a deli coffee and pastry – fifth day in a row, but who was counting – photographing them artily for her Mother Love blog, which had recently attracted a glut of new baking-and-real-crime fans. Juno then walked along Witch's Broom, passing by the village's pretty clusters of brick and flint thatched cottages, to consume her breakfast on Inkbury's famous bridge, basking in the sunshine as she fed most of the pastry to two swans.

It was the perfect moment for a romantic meet cute.

Opportunities don't happen, you create them.

She glanced over her shoulder at The Barton Arms, willing Mil to wander out.

He didn't.

Hearing pounding feet, she turned to see a runner jogging towards her, wide-shouldered and pepper haired, a George Clooney in Lycra. All he had to do was stop to catch his breath, maybe bend over to hold his knees and pant for a moment like they did in movies, straighten up, look her in the eye and...

He ran straight past, not even glancing at her.

Further along the lane, the railway crossing lights started flashing, its alarm sounding in warning that the barriers would soon come down.

Hearing a car engine roar, she turned the other way as a sporty silver hatchback accelerated towards it from the village side, trying to get across before it closed. Juno imagined the brake lights glowing red in a last-minute emergency halt, the ruffle-haired driver banging the wheel and stepping out to look across his car roof and see her on the famous bridge, the woman he was about to fall in love with.

As the silver car came flying past way over the speed limit, Juno recognised Penny Fermoy at the wheel, a tall figure sitting beside her, his mouth shouting, 'Faster!' Penny was laughing, big teeth bared, head thrown back.

They made it across the tracks just in time.

Juno was almost certain she'd seen the man in the passenger's seat before.

She plucked out her phone and added a PS to Eric, adding Kenneth Campbell's name to his search list:

> Might also go by the alias of Kendall, ex-military police.

Phoebe still hadn't read her message, now on two grey ticks, although Juno wouldn't put it past her to have sneakily peeked at it on 'do not disturb'.

She'd go and see Oscar, their antiques shop owner friend, she decided. He needed cheering up, and he was a great source of village low-down. Besides, she wanted his best price on the three-fold rococo screen in his window, painted with courting couples and winged cherubs, that she could already picture herself undressing behind, tossing bra and stockings playfully over its giltwood frame before embarking on her sexual renaissance.

Opportunities don't happen, you create them.

* * *

Phoebe

By the time Mil had left Hartridge Court, there was only time for Felix to shower quickly before setting off to the station.

Phoebe walked the dogs there with him, hurriedly taking the least muddy route along their back driveway through Hartridge Woods onto Three Bridge Lane, passing the barn conversion where Penny Fermoy's racy silver Audi was parked on the tyre-gouged gravel, its engine still ticking from a recent run.

'I don't trust her,' Phoebe muttered, gazing up at the drawn curtains. At her feet, the terriers started yapping furiously in agreement as a ginger cat padded along the high garden wall, eyeing them disdainfully.

'Pen's not involved.' Felix marched past.

'Why so certain?'

'Because she's not involved. It's all schoolgirl larks with Pen.'

Irritated, she gave him a frosty miss-kiss farewell on the station platform, like Princess Diana awarding Charles a polo cup, cheekbones clashing.

Felix kept his hand tight on her back, his forehead against hers. 'I don't have to stay in town. I can be back by six.'

'Stay, I'll work tonight,' she dismissed too quickly, eager for a sleepover with Lady Dee and Annie, already intent on making unhinged Irish aristo flapper Persephone Murphy the killer.

'Once I find out who OhFeelYa is, I will cancel them once and for all, I promise,' Felix told her from the train door. 'I'll destroy them.'

'Don't say that. I just want them to stop.'

The warning beeps started for the doors closing as Felix looked down at her on the platform. 'You don't know what they're saying about you.'

'I don't want to know,' she muttered, panic and bile rising instantly. 'I can't bear any of it. Don't tell me, Felix. Not a thing. Promise me.' The electric doors closed with a hiss in front of her.

I promise, he mouthed through the glass.

As soon as the train clattered away, she felt ridiculous for being so irritational, knocked sideways by a heart-leap of need for him, for his overprotective Felix-ness.

Heading back to Hartridge by the circular route through the village, Phoebe crossed the picturesque old stone bridge and stopped to look down at the bubbling Dunnett.

She took out her phone, cancelling its customary airplane mode, vowing to keep it that way. Lamely, she messaged Felix:

Hope today goes well

Beneath her, two McDonald's bags and a cider can floated past like evil Pooh Sticks. She added a kiss and pressed send.

On the family group chat, both their daughters had shared photos in reply to her early hours messages. She and Felix now both sent love heart reactions within moments of one another, making her feel even worse, their parental synchronicity far more in tune than their personal one.

Phoebe closed her eyes, briefly allowing herself to acknowledge how much she missed her old life, her world full of children and chatter, friends and family, colleagues and correspondence. A heady wave of nostalgia and loss almost knocked her over, sweeping her into the river before she snapped back to here and now. This was a dangerous edge she'd been to before.

Juno had messaged half an hour earlier, eager for a morning debrief:

> I've got a facial booked for ten thirty and thought maybe we could catch up first? Want to know all about these names Felix shared. Just getting a coffee from the deli – are you up for a visit? I demand full disclosure!

Leaning her elbows on the bridge wall, Phoebe replied:

> Sorry, busy working. Will call when I surface.

She gazed down into the chalk bed river, its reeds waving. With a slow, deliberate blink, she wished tech's demons away, the phubbing and trolling, the ghosting and bullying, its non-stop, life-hijacking undue influence.

Closing her eyes, she felt the phone slide from her fingers, tempted to let it drop into the Dunnett. As she did so, it vibrated. She caught its corner just in time.

It was Felix, messaging:

I'll come back.

DONT.

She replied so quickly she missed the apostrophe, then almost dropped the phone afresh when a cheerful voice called out behind her.

'Hello, it's Phoebe, isn't it?'

A group of dog walkers were crossing the bridge towards her, a tall, grey-bearded and bald-pated man at their fore with a smiling spaniel straining on its lead ahead of him.

At Phoebe's feet, the terriers went into spirals of yapping delight, leads lacing around her, tethering her there.

'Bernard Cole – this is my wife Ree.' He introduced the others by name, but she was too fazed to catch them, vaguely taking in that most were also involved with the village book group, which was meeting later that week. 'Juno has promised to bring you along. She never told us you had the most charming terriers. What lovely chaps! You must come out walking with us sometime.'

Certain she wouldn't, Phoebe said that would be terrific.

'Absolutely love your Dorothy books,' enthused one of the walkers, a handsomely sturdy ash blonde in red wellies clinging onto a yellow Labrador that was trying to goose Phoebe. 'I was so upset when I didn't win that signed set at the last meeting, wasn't I, Bernie?'

'Furious. And Beth *never* gets angry,' he told Phoebe. 'She's our book group patron.'

'That's very kind.' Glancing round, Phoebe half suspected Juno of briefing them to stage this flash mob of kindness. Then she couldn't resist asking: 'Out of interest, who did win the draw?'

'Wasted on that woman!' Beth lamented.

'Penny doesn't read anything,' explained Bernard, 'she only watches movie adaptations.'

'*Penny* won my books in the raffle?' Phoebe realised, starting to laugh.

'She asked us to draw it again, but it was her ticket the second time too,' Beth recounted enviously.

'And a third,' added Bernard.

'Bernie, that's not a very kind thing to point out,' his wife urged gently.

'No, honestly, it's wonderful.' Phoebe was still laughing, her imagination already writing its way out of her gloom. She would add a set of cursed books to her latest Dorothy De'Ath, obsessing deranged Irish aristo Persephone Murphy who murdered to sate her mania. 'I promise you it's bucked me up no end. I can give you another set if you like,' she offered Beth.

'Oh, please just sign my copies – I have them all!'

'I'd love to.' Juno was definitely behind this, Phoebe decided, loving her for it.

The dog walkers trudged off cheerfully down to the canal tow path, calling up to the bridge that they were looking forward to seeing her at the book group, and she must join them walking soon.

Head down, Phoebe marched into the village.

Up ahead, the awning of Davis and Locke Antiques was casting an oblique shadow across the pavement. Beneath it, a familiar short, round, brightly dressed figure was coming out of the door, accompanied by a tall, broad-barrelled one in tweed.

Juno. With her was the shop's owner. They were looking at something in the window, having an animated conversation.

Phoebe rushed forward, then hesitated as she heard Juno say, 'Think about it, at least. Twenty per cent off, and I'll feature Davis and Locke in an advertorial on my blog. Oh, and I almost forgot to ask, did you know the village postman well at all, or his mother?'

The cry of hello stayed in Phoebe's throat. She didn't want to think about Craig.

The cursed books were calling, and her black dog was already coming to heel again.

Cutting abruptly right along Witch's Broom, she raced home over the grass-topped bridges to catch a glamorous mass murderer.

Sometimes making everything up was the only way to make sense of it all.

8

JUNO

MOTHER LOVES HER LIFE EDIT!

Followers, I am living in a Richard Curtis movie montage!
Today, I stood on the bridge from *that* scene – and yes, I said
'let's melt the snow' line out loud! – and I watched swans and
boats and butterflies drifting by, and I could hear Van Morrison
singing 'Warm Love' in my head as I wandered back into the
village in the sunshine. And I refused to think about death and
murder, just life and love, because the High Street is so pretty
with its brick and flint cottages all jumbled up with creamy
render, thatch nuzzling between stone tiles, mullion and bay
windows sparkling.

Opportunities don't happen, you create them.

I picked up an arty magazine from the corner shop, and
now I'm having a facial in the little organic beauty salon I live
beside. Afterwards, I'll get artisan bread from the deli. Then
maybe I'll decide on impulse to buy peonies from the florist
beside my apartment, because that's what RC heroines do in

montages isn't it? She'll tell me she's just sold the last bunch to the guy before me and would I like ranunculus instead, which will make me laugh because it's such a ranunculus word. Then a deep voice behind me will say, 'Would you like these?'

And there he'll be! My ruffle-haired dream man.

That or he'll be the Poison Pen Letter Killer who I'm certain is still at large.

More soon…

Juno cast her phone aside as her beautician neighbour came back to apply the face mask.

'Will it hurt to peel off? Only I'm not good with pain.'

'You won't feel a thing, hon. This is my own recipe: organic kale and turmeric from the allotment, plus local honey and Fairtrade coconut. All natural.'

It smelt not unpleasantly like an Indian side dish. Juno's stomach rumbled. She was regretting feeding her breakfast pastry to the swans.

'Been busy?' asked the beautician as she lathered it on like pistachio icing.

'Non-stop. You?'

'Same. Got any plans today?'

'Oh, fall in love, get a job, catch a murderer. You?'

'Same.' She wasn't listening.

'Got many appointments today?' Juno asked. There were no other clients in the salon.

'A few.'

Abandoning subtlety, Juno asked what she knew about Craig the postie. 'Who did he hang out with?'

'Keep your mouth closed, okay?'

'I am completely discreet,' Juno reassured her.

'No, I mean keep it closed while I'm applying this. You don't want to swallow any.'

'I thought you said it was all natural?'

'It is! Nothing toxic in my little allotment. Although they did find hemlock in the hedgerow a while back, right behind Beth Trascott's runner beans. The Coles and Bickerstaffs helped her dig it all out. Not long before Norma Bickerstaff died, God rest her.'

'From hemlock poisoning?' Juno spoke out of the corner of her mouth, her voice distorted.

'No, she had a stroke in her sleep. Dicky heart, poor thing. Very peaceful.'

'Unlike poor Craig,' Juno mused leadingly from the opposite corner of her mouth, trying again. 'Dying from a letter bomb going off.'

Her beautician neighbour wide-eyed her in the mirror, hearing her now. 'Shocking business, that!'

'Did you know him well?'

'Only to pass the time of day with. Odd sort of bloke. Young but fuddy duddy, you know? He bought a voucher for his mum to come here once.'

Juno knew this, of course, having spoken to Craig about it outside in Wheeler's Yard only last week. Just as she knew the answer to her next question. 'Did she ever use it?'

'Funny coincidence, she was booked for her treatment today, but in the circumstances...'

'Don't tell me, she cancelled?' Juno sighed. She'd guessed it was a long shot.

'Not heard from her.'

'But I shouldn't think she'll want a pamper package now.' Even if she did, Juno reflected, the last thing Denise Jackman needed was a stranger in a green face mask leaning cross from the adjacent treatment booth asking questions about her dead son.

She might as well just relax and enjoy her facial; she'd just promised her blog readers she would stop obsessing about death and murder, after all.

'Now you sit back while this does its magic,' the beautician told her.

Juno closed her eyes, listening to the spacy synthesised arpeggios of ambient trance music. She tried to relax, to let her face mask draw out all her negative thoughts along with her skin's toxins.

But all she could think about was Craig.

Opportunities don't happen, you create them, she reminded herself.

She loved Inkbury, but since arriving she sometimes felt like she was watching herself star in the wrong movie, one with corpses and gumshoes, not kisses on bridges with ruffle-haired heroes.

For all her blogging bravado and local bonding, Juno was homesick. She missed her adopted American chutzpah. She missed welcoming Jay's family to her little colonial-style house with its back yard and walk-in closet, decent water pressure and years of happy memories. Its contents were still in transit, tied up by Customs who wanted to charge import duty on Jay's motorbikes – most of them in pieces, the metal 'hogs' she couldn't bring herself to let go – that they insisted must be part of a commercial shipment. Whilst she yearned to have her familiar things, she wasn't prepared to back down, and nor did she have anywhere to put it all. Her little rented flat next door was already crammed with hand-me-downs from her mother along with the previous inhabitant's things. Lots more stuff was stored with Phoebe and Felix.

Juno was still no closer to an idyllic doer-upper cottage in which to arrange it all, her daydream Farrow and Ball play palace in which to host future sleepovers for her unborn grandchild, seduce a ruffle-haired lover and entertain new village chums. Meanwhile, she was burning through money, the need for her to get a job pressing, her life scattered and unsettled. Thank goodness that day's negotiations for a wildly expensive antique folding screen had got her nowhere, she realised with relief. When her shipping container was released, she was tempted to thatch it and move into it.

The door tinkled out of sight beyond a three-fold fabric screen discreetly batik-printed with the parlour's logo. Juno admired it, wondering if the beautician would take an offer.

She allowed herself a brief fantasy of her ruffle-haired hero coming in to have his beautiful strong, square fingers manicured in the treatment seat beside her, their eyes meeting in the mirror. Except that her green-faced reflection currently resembled Princess Fiona from *Shrek*. Plus Ruffle-Haired Man had become increasingly unreliable and fickle in her fantasies, and now he was having daytime beauty treatments when he should be out grafting manfully at tree surgery or painting moody landscapes or performing life-saving operations on endangered species in the African savannah.

Beyond the screen, the beautician was making a lot of welcoming cooing noises.

'Make it quick.' The hoarse voice on the other side had a strong Wexshire accent, deep and impatient.

'So, so sorry for your loss.'

'Appreciated. Now bleach my moustache, love. Forget the other stuff. I'm only here 'cos my son wanted it.'

Juno's heartbeat quickened, guilty with excited anticipation. It had to be Denise Jackman.

* * *

Trapped behind the fabric screen, Juno craned to see, face mask cracking as she edged closer to the batik and listened in as her beautician neighbour started the new arrival's treatment. To Juno's relief, Denise was a talker, although she had to strain to catch what she was saying over the ambient trance music, which had now started omm-ing like a Vesak Day chant.

'One of the last things my Craig said before he died was that I had to use that gift voucher,' she was saying hoarsely, 'and no offence, love, but I'm not one for all this pampering crap. What's that bloody thing?'

'It's a light therapy mask. It prepares your skin for product application.'

'Stick it on then. Chuffing hell, I look like a Cyberman.' Her voice became muffled now, as though somebody was pinching her nose. 'Craig would love this mask. He loved this village, all its little shops and businesses. Used to tell me you needed our custom. He saw letters of claim coming in. Bought all sorts of tat from that bloke next door, too.'

Behind her screen, Juno felt a burst of allegiance with poor, dead Craig. Loyalty meant a lot. She pushed her chair back just enough to peer quickly around the screen, catching sight of a shock of burgundy hair and whiff of Georgio Armani Sí over the kale. Even in the strange Cyberman mask, she recognised Denise Jackman as the woman from the First-Class Minds team she'd seen in the loo with Bad Penny on the night of the quiz.

'He was so proud of his postal round here,' she was saying, 'always said Inkbury had the prettiest houses in Wexshire. And the nicest people. His favourite customers were the Three Bridge Lane drops 'cos he said he liked cheering up all the lonely folk there. He'd talk to Beth Trascott about gardening for hours 'cos she lives on her own and has a lazy eye and never married. And to Alan Bickerstaff about model railways 'cos he was so sad after his Norma died. Then he'd chat to Lady Penelope about high society and all her parties and freebies and boyfriends, 'cos she can't keep hold of a man more than a fortnight and they all take advantage of her. He'd even talk to that hoity author squatting in the big house about her shoddy books. He'd chat to anyone, my Craig. A people person. Above and beyond, he used to say!'

'I remember,' the beautician murmured vaguely.

'There's no way he made that awful bomb thing. I can't believe the police think it!'

'That what they're saying, is it?'

'All frigging lies! He was a victim.'

Hearing tears crack in her arid voice, Juno eyed her own green reflection, tempted to burst around the screen and tell Denise that's exactly what she and the Village Detectives were going to prove. If someone had killed their innocent, chatty postman, she was determined to help expose them.

Out of sight, the chatty mother from whom Craig must have inherited the trait was still talking, voice distorted and nasal behind her light mask, now choked with tears: 'I told that young police detective that my boy never made anything in his workshop apart from cups of tea. He couldn't work any of the equipment. He only bought stuff off the other model railway club members to please them. He just played with his train sets, read books and watched YouTube.'

Juno leaned closer, straining to hear over the ambient music.

'Hours of bloody toy trains going round and round. As if sitting in a garage watching the real thing wasn't boring enough. That's something else the police got wrong, insinuating he was looking up all sorts of mucky nonsense!'

Ask her what she means! Juno willed her beautician neighbour.

'How's that mask feeling, hon?' she purred instead. 'The red light reduces inflammation, stimulating collagen and elastin.'

'Feels like I've a flipping standard lamp taped to my face if I'm honest. Can I take it off?'

'Five more minutes. I just need to finish my other client's treatment...'

Before she knew it, Juno was being swathed in wet wipes and hot towels to remove the kale and turmeric mask. She wanted to protest that she needed to stay longer, suggest a few more pertinent questions for the beautician to ask, or offer to take over Denise's treatment while she was in the Cyberman mask so she could ask her some questions, but her neighbour was devoid of any detective instincts, leaning down to whisper, 'I meant to wash this off a bit sooner, sorry – she doesn't half go on, poor thing,' then she straightened again, saying in a loud, sing-song voice: 'The blotchiness is just temporary! The mask has drawn impurities to the surface, increasing blood circulation. And that skin discolouration is from the turmeric – nature's suntan, I call it – which will fade too. By tomorrow night, you'll be ready for a hot date, you see!'

Juno glanced at her orange, mottled gammon of a face and hoped so. Maybe it was time to give the dating app another go, after the disappointment of Kenneth Ken Doll.

As she paid for her facial, calculating she could buy sixty bags of kale in Dunford Tesco for the same price, her stomach gurgled greedily again. She could surely afford that artisan sourdough she'd promised herself? Then maybe some fresh flowers to fulfil her blog wish-list – peonies, maybe? She'd economise from tomorrow.

Face buzzing, she hurried back to the deli to pluck out the biggest, warmest loaf. Her reflection in the shiny coffee maker still looked like she was having a hot flush with a dash of acne rosacea on top. She looked quickly away, her gaze landing on something far more desirable. Forget meet cute, she was going to eat cute.

'I'll have one of those crustless blue cheese and walnut quiches,' she told the student manning the counter, 'and that wrapped wedge of Red Leicester, also a sliver of the Stinking Bishop and two of those chocolate tiffins. Did you know Craig Jackman, by the way? The postman?' *Bit weird, over-friendly, talked about his mother a lot?*

The barista apologised that no, they didn't.

Juno took another arty photo of her purchases arranged prettily on the counter: 'For my blog!'

She was half tempted to add it to her dating app profile too, the romcom montage playing in her head once more: seductive riverside picnics, a punt gliding through reeds, champagne cooling in an ice bucket. Forget fickle, vain Ruffle-Haired Man. She wanted a gorgeous, gourmand, ruddy-cheeked, round one. James Corden or James Martin.

She hurried back into Wheeler's Yard, stomach growling eagerly now.

A tall figure was walking just ahead of her in a blue beanie and red puffer coat, something about his wide shoulders and loose-hipped stride drawing her eye.

He stepped into the florist.

Juno stopped in her tracks.

After a moment's dithering and a discreet feel of her red cheeks with the back of her hand, she stepped in after him, hoping the smell of blooms would hide the Stinking Bishop.

He was buying peonies. It was kismet!

Her friend the florist also had very pink, flushed cheeks, Juno noticed, and a misty-eyed expression as she asked Blue Beanie, 'Shall I wrap those for you?'

The man gave a nod, his back still to Juno. It was a great back. Probably far too young.

Then he pulled off his beany, ruffling up a thick pelt of silvered blond hair, the square-fingered, life-weathered hands unquestionably older. Hard-working hands.

Her heart turned over and her belly revved as she pulled in her stomach and lifted her chest to say, 'Perfect choice – I love peonies. I hope those aren't the last ones.'

'I've got loads more,' said the florist, reaching for the bucket. 'How many do you want, Juno my love?'

'Just the one bunch is fine,' she told her in her throatiest sexy voice. 'I'm not very peo-needy.'

The man grinned over one wide shoulder. 'Hi, Juno.'

Dropping back onto her heels in disappointment, Juno clutched the loaf so tightly it audibly cracked. 'Hi, Felix.'

Blue eyes crinkling, he turned back to hold his phone to the contactless payment panel, waiting until it beeped before heading outside with a raised hand, calling thanks and goodbye, the door pinging behind him.

'Was that who I think it was?' the florist whispered to Juno. 'The guy from Hartridge, the one who makes the big movies, Felix Sylvian?'

'We go way back,' Juno said casually. 'They're mostly independent British films. Quite low budget. Some fail completely.'

'My life!' The florist fanned herself as she rang up the purchase. 'I heard he was lush – but, oh, his wife's a lucky woman, all I can say. Imagine what you'd do if you had a man like that all to yourself?'

'Clone him?' Juno sighed, tempted to add 'and trust him no further than I could throw him'.

Nevertheless, she felt a lurch of excitement to find Felix was waiting for her when she came out, all beetled blond eyebrows, smiling down at her. 'Are you free? Can I scrounge a coffee? Or I'll stand you a drink at the pub if you'd rather? Phoebe thinks I'm in London until tomorrow.'

We're detectives, she reminded herself. And I could probably throw his untrustworthy shadiness further than he could throw my solid dependability, so use your strength and guile, Juno.

She invited him to her flat.

* * *

'This place is amazing.' Felix admired the vintage bric-a-brac store when she let him in, its long shopfloor the only way to access the accommodation above. 'Can't believe I never came here when it was open.' Upstairs, he slumped onto her small sofa, elbows on knees, running his fingers through his hair. 'I need your help, Juno. I've cancelled today's meetings because I'm no use to anybody. I got as far as Slough and came back.'

Kevin Bacon the cat eyed Felix malevolently from the windowsill, tail flicking against a photograph of Juno's parents.

'Have you seen Phoebe today?' Felix asked.

She shook her head, reluctant to admit that she'd had just one curt reply to several long text messages. 'Both too busy to chat, but we've touched base!'

He rolled a smile away between his teeth, blue eyes troubled. 'You know that Twitter storm left her with PTSD?'

'Was it that bad?'

'Why d'you think she puts every device on airplane mode?'

Juno felt a burst of pity. She had witnessed the evasive tactics Phoebe used to avoid social media, or even going online at all.

'Publishing her novels independently means doing everything digitally,' Felix explained, 'but I handle most of the online stuff for her, leaving her to do the clever bit. She hides behind it when things get bad, you know? Work is her refuge. I lose her for weeks on end sometimes.'

Juno had only recently started to guess at the depth of Phoebe's depressive lows, aware of the hard knocks in recent years, the Stormy Cs that she played down and joked away.

'We'd hoped the scandal was almost forgotten,' Felix went on, 'that she might be remembered for more than just inciting a Twitter troll to fake a suicide, but we middlies forget digital footprints stay in the ether long after all the analogue hard work that preceded it has been forgotten.'

'Do you think Craig found out about the Virginia Woolf controversy?'

'It's possible, but he was never OhFeelYa. I'm certain that was either Otis, Gail or Seraphine.'

She recognised the three names he'd shared on the Village Detectives WhatsApp. 'Who are they?'

Felix cast her a pensive sideways look. 'Otis was a two-faced former colleague of Phoebe's at the paper; Gail is a Yorkshire yummy mummy who went from BFF to school gate enemy faster than you can shout musical chairs...' Then he winced uncomfortably before saying, 'And Seraphine is a ghost from my past.'

'You know where they all are now?'

'Yes.' He looked away, sucking his lips. 'I'd like to take a couple of days to check them all out, but I don't want to leave Phoebe alone at Hartridge overnight again.'

'I'll stay with her!'

'I've asked Mil.'

'Sensible.' Juno nodded, feeling a pinch of jealousy, because she'd also like to be part of that stake-out, safeguarding two of her favourite people with tea and treats. 'Bigger muscles.'

'Local knowledge, good with tech. He's setting up CCTV.'

'That too.'

'And I'm hoping you'll help me?'

'Me?' she squeaked, feeling an anxious stitch.

'I need someone that those three don't know. Seraphine will never talk to me for a start. I thought my PA Betsy might do it, but she's—'

'Too young to care.' She nodded sympathetically.

He closed one eye then the other, thinking about this. 'Paid too little.'

'I'm expenses only. And strongly invested.'

The handsome smile lit up his face like a beacon. 'You are priceless, Juno darling.'

Thrilled at the prospect, despite the anxiety stitch doubling, Juno held up a fist. 'I'm in!'

Not realising he was expected to bump it with his own, Felix eyed her power-salute doubtfully for a moment, then said, 'How quickly can you pack?'

'Pack?'

'Otis is in Manchester, Gail's near Harrogate and Seraphine's in Paris, so it means at least one night away.'

Juno felt a gulp of panic catch in her throat; she rarely travelled light, less so with someone as clubbable and untrustworthy as Felix. 'Is Phoebe okay about this?'

'I think she can trust us alone together, don't you?'

'Yes! I mean, you've told her about it all?' Juno had a strong suspicion Felix was making this up as he went along, a trait she knew drove his wife mad.

'She's working. Best we message on the way.'

'So what are the flowers for?' She indicated the big bunch of peonies he'd abandoned by her paltry one on the breakfast bar.

'Moving-in present.' He stood up to pick them up, swinging back to face her. The romcom fantasy had gone rogue, Juno panicked, its hero dangerously miscast. Suddenly he seemed far too big for her flat, like a jaguar in a cat carrier.

Her stitch was burning into her side now, the fear lump choking her throat.

'Shall I put them in water for you while you pack a bag?' he asked when Juno said nothing.

She stared at him open-mouthed for a moment longer, her doubts doubling then quadrupling, overlapping and illogical. She had it on authority that the husband was the guilty one overwhelmingly often. Was he luring her away to bump her off too, she wondered? Eugene Campbell had sown a seed of doubt in her mind, one that the laser-blue gaze in front of her right now could surely see.

'Are you okay, Juno?'

His eyes really were extraordinarily blue.

Calm down, Juno. Think positive, she told herself firmly. Felix is a deeply loyal, metrosexual husband, determined to root out his wife's persecutor. Far better he take trusty soon-to-be-grandmother Juno than flighty young PA Betsy. Phoebe could depend on Juno.

They were Village Detectives, Juno reminded herself, even if a niggling doubt still told her that men who buy moving-in flowers and then invite the recipient to leave them behind to go on a dangerous road trip are impractical and impulsive.

But Felix needed her, he was right. And Phoebe needed her too.

'There's a vase under the sink. Help yourself to those deli goodies while you wait!'

He'd polished off the lot and was chivvying her like a sports coach by the time she'd assembled a packable capsule wardrobe of outfits suitable for travel, surveillance, undercover work and formal occasions.

'One other thing,' he asked winningly. 'Can we take your car?'

'You have a far cooler motor.' Juno knew that there were secrets hidden beneath dust sheets in the Sylvians' coach house, aware that while Felix and Phoebe might have lost the beautiful Dales farmhouse, they'd kept the two ridiculous cars from those Turbo-charged, halogen-lit halcyon days.

'Yours has insurance and road tax.' Felix pulled an apologetic face. 'I'll pay for the fuel.'

'As long as I can choose the music.' She would message her mother later, Juno promised herself quietly, adding, 'And we can pop to see Eric first; it's practically on the way.' Her son hadn't acknowledged the names list she'd sent earlier, and she knew of old that sometimes the only way to get a response from him was in person, much as bursting into his teenage room in Brooklyn had always been more effective than shouting up the stairs.

To her surprise, Felix was delighted by the suggestion. 'Hoped you'd say that!'

Juno felt a touch more trusting.

'Where is your car?' he asked, eyeing the florist's van when they went back outside.

'In Mil's car park.'

By the time she'd asked her neighbour to feed the cat, bought yet more deli treats for Eric, and they'd walked through the village to the pub car park to collect the Jazz, it was already starting to feel less of an adventure. Lunch service was in full flow at The Barton Arms, its early diners spilling out to reclaim their cars as Juno threw her weekend bag in the boot, checking, 'Mil knows about this, yes?'

'He thinks I'm in London too.'

'We have to go and tell Phoebe before we set out,' she insisted as they buckled up.

'For her sake, we wait.'

Felix looked across at her with such smouldering sex appeal, she stalled the car twice, then almost reversed into Mil's beloved motorbike, only slamming on the brakes when Felix shouted in warning.

Turning out onto the road, the Jazz sounded so strange, graunching and grinding, that Juno half believed the engine had shifted in its casing, clunking towards Felix's sheer magnetism.

'Mind if I vape?' He produced one like Phoebe's.

They really were book ends, Juno thought fondly, lowering her window. Symbiotic lovers united in beautiful symmetry. Then she thought about the movie he'd gambled away their house on and doubt crept back in.

Her stomach let out a furious rumble, louder even than the air rushing past and the car's strange clanking. She hurriedly turned on Smiley Face Radio to cover it, the beeps cueing in the two o'clock news reminding her that she had fed her breakfast to the swans and Felix had eaten her lunch.

Feeling fabulously thin, Juno reminded herself firmly that today was a good day. They were going to find Phoebe's troll.

Opportunities don't happen, you create them.

She sent out a silent apology to her friend as they flew past the Hartridge entrance and out of Inkbury.

9

PHOEBE

'My goodness, poor Georgiana had no chance against that adder, did she? Who do you suppose could have put it under the chaise longue? It has to be the same killer that suffocated the professor beneath that scented pillow, don't you think, Annie?'

'Well, milady, I spoke to Mrs Potts, the Gilmores' house-keeper, and she told me in strictest confidence—'

'Would a lady's maid say the Gilmores' housekeeper or the housekeeper at The Grange?' Phoebe muttered to herself. 'And don't call her Mrs Potts, you prat, that's the teapot from *Beauty and the Beast*. Urgh. Think, Phoebe. Focus! Argh!'

The terriers looked up from their beds with disinterest as she left the table – still muttering to herself – to search for her vape. They were accustomed to their mistress's eccentricity whilst working.

It was only after she'd upended drawers, her coat pockets and handbag that Phoebe remembered she'd told Felix to hide her vape away from temptation.

She felt another stab of regret for their sour farewell.

His London stopover was nominally to meet distributors and see a rough cut of his latest project, although she knew that meant he'd mostly be hanging out in a Soho private members' club. Phoebe found his reluctance to let her stay alone overnight at Hartridge Court absurdly overprotective. And yet she loved him for it, especially if it meant putting fifteen stops on the Great Western Line between him and decorative Betsy.

She'd started a dozen messages asking him to come home and sent none, black clouds pressing down, refusing to be needy.

Except for needing to vape.

'Where is it?' she interrogated the dogs, who looked at her blankly.

When an intensive search unearthed nothing more stimulating than a tube of Polos, Phoebe pulled on her coat, terriers springing to attention now.

She needed cheering up.

The back door was still technically deemed out of bounds by the police, although Phoebe suspected this was because they had forgotten to remove the tape and inform her that she could use it rather than an ongoing need to preserve the crime scene. They hardly seemed to be treating the case as a priority.

Dogs at her heels, she went through the antiquated baize door into the main house, majestically still and silent, a panelled and stuccoed cathedral of abandoned grandeur, shadows and dust sheets. Her footsteps echoed and the terriers' claws scratched as they hurried to the grand front entrance.

Descending the imposing sweep of steps to the carriage circle, Phoebe envisioned Lady Dee's marabou-trimmed velvet opera cloak swirling behind her as she strode to the Alvis where chauffeur Pinkerton was holding open the door.

Waving away the fantasy with a sardonic harrumph, Phoebe

marched straight through the imaginary car, turning right to track back towards the service side of the house, through the grand archway that led to the domestic courtyard then the stable yard and coach houses beyond. There, she removed the padlock from the hasp of two tall double doors, pushing them apart and striding through the building to draw back a large canvas sheet, leaning away from the motes that danced above the gleaming yellow paintwork.

The dogs started yapping appreciatively. They loved this new ritual, which Phoebe undertook whenever she needed a speed fix shot in the arm, and a reminder that her past was still part of her.

She and Felix were currently without a road-legal vehicle, a temporary hitch which like so many had become more long-term than they'd hoped. Felix darted around the globe like Hermes on planes and trains; Phoebe walked, ran and cycled closer to home. But to her continued delight, they did have roadworthy cars – Felix's proposition again – their personal value rising in inverse proportion to their market value depreciating. It did hers good to be started up occasionally.

The Porsche roared into life. On the tiny rear seat, the two terriers waited eagerly for their mistress to reverse out of the awkward space. As soon as the roof started to concertina back, they yapped in anticipation. Then, paws upon the sills to either side, smiling mouths wide and tongues lolling, they were rewarded with a burst of speed so fast their ears turned inside out.

Phoebe floored it along the half mile of straight tarmac between Hartridge Court and its grand, pilloried entrance on the Old London Road.

A pair of moss-capped gargoyles greeted her on their plinth roosts, guarding the big wrought-iron gates they overlooked.

Attached to the far side of one tall, monolithic gatepost was a modern, lockable letter box, discreetly located beneath one of the smaller arches which housed the metal pedestrian gate. This was where the new stand-in postwoman had been delivering the Hartridge mail all week.

Phoebe's guilty pleasure was to drive there to fetch it.

She parked at a jaunty angle, groping in her coat pockets for the gate keys.

As she did so, a dusty silver hatchback on the main road braked with an audible screech and swerved sharply into the wide tarmac semicircle at the estate's main gated entrance, causing an oncoming van to beep furiously.

There was only one villager Phoebe knew who drove like a Duchess of Hazard.

It was 'Bad' Penny Fermoy, Brian Ferry booming from her subwoofer. She was wearing dark glasses and a feather fascinator.

Not noticing Phoebe, she clambered out and stalked on high heels to the post box, fishing something from her handbag to thrust in it before high-stepping back to her car.

In her hurry, she'd dropped a small black plastic rectangle attached to a large fluffy blue pompom.

Stepping through the gates, Phoebe stooped to pick it up. It was a remote car key.

'Penny!' she hollered.

Letting out a squeak, Penny slammed the driver's door shut, looking intent on driving off at speed.

Wondering what would happen if she pressed a button on the remote key, Phoebe did so. Brian Ferry stopped singing abruptly as the engine cut out.

Taking off her sunglasses, Penny first eyed the yellow Porsche through the ornate metal gates, and then Phoebe. She beckoned her closer imperiously.

Phoebe beckoned imperiously back, still holding the pedestrian gate closed with one foot to stop the dogs running out onto the road while she unlocked the box to grab the post.

It was a lengthy stand-off, made longer while Phoebe struggled to find the letter box key in the big Hartridge master set.

Eventually, Penny unstapled her red talons from the leather wheel, got out of her car and stalked towards the gate again, brandishing her tombstone veneers aggressively, two forefingers pointing accusingly at Phoebe.

'I've been wanting a word, as you can imagine.' Her voice, a media-friendly girlish drawl of rounded-down posh, could loosen fillings faster than a pitstop tyre drill. 'Is that Felix's Porsche? Things must be looking up.'

'It's my car.' No need to add that it was SORN-ed because Phoebe couldn't afford the insurance and MOT, or that she only ever raced it up and down Hartridge's long driveway.

She eyed Penny warily. Dressed in tailored coral pink with a fascinator sprouting from her hair extensions like a feather axe, the socialite looked all set to bulldoze her way to the champagne bar at a wedding.

'Just delivered your parish mag,' she announced confusingly. 'Tried to bring it to the house, but the back drive is all taped off.'

Phoebe had finally managed to wrestle her way into the post box to find the *Dunford Diocese News* on top of a pile of circulars and bills. Grabbing the lot, she pulled the gate shut just in time to stop the terriers wriggling out to throw themselves enthusiastically against Penny's super-sheer tights.

'I tried messaging and ringing,' Penny announced crossly over their yaps, 'but you seem to have something wrong with your phone. So has Felix.'

'We barred your number,' Phoebe reminded her.

Penny Fermoy's most recent spate of demands to access the

house had led even the trustees to warn her off. With a sinking heart, Phoebe guessed she was back on the warpath.

'I've sought legal advice and I suggest you do too.' Her humourless, tombstone smile was fixed beneath the cold blue eyes.

Phoebe saw *Call Me Urgently* scrawled on the parish magazine's cover in Penny's round, preppy hand, along with three different numbers.

'Legal advice on what?' As if she couldn't guess.

Glaring fixedly up at a gargoyle, Penny stepped closer to hiss, 'Boozy's legacy, of course. You are putting Hartridge Court in danger.'

Holding onto two wrought-iron bars, Phoebe regarded her warily.

'You're a target,' Penny went on through her gritted smile, 'which makes the house a target. Letter bomb one day, firebomb the next. Time to pack. We need you out.'

'But I'm holding on for the kamikaze drone...'

'I suppose that's supposed to be funny?' Penny's cold eyes narrowed. She'd never quite figured out how to handle Phoebe, who remained impervious to her overbearing sense of entitlement.

'The house is quite safe,' Phoebe told her. 'The police know who did it, and it won't happen again.'

'Well, they're wrong.' The blue eyes stretched wide again, waiting for a reaction.

Phoebe said nothing, but she identified the implied threat.

'Craig Jackman's mother is a close and loyal acquaintance of mine,' Penny drawled. 'Denise is in bits, poor thing, telling everyone who'll listen that her boy was set up. Such a tragedy.' She stepped closer, addressing her through the bars, lawyer to convict. 'Her son wouldn't have killed a fly.'

'The police aren't looking for anyone else.'

'The local plods are useless! Believe me, I have first-hand experience of their ineptitude.' Penny was well known at Dunford police station for timewasting, from setting her alarm off when drunk to calling 999 whenever her cat went missing.

Right now, she was acting as though she was addressing the witness box in court wearing a white horsehair wig, not a fascinator, her drawling outrage over-egged. 'Everyone knows Craig Jackman helped you with your novels. What sick influence did you have over that poor boy? The letter bomb that went off in his face on your doorstep was addressed to *you*.'

Phoebe flinched, witnessing his death still all too monstrously raw. But she wasn't going to let Penny see that. 'How do you know it was addressed to me?'

'Duh?' she sneered, pointing at the post in Phoebe's hands. 'I thought you were supposed to be quite clever. Somebody clearly wants you dead or hadn't you noticed?'

Phoebe didn't let her face betray how fast her mind was working, or how little she trusted Penny.

'I've seen the Twitter posts about you, the rumours that you've driven other innocent victims to kill themselves,' Penny said with relish, smile still snarling. 'They're baying for your blood out there. That means you're a threat to Hartridge Court. I've already contacted the trustees to let them know the house isn't safe with you and Felix there. I expect they'll have an emergency meeting, so you'd better have somewhere to go pronto. About bloody time. If I were you, I'd cut my losses and clear off before you receive another package.'

'Is that a threat?' It would suit Penny perfectly if she and Felix lost their temporary stewardship of Hartridge because of all this, Phoebe realised. That was a strong motive. Penny could be behind the whole ugly mess.

'How dare you? I'm a public figure with a *lot* of charity connections! The Hartridge Foundation is at stake here, the future of our cultural hub, which was darling Boozy's *dying wish*! We want you out. And don't even think you can badmouth me like you did those poor suicidal tweeters. Slur my reputation and my legal team will make things *very* hard for you.'

From what Phoebe had heard, Penny did enough slurring at village events to damage her own reputation without help, but she kept quiet.

The socialite was glaring at her expectantly now. 'Hand it over!'

'What?'

'The key, of course!' She reached up to straighten her fascinator. 'Come on, I'm in a hurry.'

Phoebe wondered if Penny imagined she was going to surrender the Hartridge master set before packing up and leaving straight away.

'Do you always wear a hat to deliver the parish magazine?' She stalled for time, determined not to show how rattled she felt.

'What?' Penny was tapping her pointed toe. 'I'm off to the races if you must know. Evening meeting at Salisbury in aid of sick kids or lame donkeys or some such.' She glanced at her watch. 'My date will be waiting at Marlbury station, so if I can have my car key back?'

That's when Phoebe remembered she still had the Audi remote. She held on to it, angrily tempted to hurl it into the busy road for a lorry to crush, although she worried that this might also crush Penny if she went after it.

'Don't be silly, Phoebe.' The small eyes blinked coldly. 'We all know Boozy's family leeches aren't going to inherit Hartridge. You and Felix must vacate the place sometime. Why not now?'

'And if we don't?'

'Then you only have yourself to blame for what happens next.'

That was unquestionably a threat.

Having heard enough, Phoebe offered the key through the bars.

'Call me when you're ready to clear out.' Penny snatched it, turning to stalk back to her car.

It was only after Phoebe had returned the Porsche to the coach house, ducking under the police tape to short-cut back past the scene of the crime, that she realised what she'd just picked up in the bundle of post along with the parish magazine.

It was a rigid, luxuriously textured cream envelope. Another stiffy.

The extravagantly feminine loopy blue handwriting on the front was the same as the previous one.

Inside, picked out in embossed gilt and black letters on thick card, she read:

MEMORIAL SERVICE
Your invited to celebrate the life and works of moaning mummy Karen, ex-columnist and self-published crime novelist, Phoebe Fredericks.

Phoebe put it down on the table with the parish magazine.

Even supposing Craig had posted it from beyond the grave, he would never have let 'your' past his grammar-checking pedantry.

She grabbed her phone to photograph the invitation. About to share it with the Village Detectives WhatsApp group, she stopped herself, calling DI Mason instead.

As she waited to be put through, she slipped the SOS wristband over her hand.

10

JUNO

Juno had been worrying non-stop that she was doing the wrong thing since leaving Inkbury. At Milton Heights Services near Didcot, she almost messaged Phoebe from the privacy of the Ladies' to confess that Felix had persuaded her to take her mother's car on a magical mystery troll hunt, but that somehow made it seem worse. And weirder.

Instead, driving north again, she allowed herself the daydream that it wasn't her friend's notoriously wayward husband sitting beside her, a man with whom she was skulking off to dig up things Phoebe would rather leave in the past. This was her crime-fighting buddy, the Crockett to her Tubbs in *Miami Vice*.

Ignoring the Jazz start to rattle yet louder as the speedometer crept above seventy on the A34, Juno fantasised they were off to catch a criminal mastermind, and that she was behind the wheel of whatever sportscar Felix kept tantalisingly hidden beneath a dustsheet beside his wife's yellow Porsche. Snarly, vintage and low-slung in British racing green, she was certain.

The Jazz's graunching and clattering noises were starting to

give her a headache, and she quashed a guilty conviction that she
might be enjoying it much more if she was with Mil.

Felix didn't say a lot. He was far tougher to make laugh than
Mil and had demolished all her mother's car sweets, but at least
he didn't criticise her driving or bore her about engine capacity.
His phone rang a lot, but he said he'd call back when it was
quieter. They had Britpop blaring, dark glasses bobbling, justice
on their sides.

First stop, high-tech intel. They made a quick detour to a
pretty ironstone village near Banbury where Eric's houseboat,
Atlantis, was currently moored along a quiet stretch of the Oxford
canal.

'I'll go dig him out,' Juno told Felix. 'I need to talk to him
alone about something.'

Leaving him pacing around the Jazz returning calls, she
hurried along the towpath to find her lion cub. He was napping
in the afternoon sun on his roof.

'I have five minutes!' she apologised, panting up to him.

Golden haired, big bearded and athletic, Eric was what Juno
had come to understand was a 'hot geek', although she struggled
to see beyond her single-mindedly quirky cool kid, a computer
savant and tech junkie who had once dismantled everything
mechanical within reach, including her beloved squeezebox.
Obsessed first with Ben 10 and Alex Ryder, later Matthew Bourne
and James Bond, he'd feared nothing, setting his heart on a
career in espionage. He'd come to England to take his master's at
Oxford with that express intention, soon winning a coveted post-
graduate training place at GCHQ. Except that her cool kid hot
geek was currently suspended for breaching protocol.

He was biding his time awaiting a tribunal by competing on
an eSports team. Juno didn't understand how these tournaments
worked at all, just that they had eye-watering prize pots, a share

of which was keeping her son afloat in his narrowboat with its secret high-tech gaming den and 5G roof antenna.

Nor did she understand how one went about tracking down anonymous online trolls, but she had no doubt Eric could do so without breaking a sweat.

'Have you found OhFeelYa?' she asked after hugging him thoroughly, gifting him a big bag of Inkbury deli treats and telling him he needed a wash. 'Are they any of those names I forwarded to you?'

Eric was quick to burst her bubble, yawning sleepily and apologising that he hadn't yet looked into it before explaining, 'It can be real tricky to trace an IP address masked behind a VPN, especially without a subpoena. Impossible most times.' He turned away to ride out another jaw-breaking yawn. Rumpled in an Iggy Pop T-shirt and surfer shorts, he looked – and smelled – like he hadn't slept in days. He told her he knew people who knew people who might bend the tech giant rules to look behind those data walls, but not to get her hopes up. 'I've got twenty-four hours before I compete again. I'll try my best.'

Thanking him, Juno hurried on to the ulterior motive of her lightning visit. 'I also brought you this.'

Fishing in her bag, she drew out the solicitor's letter she'd reread multiple times in the past week. 'You have rights, Eric. They say Anita can't cut you out of your own child's life.'

His former boss – tough, formidably bright, career-driven – had surprised all her GCHQ colleagues by getting pregnant in her forties, at first passing it off as an anonymous donor, until a heartbroken Eric – who she'd dumped as soon as she got a line on her Clearblue window – pointed out that he was the father. He'd pointed this out on every screen in the Doughnut, a hacking stunt that had briefly scandalised British Intelligence, triggering Eric's unpaid furlough while the mother of his unborn child retreated on gardening leave, guarded by a fierce extended family. Juno was proud of her son for standing up for himself. Their short, passionate affair had thus far been his greatest love story. But now he seemed to have accepted the brutal truth that Anita had merely used his healthy young gametes and wanted him to play no part in her motherhood journey.

'We're cool, man,' he insisted.

'Please don't call me man. And she must be so close now, another six weeks, is it? This letter explains that while you may have no rights during the pregnancy, after your little person is born you can apply for a Parental Responsibility Order. Anita may insist on a DNA paternity test, and that can happen at any time.'

'We're cool, ma... Mom.'

'Do you two even speak?'

'We're—'

'I know you're cool, Eric. But I am finding all this deeply uncool. I'm about to be a grandmother – which I'm frankly far too young to be – and I have no idea if I'll ever even meet my grandchild.'

'I'm working on it. I thought you said you had to go?' Crabby and bug-eyed from gaming all night, he reminded her so acutely of his father, she wanted to hug him even tighter. Jay had been just as uncommunicative and truculent.

She pressed the letter on him. 'Read this when you feel ready.'

'Thanks.' It disappeared into a pocket of his board shorts, where Juno feared it would stay indefinitely, although the fact he so rarely did laundry meant it was at least unlikely to be destroyed in the wash.

Eric walked her back to the village layby where she'd abandoned the Jazz.

Felix had wandered across the canal bridge to get better reception, waving to them, then turning away as he talked into his phone.

'Say, who is the Brad Pitt dude?' asked Eric, turning to hug her farewell.

'You've met Felix before,' she reminded him. For a man who almost became a spy – and still might if GCHQ reinstated him after the hearing – her son had a terrible memory for faces.

By contrast, he had a photographic memory for cars. 'Why are you still driving Grandmom's clunker?' He then cracked an enormous yawn, telling her, 'I gotta get shut eye. I'll see what I can find out about your Twitter trolls, but don't get your hopes up, Mom man.' He gave her a final squeeze, raised an arm to Felix and loped off.

Still talking into his phone, Felix was now coming back along the lane. 'I've really got to go, my darling, but thank you a million times for having my back; I'm so grateful to you... Yes, yes, I know it's tough on you, but you are holding everything together brilliantly... Don't say that, you are! You are strong and you are brave and you are brilliant. I'm so proud of you. I'll call later... yes, yes, I promise... You too... Gotta go, bye... bye... you too.' He rang off, rolling his eyes and smiling apologetically to Juno. 'Did I miss Eric?'

'He's usually much friendlier but he was exhausted, poor love,' Juno told Felix as they drove away, the Jazz making even more ominous rattling noises now. 'What did Phoebe say?'

'No answer – I left a message.'

Juno digested this for a moment. 'Weren't you just speaking with her?'

'That was Betsy. Mind that tractor.'

Juno swerved just in time, grateful to Garbage for bursting into song through the car's speakers with 'Stupid Girl'. Too right.

She was back to not trusting him again.

Phoebe

Detective Inspector Mason put the memorial service invitation in an evidence bag. 'I'll get forensics to run checks on this asap, so to speak, to coin a phrase.'

'Don't you want to take this too?' Phoebe offered the parish magazine.

'I'm not a churchgoer myself but thank you.'

'For forensics to check.'

He smiled patiently, tram braces glinting amid his downy young beard. 'Taking everything into account, speaking candidly, I don't think that will be necessary in a nutshell.'

'But I told you I witnessed Penny Fermoy put it in the post box,' she said, frustrated that he seemed to think this was a trivial detail. 'And that stiffy – I mean memorial invitation – was immediately below it when I took everything out. Compare the handwriting on that envelope with Penny's note on the magazine cover. It's the same, isn't it?'

'It's a little similar,' he conceded, studying the handwritten address through the clear plastic bag. 'Different ink. Different Ps. We'll trace the barcode on the stamp and see if we can track down its route here, in essence.'

'But Craig can't have sent it, can he? He's been dead over a week.'

'My sister received a Christmas card in March this year.'

'Do you still think Craig was the one trying to harm me?'

'We are still investigating all possibilities, although in fairness, when push comes to shove, the balance of probability suggests that the direction of travel is indicating that there's unlikely to be—'

'Penny Fermoy threatened me today.'

He looked pained. 'We must handle Ms Fermoy delicately.'

'Why? Because she has expensive lawyers? Penny knew all about the Twitter trolling against me, which suggests she's actively invested; she might even be part of it.'

He gave her a soothing smile, flashing his brace. 'The NCA cybercrime team are investigating that side of things, although I must warn you, they have something of a backlog.'

It had been the same story when OhManiacNymph and OhFeelYa had been at their worst, the path to the truth blocked by small, slow police teams and big, fast tech.

'Rest assured, Ms Fredericks, we have passed on the information that your husband kindly furnished us with in respect of the online abuse and, whilst I gather that the names he supplied are, to all intents and purposes, perhaps not those that you yourself would concur are behind these salacious—'

There was a crashing noise beyond the kitchen door, then DS Alsop burst in dragging a beefy figure in a neck-lock. 'Caught this one up a stepladder trying to peer in on the place!'

'I was fixing a camera up on the wall!'

'This is private property, buster!'

Phoebe recognised the broad shoulders and thinning, tight-cropped blond hair. 'That's Mil! He's a friend! Mil Winterbourne.'

'Drop him, Sergeant Alsop,' sighed Mason, 'that's the village publican.'

Released, Mil flopped down with relief, feeling his sore neck with his hand and explaining, 'Felix called half an hour ago and asked me to fix the cameras up asap because he's not here tonight.'

'Your husband is away?' DI Mason asked Phoebe, making another note in his pad.

'In London.'

'Manchester, he said,' Mil corrected affably. 'With Juno.'

Phoebe took a moment to absorb this.

'Of course,' she said coolly, already molten with indignation, wondering why she knew nothing about it. Felix lying by omission she was accustomed to; he bent truths all the time. But Juno... 'Will that be all, officers?'

'I think so.' Mason picked up the evidence bag. 'You might want to ask a friend to stay with you tonight, just to put your mind at rest. Big old place this.'

'I won't let her out of my sight,' Mil assured them.

'You have a pub to run,' Phoebe protested as soon as the police had left.

'And I'll be back over straight after last orders,' he insisted. 'Before that, we'll get this place on CCTV surveillance and we can watch a live feed anywhere on our phones.'

'If only we had Felix on that too.'

'He is!' Mil boasted. 'Felix downloaded the app this morning.'

'That's not what I meant,' she muttered, picking up her phone and noticing that she had a voicemail.

When she listened to it, the ebullience in her husband's voice and his overexcited action-hero energy left her feeling too crabby and caged-in to return the call.

Mil was back outside, up his ladder again, fixing a camera onto a support beam of the open barn to overlook the rear entrance.

'Can Felix really see what this thing is filming on his phone?' she asked, peering up at its fisheye.

'If he opens the app.'

Phoebe gave it her most exasperated look and flicked up a few V-signs, which made her feel slightly better.

'Do the Haka,' Mil suggested, amused.

'Juno would accuse me of cultural appropriation,' she pointed out, although she was tempted.

She let Mil moon at it instead.

Felix phoned again an hour later, by which time Phoebe was alone once more, relieved Mil had pushed off for the evening rush. There was a terrific racket in the background, as though he was calling from inside a sawmill. He sounded surprised to hear her voice. 'I was expecting to leave another voicemail.'

'I'm no longer using airplane mode or do not disturb,' she told him, 'which perhaps explains why I've come down to earth with a bump and I'm finding so many things disturbing. Like you going rogue.'

'Which you knew I would.'

'Not with Juno!'

'We need someone... don't know. We'll invent a co... ry.' The background noise got louder.

'What?'

'Cover story!'

'Felix, this could be dangerous. I don't want Juno getting hurt. If one of those three is involved—'

'Ah, so you now admit it's worth checking out if they are involved?'

'Just look after Juno.'

'We'll be careful, I promise.' He was shouting even louder, the sawmill clanking and groaning, accompanied by a strange thudding.

'What *is* that noise?' she asked.

'Britpop meets Jazz.'

11

JUNO

By the time Juno had circumnavigated Birmingham to join the M6, the Jazz sounded like a cement mixer full of hammers.

When the Bluetooth announced an incoming call from 'MUM – MOBILE', the car's proud owner, Juno longed to let it go to voicemail. But she had just spent a chunk of the journey telling Felix that the primary reason she'd moved back to the UK was to look after her elderly mother, so ignoring it seemed heartless.

'Hi, Mum! Are you okay? Can't really talk right now!'

'You don't need to, Pusscat, I am. I wanted to let you know that Eugene is working on Kenneth. I promised him I'd check what dates work best for you to meet again. I've told him you're *super* keen.'

'*Mum!*'

'We thought a picnic, possibly open-air theatre – there's an al fresco Gilbert and Sullivan here at Godlington this coming week-end, by coincidence – or would you prefer an afternoon on Dennis's boat? Better for seduction, eh, Doobee?' She growled with laughter as Dennis said something inaudible behind her.

'I'm easy.' Juno glanced across at Felix. 'I mean, not *easy* easy.

Not bothered. Actually, the thing is, Mum, I don't think I really
want to meet Ken—'

'What's that awful noise? Not my car, I hope!'

'Roadworks.'

Felix laughed at this, his customary tiger growl.

'Have you got someone with you, Pusscat?'

'Just a friend, Mum.'

'Hello, friend! I'm Judy.'

'Hi, Judy.'

Judy let out a small squeak of excitement before covering the
phone again to whisper urgently to Dennis. Then she said, 'Say
no more, Pusscat,' and rang off.

How did Felix even *do* that, Juno wondered? He'd spoken just
two words, via Bluetooth, in a car that sounded as though it was
falling apart, and yet his weird, seductive charm had bewitched
and silenced her mother.

Juno was quietly grateful; the car's grinding noise was
suddenly sounding even worse.

'Do you think it's the brakes?' she asked Felix anxiously.

'I know nothing about cars.' He was flicking around on his
phone again. 'According to this, we'll be in Manchester around
seven. Otis has got a little place near Media City he stays in when
he's up presenting his radio show three days a week.'

'Otis worked on the same Sunday paper as Phoebe, you said?'

'That's right. Their rivalry goes back years, decades even. Otis
was a hotshot features writer when Phoebe joined as a columnist.
He made no secret of the fact he thought she was a waste of
newsprint. Even when her Undomestic Goddess column was at
its most popular, he slagged it off. He and Phoebe had a lot of
spats in person and online. Otis never let up. It became a running
joke in the end. He even created a regular slot called Phoebe
Jeebies to take the piss out of her on his podcast, Tis News.'

'I used to listen to that,' she remembered, although she didn't recall Phoebe being mentioned.

'It's been going for ages, Otis and his middle-aged man-boy mates trading soundbites and schoolboy pranks. He writes a lot of the big celebrity interviews for the paper, and he's adept at toadying and networking, so the podcast guest list is impressive. A few A listers are regulars by Zoom. It's also where Otis found a ready supply of young, ambitious girlfriends who he recruited to build his Insta and TikTok following, then seduced.'

'What makes you think Otis might be OhFeelYa?' asked Juno.

'One of Otis's girlfriends was an online influencer who'd been paid a megabucks advance for a steamy fantasy series set in a lost underwater city. It was being hyped everywhere, a film deal under negotiation. Phoebe often reviewed for the paper's books pages, with a reputation for making bestsellers. When she read something she loved, she championed it and her readers bought it in droves. There was a lot of nepotism at the paper, so Phoebe was expected to give Otis's girlfriend's fishy sexsploits a rave write up. But she hated it so much, she asked them to find somebody else to review it rather than blast it in print.'

'And you think that's the reason Otis trolled her?' Juno thought it pathetically petty.

'The other reviewer hated it even more.'

'Was it that bad?'

'"Vomit-inducing" was one of the kinder comments, along with "mermaid porn". It became an industry joke. It made Private Eye's Bookmen column. Everyone panned it after that. Otis went berserk, accusing Phoebe of orchestrating a deliberate hatchet job, passing it onto a crony to do her dirty work. He didn't believe that she'd never heard of the reviewer. He blamed her for the fact his girlfriend was on antidepressants. This was just before the Woolf thing happened. Otis went for the jugular on Twitter from day one over that, stoking up his army of followers. And he has a million of those. It's easy enough to imagine him inventing OhManiacNymph and OhFeelYa; the names are just his style, and he reposted everything they tweeted, even the drowning countdown stuff Twitter banned.

'When OhManiacNymph's account went suddenly inactive, and the conspiracy theories started about Phoebe inciting them into suicide, Otis was instrumental in her departure from the paper. He circulated a secret petition around the staff, saying they felt threatened by her views. He also told the bosses he'd walk if she stayed. At the time, he had exclusive interviews lined up with *that* ex-Royal, *that* e-tech billionaire and *that* vengeful pop princess, so she stood no chance.'

'The holy trinity.' Juno whistled. 'And since then?'

'As soon as she left the paper, he piped down. We thought that was the end of it. He'd have been aware of Phoebe's illness; close friends at the paper knew. His girlfriend was soon happily distracted by their new baby, then less happily by Otis dumping her for someone younger. The mermaid porn series bombed and the film will never be made, because it *was* bloody awful.

'It was a couple of years until we noticed every book Phoebe published as Dorothy De'Ath was getting a rash of one-star reviews online the day it came out, all slanderously bad. The phrase "vomit-inducing" was pointedly over-used. We're talking ten, twenty-plus reviews landing at once. And every one of those reviewers had given Otis's girlfriend's salty little erotica five stars. Eventually, I flagged them up and they were all traced to one source.'

'Otis?'

'They wouldn't say, but they took them straight down.'

Aware of her friend's literary modus operandi, Juno ventured,

'Please tell me Phoebe didn't base a character on Otis New in a Dorothy book?'

Felix looked away, trying not to smile despite himself. 'He was neurotic social climber Otto Numan in her debut, demented opium addict Omar Nasir in the sequel, and half-wit peeping tom gardener Odin Nettlebed after we uncovered the sock-puppetry. All three died horribly.'

'I love her!' She clapped her hand against the wheel.

'As do I, my darling, although she doesn't help herself. I think sex trafficker Oswold Newton in P. F. Sylvian's latest, *The Three Hares Murders*, might be one too many. He got castrated by a *grandes* cigar cutter.'

'Ouch,' Juno winced.

'OhFeelYa's reappearance on Twitter coincided with its publication.'

'Otis wants revenge,' Juno breathed, nervous excitement mounting.

'That's my guess.'

As they closed in on the converted dockside factory where Otis had his work flat, her phone rang with a call from Eric.

She answered it over the Bluetooth. 'Any luck?'

'I'm doing the easy stuff from bed,' he yawned. 'So this guy you're going to see in Manchester, Otis New, is an asshole: NDAs everywhere, tax avoidance and a *lot* of rumours about underage girls.'

'What about his ex-girlfriend who wrote the book?'

'No trace of her for eighteen months.'

'Okay.' Juno rattled the groaning Jazz around the outskirts of Salford Quays. 'Let's go get him. With luck, if he's our culprit, we'll be home in time for last orders at The Barton Arms.' She tried to hide how nervous she was, although her hands were so clammy on the wheel, parallel parking was out of the question.

When they finally stopped in a back alley near the apartment building, she turned to Felix eagerly. 'What's my cover story? I thought Australian reporter – I have a bonza accent, mate – or something more personal, a flirtatious new neighbour maybe?'

'I am your cover. Felix Sylvian, filmmaker. I never do interviews.'

Juno scoffed, then pulled back her chin, staring at him. 'Seriously?'

'I'm the honey trap. You're the detective. I'll cue you.'

* * *

Otis New lived on the fourth floor of a converted industrial dock building. To Juno's surprise, he buzzed Felix straight in when he announced himself over the intercom with a whoopy 'Sweet!'

'Felix, my man!' He went into an elaborate shoulder banging, back-slapping high five welcome like a seventies disco dance. 'Looking boss, bro! Great drip! Who is this bougie lady?'

In a clingy gunmetal velvet singlet and joggers, faded tattoos stretched over gym-pumped guns, with a full set of bright white Turkish teeth implants, heavy-rimmed glasses and fingers weighed down with silver rings, Otis New was part gangster rap pretender, part ageing Costa Blanca strip club manager.

'Juno, this is Otis,' Felix said, introducing her.

'Enchanté!' He kissed her hand, beckoning them in.

'Is he *expecting* us?' Juno hissed out of the corner of her mouth as they were led through an open-plan monochrome apartment, furnished only with glass shelves lined with media awards, and white leather sofas stranded like sea ice on a vast expanse of grey shagpile rug.

'Play along,' Felix murmured back.

'I'm all set up.' Otis opened a door through to what was probably once a small bedroom, now set up as a recording studio. 'Take a seat, my man. Lovely lady, can you fetch us all some beers from the fridge?'

Juno gaped at Felix, who gave a ghost of a wink, or it could just have been his eye twitching with the effort of not lamping Otis. Juno liked to think so.

When she came back from raiding a glossy white fridge containing nothing but Punk IPA and Voss water, Otis and Felix were in headphones, two pop-screened microphones and a bank of monitors, audio interfaces and button decks between them. Otis pressed a ringed finger to his lips and waved at her to leave the bottles and take a seat in the corner while he started recording the intro.

'Hey, guys, so today I have my holy grail with me on Tis News! The one, the only, Feeeeelix Sylvian. I can't tell you how long I've been asking this guy to come talk making movies and shaking, grooving and moving. Spill, fella.'

They bantered for a few minutes, Felix's soft, deep voice hypnotising, his anecdotes on point, his name drops and indiscretions noticeably sparse despite Otis wheedling for more.

'My man, my legend, my days – Felix Sylvian is in the house, people! He's partied with Hollywood bad boys, skinny dipped with supermodels and shared a cell with rock stars! Check it out.'

His was the ubiquitous fast-talking, streetwise mid-Atlantic patter synonymous with middle-aged journalists and radio presenters desperate to stay relevant. 'Tell me about your leading laaaadies, bro – you've had some beautiful women in your films and what's more, let me tell you, folks, rumour is they work for this man for peanuts! You heard it here on Tis News, Felix Sylvian casts A-list talent at pound shop prices. What's your secret, man? What do you *do* to those babes?'

'I guess I'm nice to them. Astonishing how few people in this industry are. Some are downright bullies.' That's when Felix casually dropped the bomb. 'Which reminds me, why are you still persecuting my wife?'

Otis's smile froze.

Calmly recounting the story he'd told Juno in the car, Felix edited it down to the pithiest highlights, concluding with, 'How can you justify hounding her out of a job and then becoming a sock puppet?'

'That's not my shit, mate!' The white Turkish teeth implants flashed imploringly. 'That was the girlfriend. *Ex*-girlfriend.'

Felix stared at him in silence, waiting.

'Okay, it was my shit at first, yeah, but I've moved on, you feel me. Matured. *Namaste.*'

'You punished Phoebe for a review she *didn't even write*?'

Otis was truly squirming. 'I hear you, bro. I own that.'

'Too right you do. Tell me, Otis, when Phoebe asked that someone else be assigned to review your girlfriend's fishy book on the paper, who wrote it in the end?'

Otis shrugged, ringed fingers clanking together as he rubbed his face. 'Paige Turner, I think her name was.'

'Paige Turner?' Felix repeated incredulously.

'Yeah. Nasty bitch.'

'It was you, wasn't it?'

Otis shrugged.

'Admit it was you.'

Otis shrugged again, then grimaced. 'Bro, I *hated* that bloody book! The missus was always on Zoom to Hollywood, and putting our lives on Insta non-stop, and her pretty little head got so damned big. And for *what*? Muscle men with scales and fins getting it on with hot aqua nymphs? I was relying on Phoebe to pull it apart. When she didn't, I had to do it myself under a false name.'

'Yet you still blamed Phoebe?'

'Deflected attention, innit? Besides, she pissed me off, bro.' He polished off his beer, rings and bracelets jangling. 'I can't believe you two, like, you're still... together?'

'Why wouldn't we be?'

'Man like Felix, all those pretty actresses to choose from.' He glanced at Juno, thrust out a doubtful lower lip, then looked away. 'And Phoebe, she's fierce, which ain't no fun. So when you called me to come on the show at last, I thought you'd moved on, and about time, bro.' He held up his empty bottle to Juno. 'Another of these, please, darlin'!'

'Get lost.'

'Gotta be honest, Felix man, but your assistant here is suboptimal.'

'Juno' – Felix turned to her, blue eyes luminous – 'tell Otis who you are.'

She watched his direct gaze, so mesmerised, it took her a moment to recognise her cue. 'I'm a detective, mate.'

She realised too late that she was using the Australian accent, but she'd go with it, she decided.

Otis's mouth had fallen open, white teeth being circled by a pink tongue.

Aware she had the floor, Juno improvised. 'Listen carefully, Otis, we know you hounded Phoebe out of her column and faked reviews; we know you have tax dodges and lawsuits up to your ears, mate, none of which you probably want to be investigated too deeply. Then there's the young girls... So what we need to know is if you – or your ex – are OhFeelYa and Nymphomaniac?'

'OhManiacNymph,' Felix corrected under his breath.

'That's right. OhNymphManiac.'

Otis still had his mouth open. He closed it slowly, eyes troubled and furtive.

'Let me try to understand this, lady – are you're asking if I know a nymphomaniac called Ophelia?'

'Close enough.' Juno didn't want to lose momentum. 'And did you send Phoebe a funeral notice followed by an exploding package full of poison-tipped pen nibs?'

He let out an astonished, belly-deep laugh. 'Never!'

'What about your ex, the mother of your child? The one whose book you trashed,' Juno demanded. 'Tell the listeners where she is now?'

Realising they were still recording, Otis turned off the feed, dark eyes soulful. 'She's living off grid in Wales.'

'You expect us to believe that?'

'I go there to pick up my boy every other weekend. Her new fella makes harps. They're happy crusties. They have a flock of sheep and make music and felt art. When we split, it was nasty for a bit, but now I like to think we're mates. She had me all wrong. She's got a memoir coming out for Christmas. Apparently, I'm Chapters Ten to Fourteen.' He looked proud. '*Namaste.*'

Juno anticipated he was in for a shock in Santa's stocking.

'So you weren't acting like a paranoid, self-obsessed control freak who hates grown-up women when you targeted Phoebe?' Felix asked.

'Swear on my life, I didn't do any fake account trolling and I didn't send her any of that shit through the post. I admit those online book reviews were me and the wife when we were still together, but it was just for jokes. We did the same to Sally Rooney and The Yorkshire Shepherdess. It's true I always thought her column sucked; I wasn't alone.' He explained that he had never intended to put Phoebe in danger, but that he found her outspoken Undomestic Goddess pieces pointless: 'She was wanging on about her kids and ageing parents and sagging tits while I was, like, wake up and feel the vibe! We're the same age and I'm still young! My girlfriend was twenty-three, FFS. Phoebe was so easy to laugh at.'

'Yes, her column made millions of readers laugh,' Juno muttered, the irony lost on him.

'Let's hope they had their Tena Lady pads in!' he guffawed.

She was tempted to garotte him with his headphones.

'Before she left the paper,' Felix dived in quickly, 'you retweeted almost everything OhFeelYa and OhManiacNymph said. Surely you remember them?'

'Everyone had it in for Phoebe back then. I didn't bother reading most of it if I'm honest. I just liked and shared, took the piss. Lots of gobby tarts talking about mental health and menopause. Almost as bad as her bloody columns. She given up writing now, has she, Felix, bro? Bet you're relieved.'

Felix pursed his lips and for a moment Juno thought he was going to throw that punch at long last, but he just turned away, catching her eye. 'It's not him. Let's go.'

As they left, they could hear Otis re-recording a banter-laden intro telling listeners that the legendary Felix Sylvian had just behaved like a jerk. 'Listen up, guys, you are not going to *believe* this, but one of London's biggest nineties party animals is officially a boring. Old. Man! Not da bomb but a BOM, guys!'

Heading down in the lift, Juno said, 'You're right. I'm 99 per cent certain he's not our OhFeelYa.'

'I'll raise you the other 1 per cent. Thanks for roasting him.'

'He got off lightly,' she grumbled. 'You could have briefed me better.'

'I'll try next time. And I'll drive,' he offered as they reached the Jazz.

'You're not insured.'

'Third party. And it's okay, I drive like a boring old man.' He winked at her over the roof before climbing into the driver's seat, sliding it back as far as it would go to accommodate his long legs. 'I want to buy you a thank you drink. You were brilliant. We'll make last orders if we don't hit traffic.'

'Try not to hit anything, you third-party animal, you.' She was too tired to argue, quietly wishing they were going home after all. She longed to see Mil's cheery, craggy face and check Phoebe was okay.

But no sooner had Primal Scream come on the car stereo singing 'Movin' On Up' than Juno started to rally. It never took much to make a believer out of her.

'Harrogate next?' she checked, nerves tingling with excitement once more as Felix headed north out of Manchester.

'Close enough,' he nodded. 'We're off to the Dales. The most beautiful valley on earth. Here's the brief: Your cover is a hotel inspector. I want you to go online and book two rooms at The Poacher's Inn in Nidderdale for tonight under a false name.' He crashed the Jazz's gears, speeding around a roundabout into Charlestown. 'Then message Phoebe and let her know we're going to see Gail Lamb.'

12

PHOEBE

Mil returned to Hartridge before ten, issuing his special knock at the back door. He'd brought a bottle of wine for Phoebe, alcohol-free beer for himself, and several foil-wrapped packages from The Barton Arms kitchens, 'because I know you never eat.'

He laid the feast out on the table, stifling yawns. 'We were quiet, so Albie let me knock off after food service finished. I've asked around the regulars and have fresh intel. Grab a fork and I'll tell all.'

He'd made voice notes and recorded interviews on his phone, which he played back as prompts, his skill at deciphering the faint voices over the pub hubbub astonishing Phoebe, like dentists who have conversations with open-mouthed patients.

His in-depth Craig Jackman character profile was shaping up, he explained, although pub regular Rachel, who was Craig's mother's best friend and the third member of the First-Class Minds quiz team, reported that Denise wouldn't welcome an approach from the Village Detectives. 'She's all talked out, Rachel says. Literally. Strained her throat telling people he was an innocent victim and the police are wrong saying they're looking no further for suspects.'

He played another series of burbling voice notes, translating: 'Some of the model railway club were in tonight and they raised a glass to him. Alan and Bernard say Craig was a top model maker and a lovely bloke, although Bernard's wife Ree says Craig looked at her funny sometimes.'

Mil paused the playback. 'All the villagers on Craig's round said he talked for England, but they'd never heard a bad word from him. Something Graham from Inkbury Mill told me about the day it happened might be of interest. I got that recording time stamped.'

He located and played it. Phoebe shook her head, unable to make out a word.

'He says Craig's code scanner was definitely working when he received a tracked package that day.'

'So it broke somewhere between Inkbury Mill and here?'

'Might be insignificant, but that can't be more than half a dozen stops – Station Cottage, Bridge Row, Home Farm—'

'Hartridge Holt Barn,' Phoebe finished darkly. That was where Penny Fermoy lived. 'Did you ask Alan about his doorbell-cam footage?'

'Forgot, sorry. We can ask tomorrow. I thought we could retrace the last few calls on Craig's round first thing, see if we turn up anything useful.'

Mil had already eaten his way through the contents of two foil trays, opening a fresh beer. 'Drink some wine. Our best Merlot, that is.'

Phoebe took a sip to appease him.

'What's your beef with Penny?' he asked, ears and cheeks flaming red.

'It's not something I like talking about much. Probably like your romantic history with Penny, I'm guessing?' she fished.

'I asked first.'

While Mil helped himself to chips, Phoebe pushed her wine glass around like a Ouija counter before reluctantly confiding the truth that largely still eluded the Inkbury grapevine: 'Penny wants us out of here. She's convinced Felix is trying to muscle in on the Hartridge inheritance and scupper her plan to make this place into some sort of cultural hub. Apparently Boozy Faulkland wrote a Letter of Wishes before he died saying that's what he wanted for it.'

'Isn't Felix in line for Boozy's millions then?' Mil asked in surprise. 'Everyone in the village thinks so.'

'No way,' she laughed, always astonished how wrong the jungle drums could be. 'They weren't even blood relatives. Boozy's father and Felix's grandmother fell in love across the bridge table in the genteel Wiltshire nursing home that their respective self-made, self-centred children had packed them off to. They married in their eighties. Both were widowed, working-class Mancunians; he'd spent his life in the textile industry; she'd been a Tiller Girl. Their union made Boozy and Felix's father Jocelyn middle-aged stepbrothers. Felix was in his twenties when he met "Uncle Boozy". They got on famously, but Boozy already had six children and several grandchildren by then, and he certainly didn't see Felix as an heir. He had even more by the time he died – over twenty claimants on the estate at last count including Penny, and Felix isn't one of them.'

Mil nodded. After a long, thoughtful pause, he said, 'Nope, sorry, you lost me at Tiller Girl.'

'Boozy was only Felix's uncle by marriage. It's hardly a blended family. They used to all get together on landmark occasions, and Felix and a couple of his stepcousins are now close friends – hence we're here as house-sitters, or kitchen sitters – but he's not inheriting anything.'

'Penny knows all this?'

'It's no secret. Felix and I think she just wants us out of the way so she can have the run of this place and throw parties.'

'She knows what she wants, that woman.' His ears reddened.

'Now it's your turn to tell me what the story is between you and—'

'Any news from Felix and Juno? WhatsApp is a bit quiet.' Mil knocked back more alcohol-free beer, ears and cheeks aglow.

Phoebe studied him closely. His noble, battered face was cross hatched with deep folds of tiredness, his good eye bloodshot alongside his glass one. Mil worked long hours, and he was here to protect her out of kindness and loyalty, even though she'd rather he'd stayed home. He didn't owe her any secrets, she realised.

'They're heading to the Dales for last orders.'

'Beautiful spot.' He cracked another wide yawn.

'It's where we lived before we moved here.'

'Yeah, Felix said. Big old farm in the middle of nowhere, wasn't it?'

'The village was only a couple of fields and a hop over the beck away. I used to walk the girls to school across the meadows when they were little, all of us in wellies.'

'Sounds idyllic.'

'It was.'

'Not as grand as this big old place, though, your ladyship?'

'We didn't just live in the kitchen,' she sighed, 'and we owned it. Well, the little bit that wasn't mortgaged.'

'Tell me about it!' Mil chuckled, standing up and gathering up all the now-empty foil containers to bin. 'Being in pubs is no bloody fun right now. Bank owns everything but the beer froth.

Lucky to be still clinging on. You sold up that place to come down here, am I right?'

'Something like that.'

'Gather you had a bit of a rough ride before that.' Mil stifled another yawn, heading for the big open fire to throw on another log. 'Shall I kip on this sofa?' He was on it, in foetal position, terriers on board before she could answer. 'Heard a big movie of Felix's went bust. Wasn't Kate Winslet in it? What went on there?'

'Felix told you that?' Phoebe's defences shot up, although she guessed Mil knew the truth of it. Felix had always been refreshingly honest amongst his trusted few. The movie that got away.

It had been his baby, an adaptation years in the planning, a step up from anything he'd produced or directed previously: household names, mammoth budget, blue-chip investors; a four-month shoot in New Zealand. Felix's biggest film to date by far. Then Phoebe had got ill. So ill, doctors gave her fifty-fifty odds at best. They told the Sylvians that a radical hysterectomy, then chemo, was the only thing that could save her.

'I'd been out of hospital a few weeks when production began,' she confided as she heard Mil's breathing deepen to sleep. 'My sister was staying with me while Felix was away filming, but then her partner had a serious bike smash and she had to go back; the girls had just started at university; friends stepped in, but that was intermittent and I wasn't responding well to chemo. Felix flew home and flatly refused to leave. He stayed through my treatment, all four months, the same as the shoot, telling the big names and big investors to get lost because his wife came first. That's why his movie went broke; that's why we had to sell up; that's why we're here. Because he stayed with me and willed me to recover. And I did recover, but he lost his film and we lost the house.'

Mil was snoring loudly now.

'I'm not sure he'll ever forgive himself,' she said to herself, 'or me.'

'Whoa!' He spluttered awake, woken by his own snoring. 'What was I saying?'

'Nothing – it's not important.'

'Oh, yeah, the movie Juno told me about that lost you all that dosh.'

'Juno told you?'

'Was Kate Winslet really in it? Felix must have been gutted. Proper actress, she is.' He sighed, turning over and snuggling down again. 'Who are they off to see in the Dales, then?' He yawned.

'Gail Lamb.'

'What's the story there?'

She could already hear his breathing changing, the telltale somnolent rasp.

This time she didn't confide.

It still hurt too much.

Juno

Felix hurtled the Jazz towards the Dales as though he was on the last leg of the Pennine 1000 rally. Juno squeaked in alarm more than once, drowned out by Britpop, engine noise, and a timpani of vehicular decimation.

'I thought you said you drove like a boring old man?' she called over the din as they tore along the A59 towards Skipton, her phone's map now dark themed for night and telling her they were crossing the Leeds and Liverpool Canal.

'It's how my father drove. He always seemed ancient to me.

Not that he lived to be much older than I am now. That's when I finally bothered to find out he wasn't boring either.'

'The brakes sound like they're shearing off!' she cried as they rattled through picturesque Grassington as though negotiating a series of chicanes, Pulp singing 'Do You Remember the First Time'. Juno worried it might be the last time she ever heard it.

'It's handling fine!' Felix yelled back, powering on through the moonlit Dales, along die-straight walled roads towards the village of Dallowbeck, on which Phoebe had based Dingledale in her Dorothy De'Ath series.

'Gail's a big character,' he shouted across to Juno. 'Used to be in music PR, claims she helped invent the Manchester scene. Cashed it all in at forty to buy into the rural dream with her partner and their kid. She and Phoebe hit it off straight away. Our twins and her daughter were as close as cousins for a while.'

'What went wrong?'

'When Gail bears a grudge, it's for keeps – just ask some of the bands she once promoted.'

They turned off the main road, a narrow lane snaking up into the ink-dark sky above the valley, a village glittering in the distance beneath them. Then they turned right to plunge back down a wooded, sunken road, the car lights bouncing back through its tunnelled twists, Juno's stomach in her throat.

As the woods cleared, the lane flattened out and they were racing between dry-stone walls again, a beck running alongside.

'That's our old farm drive.' Felix slowed a little to point out a pair of gateposts marking an entranceway, an old stone milk-churn stand alongside, and a long drive curving away into the dark distance, the house out of sight. 'Phoebe loved it here. Big on remote living, my wife.'

'You must miss it,' Juno said carefully. 'Huge wrench to have to sell up.'

He said nothing, and it struck afresh how irresponsible he'd been, selfishly gambling his family's home on a movie.

They drove on, accelerating away at even more breakneck speed, bouncing over a humpback bridge and careering round a dog-leg bend before dropping down another hill into the village.

Crossing a larger bridge over the Nidd, Felix parked by an ivy-clad pub, its stone gables gleaming in the moonlight like hammered pewter, a carved plaque on one reading 1567. An A-frame sign by the entrance boasted five-star reviews, four-poster beds and a three-rosette rating.

'Half an hour to spare.' He checked his watch, delighted.

Juno took a few deep breaths to recentre herself, motion displacement still making her head spin as she tried to focus on Felix's quick briefing.

'Gail will still be at the bar, so I'll stay here while you check in and order that nightcap. She'll be straight onto you; she's incurably chatty.'

'How do you know she'll be at the bar?' Juno asked. 'Bit of a dipso, is she?'

'Gail owns the pub, Juno.'

'You could have told me,' she grumbled, sensing his briefing skills still needed improving.

'Officially, I'm barred for life,' Felix explained, putting on a baseball cap and tilting the brim down over his nose, 'which is why I'm lying low for now. Don't hang back with the cover story; *Conde Nast Traveller*, boutique hotel expert should do it, last-minute change of plan recommended by a friend. Tell her you have a senior colleague outside making calls. She mustn't see me.'

'Why senior?'

'Sorry?'

'Why are you my *senior* colleague?'

'We need her eager to please.'

'Then I'll be the senior colleague.'

'Absolutely fine.' The winning smile flashed below the base-ball cap peak. 'Message me our room numbers when the coast is clear and I'll meet you upstairs for that drink. Mine's a large Filey Bay Double Oak whisky. Good luck.'

Feeling fabulously spy-like – if under-briefed – Juno applied more lipstick and sauntered inside.

* * *

There were just a handful of drinkers in the bar of The Poacher's Inn, which creaked with gloomy Elizabethan authenticity from its historic beams to its worn flagstones, along with incongruous indie rock touches. Framed gold discs hung on wattle and daub walls amongst coats of arms, and carved priest's chairs and pews had seats upholstered in punky yellow tartan.

A surly barman told Juno in a strong Polish accent that the boss was the one who handled the online reservations and she wasn't in tonight, so their rooms wouldn't be ready. 'She has booking app on her phone, but I hear nothing. There is nobody here to make up beds now.'

After much sighing and eye-rolling on his part, and a lot of mentions of *Conde Nast Traveller* on hers, he reluctantly sloped off to see if any unoccupied rooms were habitable, coming back to hand over a keyring shaped like a massive wooden hare in Dr Martens. 'I find only one room made up, but it is a big suite so I think is okay, yes?'

Assuring him it would be, Juno asked when he was expecting his boss back.

'In the morning. She lives with her fiancé in the village. Busy lady.'

Thanking him, she ordered Felix's malt whisky and herself a large brandy to take up, messaging him that Gail wasn't in situ, so the coast was clear.

A few minutes later, she let him in to a vast oak-panelled Tudoresque bedchamber with eighties goth sex dungeon design touches. The wrought-iron four-poster had black lace curtains; a suit of armour in the corner was wearing a leather biker's jacket.

'The guy in charge said this is a suite,' she explained, 'but I can't find the connecting bedroom.'

Felix's eyebrows shot up. 'That's because this is the honeymoon suite, Juno.'

Juno looked around her again, realising she should have guessed. There were moody black and white close-ups of rock-'n'roll couples framed on the wall, tattoo hearts and flowers fabric on the bedding, and cascading fairy lights everywhere.

'Bit clichéd,' she muttered, spotting a chandelier made of chains and barbed wire hanging above them.

'Yeah, the old one bed trope,' he agreed.

Juno did a double take, not caring if that was clichéd too. 'I didn't *orchestrate* this!'

'I wasn't suggesting you did.'

Juno fumed silently, certain he had insinuated just that, and feeling mildly paranoid that perhaps she had invoked it with all her stupid wishful thinking on the M6 earlier. Which was awful because – whilst Felix in a one bed trope scenario might have been her generation's fantasy over thirty years ago – he was now her lovely friend's handsomely shabby husband, and Juno had absolutely no desire to share anything with him apart from some home truths. Also, she had some middle-aged bedtime, bathroom and sleeping habits she preferred to keep private.

Feeling her cheeks glow pinkly, she eyed an uninviting studded black leather settee. 'I'll take the sofa!'

He eyed it too. 'Wouldn't dream of it. That's mine.'

'I'm already on it!' She threw herself aboard. It felt like a bed of nails.

Felix perched on the arm, amused. 'Mil's kipping on a sofa at Hartridge tonight. The Village Detectives are wife-swapping.'

Not knowing quite what to make of this, Juno blustered, 'Mil's hardly my wife! I mean—'

'I'm glad he's there.' Just for a moment, the nonchalant guard slipped and Juno saw his preoccupation, face etched with love and worry. 'Phoebe thinks she's tougher than she is.'

'Mil will look out for her,' she reassured him.

'He'd better behave.' He pulled out his phone. 'I'll message to let them know I have you cornered in The Poacher's Inn honeymoon suite as collateral.'

Juno found this strangely bolstering. Even if the Polish barman had bothered to put champagne on ice, scattered a rose petal welcome on the bed and run them a deep foaming bath for two, she could never be in doubt she was safe with Felix. And she was grateful at least for the chance to ask him more about Gail Lamb.

Over her brandy, she quizzed him about Phoebe and their absent landlady falling out. 'They were close once, you say?'

Felix was woolly on the finer detail, admitting he'd been away working a lot of the time, but he knew enough to recount that she and Phoebe had been terrific mates, especially when Gail's relationship started breaking down – 'Her partner hated it out here, it was a messy, angry split.' Their daughter Leah often stayed at the Sylvians' farm for after-school sleepovers with best friends the twins to protect her from the crossfire at home in the pub. 'Gail was all for it.'

What the adults failed to realise, he went on, was how threatened

Leah felt by the twins and their close bond: 'Leah was a live wire like her mum, a lot more streetwise than our kids but obviously traumatised by what was going on at home. We found out later that she'd picked on Maud from the start, always the quietest of the three, constantly isolating her. It was subtle at first, but gradually became full-on bullying, which Maud was too frightened and ashamed to tell anyone about. It went on for years. In the end, Amelie blurted it all out after her sister almost drowned because of something Leah did.'

'What happened?'

Felix sucked his teeth unhappily and glanced at the curtained window, beneath which the river babbled. 'The girls were ten, almost eleven. They all loved the outdoors, rattling round the fields like buccaneers. Phoebe and her sister were raised like that, so she encouraged it. There'd been a godawful storm. I was stuck in London because the trains weren't running. Phoebe thought the girls were all playing in the farmyard, but they'd gone to the beck. We found out later that Leah had dared the other two to walk across a tree trunk that had come down over it and Maud fell in.'

Lifting his whisky glass to his lips and finding it empty, he stood up and looked round for a mini bar. Not finding one, he filled the kettle.

'The beck was swollen from the storm and she was swept straight under.' He started making them both tea, clattering cups and spoons angrily. 'While Amelie waded in, desperately trying to pull her sister out, Leah said she'd go for help. Instead, she just ran home here to the pub and said nothing.

'Thank heavens, Phoebe had got worried and was already searching for them. She found them by the beck. Both were soaked through. Amelie had got her sister out but was hysterical and badly cut; Maud had a broken wrist and she was close to unconscious with hypothermia. Amelie swore she'd seen Leah push her, although Maud later said she'd slipped.

'Either way, Leah not raising the alarm was an unforgiveable act. When we heard about the bullying that had come before, there was no way I was letting that child near ours again. Phoebe insisted on talking it through with Gail, even though I told her it was a waste of time.'

Hearing the anger in his voice, Juno could imagine him laying down the law. Yet she also knew how children in a blind panic did illogical things. As do unhappy, damaged children with tough home lives. They need help, she thought. But she kept schtum because Felix was still plainly furious about it.

'Gail's attitude made it worse,' he went on, pouring boiling water into cups. 'When we tried to talk to her about it, she refused to accept that Leah was anything other than the victim in the whole situation. She blamed Amelie for what happened at the beck, claiming our daughter had tried to push *Leah* in and she'd run away terrified.'

Again, Juno sensed shock muddling memories, a frightened child not wanting to be told off, powerless parents in need of somebody to blame.

'The girls had their birthday party coming up the following weekend,' Felix said, peeling open a UHT milk miniature with enviable ease, 'a disco in the village hall. They begged us to stop Leah coming. They were both scared of her. I was right behind that, but Phoebe wanted to cancel and do something with just the family.'

'Sensible.'

'In the end, we let the girls decide, and they chose the disco. They'd been planning it for weeks, making playlists and designing outfits, devising games for all their friends. Maud wanted to get her plaster cast signed by everyone. The whole of their school year had been invited, so Phoebe went to see Gail to talk through the situation.' He handed Juno a mug of tea, settling on the sofa beside her. 'Big mistake. You can guess what happened next.'

'I can,' she sighed, having navigated the parental back-stabbing around children's birthday parties in her day, without the added complication of near-drowning. But she also sensed that it was not as straightforward as Felix was painting it, that Phoebe's friendship with Gail was more nuanced than two school gate lionesses snarling over their cubs.

'Retaliation was instant,' he laughed hollowly. 'Rumours flew around the village that our girls were bullies, that excluding Leah from their party was another example of how cruel and stuck up they were. Gail's a persuasive character and being the pub landlady put her in pole position to mudsling. The twins were devastated when only a tiny handful of local friends turned up to the disco. The rest had been told not to go; Phoebe was incandescent.'

Juno winced, feeling her pain. Nothing hurt so much as your children being punished by an adult's spite.

The feud had then simmered on for years, Felix told her, his low husky voice hypnotic. 'It divided the village, long after the twins and Leah had gone off to different high schools, and moved on to teenage tantrums and boyfriends, attending many more parties in the village hall where they'd all been on the guest list. Gail wouldn't ever let it go, dispensing malicious gossip with every pint. She's a great yarn-spinner – it's one of the things Phoebe had adored about her at first – so the stories she invented about us to keep the myth alive and drinkers here entertained got increasingly wild.'

'Such as?' Juno wondered what fire lay behind her smoke screen.

'Trust me, we were the Borgias by the end.' His evasion made her suspect there was plenty. 'It didn't help both being in the media spotlight, especially Phoebe, whose Undomestic Goddess column was about our home life. Phoebe's revenge had been to put Gail in it, heavily disguised as a fantasist village WI zealot whose compulsive lying and social media trolling kept catching her out.'

'Victoria Sponger!' Juno recognised the description. 'I loved it whenever she got mentioned. Did Gail realise it was her?'

'Must have. The online abuse had started getting more vicious. Long before OhFeelYa and OhManiacNymph debuted, there were forerunners which we suspected were Gail. Then, when all the Twitter nastiness started around Phoebe championing the Virginia Woolf bench, Gail wasted no time recounting the story of what had happened between the girls at the beck to her pub regulars, claiming that the twins had both tried to drown Leah. That was too much for me. I came here to demand she put people right or we'd sue her for defamation.' His handsome face was pure granite.

'Which was when you were barred, I take it?'

He nodded. 'Within hours of that, the OhFeelYa and OhManiacNymph tweets rocketed in frequency from once or twice a week to twenty times a day.'

'That can't have felt like a coincidence.' Juno could hear Phoebe's voice in her head: *Felix doesn't think before he acts.*

'Exactly. The death announcements started appearing in the local paper around the same time, although we didn't know that until later. We had way too much shit going on. By the time we found out, Phoebe had just had her last round of chemo and the house was on the market.'

Juno's fingers tapped on the cup rim. 'You must have felt bad about that.'

'Apoplectic.'

'You losing all that money on a movie, I mean.'

'Oh, that.' He nodded curtly.

'Awful timing.' She couldn't let this one pass, a small fireball of brandy still in her belly. 'Being forced to sell the house.'

He said nothing.

'Bit reckless when your wife was ill.'

Staying silent, he pressed his palms together, forefingers to his nose, eyes darkening.

'No wonder Gail's newspaper nastiness hardly registered,' she said, losing her nerve.

There was another aching pause. Juno cracked first, gratefully hurrying back into detection: 'But if it is Gail, why bring it up again now? Why resurrect OhFeelYa? Why the funeral notice, the newspaper announcement, the poison pen bomb?'

'That's what we're here to find out,' he said carefully.

'Need some sleep first!' She wasn't remotely tired, but she didn't want to talk any more, heart thundering from her minor altercation, that night's garage sandwich supper squirming anxiously in her belly. She sensed Felix ticking beside her like an unexploded bomb.

'I'll take the sofa.' She patted the studded leather showpiece beneath them.

'You won't.' He stayed put.

They finished their tea in silence, both trying not to look at the big four-poster bed. Juno's stomach did all the talking, gurgling furiously.

'I'm honestly fine on here,' she insisted again.

'Me too.' He refused to concede.

There was another pause, neither of them budging.

'Well, this isn't awkward,' she joked eventually.

Felix muttered under his breath, standing up at last. 'Tell you what, I'll sleep in the car.'

'You will not! That's my mother's car. If anyone's going to sleep in it, I am!' She sprang up too.

His phone vibrated and he read a message on it, with a quick, tired smile. 'Okay, I'll take the bed. I don't think Phoebe will be letting me back into the marital one for a while, so I could use a good night's rest ahead of that.'

* * *

Finding herself illogically piqued that he hadn't fought harder to give her the bed, and worrying about what Phoebe's message had said, Juno sulked on the sofa, unable to sleep at all. Feeling guilty, she texted Phoebe a badly typed apology for agreeing to this road trip. She then opened *Possession* on her phone to try to read some more ahead of that week's book club gathering, just two days away, but gave up after three pages, still only 10 per cent in.

Finally, to pass the time, she looked up Phoebe's old newspaper columns, forced to take out a trial subscription to get behind the paywall and access the archive, following the antics of the Sylvian family and their village neighbours, including the glorious Victoria Sponger. It was a surprisingly affectionate caricature. Juno sensed in it the unspoken pain of a lost female friendship.

Just as yawns were finally starting to tug at her jowls, she read a column that made her sit up in shock. 'Gotcha!'

13

PHOEBE

Mil snored. Ripely. A big-engine, eight-cylinder, three octave petrolhead snore.

The dogs found his presence unsettling. Restless and squeaky, they had wanted to go out more than once.

Yet Phoebe found overnighting with a sleeping giant surprisingly comforting, especially given the Hartridge kitchen bedsit already had such a Bedouin communal living vibe. Not bothering to pull out the sofa bed that she and Felix usually inhabited, she'd catnapped on the big couch opposite Mil's, read a lot, written some notes and thought deeply about Craig's plight, the sinister hate mail invitations, and how Penny Fermoy might have orchestrated it.

Mil snored on, rhythmic as the kitchen clock's tick.

Just after midnight, her phone had buzzed with a message from Juno:

> I am in the honeymoon suite with your husband and I can't sleep. I promise I haven't touched him. Sorry I agreed to this. How mad are you at me?

Phoebe had smiled to herself. She knew how persuasive Felix could be.

> Ish.

Juno messaged again an hour later, sharing a screenshot.

> Was this based on truth?

It was an old Undomestic Goddess column. She reread it now, the first time since its publication, marvelling at her breezy bon mots and petty woes. Written a year before the Stormy Cs started arriving, she'd been doing the rounds of university open days with the twins at the time, all mutually horrified to find themselves being shown around one in the same tour group as village frenemy 'Victoria Sponger' and her daughter.

She messaged Juno back:

> Ish.

A second screenshot came of the expanded comments section beneath the column with a red circle drawn around one that started:

> Will this moaning mummy Karen ever shut up?

It was the same phrase as the invitation Phoebe had just been sent to her own memorial service, she realised with a start. But Juno hadn't seen that, and it wasn't what she was drawing her attention to. It was the reader name by the comment: Lamb to the Slaughter. Beneath it, she'd written:

Gail Lamb?

Phoebe had never accepted Felix's belief that Gail could be behind OhFeelYa and OhManiacNymph. Yet in her darkest heart, she realised she'd probably always secretly dreaded it.

She messaged Juno back now to explain that this column had been an olive branch of sorts. The open day encounter was real enough: business-brain Maud and fashion-mad Leah had both set their hearts on studying marketing at Bath University. Finding themselves touring around the department in a group of just six had been excruciating, although perhaps not quite as she'd depicted it in print. The two girls had got on quite amicably; it was Gail and Phoebe – the supposed adults – who couldn't look at one another. In her column, she'd called the encounter out as a painful reality check. She'd lamented the long grudge match and the harm it had done, although, as she told Juno now:

Bringing pathos to Victoria Sponger was tough in a thousand words.

Especially with that twist! More stake through the heart than olive branch.

Juno's reply was followed by a row of shocked face emojis.

Later in the same Undomestic Goddess column, Phoebe had told her readers how she'd agonised for days before sending 'Victoria Sponger' an email suggesting they put the feud behind them, confessing how much she missed their friendship and wanted their daughters to make peace too, especially as they might soon be studying together far from home. The reply was short and swift:

TL;DR.

Too long; didn't read.

Phoebe told Juno now:

> That happened, although it was a handwritten
> letter, not an email. I'm analogue.

You'll always be my Lady Dee Jekyll.

Juno added a cluster of love heart hands emojis to this.

The dogs wanted to go out again. Phoebe wandered outside with them, admiring the full moon.

She fell over Mil's boots when she came back in, cursing.

From the sofa, his sonorous rasps continued uninterrupted. Anyone could have broken in to abduct her, whisking her off to acupuncture with poisoned pen nibs and bury alive, and he wouldn't have stirred. It was reassuringly rather like having Felix home.

Phoebe opened her laptop, refusing to let herself think about Felix, who she remained deeply aggrieved with. Instead, she returned to Dingledale, where her flapper sleuth was much further ahead in her investigations than the Village Detectives.

She broke off to take a shower at six. By the time she came out, Mil was sitting up awake, sparse hair on end, reading a long incoming update from Juno on the WhatsApp Group Chat. 'Do you two never sleep?'

'We're both menopausal women, so not much.'

'Juno says Otis New was a false lead, but this Gail woman they're about to meet is looking highly suspicious.'

'I know,' sighed Phoebe, wishing it wasn't so. She'd so adored Gail, a rare best friend made in adulthood. A bit like Juno.

Unlike Felix, Mil was both night owl and early bird, sleepily good-tempered, soon amiably tea making and breakfast prepping while planning their crime reconstruction.

'This morning, we'll retrace Craig's round, starting from Inkbury Mill,' he recapped. 'See if anybody spotted anything unusual. We can plan out some questions over breakfast, and I'll fill you in on who everyone is. I'll just check last night's motion-activated CCTV.' He took out his phone.

Moments later, he was letting out a shout of alarm. 'Call DI Mason! We had a prowler last night! Tall, spooky-looking geezer creeping about at 3 a.m. Look!'

Phoebe looked.

'Mil, that's me.'

* * *

Juno

Having stolen around the honeymoon suite for half an hour, getting washed and dressed in the privacy of the bathroom, Juno had showered, eye-dropped and tooth-pasted away her fatigue to ensure she was at her most perkily, platonically professional to wake Felix, delivering a cup of tea to the bedside.

'Morning!'

'Oof.'

'Sleep well?'

'Ugh.'

'I'm going down to breakfast now to pretend I'm a hotel reviewer and suss out Gail!'

'Uh?'

Phoebe had mentioned he wasn't a morning person, but now that Juno witnessed first-hand just how uncommunicative he was – mere monosyllables emitted from beneath the Egyptian cotton – she realised she was on her own. 'Stay here, understood?'

'Oof.'

'I'll message if I need you.'

Quietly grateful she had this assignment to herself, she painted on a slick of *Conde Nast*-worthy lipstick. She already knew her mission objectives.

Leaving him still deep in bed, an exquisitely primeval man-mound beneath the covers, his phone playing 'Mr Brightside' for the second time, she hurried downstairs for breakfast, hoping Gail was in charge, and that she'd be easy to identify.

She'd been frustrated to find no photographs of their land-lady on The Poacher's Inn website, nor Gail's social media, which was surprisingly limited and tiled with her food, pub decor, dogs and fiancé, who was, by uncomfortable coincidence, a postman.

Or *was* it a coincidence?

Juno braced herself for a virago. All Felix's talk of her Hacienda-partying past, loudness and threats had conjured a plus-size Mancunian firebrand in a baseball cap shooting her mouth off.

But the woman who greeted her in the breakfast room was a Botoxed pixie dressed in a Kate Bush hippy tribute of floral smock, corseted leather waistcoat and cowboy boots, button-nosed like a Disney fairy. Hair dyed unfeasibly black, big manga eyes blinking out through an over-long fringe, she looked genuinely thrilled to see Juno in her pub.

'You must be our surprise guest! Have the table in the window, flower.' She was warm and gushy with a sing-song Lancashire accent. 'Lovely view of the Nidd from here. That's a dead nice top. Can I get you a brew? Tea, coffee, juice?'

Remembering her travel expert cover story, Juno asked for a decaffeinated latte with warm oat milk on the side and pink grapefruit juice, 'but anything freshly squeezed will do if you don't have that.' She beamed in what she hoped was a warm Alex Polizzi way.

'Sorted. Mint!'

'Yes, mint's fine.'

'No, I mean you've good taste, flower!' She laughed, a delicious, throaty descant. 'Coming right up. Breakfast menu is there on the wall, but just say if you want something special.' She spoke breathlessly fast, eyes blinking rapidly before she turned to waft out, calling over her shoulder, 'Nothing's too much trouble at The Poacher's Inn!'

Felix was wrong about Gail, Juno had already decided. She was all heart and fire, not smoke and mirrors. She reminded Juno of someone, an icon from another generation she couldn't quite place with the same cartoon eyes and wicked giggle.

Scurrying back with the coffee and strange-coloured juice, Gail apologised for being caught out by a late booking. 'My bar manager told me that you were let down by another hotel?'

Having done her research for this already, Juno named the region's five-starred, go-to boutique destination.

'Shocking, flower! And you a top reviewer!'

'They didn't know that, but I thought it was only fair to declare it here given we were so last minute. A friend recommended it. And she wasn't wrong – it's delightful. Very authentic.'

'We are that.' Gail beamed delightedly. 'It's not like me to miss a booking, but I'm getting married in a fortnight and it's all a bit topsy turvy.'

Juno would have liked to jump in to ask about this – the postman fiancé was of interest – but she'd just sipped the juice and was struggling to swallow it, eyes watering.

'We had no pink grapefruit,' Gail explained, 'but you said an alternative was fine, so I blended beetroot with Apple and Mango J2O. It's the same colour. Is it okay, duck?'

'It's unique.' Juno swigged some of her coffee to take the taste away and gagged afresh. The 'oat milk' seemed to be blended

Quakers and water, floating on Nescafe instant. Juno guessed they didn't have any of that in right now, either. Nor avocados to smash, blueberries to drizzle in maple syrup or muffins to top with poached eggs, judging from the number of lines through the specials on the breakfast board.

'What can I get you to eat, duck?' Gail offered eagerly, waving at it.

Staying in role, Juno ignored all the tempting artery-blockers listed there and asked for an egg-white souffle omelette with morels – 'or any wild mushroom will do, darling' – and sourdough toast. When Gail skipped back to the kitchen once more, she hurriedly visited the continental breakfast buffet to scoop some pastries, cereal bars and a pot of yoghurt into her handbag for Felix, observed closely by an elderly couple eating full Englishes in the corner.

Juno then messaged him:

> Have identified suspect and will be engaging in convo shortly. Do not come down.

A few minutes later, Gail returned with a small, anaemic yellow omelette and slices of burnt baguette. 'Enjoy!'

Juno, who was big on small talk, wasted no time engaging her target, asking Gail if she'd owned the pub long, whether it was a friendly area, had any TV shows been filmed round here, whether any celebrities past and present lived locally and if the Brontës had ever eaten in The Poacher's Inn.

The answers were deliciously unexpected – funny, indiscreet, adorably irreverent – and scattered with sarcastic asides about hill walkers and James Herriott fans. Her favourite Brontë book was *The Tenant of Wildfell Hall*. 'Everyone picks *Wuthering Heights* but the Earnshaws were all nutjobs.'

Juno couldn't agree more. Her stomach let out a bellow,

reminding her that she'd been enjoying the conversation too much to eat, and she crammed a mushroom in her mouth. It wasn't a morel, but it was delicious.

'Breaded garlic mushrooms,' Gail explained. 'We do them as a starter in the pub. I'm afraid the larder's a bit low on supplies.' She dropped her voice. 'My bad. Brain fog meets bride-brain.'

She hovered lovingly for a few moments, but Juno was too hungry to interrogate further, grateful that the elderly couple chose that moment to request mustard, HP sauce and two steak knives.

'Very tough bacon!' they told Juno conspiratorially.

'I'll inform *Conde Nast* subscribers,' she promised, polishing off the breaded mushrooms.

Wishing she'd ordered the Full English too, Juno demolished the omelette in seconds, challenged her veneers with the bread and discreetly reclaimed a Danish pastry from her handbag to stave her ongoing hunger pangs.

When Gail returned to deliver condiments to her fellow diners, Juno quickly asked after her wedding. 'That must be so exciting! Are you having it here?'

'No, a beach in the Caribbean.'

'Wow! You must both be so excited.'

As she chatted happily about her gorgeous husband-to-be, Gail dropped plentiful information for Juno to scoop: daughter Leah was now in fashion promotion and had scored her mother a haute couture wedding dress; the pub was currently taking second place to the wedding but they had big renovation plans; the postman's divorce had been long and dirty, much as hers had been years ago. 'I was crazy as an Earnshaw back then.'

Juno warmed to her even more. Gail was funny and indiscreet, and to her surprise, Juno sensed a kindred spirit. They giggled over their savvy children – 'Our Leah has my thin skin and a filthy temper like her dad, but she can get a drop waist, super-size sleeve silhouette trending in a heartbeat' – nostalgic musical taste – 'I was twisting my melon before Bez had his maracas out' – and hopeless romanticism – 'there's someone for everyone, Juno, flower' – fast discovering a surprising amount in common, including a stand-up comic mate from nearby Harrogate.

'We must swap numbers!' Gail gushed, fishing in her apron pocket for her phone and unlocking the screen before handing it across. 'Put yours in there, flower. I'll just show these guys to their table.' She jumped up to greet a couple in walking gear coming into the breakfast room.

Grateful she'd booked under her maiden name rather than making something up, Juno added it to Gail's contacts and ran a hasty eye along them. While Gail was noisily taking an order for two pots of tea and vegan breakfasts, she stealthily checked out the apps, surprised to find X wasn't even downloaded. When Gail disappeared into the kitchen without reclaiming her phone, Juno also hurriedly checked out her recent messages. Those she'd sent were fully punctuated with minimal spelling errors, she noted. Most were to the postman fiancé who, to Juno's alarm, liked to share intimate photos of himself. Racing on, she found Gail's exclamation-heavy replies to her daughter who obviously communicated in voice notes, like Mil, while she stuck doggedly to texts like Juno. Scrolling up the exchange, she spotted snaps of a corseted lace wedding dress on a mannequin in front of a window, clearly staged for Instagram with billowing net curtains and what appeared to be Blackpool Illuminations against a moody sky beyond.

The kitchen door swung open. 'Made your brews, flowers! Vegan brekkies on the way.'

Juno hurriedly cast the phone aside as Gail swirled past with mugs of tea for the walkers. On the way back, she perched in the chair opposite Juno to reclaim it, navigating to the newly added number. 'Nice one. I'll message you so you have mine. Lend us your reading specs, Juno love. Ta!'

Juno watched the slow, punctilious way she messaged. She was no lightning-speed tweeter.

'I hate these bloody things, don't you? There! Who's your mate by the way? The one that recommended The Poacher's Inn to you? Do I know them?'

'Phoebe Fredericks.' Juno said it before she could stop herself. This wasn't in the plan. Felix would be furious, and probably Phoebe too. But it just felt right.

'Phoebe?' The big, dark eyes filled with tears.

'You know her?' Juno bluffed, although the surprised note in her own voice was genuine; she hadn't expected Gail to be so visibly upset.

'She was once my best friend.' The tears were already working their way up the long lashes onto her Claudia Winkleman fringe.

This might not be in Felix's plan, but Juno was certain her gut feeling was right. Within moments, Gail was pulling the seat closer across the table, eager to hear how Phoebe was. 'Is she really okay? You know she was ill? I was dead worried.'

'She's fine now.'

'I'm so relieved to hear that! We don't talk any more. Not for years. I was a right cow, we both were.'

Again, Gail's warm, confessional character was unfiltered. 'We fell out, and it was right awful, I couldn't make it better. I was just so hurt, and it was a shit time for me personally. My first marriage bombed. Our kid Leah looked up to Phoebe. She went right into herself when we fell out, it shredded her confidence.

There was us two hand-bagging at dawn, not noticing how much our kids were hurting.'

Hand-bagging at dawn made Juno blink in recognition. She'd heard Phoebe use it more than once. A silly phrase, coined by eighties sexist football pundits, later bought out by nineties women who kept their cash in their bras and partied 'til dawn. Women like them.

'I heard a bit of what happened,' Juno said sympathetically, in no doubt Gail and Phoebe had been best friends, both still grieving its loss.

The tears thickened. 'You know Phoebe well?'

'We go back a lifetime, although I was based in the States when she lived here. We're super close now.'

'So you know Felix too?' The pixie features sharpened.

'Not so well.'

Gail gave a bitter laugh. 'When that man bears a grudge, it's for life.'

Juno started, recognising this was almost exactly what Felix had said about Gail. She watched her closely, those big cartoon eyes still tear-starred bright, the rushed voice confiding.

'Phoebe was such a mate through my marriage bust-up; I escaped to her place all the time. When Felix was away, that house was a right laugh. Leah and me both stayed over the nights my ex was being an arsehole. Me and Phoebe talked and talked once the kids were in bed. But whenever Felix was home, I knew I wasn't welcome. Phoebe always made a point of treating all three girls as equals, but Felix made it dead clear he just wanted time with his daughters. He treated Leah like crap. He didn't like me much either, I could tell. Different story when he was in here, drinking after hours, charming everyone, flirting his arse off if his wife wasn't around. I saw it all. Everyone round here did.' Gail mopped her eyes with a napkin. 'You heard what happened with Seraphine, I take it?'

Juno nodded vaguely, recognising the third name from Felix's list: Seraphine Delauney-Roche. Felix's briefing had been predictably sparse – 'a ghost from my past'. Apart from the fact she lived in Paris, Juno knew nothing, although she had a shrewd suspicion Seraphine was an ex.

'I don't know how poor Phoebe held it together,' Gail whispered. 'He behaved right badly over that whole business.'

'Behaving badly is in the genes,' said a husky voice behind them, tinged with steel.

The pixie face across the table from Juno hardened from Tinkerbell to bad fairy. She stood up slowly, stretching up to her full five feet three, bangle jangling as she pointed a finger at the door. 'Get out of my pub!'

Juno closed her eyes. Now she knew who Gail reminded her of. She was a younger, northern reincarnation of the pint-sized actress who had played a legendary soap opera landlady, a sparkly-eyed naughty giggler with a penchant for life's good times, bad boys and ugly tempers.

And Gail's temper had just turned very ugly indeed.

* * *

When Juno opened her eyes again, Felix had drawn up a chair, impressively washed and buffed and in a knitted turquoise shirt that made his blue eyes pop bright as laser spots. 'Hi, Gail.'

'You're barred.' Gail was glaring at him, wet lashes like anti-trespass spikes.

'A breakfast bar doesn't count.' He turned to look at the menu board. 'I'm hungry.'

Dismayed by his arrogance, Juno was back to not liking him much.

'I see you've met darling Juno.' He turned back with a smile that would melt icebergs. 'Isn't she lovely?'

Gail's teary catchlight gaze was switching back and forth between Juno and Felix, betrayed.

'She's a two-faced bitch!' she hissed. 'You two are together, I take it?'

'Not romantically!' Juno bleated.

But Gail's fast love had flipped to enmity. 'Pull the other one, flower! You two lovebirds shared our honeymoon suite last night! Does Phoebe know about this?'

'My wife is as keen as Juno and I are to know why you're tweeting slander against her again,' Felix said softly. 'And why in hell did you send her an invitation to her own funeral? There's more...'

'I never!' The tears plopped out at speed. 'Honest to God, Felix, I'd never do that to her!' She put her face in her hands, sobbing loudly now.

'I don't think she did!' Juno told him urgently.

'You said you thought she *did* on the WhatsApp group last night,' he snapped back. 'I just read it!'

'What WhatsApp group?' bleated Gail.

'That was before I met her!'

With a lot of throat clearing, a shadow fell across them. 'Any chance of that vegan breakfast? Only we're planning to walk up to Brimham Rocks this morning.'

'Can't you see I'm busy!' Gail wailed.

Juno's phone had started ringing. It was Eric. She dismissed it. He messaged *Answer!* and it rang again.

Gail was shouting at Felix: 'You've always hated me! Ever since that Bonfire Night party...'

Juno took the call away from the table, forcing a reassuring smile at the elderly couple in the corner who were watching proceedings open-mouthed, Full Englishes barely touched. Her stomach grumbled again. It had no sense of timing.

'S'up, Mom!' Eric sounded buzzed. 'Listen up, you've got lucky on the ISP for OhFeelYa's recent online activity. It's coming from Paris. Public access, so no specific ID, but definitely there.'

'They're tweeting from France? Not somewhere like, say, Yorkshire?'

'Nope. La France, man.'

'Thank you, darling! And please don't call me man.'

Felix was still sitting at her table, arms crossed and stone-faced as Gail flew at him with a barrage of insults, hippy pixie transformed to howling harpy. 'You think your mingin' nepo-baby twins are so much chuffing better than my girl! Well, my Leah is in high fashion now, following this queen into PR' – she stabbed a finger into her chest – 'and she's good, our kid, swear down she's going places! She interned with Tom Ford. She was poached by Chiuri. The fashion houses all love her. She's a digital genius, a designer label meta-tagger, an algorithm alchemist. She took me to Kate Moss's fiftieth as her plus one! Buzzin', it was! Where were you that night, eh, Felix? I looked for you both, but maybe the invite went missing in the post, eh?'

'Phoebe hates parties.'

'Any chance of those breakfasts?' the male walker tried again, turning to Juno. 'This really isn't good enough. I'll be recounting this breakfast experience on TripAdvisor.'

Juno missed what Felix said next, but whatever it was poured lighter fluid on Gail's fire.

Standing up, Gail picked up Juno's lurid pink juice and threw it in his face. 'Do one, you tosser! Sling your hook! You too, you cow!' she screamed at Juno, who was starting to see a different side to her.

'I'm so sorry!' she babbled, hating conflict. 'I know it's not you! Whoever it is, seems they're in Paris.'

'Then we're going to Paris,' muttered Felix.

Gail's eyes were saucers. 'Go to hell on a pogo stick for all I care!'

There was a clatter of dropped steak knives from the elderly couple's corner table as their landlady marched back into her kitchen, shouting, 'If you're not out of this pub in five, you're getting two vegan breakfasts where the sun don't shine.'

'She meant us, not you,' Juno reassured the pale-faced walking couple.

Still sitting at the window table, face dripping, Felix closed one eye and cast Juno a contemplative look with the other, sooty lashes starred with pink liquid. 'Now do you believe me?'

'You wound her up. She's not who we're looking for.' Juno thought back over the slow texting, the careful grammar, the kindness and innocence and obvious deep, mournful affection for Phoebe. 'She's not our troll.'

She gathered her key card and stomped up to the honeymoon suite, not trusting him. She was no longer certain that Gail was best friend material. But she did know she couldn't be OhFeelYa.

* * *

Phoebe

'Almond, coconut or filtered organic cow's milk? Brown, white sugar, natural sweetener. Lemon slice?'

Phoebe and Mil were already on their fourth cup of coffee as they retraced Craig's last round. The phrase 'Craig loved to chat' was a running theme. The residents of Inkbury Mill, a creative, semi-retired WFH heartland, liked to chat too.

They'd started with Graham on the ground floor, soft-spoken and gull-eyed, who had served them Nespresso Lungo from a noisy machine whilst reporting that Craig had been in high spirits on the day he died, delivering several circulars and a tracked package. 'He was very talkative, and his barcode scanner was working. I received my printer cartridge subscription and *New Scientist* and we chatted about the pub quiz. He wasn't at all keen on the new host.'

In the apartment next door, retired physiotherapist Maya had proffered decaffeinated fair trade filter coffee in a cafetière and told them Craig had personally handed across her *Women's Health* magazine and magnesium supplement-by-post. 'He was ever so excited about his new electric van.'

A floor above, Henry and Carol had pressed instant Douwe Egberts on them, appalled that their postie had met such a dramatic end. 'Only that day, he was so full of life! He said he was looking forward to the new series of *Great Railway Journeys*.'

Now they were with Gigi in Inkbury Mill's book-lined penthouse, her red bun artfully pierced with a Staedtler pencil as she performed a balletic pas de deux with her state-of-the-art bean-to-cup machine, recalling that she and Craig had gossiped about Bad Penny's much younger boyfriend. 'He told me that the day before she'd signed for a *lot* of beauty products and something in a chill bag from an online pharmacy that we both agreed might be skinny pens. He had more packages for her that day. Craig thought she was giving her toyboy gifts.'

'What toyboy?' Mil demanded gruffly.

'As I told Craig then, I've never seen him. She meets up with him at odd hours. Half suspect he's made up.'

'But you saw him that day?' asked Phoebe. 'Craig, not the toyboy.'

'He brought me a pile of book proofs to review for *Wexshire Life*. Mostly historical schmaltz and cosy crime.' She gave her a condescending smile.

'Did he use his scanner?' asked Mil.

'I didn't notice,' she said vaguely, vulpine eyes lingering on Phoebe, demanding to know if she was coming to tomorrow's book club. 'Has Juno told you we're discussing *Possession*?' When Phoebe didn't immediately react, she added a condescending, 'Byatt.'

'I already own it,' she joked.

'A. S. Byatt is the name of the – ah. Very witty. Have you read it?'

'A while ago,' Phoebe conceded.

'May I suggest you revisit it if you're joining us,' Gigi instructed. 'It'll be a lively discussion. Don't want you to get left behind. And please don't plug your own books.'

Coffees taking their toll, Phoebe would have liked to ask to use the loo but wanted to get away too badly. The dogs, tethered outside, were yapping impatiently.

* * *

The next stop Phoebe and Mil traced on Craig's round was boxy little Station Cottage wedged between the railway and canal, but Bernard and Ree Cole weren't in.

'They'll be at their allotment.' Mil yomped onwards. 'We'll have better luck at Bridge Row, I reckon.'

A hundred yards further along Three Bridge Lane, the lopsided run of three thatched cottages beside the smallest of

Inkbury's river bridges were much-photographed welcome mats to the village, although they flooded regularly.

So, Phoebe worried, would her cropped chinos if she didn't find somewhere to wee soon.

She shifted her weight from foot to foot on the doorstep of Number One with gritted teeth as they waited for an answer. Nobody was home.

Number Two was also deserted.

'They're weekenders,' Mil explained.

By Number Three, Phoebe was dancing on the spot, four coffees swooshing ever lower inside her.

'You're chomping at the bit to investigate this, aren't you?' Mil chuckled. 'Felix said this was just what you needed to get you out of your shell.'

'Hello, Mil!' Number Three's owner welcomed them, bright eyed and bearded like a westie. 'You must be Mrs Sylvian, Alan Bickerstaff.' He shook her hand firmly. 'I hear you're a great puzzle solver.'

'Call me Phoebe.' She admired his snowy white hair and crisp Tattersall shirt, motifs he shared with her father, along with intelligent nervous energy.

'What wonderful dogs.' He stooped to pat then, then beamed up from them to Phoebe. 'Do bring them in. Coffee?'

'Would you mind if I—'

'Straight through there on the left.' He smiled sagely.

In a downstairs loo moments later, Phoebe thanked Alan for saving her dignity, and the framed *Private Eye* covers on its walls for reviving her sense of humour. Her eyes were level with a cover from the 1970s featuring the headline 'Water Shortage' above a photo of Queen with a speech bubble saying, 'Let them drink cake.'

Again, it made her think of her father, who had never missed an issue. Her parents' downstairs loo had been just as eclectic too. This room was L-shaped, a large bookshelf in its recess housing hundreds of Giles cartoon books and *Punch* annuals, an antiquated wicker pet carrier balanced on top alongside a diver's helmet wearing a fez.

Feeling thoroughly nostalgic, she washed her hands – Imperial Leather, the smell of the seventies – and joined Alan and Mil in a dated pine kitchen with multicoloured tile splashbacks and dried flower garlands along the beams.

'...And mark my words, Maximilian,' Alan was saying, 'the policemen are getting younger! That DI Mason should still be in short trousers. Ah, Phoebe! Let me sort your beverage and then you and Mil must tell me everything and ask whatever it is you need to know.'

They politely accepted a frothy Dulce Gusto each. 'Norma's last ever birthday gift, this contraption.' Alan patted it fondly and then indicated a framed photograph of a kind-eyed, long-nosed woman on the windowsill above the sink watching them all perceptively. 'She loved her flat whites. What are the dogs' names?' He stooped to fuss them again. 'Always liked Jack Russells.'

As she told him, Phoebe finally twigged why Alan looked familiar. It wasn't just that he had an air of her father, or that she'd seen him around the village and drinking in the pub. He'd also shouted at her when she was running along Three Bridge Lane with the dogs off the leads once. If he recognised her, he gave no indication.

They settled at a round kitchen table with a William Morris pomegranate oilcloth on it, a cruet set balanced on a platform of place mats and coasters in the centre. A row of vintage bears were lined up on the window seat along one side, as though joining in the conversation. Phoebe guessed Norma had once collected them; Alan was an out-and-out gadget man, asking Mil eagerly:

'How's the CCTV working out?'

Mil proudly showed off the app with the live Hartridge footage on it. A spider had woven a web across the camera covering the rear entrance. In turn, Alan pointed at the Alexa smart screen on his kitchen surface that was alternating between the weather, recipes, and footage from his doorbell, garden and shed roof cameras. 'There's my spaceship deck, right there! Bernie has the same one, and the old rogue pranks mine every time he's here. Set it to play a steam train sound effect each midday last time. Always the mischief-maker!'

He and Mil were soon deep in the tech talk.

Phoebe discreetly checked her own phone, concerned that there was still no update from Felix or Juno.

She glanced around, spotting an old-fashioned rattan dog basket with a tartan blanket, but no sign of a dog.

There were several vintage steam railway posters on the wall, one for the *Golden Arrow*, a luxury boat train that had run between London and Paris in the 1920s. She'd featured it in a Dorothy De'Ath novel *Blood on the Tracks*. Craig had made a lot of margin notes on that one suggesting missing details, plus extra Post-it notes and a separate indexed jotter pad.

'Magnificent, isn't it?' Alan was following her gaze. 'Craig had the engine. He was an exemplary railway model enthusiast, had an impressive layout. Have you seen it?'

'Not yet. I gather you and Bernard sold him some of your unwanted stuff?'

'Keen interest in N Scale Graham Farish locomotives with manual points.' Alan got up to fetch a biscuit barrel.

'Could he have made an explosive device with the equipment he had, in your opinion?'

'Tiny pliers and screwdrivers are better suited to mending spectacles,' he explained, offering her the barrel.

She shook her head. 'But he had the skills?'

'He spent a lot of time in that garage of his. Possibly trying to get away from his mother, hey, Mil?'

'Denise Jackman is a difficult character,' Mil conceded, adding to Phoebe, 'I told you that. Speaks her mind. She's been through a lot of jobs. Bit of an oddball, but clever with it.'

'She was briefly even a lab assistant at St Cuthbert's when I was on the science staff,' Alan told them with a chuckle, 'a most unfortunate appointment. My dear wife lost her eyebrows and lashes whilst teaching a Chemistry A level group thanks to Denise.'

'So Craig's mother knew about chemistry?' Phoebe wondered if she knew enough to set a detonator.

'Hardly. She lied to get the job, which I gather was not the first time. When she was on the gamekeeping team at Barton Court, they had her loading guns during one of their shooting parties and she almost finished off Richard Branson. They moved her across to the office staff after that.'

'Yeah, she worked there right up until old Boozy died,' Mil nodded, 'answering emails and whatnot. Loved the place. Worked with Penny, I think. In fact – light bulb moment – what if they were in it together?'

'Penny and Denise?'

'Craig and his mum!'

'Let's not jump ahead of ourselves, Mil.' Phoebe cleared her throat, smiling reassuringly at Alan, who was looking agog at it all. 'Can you tell us what you saw of Craig on his postal round the day he died, Alan?'

He apologised that he wasn't going to be much use to them. 'I did spot Craig's van go past, but I had no mail that day. So few things arrive by post nowadays, don't you find? I do miss old-fashioned hand-addressed correspondence, don't you?'

Phoebe's smile tightened. 'I'm not wild about receiving those.'

'Oh, come, come! I'm sure poor Craig must have been bent double on Valentine's Day, my dear.'

'Laughing, maybe!' Mil ribbed.

'With the weight of cards,' Alan said with a flourish.

Phoebe appreciated his jollying efforts, anachronistically condescending as they might be, but it wasn't helping. 'What time did you see his van pass?'

'I'm not certain.' Alan looked apologetic.

'We thought you might have CCTV footage, though?' Mil remembered excitedly. 'I was telling Phoebe and her husband about those new cameras of yours, Alan.' He indicated the Alexa screen, which was uncooperatively showing a chicken tray bake recipe.

'As recommended by Bernard Cole and *Which* magazine! BellSpy at the front, GardenEye at the back, two ShedCams with movement tracking and night vision – which is one more than Bernie has – and a miniature fisheye in every room,' Alan told Phoebe proudly. 'This place is constantly monitored.'

'Impressive.' She looked around warily for hidden fisheyes. Then she spotted that the terriers were sharing the rattan dog bed, playing growly tug of war with a rope toy. She whistled them out, apologising to Alan.

'No, it's charming to see them here.'

'Where's your little dog?' asked Mil.

'He passed away a couple of weeks ago.' Alan's face twitched sadly behind the neat white beard.

'Oh, I'm sorry, I didn't know that.' Mil put a comforting hand on his checked cotton shoulder.

'He belonged to my wife,' Alan told Phoebe, 'and was a great comfort to me after she died.'

With a pang, she remembered the story of the dog who took himself out on his mistress's favourite walks.

Alan was looking indulgently at the terriers. 'You know, I might get another.'

'Yes, you must,' she urged.

'And maybe another dog while you're at it!' Mil gave the checked shoulder a jocular slap that almost knocked Alan over.

There was an uncomfortable silence as his joke fell flat. Uncertain where to look, Phoebe managed to croak out some polite farewell noises. 'We must leave you in peace now. Thanks so much for all your help.'

'And you can get us that CCTV footage from your doorbell camera?' asked Mil, who didn't seem to realise his blunder.

'The BellSpy 6000 4K.' Alan nodded, still looking slightly pole-axed. 'If you think it'll be of any help, I can copy the micro-card footage and drop it off to you in the pub later.'

'No harm in it,' Mil agreed. 'There'll be a pint waiting in thanks.'

'Excellent!' Alan seemed revitalised by the thought. On the way to the door, they had a protracted mansplaining banter about motion sensor digital imaging, which left him positively animated, waving them off cheerily. 'Good luck with your investigations!'

Walking up the long drive to Home Farm, part of the Hartridge Estate, Phoebe told him off for the new wife/dog joke. 'That was in very poor taste!'

'Alan never holds a grudge,' Mil said cheerfully. 'Although he and Bernard did have a long stand-off once about Sunday bonfires, and he gets pretty aerated about traffic speeding along the lane.'

Behind them, they could hear a throaty sportscar snarling the length of Three Bridge Lane.

'Had a go at me more than once,' sighed Mil, who Phoebe knew regularly opened his Ducati up to seventy between the level crossing and the Old London Road.

'Good for him,' she upbraided.

'We don't all have a private estate we can race around, ma'am,' Mil teased.

Looking ahead along the dragstrip-straight Home Farm drive-way, a miniature tree-lined version of Hartridge Court's, she acknowledged that having a drive long enough to speed along was an exceptionally rare privilege, especially if one couldn't afford road tax.

There was nobody in at the farmhouse to ask about Craig's last round.

They trailed back up the drive, Mil recounting more instances of Alan and best friend Bernard at loggerheads.

The penultimate address that Craig had delivered post to before his tragic demise on Hartridge Court's back doorstep was Hartridge Holt Barn on the opposite side of Three Bridge Lane. Built from the same mellow brick as the big house, with flint panels and limestone mullions, it was a *Country Life* cover, status symbol of a barn conversion.

Penny Fermoy took forever to open the door. Phoebe found herself hoping she'd be out.

At her feet, sensing cat, the terriers were growling furiously under their breaths. Beside her, Mil was hammering the horse-shoe knocker against its plate like an overenthusiastic black-smith. He had his red-faced machismo look on, making Phoebe apprehensive. He'd come on too strong in the past, fantasising himself DI Lowe from her gritty eighties crime series. And she still hadn't got to the bottom of exactly what the deal was between him and Penny or why he blushed so ferociously whenever her name came up.

Just as they were about to turn away, Penny finally answered his knocks. She was wearing scanty, clingy designer gym gear and dark glasses, breathless from a work-out, baring her big teeth aggressively on the step.

'Need a word,' Mil started predictable bullishly.

Penny looked from him to Phoebe, peeling back her lips to show yet more expensively veneered dentistry. 'Are you moving out of Hartridge?'

'This is nothing to do with that,' Phoebe said quickly.

'Then I'm not interested.' Penny made to close the door.

'Wait!' Mil put out a hand to stop it. 'We need to ask about Craig the postman.' He cleared his throat, adding a cajoling, 'Please, Pen.'

The door opened a little wider, red talons creeping around it.

'Did you sign for anything the day he died?' asked Phoebe.

Penny's head reappeared. The dark glasses reflected Phoebe's stern face back at her. Beneath that, Penny's horse smile had disappeared. 'Possibly. Why?'

There was sweat on her upper lip, Phoebe noticed, and on closer inspection, it didn't look as though she'd been working out so much as passed out. Her skin was a waxy grey, the blonde helmet dirty as well as sweaty.

'Can we come in?'

'I'm very busy!' she snapped, then eyed Mil again. 'Hi, Mil darling.'

He smiled craggily, cheeks deepening to damson.

'One gets all sorts of freebies being delivered,' she told him, admiring his shoulders. 'Being in the public eye, everyone wants one to play with, wear or promote something.'

'I'll bet,' said Mil in his gruff detective voice.

'We're just trying to find out if Craig's scanner was really broken the day he died,' Phoebe impressed.

Ignoring her, Penny stepped closer to Mil, the smile curling back again into full toothy force as she linked her fingers behind her neck and stretched extravagantly. 'Yah, it might have been broken, actually. He was terribly pushy. Made me fetch ID.'

Mil's one working eye was struggling to look the same way as his glass one as Penny now stretched both arms over her head, bust lifting like a JCB bucket.

'Everyone around here knows who I am! I've been on magazine covers, red carpets and *Loose Women*. And my godmother gets to wear ermine in a state carriage. I'm a village celebrity, aren't I, Mil darling?'

'You are,' Mil agreed, hypnotised as she lowered her arms to put her hands against the small of her back to arch it, the JCB bucket thrusting forward.

'Craig loved hearing my glamorous stories; he'd do anything for me.' She glanced behind her into the house.

Something about the gesture made Phoebe suspicious. She elbowed Mil, who asked in his sexiest gruff detective voice: 'May we come in?'

Penny looked as though she was about to tell them to clear off, but somehow Mil's broad-shouldered charisma and obvious admiration got them over the threshold this time. 'Those dogs must stay outside. Damian is around somewhere and can't abide them.'

'Your boyfriend?' asked Phoebe, remembering the toyboy Gigi had mentioned.

'Cat,' Penny told Mil, turning to lead them into the house. 'Forgive the mess. The char's not been.'

The double-height reception hall was interior-designed shabby Mayfair bordello chic, with long velvet upholstered benches beneath fake rococo panelled walls, an ageing flower arrangement dropping its petals on a circular marble table. A grand staircase curved away to a galleried landing.

Its polished oak floor was also a bombsite of shopping bags, goody bags and lots of parcels, some unopened.

'Order things online a lot, do you?' asked Phoebe, gazing round at them.

'These are mostly gifts and samples,' Penny said breezily, taking off her dark glasses. 'I'm very popular.' The eyes that shot Phoebe a scornful look were bloodshot, pupils overlarge, the hard-partying habits harder to hide over fifty.

Phoebe noticed an unread copy of *Possession* poking from a Waterstones box. On top of it was a smaller, squarer package with a US mailing label. She picked it up to examine. 'What was in this one?'

'Some beauty product or other, a supplement, I think. Gummies. Rather good. That might have been one of the things that came that day. Been taking it all week and feel jolly peppy. Not sure it's legal.'

'Ashwagandha?' suggested Phoebe, reading the import label.

'I don't smoke, thanks.'

'I don't suppose you noticed it's addressed to me?'

'Is it?' Penny said it so nonchalantly, Phoebe sensed she did know.

'Not like Craig to slip up,' observed Mil, examining the other boxes.

'He was always jolly keen to come inside. Craig liked to watch me open the parcels he delivered, so he often lingered. He once told me I should make unboxing videos for YouTube. He was addicted to watching them, apparently. That and reading trashy books.' Penny's cold blue eyes bored into Phoebe's for a moment.

Phoebe smarted. 'Did you ever have a physical relationship with Craig?'

Penny hooted with forced laughter. 'In his dreams!'

'We heard you have a toyboy.'

She snorted again, genuinely amused now. 'Hardly a toyboy! Still, one must give the village something to gossip about. It's true I like playing with expensive toys in secret. And sometimes with boys too.' She gave Mil a lingering look.

'Was Craig trying to blackmail you?' Phoebe asked.

'Quite the reverse. He'd do anything for me. I told you. He doted on me,' Penny dismissed airily, turning away towards the kitchen. 'I'll fetch those magic gummies for you, Phoebe. Terrific for the libido. I'm sure your need is greater, whereas mine is...' She glanced back over her shoulder, striking a pose in the doorway. '...all natural, eh, Mil?'

'Unlike your hair, nails, skin, lips and breasts,' Phoebe muttered as she vanished from sight. Then she eyed Mil, taking in his anxious expression, the beetroot cheeks. 'You and Penny?'

'While ago now,' he breathed, glancing towards the kitchen. 'Just a casual thing.'

'Maximilian!'

'She's a good-looking woman.' He avoided her gaze, dimples deepening at the memory. 'We were both blootered, so it got a bit wild.'

Phoebe heard a clatter in the kitchen, like something glass being dropped in an enamel sink.

'I like a bird who knows what she wants,' Mil was sighing, wiping his forehead as he glanced at one of the long velvet ottomans, then up to the vast, beaded chandelier, then across to the other ottoman.

Phoebe decided it was best not to ask.

'Please don't call women birds,' she whispered, a plan forming. 'Penny's not going to open up about anything with me here, so I'll make an excuse to push off while you stay and probe for some more info. Use your rugged charm.'

'You expect me to—'

'Probe her, yes. You know what to do.' His tough DI Lowe act might just rattle Penny into indiscretion, she hoped.

Mil gave a nervous laugh, about to say more when Penny curled back round the door frame, rattling an oversized pill bottle.

'Don't take them all at once, Phoebe!' There was an unpleasant glint in her eye. Phoebe couldn't be sure, but she had a suspicion Penny had been up to something furtive in the kitchen.

'Thanks.' She grabbed the bottle. 'I've just remembered I must dash, but Mil here wants to ask you something, don't you, Mil?' She started backing at speed towards the door.

'I do?' He turned to look at her pleadingly. 'I do!'

'Super!' Penny swung back round towards the kitchen, arms aloft to beckon him after her. 'I'll fix us both a drinkie. Show yourself out, Phoebe.'

Mil was still gaping at Phoebe, his face like a small boy being abandoned alone in the front car of a rollercoaster.

Mouthing 'Probe her hard!' she ducked through the front door to gather the terriers and hurry away across Three Bridge Lane.

It was only when she was walking back through Hartridge Woods, reflecting on Mil's shocked face, that Phoebe wondered whether her instruction might be open to interpretation.

He was a grown-up, she reminded herself, and headed home to flush the ashwagandha jellies down the loo.

* * *

When Mil gave his special knock at the back door less than an hour later – still crimson red in the face, now swaying and faintly dishevelled – he reported that Penny had no more to say about Craig or parcels, 'so I cut my losses.'

He went to the sink to splash water on his face and gulp some down.

'She mixed Bloody Marys strong enough to tranquilise a rhino, told me that this place should be hers by rights but that you and Felix got in her way, or was it Felix should be hers but this place and you got in the way? Either way, not your biggest fan. In fact, I think she did say she hates you. Then she told me she was going upstairs and to give her five minutes before following.'

'I won't ask what happened next.'

'This happened! I scarpered. I can't probe.' He staggered to a sofa to sink down into it, pulling a cushion over his face. 'Don't ever ask me to that again. That woman has a *serious* drink problem.'

Which explained her grey, sweaty appearance opening the door to them, Phoebe realised. She'd guessed Penny was knocking something back in the kitchen too. Her reputation for intoxication was well known locally, part of the ageing party girl package, but the extent of the addiction made sense; the badly typed late-night emails; the illogical belief that she was owed a living by Boozy's estate; her graceless dependence on favours.

But was she desperate enough to send a poisoned nail bomb through the post? For all she didn't trust her, Phoebe sensed not.

Mil had reemerged from the cushion to look at his phone. 'There's nothing new on the Village Detectives WhatsApp. I'm going to write up a report of us following Craig's last few deliveries. I wonder how Felix and Juno are doing in the Dales?'

Phoebe checked her phone too. There was a private message from Felix sent an hour earlier:

> I'm breaking a promise, forgive me.

Another from Juno sent five minutes after that.

> Eric says OhFeelYa was posting from Paris. We're on the case!!! I'll bring you back some chocolate from La Mere de Famille. Not v keen on your husband right now btw. But it's Paris!

Bile rising, Phoebe hurried outside, gulping fresh air. Leaning back against the cool bricks of the house, she looked up at the cirrus, imagining them flying high above it.

Of the three names on Felix's OhFeelYa shortlist, she'd never been in doubt that Otis despised her the most, or that Gail had always been the most hurt by what happened between them. But it was Seraphine that Phoebe feared the most. And Seraphine alone had a hold over Felix that Phoebe was helpless to alter.

14

JUNO

There were plenty of reasons Juno almost hadn't come to Paris with Felix.

First, there was the blazing row that they'd had in The Poacher's Inn honeymoon suite, which quickly transferred to the car park, then into the Jazz, during which Juno had told him she didn't like or trust him much right now and argued that they must go straight back to Inkbury, not the City of Light.

But Felix had a persuasive charm like no one else she knew. He'd insisted that it wouldn't take long; that he knew where Seraphine lived; that he must do this urgently for his family's sake and that he needed her help.

And, as Juno had secretly acknowledged to herself, it was Paris! Beautiful, iconic, unforgettable Paris. Who could resist a free trip there?

Secondly, there was the lack of flights. Whilst they were still arguing, Felix had searched for them on his phone, discovering that everything from Manchester and Leeds Bradford was fully booked, but there was one leaving Luton late morning that they could make, and then they could catch the last flight back there.

The Jazz struggling to make it from Yorkshire to Bedfordshire
had almost foiled them, rattling and groaning towards Luton
Airport sounding like a traction engine. Juno had been tempted
to stop on the M1 hard shoulder multiple times to call the AA.

But it was Paris!

There was also the fact that her attempts to quiz Felix about
Seraphine in the car had been met with the usual taciturn
response. He'd shouted over the engine noises that he would
explain everything in the plane. When Juno told him she
wouldn't get on the plane unless he spilled the beans beforehand,
he'd closed his eyes, pretending to sleep. Which was equally
maddening because his phone was navigating, forcing her to rely
on its faintly audible voice instructions from his lap the rest of
the way.

Paris!

Then they had almost missed their flight, checking in so last
minute that they were allocated the final two seats at opposite
ends of the plane. Up front, Felix had read a thriller by a window
seat alongside two willowy French students. Twenty rows back,
Juno had been crammed between a silent, goliath-shouldered
teenager reeking of Lynx Africa and an even larger, un-
deodorised businessman called Pete who had greeted her by
saying: 'Cheap flights aren't designed for fatties like us to sit
together, are they?' Then he'd told her Paris had a severe weather
warning: 'We're lucky they're still flying.'

Exhausted from her sleepless night on a studded sofa
exchanging insomniac messages with Phoebe, Juno had fallen
asleep with her mouth open until the storm woke her up.

Then there was the storm. It had thrown the plane around
like a paper bag over Charles de Gaulle. The passengers had
gasped and screamed – Juno possibly loudest of all – applauding
and whooping when it finally touched down. It was a named

storm, Pete told her cheerfully. 'Prunella. Over from Africa, apparently. Once in a decade rainfall. Won't stop any time soon.'

It hadn't.

After a taxi ride through the floods that felt more U-boat journey than Uber, they were now in the Left Bank's trendy, touristy Saint-Germain des Prés, drinking pastis in a side-street bar. French pop music was playing, chic-looking Parisians were chatting around her, raindrops snaked down a window with gold-etched letters that she read back to front: *Vins au Verre, Bieres, d'Absinthe, Chocolat a l'Ancienne.* And Juno felt cooler than she had in years.

Despite everything, she was in Paris!

Typically, Felix fitted right in, impossibly cosmopolitan in his wet-shouldered jacket with the collar turned up, all broody-eyed angst as he finally filled her in on the mysterious Seraphine, who he'd only previously described as 'a ghost from my past'.

'Her apartment's just along the road from here on Quai Voltaire,' he told her. 'Amazing place, views across the river to the Louvre. It belonged to her mother. Seraphine might not be home, and if she is, she probably won't be alone, but you'll have to risk it.'

'I will?'

'I promised I'd never go there again.'

'Why? What did you do to her?'

'Nothing, I hardly know the girl.'

'But you know her apartment.'

Shrugging in a very French New Wave way, he muttered, 'Yes, I know it.'

'Tell me everything you "hardly" know about Seraphine.'

'She's twenty-seven. Very beautiful, fiery, independent, probably in the genes. Party animal. Occasionally freelances in something arty, although she doesn't need to work. Never held down a serious relationship as far as I know. She no doubt blames the genes for that too.' He smiled, eyes sliding away. 'Her mother was an actress, famously wild too.'

Juno was quietly appalled by his attitude. 'So it was a one-night stand sort of thing?'

'A little more. A few months. Very on and off. Very shallow, I admit. It was just about sex and aesthetics. My French is lousy, her English non-existent, so it was never going anywhere.' He toyed with the glass water bottle that had come with their anisette. 'Big age gap too.' He looked up at her, blue eyes intense and troubled. 'And then there was Phoebe.'

Juno harrumphed disapprovingly.

'When it ended, I didn't think I'd hear from her again.'

Juno glared across the table at him, even more astonished by his gall. 'Gail was right, you are a complete tosser!'

'I've been called worse.'

Outside, the rain was hammering so hard it was bouncing off the pavements like ball bearings, the sky black as dusk.

Juno had guessed at infidelities. Phoebe was tight-lipped, fiercely loyal and self-confessedly jealous, but the film industry was notorious; those long location shoots, the company like a band of brothers, pretty young actresses and adoring assistants. This might be Paris, but she wasn't in the mood to play Madame Claude, the city's legendary keeper of brothels and powerful men's secrets.

'I can't believe you expect me to go in there and ask your casual shag if she's targeting your wife online!'

Felix looked away again, sucking his lips, his eyes narrowed. 'I thought you knew.'

'Knew what?'

'Seraphine is my *daughter*, Juno.'

She gaped at him.

'Her mother was my "casual shag".' He picked up his pastis glass then put it down again. 'No, that's wrong; Belle was amazing, I was *her* casual shag. It was in the nineties. I was dumb and wild. She was ten, fifteen years older than me. What we had ended the night I met Phoebe. Turns out Belle was ten weeks pregnant at the time, not that either of us knew that.'

Juno let out a squeak of shocked surprise.

Leaning across the table, voice low, he told her that he hadn't heard from her again. 'Belle always used to tell me she couldn't have kids after a messed-up abortion in her twenties. I had no idea Seraphine existed until a few years ago. That's when I got a call out of the blue from Belle's old manager, Guillaume, telling me that she'd died. He was in bits. Turns out they'd married – that came as a shock – and had three kids, bigger shock still. Then he broke it to me that one of those kids was mine. Biggest shock of all.'

'So Seraphine is your biological daughter?'

'By the time Belle finally found out she was pregnant with her, it had been too late to do anything about it. She'd just started shooting a movie, her first decent role in ages, so she kept it secret. She'd long struggled with her Catholic upbringing, had believed she was being punished for her sins with infertility, so this baby felt like a gift from God. After the film wrapped, she married Guillaume, who had been loyal for years, looking out for her since she was a kid. Lovely guy, big on the sacrament, firmly in the closet. He'd trained in the priesthood, but he coveted filthy lucre and freedom too much. Belle quit acting and they brought Seraphine up on a vineyard in deepest Bordeaux and adopted two more kids; Guillaume is terrific father by all accounts. Belle wasn't so great at parenting. She'd always been a hothead, impulsive, yet another kid for Guillaume to manage. She didn't miss work, but she hated giving up fame, although the truth is that last movie bombed and the decent roles had dried up since *Pas Fumee.*'

Juno let out a squeak of recognition. 'Hang on, Seraphine's mother is *La Belle Delauney*?'

All drooping pout and come-to-bed eyes, French actress Isobelle 'La Belle' Delauney had been a huge pin-up in her student days, her legendary X-rated movie *Pas Fumee* famously smoking hot.

'*Was* La Belle Delauney,' he reminded her. 'She died.'

'Of course.' She vaguely remembered seeing a news obituary in New York. Americans had loved the wild French actress with her rock-and-roll lifestyle, a raven haired badder-than-Bardot, madder-than-Monroe femme fatale whose well-publicised volatility and mental health struggles had outlasted her short, sexy movie career. 'Her poor children. She couldn't have been much older than sixty. What did she die of?'

'She drowned.'

Juno covered her mouth, connections starting to click unpleasantly together.

'The vineyard was on the banks of the Garonne. One day, when Guillaume was away, she drank a bottle of their finest cru, put her Best Actress César in one pocket, her Best Foreign Language Film BAFTA in the other and waded in. It wasn't her first attempt – there had been several throughout her life – but it was her last one. They found a note in her pocket. The ink had run too much to be legible. The official line was that it was an accident, but of course it wasn't.'

'Oh, those poor children,' Juno repeated through her fingers, tears already landing hot on her knuckles.

'Seraphine had just graduated from the Sorbonne; the two younger boys were both away at school. Guillaume tried to protect them all after her mother's death, but Seraphine was already following in La Belle's – and my – footsteps, living here in Paris in her mother's flat with a bunch of friends, partying too hard. Harder still after they buried Belle.

'That's when Guillaume contacted me and asked to meet in London, breaking it to me I'm her biological father. Seraphine had gone seriously off the rails, been arrested twice, and was refusing to talk to him. She'd always known he wasn't her birth father – his and Belle's marriage was entirely platonic – but Belle had built this myth around her real father's identity, naming a movie star one day, a musician the next, then artists and stunt men and directors until there was a who's who of serial shaggers. It's quite possible Belle didn't even know for certain; I wasn't much more than a notch in her bedpost. A few notches, maybe.' He gave her a sheepish look.

'But you are definitely Seraphine's father?'

'Guillaume was in absolutely no doubt; Belle might have been crazy, he said, but she was faithful. And he'd been around the whole time La Belle and I were together, making sure I didn't screw up her career or PR. We used to call him Papa Pontiff back then. He was Belle's hot priest, and he later brought their children up to be believers. He hoped telling Seraphine the truth about me might help her. He gave me a lot of Catholic spiel about her faith being tested. But he wanted to forewarn me first, explained how volatile she was. He knew I'd demand proof, so he'd brought a DNA kit with him. He said he was going directly to Paris to talk to Seraphine after me, and promised to act as a mediator for our initial contact once we had the results.

'I went straight home and told Phoebe. I was in shock. She was fantastic, completely calm. We agreed not to say anything to the girls until we knew for certain. I had to go to Ireland for work for a few days. We knew the results would take longer. So we just waited for Guillaume to get back in touch.'

He pressed his palms one over the other across his mouth for a moment, his eyes far away, and Juno felt a chill abseil down her spine, guessing what was coming next would be bad.

Felix had turned aside to order another round of drinks from the waiter. Then, muttering an apology that he'd be right back, he sprang up to stalk outside where, sheltering under the rain-hammered awning, he smoked a Gauloise from the packet he'd bought as soon as they got here.

That bad, Juno realised.

* * *

'Carry on,' she urged a few minutes later, watching the pastis in his glass turn from golden to cloudy as he added water.

Felix watched it too, his hair and shoulders jewelled with raindrops despite the shelter of the awning. 'While I was away in Ireland, Seraphine turned up at the farm out of the blue in the middle of the night, hammering on the door. Phoebe guessed who she was straight away and tried to calm her down. She speaks some French, but Seraphine was high on something as well as distraught, screaming a torrent of insults, going berserk when one of the dogs bit her, kicking it and threatening to kill it. The girls were terrified. Maud called the police, Amelie texted friends in the village for help. Apparently, it was being shouted round the pub in minutes that the Sylvians had a mad stalker on site, regulars jumping into pickups with cricket and rounders bats.'

'You mean they formed a lynch mob?' Juno gasped.

He shook his head. 'By the time the menfolk of Dallowbeck stormed to the rescue, Seraphine was already being sectioned in the back of a police car. Guillaume drove through the night to accompany her home. They were back to France before my flight had even landed in the UK the next morning.

'He called a few days later to confirm that the DNA test was positive. He told me Seraphine was in rehab at a convent close to the vineyard, and that she had now decided she didn't want to meet me. We agreed it was for the best until she was feeling stronger. He said I should wait for her to make contact.

'That's when OhFeelYa and OhManiacNymph started popping up more often on Phoebe's feeds. She refused to take it seriously at first. Naturally, Gail in the village pub had told everyone who would listen that the beautiful young French nutter was one of my many mistresses. We were the talk of The Poacher's Inn for weeks.' He sat back, raking his hands through his hair and staring up to the ornate ceiling lamps as if in prayer. 'And then the Woolf thing happened. Foolishly, I didn't even connect the two at first. By the time the trolling escalated, it was too late to warn Phoebe that Belle's death had been no accident.'

Juno pressed her hands to her face, shocked to find it icy and sweaty. 'Phoebe didn't know?'

'I should have told her sooner; I realise that now. I wanted to protect her.'

Juno thought about his long absences, his crazily timed career gamble that had cost them the house Phoebe loved, his high-handed treatment of Gail and Leah, and their current reckless mission to seek out OhFeelYa, who he had goaded back into a frenzied state on Twitter, and who might be his mentally fragile daughter.

'To quote Gail again, you are a tosser, Felix.'

He looked down, half-smiling. 'I deserve that.'

'But you're right to suspect Seraphine,' she conceded. 'We know whoever is tweeting OhFeelYa's recent rants is doing so from a Paris ISP. I also think they're under thirty, and a digital native. The language is Gen Z, slangy; it reminds me of Eric's crew. Like using "Karen" as an insult which came over from the States, what, five years ago? Seraphine speaks good English, yes?'

'I believe so,' he said vaguely. 'She shared the apartment here with a Brit and an American.'

'Okay, so that adds up. There's no doubt she's emotionally unstable and very probably thinks Phoebe was having direct digs at her mother in her column when she brushed aside Woolf's suicide. She might also think it was Phoebe who had her sectioned, ruining her chances of having a relationship with you, her birth father.'

Felix stared out at the sheets of rain, at Parisians hastening past the bar windows with umbrellas and newspapers over their heads.

'I think the weather's easing,' he said, even though they both knew it wasn't. 'We must get on with this. We've only a couple more hours before we need to set off back to Charles de Gaulle. I don't want to leave Phoebe another night.'

Juno felt the chill crawling back up her spine again, right to her scalp. 'I'm not going to see Seraphine alone, now I know all this! She sounds dangerous, for a start.'

'I genuinely don't think she's violent.'

'Yet you do think she might have sent Phoebe an exploding box full of poisoned pen tips?'

'I think she trolled her online.' He stared at her imploringly.

'You go!' she demanded.

'I can't.' He grimaced, picking up his pastis to drain its last dregs. 'There's just one more thing I haven't mentioned.'

Juno groaned, closing her eyes. 'Spit it out.'

'Nobody knows this. Not even Phoebe.'

She waited, watching as he moved the water bottle around the table in a courtly dance before finally speaking.

'I've come here to find Seraphine before; I went to the apartment. It wasn't long after Phoebe's cancer diagnosis. The Twitter storm was at its worse. I wasn't thinking straight.'

'What happened?'

'I was here in Paris for the Nuit de César; I hadn't wanted to attend, but we were up for two awards and Phoebe was adamant, excited for me. My hotel was just a few minutes' walk from here. I'd probably had too many of these.' He lifted his empty glass. 'I didn't plan it – I just set off on foot. Before I knew it, I was crossing Pont Royal and standing outside La Belle's apartment. Fate does that sometimes, don't you find? Like a ghostly GPS taking you back to previous destinations. I'd been there plenty of times in the nineties; Seraphine might have been conceived there.'

Juno said nothing, although she suspected that her ghost GPS, like her recurring dreams, wouldn't take her to the TriBeCa loft apartment where she and Jay first shared hedonistic happiness in New York. More likely Spaghetti Junction or Wembley IKEA.

'When she answered the door, I blurted a lot of stuff out about feeling bad about what happened, that I had never known I was her father, and was wretched that we had never even met. I said I had to know if it was Seraphine trolling my wife. I told her how ill Phoebe was. She was the first person I'd admitted it to out loud, that I was terrified she would die. Then I cried.'

He was staring at Juno across the table as though admitting he'd spontaneously combusted. She imagined Felix could probably count the number of times he'd cried in his life on one hand. 'I was quite drunk.'

'What did she do?'

'She asked who I was.'

'No!'

'You're right, she didn't.' He smiled stiffly into his empty glass. 'Sorry. Cheap joke. Default mechanism. She invited me in. She looked terrible – gaunt, no make-up, drab clothes. The place was spartan, like she'd sold everything. Then she said...'

Juno waited.

'She said...' He rubbed his mouth unhappily.

Juno waited longer.

'What did she say?' she cracked. 'Was it "*Je ne comprends pas l'anglais*"?'

'I wish.' He gave a gruff little cough of laughter, appreciating the cheap joke coming back at him. 'She said that I was not a father to her, nor had I ever been, but that she would pray for Phoebe and for me and our girls. Then she told me that I must never come back because she'd be joining the Holy Father before I made it through the door. She said she wasn't afraid to sacrifice her life.'

'She threatened to...?' She couldn't say it.

He nodded.

'Like her mother?'

'That's what she said.' He nodded again. 'Then she told me that I deserved to be with God too. That's when she hit me. Quite hard, actually.' He winced at the memory. 'An hour later, I was sitting between Timothée Chalamet and Léa Seydoux, nursing a black eye.'

'Do you think she was on drugs? Maybe she sold the furniture to pay for them?'

He shrugged. 'I tried to contact Guillaume, but he never got back to me. After that, I just focused everything on Phoebe getting well; it's all I cared about. The trolling died down; life moved on.'

'Only now you think Seraphine's targeting her again?' Juno chewed her lip.

He glanced at his watch. 'We've not got much time.'

'What if I turn up and she does something to herself? Or me?'

'Not if you claim to be from Interpol investigating online hate crime.' He reached in his pocket. 'I have some false ID for you.'

He handed across an official-looking wallet badge. Juno looked at it.

'This says Gina Vanderbilt, FBI, and that photo looks like Florence Pugh.'

'It's a prop from a movie but flash it fast enough and she'll never know.'

'Do you normally carry round props from your movies?'

'I did sort of plan this one ahead just in case,' he admitted, and Juno felt a little flush of pride despite herself that he'd formulated a cover story especially for her.

'I trust you, Juno. You're ingenious and intrepid. And you do look a bit like Flossie Pugh.'

Juno was a sucker for flattery. Feeling her icy cheeks warming, she gazed out at the stair-rodding rain, which seemed fantastically dramatic and French and film noire atmospheric right now.

This was Paris!

'I need another drink first.' She turned back and found one was already in front of her. Felix gave her his most heart-stopping, reformed bounder smile.

'You can do this.'

Downing it and picking up her phone, Juno summoned Citymapper and grabbed her brolly. 'If I'm not back in an hour, call the gendarmes.'

'They're rural. It's the Police Nationale in Paris.'

'Call MI bloody 5. Interpol. The FBI too. And make that half an hour.'

* * *

Juno was back in ten minutes. 'She's not there.'

'Did you ring the bell?'

'Of course I rang the bloody bell. Several times. The person who came out has been renting the apartment for over a year. We had to use Google Translate on our phones, and I found out it can't be Seraphine sending poison pens or tweeting.'

'How can you be certain?'

'She's not lived in Paris for two years. Guillaume should have bloody well told you this by now. Seraphine's been in the Congo helping run an aid camp for Secours Catholique. She's taken Holy Orders, Felix. Your daughter may not be a saint, but she is a nun.'

Felix stared at her for a long time, handsome face frozen. 'Are you sure?'

'Some of the detail may have been lost in translation,' she admitted, 'so maybe she's not the full *Sister Act*, but she is definitely working for an NGO. And the apartment wasn't barren when you went there because she'd sold the furniture for drugs money. She was clearing it to rent it out. She's not our troller.'

Sitting back in his chair, he started to laugh. 'This calls for another drink.'

'I don't want another drink!' Juno was very wet and very angry. 'You drag me to Paris – Paris! – and bang on about yourself yet again, when we could have said all this in the pub or the car. Do you make a habit of this sort of thing?'

'Phoebe thinks so.'

'With respect, Felix, you're very gorgeous and I know Phoebe loves you very much, but you aren't worthy of the Village Detectives. Consider yourself fired. Now put on your coat. We're buying chocolates, then going home to catch the real Poison Pen Killer.'

* * *

Juno gave him the silent treatment in the taxi, gazing out forlornly at beautiful Paris which she had barely breathed in.

Their driver took them across Pont de la Concorde and alongside the Seine, affording Juno the briefest eyeful of a rain-lashed, illuminated Eiffel Tower, her view strobed by the dark trunks of elm trees that lined the right bank.

Craning round, she took one last lingering look at it before they swung away towards the Arc de Triomphe and on to the Périph, racing north to try to make it to Charles de Gaulle in time for the last Luton flight.

It had jogged a memory that she couldn't pin down, a flash of déjà vu. She hadn't been to Paris for decades, and yet she was certain she'd looked at that same view recently.

The time difference meant Juno and Felix landed in London ten minutes after they'd taken off from France. Although they'd sat together in the plane this time, they hadn't spoken for the entire flight. Juno was wrung out with exhaustion, hollow-bellied from hunger and dizzy from turbulence.

Storm Prunella had crossed the Channel to Great Britain in the few hours since they'd been gone, lashing Blighty with rain that was somehow less sexy, drabber and greyer than it had been in Paris.

Felix drove the Jazz from Luton to Wexshire, wipers at top speed, engine and brakes clanking ever more industrially. Even shouting, it was hard to be heard, so Juno didn't bother trying now either.

Her phone had run out of charge in Paris. She plugged it into the car charger and as soon as she had enough battery to switch it on, she posted an uncharacteristically concise message to the

Village Detective WhatsApp group saying they were coming home. She didn't want to think how much their wet day trip to Paris must have cost. Felix had paid for it all, but she knew he and Phoebe were perpetually broke. Her thoughts kept returning to the big movie he'd lost so much money on that meant they'd been forced to sell their house.

For all his charisma, what Phoebe put up with from Felix astonished Juno. More so now she knew the truth about Seraphine. Admittedly it wasn't Felix's fault that he'd fathered a daughter he'd not been told about until she was an adult, or that she was a crazed Joan of Arc type, although he was probably right that it was in the genes. From what Juno knew about Felix's twin daughters, both were lucky they had inherited their mother's cool head; poor Eric had his father's mulish one, along with Jay's nomadic streak; Gail Lamb had told Juno that Leah had her father's filthy temper.

A loose connection in her memory niggled again, but she couldn't place it.

'Can you check Twitter?' Felix bellowed, making her snap back to the present.

They were somewhere dark on the M4, her screen glowing in her hands, a portal to humankind's darker psyche. Although occasionally addicted to @VeryBritishProblems, Juno wasn't much of a tweeter, preferring her social streams without character limits or assassinations. One look at OhFeelYa's feed reminded her why.

'Oh, Christ, they've been tweeting non-stop all day and they're taking Phoebe apart!' She read a few out to Felix, threats of witch-burning, drowning, social justice and revenge for OhManiacNymph, many hash-tagged #DieDorothyDeath. 'This one says: *Why can't Phoebe Fredericks do the world a favour, pussy up and kill herself.* And this: *The Undomestic Goddess might have sunk without trace, but its author is still a grasping bottom feeder, #Drown-TheWitch.* I'll report that, shall I?'

'Report them all!' He drove faster. 'First, call Phoebe and check she's okay.'

'There's a new one just been posted. *Does she know her husband is cuddling up with his curvy new mistress in Paris?* Oh my God, Felix, they know we were in Paris. OhFeelYa knows we were in Paris!'

She speed-dialled Phoebe's number, relieved when it was answered within two rings for once, her friend's curt voice demanding, 'How close are you?'

'Why? Has something happened?'

'No, I just wondered whether to put the kettle on. Have you bought back those chocolates?'

'Yes. Are you sure everything's okay?'

'Well, I can't get rid of Mil. He's napping, thank God. Let's talk when you get here. I'm reading. Want to finish this chapter.' She rung off abruptly.

'She's fine,' Juno told Felix, although she always sensed disquiet when Phoebe was chippy.

'She's not.' A muscle was pulsing in the hollow of his cheek, telling her Felix felt the same way. 'This is my bad. I wasted your time,' he said eventually. 'I was certain it was one of them. I'll make sure Phoebe knows none of this is down to you.'

'Let's show a united front,' Juno suggested. 'And it wasn't wasted. In detection, dismissing suspects is just as important as gathering them; sometimes it's only when you've taken the brightest bijoux out of the jewellery box that you see the tarnished trophy behind.'

'I like that.'

'Annie Logg in *Blood on Her Hands*. My favourite Dorothy

De'Ath novel. Your wife's words, not mine. Dennis is trying to find a television production company to option the series.'

'Good for Dennis,' he said a touch too lightly.

But as they came off the motorway to bypass Newborough, hurtling westwards into the darkness along the Old London Road, she sensed his tension mounting.

She reconnected her phone to the car's Bluetooth and selected a mellow, retro playlist to soothe him, although it was hard to hear much over the wailing, moaning brakes. Halfway through Texas's 'I Don't Want a Lover', 'MUM – MOBILE' called over the car speakers, sounding zealous. 'Pusscat! Where have you *been*? Are you alone? Tell me *everything!*'

'Still with a friend!'

'That noise is awful! I've been ringing all day. Where *were* you?'

'Paris.'

'Say no more. Call me *very* soon! And bring my car back!' She rang off with a fresh squeak of delight.

On reflection, Juno sensed she shouldn't have mentioned Paris. Chewing her lip, she asked Felix if he could recommend a mechanic, but he was in no mood to chat.

When they finally careered into the Hartridge courtyard, he was out of the car in a flash, running across the rain-pounded cobbles to the back entrance.

While Juno hadn't expected him to walk round and open the passenger door with a golfing umbrella held aloft, she was mildly annoyed at his rudeness. She'd thought that they were putting on their united front. But when she squelched inside to the back corridor, grateful at least that he'd left the door on the latch, she found the two terriers waiting outside the shower room, tails wagging furiously as a loo flushed beyond it. Then hand basin taps ran. A moment later, Felix emerged, having clearly rushed in to take a pee.

Juno might not like him much right now, but the middle-aged bladder was a uniting force.

The big, echoing house was so thick walled, only the dogs had heard them returning. They could hear music coming from the kitchen, Morcheeba's spinny, trippy 'The Sea' coming to a close, then Puccini's 'Musetta's Waltz' striking up; Phoebe had notoriously eclectic taste.

'Juno, I want to thank you,' Felix said quietly, smiling down at her. 'You've been quite brilliant; my sanity and the voice of reason.' Then he hugged her, which was surprisingly lovely and brotherly.

'I'm only sorry OhFeelYa wasn't one of the three,' she said.

'Phoebe knew that all along,' he reminded her. He scooped an ecstatic, wriggling dog under each arm and kissed their heads before catching her eye and whispering, 'Don't mention tonight's tweets to her just yet, okay?'

Juno didn't like secrets, but she understood why, nodding reluctantly.

'Ready?'

In the cavernous Hartridge kitchen, Mil was snoring on a sofa. Opposite him, Phoebe was reading *Possession*. She looked up, green eyes mistrustful.

'Well, it's almost certainly not Gail,' Felix said, crossing the flagstones to stoop and kiss her. 'So Yorkshire was a wasted trip.'

She pulled back. 'I could have told you that.'

'Then we went to Paris,' Juno took over breathlessly, 'but Seraphine wasn't in and it turns out she has been a humanitarian nun for two years, which means it's not her either. So I've fired Felix from the Village Detectives.'

Phoebe's eyebrows shot up.

'And we bought you the chocolates!' Juno held them up.

'Not such a wasted trip then,' muttered Felix, going in search of a drink. 'Whisky, anyone?'

'Or tea?' suggested Juno, who'd been desperate for a brew since leaving Yorkshire.

'I forgot to boil the kettle.' Phoebe looked distracted. 'Don't think we've got any milk, mind you. Or whisky.'

Felix was slamming cupboard doors open and shut.

Mil continued snoring.

Juno was watching Phoebe closely, not liking the dark smudges beneath her eyes, the distracted La Boheme pallor. She'd expected a scathing telling off for her and Felix – but mostly Felix – for recklessly wasting time and money on a wild goose chase. Subdued Phoebe was even more worrying than chippy Phoebe, thoughts of her illness never far from Juno's mind, along with the mental scars left by suffering trolling and cancellation.

She sat down beside her. 'How about you? Have you found out anything new?'

Phoebe closed her book, pushing her glasses up onto her head, pulling a frustrated face. 'Not much. It's possible Penny might have been helping herself to other people's packages, maybe in collaboration with Craig, who she stringently denies was her mystery toyboy. From what Penny says, hers is more expensive adult toy than boy. She also tried to help herself to Mil, who claims it's not him either.'

On the opposite sofa, Mil awoke with a start, blinking at them. 'What's that?'

'Penny's *toyboy*,' Phoebe repeated slowly.

'It was only a one-off, I told you!'

Juno turned in shock, heart thudding a hollow gong of disappointment in her chest.

Still searching fruitlessly for something to drink, Felix let out a surprised growl of laughter under his breath. 'You dark horse, Winterbourne.'

'I was just updating Juno about Penny's secret toyboy,' Phoebe was explaining to a sleepy, blinking Mil, 'along with the online retail addiction, daytime drinking problem and possibly more.'

'Oh, yeah, hi, guys.' Mil yawned widely, running his hand through his crew cut and sitting up, still looking dazed. 'Yeah, Penny's got a lot of gear in that house. Clothes, bags, beauty products, supplements...'

'Not all of it hers,' Phoebe muttered. Pulling her reading glasses down from her head, she picked up the novel again. 'I've decided I will come to the village book club tomorrow night after all, Juno. I have several things I want get off my chest about *Possession*.'

'Wouldn't it be better to tackle Penny about the packages in private?'

'I'm not tackling Penny about the packages; I'm going to say what I think about *Possession*. I doubt she has a clue what's going on there.'

'It's a matter for the police, surely?'

'*Possession* the book, Juno.' She held it up. 'Byatt!'

'I don't need to. I've borrowed it from the library.'

'I've already done that joke.'

Yes, there was definitely something not right about Phoebe, Juno decided anxiously. In her experience – when solving who murdered poor Si Locke, at least – Phoebe always read vociferously when she was close to a breakthrough.

15

PHOEBE

For once, Felix was as sleepless as Phoebe, shifting position in bed every few minutes like a life model posing for quick sketches, unable to settle, phone screen glowing on and off.

'You shouldn't try to sleep with that thing close by,' she grumbled.

He blamed a sudden influx of urgent messages from LA where his latest film's backers and distributor were based, but Phoebe sensed there was something else too.

There was a specific way Felix scrolled when he was on Twitter, a certain face he pulled that was like no other.

Phoebe turned her back to him, listening to Storm Prunella still throwing rain at the high windows like gravel, gusts rattling the loosest window fittings, grateful it was drowning out Felix's finger tapping on his screen. She was half tempted to grab her own phone and tweet him to stop, but that would mean walking back into her least favourite storm, far wilder than the one outside.

They'd been jaw-achingly polite to each other since he'd got home from Paris, often the case when a big row was cooking between them, neither prepared to give ground. Before coming to bed, they'd talked in circles, skirting around the big stuff.

She reached back for his hand, feeling his fingers slot between hers. Folding hers over them, she held onto their warmth, reassured that while she did, he couldn't type.

It worked like a sleeping draught.

Phoebe awoke to find they were curled tightly around each other, not so much big and little spoon as two forks with their tines tangled, teaspoon terriers fitting into the gaps. Sunlight flooded the kitchen.

Someone was hammering on the back door.

She reached for her watch and let out a cry of surprise. It was after ten. They'd both overslept. Her eyes hadn't snapped open at four with the usual urge to write; Felix's maddening alarm hadn't gone off; the terriers hadn't noisily demanded breakfast and a walk.

DI Mason and DS Alsop were outside, standing on shiny storm-soaked cobbles now drying in the sun, bright blue sky behind them.

'That was some weather last night, man!' said Mason, holding up a smart tablet in a Wexshire Constabulary case. 'The Chief Super has given us the go ahead to share something which I'm afraid to say you may find in all honesty, how shall I put this – somewhat, um—'

'Ick,' Alsop told Phoebe over his shoulder. 'It's pretty ick.'

'Unsettling,' he suggested instead. 'We believe you may be able to help us understand certain coded messages, images and connections.'

'The nudey wall of death, we call it down the nick,' Alsop nodded eagerly.

Phoebe took a moment to realise. 'You're talking about the noticeboard that was on Craig's workshop wall?'

'We would like you to look at photographs of some of the evidence found in Mr Jackman's garage, yes.' Mason coughed awkwardly. 'In order to establish incontrovertible culpability, so to speak, it is necessary to categorically identify certain, erm, figures therein.'

'You'd better come through to the kitchen.' She stepped aside to let them in. 'Felix will want to see this too.'

'You might prefer to look without your husband present initially.' DI Mason cleared his throat again. 'Would you like DS Alsop as support? She is recently Sensitivity Trained.'

'It's pretty tame stuff, don't worry.' Towering over her boss, DS Alsop gave her encouraging gummy smile. 'I've seen much worse. And Craig Jackman's dead now, let's not forget.'

'That's reassuring,' Phoebe said lightly. She might feign amused indifference, but she was extremely anxious, the prospect of seeing what she recalled Mason describing as 'compromising material' making her palms damp.

'I'd like my husband with me,' she said, turning to beckon them on.

'With respect, Ms Fredericks, given the nature of some of the photographs, I'm not sure that's wise until you have availed yourself of the opportunity to—'

'Felix!' Phoebe called brightly, marching along the corridor. 'The police have brought some pictures of Craig's workshop. Do you want to see them?' She knew she sounded as though she was suggesting they look at the neighbour's holiday snaps, but she couldn't stop her self-protective flippancy.

'Sure.' He smiled sleepily as they went into the kitchen, dressed in sneakers and board shorts, the sofa bed already folded away. 'Why not? Coffee first?' His voice was honeyed and easy. 'Has to be black, I'm afraid.'

Phoebe felt a flash of gratitude because she knew he got it completely; he felt much the same need to play it down.

'Thank you, but I have my own thermos and Alsop has a Monster,' DI Mason reminded them before sitting at the table with the tablet.

Phoebe and Felix stood behind him to look at the screen, shoulders touching, bracing themselves.

The first photograph showed a large sign running across the top of the noticeboard that read:

PHOEBE FREDERICKS'S DEATH.

'That's unambiguous,' Felix muttered tightly.

The board was, as Mason had told her, enormous – stretching most of the height and half the length of the garage side – and densely covered with notes in Craig's distinctive small spiky hand, along with photographs and a *lot* of red string. There was so much red string criss-crossing between Post-its and pictures, it resembled a macrame artwork.

Most striking amongst the pinned images were the multiple photographs of guns and knives, bottles with poisonous substance labels and even one of a kinky-looking torture chamber.

'Very disturbed mind,' DS Alsop muttered under her breath.

Many of the other pictures were of places: grand houses, town squares and rural views.

'Do you recognise anywhere?' asked Mason.

'I'm afraid not. Hang on, does that one say Dingledale?' She pointed at a hand-labelled postcard of an idyllic-looking village.

Mason zoomed in, but it was too blurred to tell. 'How about these people? Any familiar faces and, er, bodies?'

Amongst a great many grainy-looking monochrome

photographs of men and women Phoebe didn't recognise was a small collection of black and white nudes, all apparently of the same model, along with several sexually explicit close-ups.

'Blimey.' Felix eyed them with interest.

'I've seen far worse,' Alsop reminded them.

'Do you recognise this woman, Miss Fredericks?' asked Mason, pointing at the naked beaky-nosed brunette with elfishly short hair and distinctive curving Cupid's bow lips.

She and Felix both tilted their heads, studying the fierce kohl-rimmed eyes and smooth naked skin.

'I think I do,' she admitted.

'Looks a bit like you when we first met,' Felix pointed out.

'You don't seriously think that could be *me*?' Phoebe peered closer.

'Have you heard of "artificial intelligence" at all, Ms Fredericks?' Mason made quotes around the phrase, as though asking a Chelsea Pensioner if they'd heard of K-Pop.

'I'm a writer, DI Mason, AI might soon be putting us all out of business; I know what it is.'

'We believe these erotic images may have been AI generated,' Mason explained. 'Using a... ahem... somewhat younger picture of your face, shall we say.'

'That's not my face!' she insisted. 'Young or old.'

'Who is it then?' asked Felix.

'She *is* familiar.' Phoebe racked her mind as they both peered closer.

'Could this be the same person...?' Mason gestured at one of the explicit photographs in which only the woman's distinctive curved lips were visible.

'That's graphic,' murmured Felix, tilting his head the other way. 'Arty, though.'

'It would be.' Phoebe realised as the missing piece fell into place at last. 'It's by Man Ray. The lips are thought to belong to Kiki de Montparnasse, his muse and lover. The other body part in this shot is his. These images appear in a very rare poetry collection called *1929* that scandalised Paris between the wars. The whereabouts of a copy is central to the plotline of *Blood on the Tracks*, my third Dorothy De'Ath mystery. Copies once sold for almost as much as a Bugatti Royale. Nowadays, you can download it on Kindle for a couple of quid.'

'So it's not a recent photograph then?' asked Mason.

'Almost a hundred years old.'

'They took dirty selfies like this that long ago?' Alsop looked amazed.

'Shocking,' whispered Felix, catching Phoebe's eye, relief flooding his face.

'Can we zoom in on what's written on the notes beside it?' she asked, studying the pinned paper squares: *asphyxiate her with a silk stocking*; *cyanide in her glass of champagne*; *throw her from a Pullman carriage*.

'Craig Jackman must have fantasised about your death a lot,' Alsop said cheerfully, then remembered her sensitivity training and added, 'But best not dwell on it, eh?'

'Although not one of these mentions a letter bomb, which is odd,' DI Mason conjected. 'I can't help feeling that, despite the evidence pointing to what we might call, for want of a better word, homicidal obsession, we're missing something.'

'Go back to the first picture,' Phoebe told him, 'and zoom in on the word "death".'

'Don't punish yourself,' Alsop soothed.

Ignoring her, Phoebe spotted the small black curl between the E and the A this time.

'That's what you're missing!' she said triumphantly, pointing at it. 'An apostrophe!'

Mason and Alsop looked astonished as she broke it to them that Craig's garage wall wasn't covered with his murderous masterplan at all; it was an investigation board he used whilst fact-checking her books. 'Phoebe Fredericks's *De'Ath*, not Death. This board isn't anything to do with planning my demise – it's scrutinising my whodunnits. These are the plots of the four Dorothy De'Ath mysteries Craig read and corrected. The three victims in *Death on the Tracks* die from strangulation, poisoned champagne and falling from a moving train. The killer thinks each has stolen his valuable copy of *1929*. It seems Craig also downloaded that in order to' – she paused, not doubting it for a moment – 'fact check.'

Both police officers made sing-sing 'of course' noises in their throats.

'Now why didn't we think of that?' whistled DS Alsop.

'The question is' – DI Mason took charge, tram braces flashing in a quick smile – 'when it comes down to the pith of the matter, in a nutshell, what we should be asking ourselves is *did* Craig Jackman wish you ill, Ms Fredericks? I still believe so.'

Having once longed to swallow this explanation, Phoebe found she no longer could. She felt a surge of pity for Craig, and appreciation that he'd been so passionately invested in her books. Far beyond that, he'd saved her by dying. She owed it to him to find out the truth.

'I don't follow your thinking.' She glanced to Felix for support, but he'd turned away to read a message on his phone screen, the hunch of his shoulders telling her it wasn't good news.

The detective's braces flashed again. 'Reading your novels clearly triggered his obsessive interest in murder and vintage pornography, Ms Fredericks. In which case, it's my belief that, all things taken into consideration, he intended to harm you.'

'And yet he still had two more Dorothy De'Ath books to go,'

Felix pointed out, coming off his phone. 'Plus the one Phoebe's writing now.'

'Fair point.' Mason nodded. 'Make a note of that will you, Sergeant Alsop?'

He deferred to Felix far more eagerly than he did to her, Phoebe noticed as DS Alsop got out her pad.

'Perhaps I'll write a poison letter bomb into Dorothy's latest mystery,' she said drily. 'It might provoke the real killer into revealing themselves.'

'Nice call!' DS Alsop wrote that down on her pad too.

'Except that whoever it is that really wants you dead might just try again first?' suggested Felix, smile dropping to reveal the dark expression beneath.

There was a brief, uncomfortable silence.

'I've said it before; I think we need look no further,' Mason summarised surprisingly succinctly. 'Craig Jackman had the means. And while we've established this board doesn't contain explicit images of Ms Fredericks, it is nonetheless damning evidence.'

'I disagree!' Phoebe said hotly, frustration mounting. 'Craig liked watching model railway footage and unboxing videos. He was a fact checker, a trivia boff and a devotee of authenticity. Sending crank invitations and exploding packages is just not his gig.'

Mason looked unconvinced. 'If not Mr Jackman, whose "gig" do you suggest it is?'

'Penny Fermoy.' As soon as she said it, Phoebe realised how fanciful it sounded.

'You have proof of this?'

'She hates us.' She looked round helplessly, wishing she hadn't flushed the ashwagandha gummies away which she'd suspected Penny had tampered with while she was clanking around in the kitchen. 'She wants us out of here, whether by threat or blackmail.'

Felix was back on his phone again, she noticed disconsolately. He'd never agreed with her on Penny.

'With respect, Ms Fredericks,' Mason sighed, tucking the tablet under his arm like a clutch bag, 'while I appreciate Ms Fermoy is a colourful local character with significant, shall we say, personal interest in the future of Hartridge Court, you cannot make wild accusations against her. Unless you have something concrete, may I suggest you leave the investigation to us and focus elsewhere?'

Defeated, she nodded, glancing across at the book open on a sofa arm. '*Possession*.'

'Possession, you say?' Mason was suddenly animated, as though he'd long suspected as much.

'What drugs exactly? Cocaine, marijuana, party pills?' DI Alsop still had her notepad out.

'It's the title of tonight's book club novel.'

'That's not a criminal offence,' Mason sighed.

'It is if you don't read it beforehand, and just watch the movie.'

Juno

Juno switched tabs from Wikipedia's *Possession* Plot Summary to read back through her latest blog draft, suspecting A. S. Byatt had crafted shorter sentences and was more sparing with exclamation marks:

MOTHER LOVES FREEDOM!

I'm writing this in blazing (yes, British and blazing) sunshine on the terrace of The Barton Arms, overlooking the gorgeous, glittery River Dunnett with the silk ribbon of the North Wessex Canal beyond, and the magical, mythical chalk downs in the distance. We're out in the wild, guys!

(Office_view.jpg)

The laptop fan is purring because I've just applied for a bunch of jobs online and – you heard it here first – this blog may soon be authored by an official 'director of first impressions' or 'head of verbal communications'. (No idea what these are, but I match the skill set.) Meanwhile, my friend Mil says he can give me plenty of bar work and waitressing shifts. *And* I've just signed up for an online Life Coaching course! Bring it on...

As for all of you who have messaged me about the village murder, I salute your enthusiasm, suggestions and big hearts! Thank you! Investigations remain ongoing. On the down low, I'm going deep undercover tonight to stake out a village cabal that might just contain the murderer. Wish me luck!

Anxiety spiking, Juno switched back to Wikipedia and read to the end of the book synopsis, feeling a bit teary because even reduced to four paragraphs, it was terribly sad. She was grateful to hear her phone ring, more still to see the name on screen.

'Eric baby, what news?'

He sounded smiley and yawny. 'Hey, Mom, so I checked out the rest of those names you gave me. Gail Lamb is a total lightweight online, Seraphine Delauney-Roche is in the Congo.'

'We've already done the fieldwork on that, sorry, we know all this.'

'No sweat. So you know Kenneth Campbell is shadier, I guess?'

'How?'

He told her that Kenneth 'Ken Doll' Campbell went by several aliases on dating sites, drifting between jobs since leaving the military police. 'He was a serious high-flyer there. Officially, he resigned with a pat on the back, but he's on a five-year driving ban, so chances are a serious dangerous driving offence was hushed up. It's too deep in red tape to get at, but my guess is someone got killed. Ken's sitting pretty. Lots of covering fire from friends in high places, new places and safe places.'

'Like his parents,' Juno identified. 'Any rumour of him being a hired escort or undertaking mercenary work?'

'This isn't a Richard Gere movie, Mom.'

'I wish,' she sighed.

He asked her how she was, and she recounted the madcap Pennine road trip via Paris with die-hard rogue detective Felix. She also confessed to making multiple online job applications she didn't understand, hamming up the comedy, loving his laughter.

A call waiting alert had started pinging in her ear. 'I must go, darling, Granny's on the other line!'

'Stay strong, Mom. Love you. You so sound like a *head of verbal communications*.'

'What even *is* that?'

'Receptionist, man. But you knew that, right?'

'Totally! Love you too. Don't call me man. Bye!' Juno swiftly switched calls. 'Mum! Hello!'

'At last!' Judy boomed in her ear, the Rolling Stones singing 'She's a Rainbow' in the background. 'I'm in the hot tub with Dennis and we're *dying* to know about you and your "friend" in Paris! Honestly, here we are lining up handsome Kenneth for a sexy picnic, and you're being whisked off to *la Ville d'Amour*!'

'I was in Paris with Felix, Mum.'

There was a lot of splashing and gasping at the other end. 'You were in Paris with *Freddy's husband*?'

'We were on Village Detective business.'

'Ah! Then perhaps we'll forgive you. It's okay, Doobee!' Judy called out amid more splashing, the Beatles' 'All You Need Is Love' now their backtrack. 'Kenneth is still a goer!' She came back on the line. 'How are you fixed the day after tomorrow? Eugene got a cautious "yes" his end to joining us with their son for a champagne picnic and Gilbert and Sullivan here in the walled garden.'

'Mum, I've changed my mind about that.' Juno heard Eric's warning like a siren echoing in her ears. Also, she hated Gilbert and Sullivan.

'But he's so *divine* and beefy and shy. And entre nous, the Campbells are big hitters at Godlington. Doesn't play to get on their wrong side. Doobee's set his heart on a place on the residents' board.'

'It's still a no.'

'Such ingratitude! Pusscat, you are horribly spoiled and I blame myself.' The rant that followed was largely lost to splashing and the 'All You Need Is Love' refrain alternating with its da-da-da-da-dums. But Juno distinctly heard her mother splutter: 'And I want my car back!'

This played straight into her daughterly shame and guilt. Although Judy hadn't driven in five years, the orange Honda Jazz was a portal to her past and she was enormously sentimental about it. She also liked hiding impulse purchases in its boot.

Juno hadn't told her mother how bad the little car was sounding. She knew its current state was her fault and she was determined to put it right without causing parental stress.

As soon as they'd testily rung off, she asked Mil to recommend a mechanic.

Juno's recent experience with her Mini being kept hostage had put her off large corporate garages. Mil suggested a young husband and wife team who had recently set up shop in a repurposed filling station on the Newborough road called Garage Drum 'n' Brakes. Eager for business, they agreed to check the car over that day and Juno clanked the Jazz round there now, groaning and grinding all the way.

They told her the brake pads and discs were totally shot, but they could fix it at a fraction of the manufacturer cost.

'Can we photograph you for our social media?' they asked. 'Maybe you can tag us back? You've a big following, Mil says.'

Flattered, Juno agreed, although she felt compelled to point out, 'They're almost all in the States.'

She posed for a selfie, embarrassed to find herself draped over the Jazz bonnet like an ageing eighties glamour model while the cool young couple leant in to either side of her in one-strap dungarees making hang loose signs with their hands.

Garage Drum 'n' Brakes had all available social streams covered, posting the picture on them all at once via a clever app and tagging in Juno.

The first response which pinged back was:

Shame it didn't crash in the Nidd #DrownTheWitch.

Juno let out a cry of anguish.

She called Felix from her flat, bolstered by tea and deli muffins. The moment he picked up, she blurted breathlessly: 'Look at Twitter! OhFeelYa hasn't just figured out we were in Paris; they knew that we were in Yorkshire too! It's like they were *following us*! And now they are literally following me – they're trolling my Mother Love stuff!'

'Calm down, Juno. We'll get to the bottom of this, I promise.

Listen, I'm going to have to call you back; I'm in a meeting in South Bank right now.'

'With whom?' she demanded mulishly, wondering if it was Betsy and feeling angry on Phoebe's behalf.

'Head of funding at the British Film Institute.'

'I'll let you go,' she said in a small voice. She was starting to feel cold and shaky.

She scrolled paranoically through her social media, but there was nothing more from OhFeelYa directed personally towards Juno. They were quiet on X too, last night's savagery no doubt having exhausted them.

Yesterday's Parisian exploits in the cold and rain had left Juno with more than just tiredness. The shivers were taking hold. She had a sneezing fit now. Making herself a hot lemon drink, she sank into the sofa and wrapped a throw around her shoulders, grateful for Kevin Bacon's warmth as she phoned Phoebe.

'I might have to give book group a miss,' she told her. 'Got a chill.'

'Don't be so wet,' snapped Phoebe. 'I'm certain the clue to Craig's killer is right here under our noses in Inkbury. I need you there. Now buck up and read the book.'

Phoebe was right, Juno reminded herself, going in search of Olbas Oil. They mustn't give up now. And Gigi had laid on fantastic wine and nibbles last time.

16

PHOEBE

That evening, the Village Detectives met for a quick drink in The Barton Arms before the Inkbury Book Group discussion.

Felix was stuck in London in crisis meetings, Phoebe explained as Mil lined up two large gin and tonics and his customary alcohol-free beer on a table in the quietest corner of the bar. 'This always happens in films. Last week, they had Apple TV and a Venice Film Festival premiere lined up; this week there's no distributor, no money left, an over-long first cut and an unmeetable festival deadline. He's pitching for BFI funding and aiming for Sundance instead.' She didn't add that this meant she'd have to write twice as fast to cover the income delay.

'I knew I should have stopped him dragging me to Paris,' Juno fretted now, stifling a sneeze.

'You did fire him for that.' Phoebe was still crotchety about their wasted trip, although mildly appeased that Juno seemed to have picked up a head cold there.

'But it's seriously triggered OhFeelYa, and all the noise on Felix's Twitter feed can't be helping,' Juno sympathised. 'I mean his X.'

'Felix's ex?' Mil looked confused. 'I thought the French one was his daughter?'

'She is!' Juno swigged more gin. 'And if Seraphine's not OhFeelYa then who else could be in Paris? They knew we were there!'

'Maybe they have a contact over there,' Mil suggested.

'I wondered that. What if it's an insider? They also knew we were in Yorkshire!'

'By insider, do you mean one of us?' asked Phoebe, bemused.

'A local, perhaps.' Juno cast her eyes left and right, although the pub was still quiet, just a few tables occupied.

'Let's not get fixated on OhFeelYa,' Phoebe urged. 'I'd like to find out more about what was in Craig's workshop, also more about the IED that killed him.'

'Yeah, I googled that.' Mil picked up his phone. 'I meant to put it on the WhatsApp chat. To make an improvised explosive device, you need PIES, which stands for power, an initiator, explosives and a switch. Packing it with additional stuff, like shrapnel or nails, causes more damage. In Craig's case, poisoned pen nibs.'

'Surely the police checked out where those fountain nibs came from? It's not something you can easily buy in bulk.'

'You can, actually,' he said. 'I looked that up too. Sold by the bagful on eBay for jewellery making and crafters.'

'What about the hemlock?' Juno asked. 'I heard that grows wild in the hedgerows locally. There was even some in the village allotments.'

'Then we definitely need to focus our investigations on the village,' Mil agreed, looking relieved. 'I'll do some more asking around in here this evening while you're both over at Gigi's.'

'And we'll find out what the literary gossips have to say,' Juno agreed. 'The book talk is usually over pretty quickly.'

'I hope not.' Phoebe thought of the heavily annotated copy of *Possession* in her bag.

Several white-haired village elders were coming into the pub, hailing friends at a far table.

'Excuse me, ladies,' said Mil, jumping up to man the bar. 'Evening, Alan, Bernard – looking lovely, Ree and Beth! What can I get you folks? The usual?' He reached up for two tankards hanging over the bar.

'We must be alert, Freddy,' Juno breathed, looking around, lowering her voice. 'That's Beth Trascott with the Coles and Alan. Pale bob and lazy eye. She's the book group patron, her family ran it for years. Very quiet, big crime fan. *She's* the one who had hemlock in her allotment.'

'I've met her.' Phoebe remembered the Dorothy De'Ath enthusiast from her encounter with the dog walkers on the bridge.

'And the Coles are in the book group too. Bernard was an engineer. He's known to have a bad temper. *And* he's in the railway model club, so could be worth a closer look.' She started making little gasps in the build-up to a sneeze, turning away as it reached its crescendo. 'Chew! Sorry about that. I think the Coles just go to book group for the catering. The food's sensational, and Penny supplies amazing wine.'

'No surprise there.' Now she'd discovered how bad Penny's drink problem was, Phoebe couldn't kick the sense that her high-society life had derailed, and she was no longer in control. Perhaps she never had been. For all her bravado and connections, there was a chaos to Bad Penny that bothered Phoebe, the unalloyed partying more teenager than mid-lifer. Boozy had looked after her as though she was an adopted child, not a former mistress. 'That woman's hiding something,' she told Juno, 'and not just her mysterious "adult" toyboy.'

'I have a faint suspicion I might know who that is.' Juno bit her lip guiltily. 'Sorry, meant to say: Kenneth Ken Doll.'

'The newsreader? He's been dead years.'

'Who? I'm talking about my dating app gigolo Kendall, who turned out to be called Kenneth, you remember? Asked me to pay for a night in a hotel, then came to Mum's for lunch and ate too much to talk? I'm sure I saw him in Penny's car the other day.' She swigged more gin and tonic, frowning in thought. 'You know, I think I *do* remember a Kenneth Kendall on telly.' She launched into a reverie about a show involving a blond, jump-suited star looking for treasure in a helicopter.

Accustomed to Juno's butterfly mind flitting from suspicious villagers to random eighties TV nostalgia, Phoebe picked up her own drink and watched as Mil waylaid Alan Bickerstaff on his way past to ask whether he'd copied the CCTV footage from his doorbell camera showing Craig's final round. 'You'd be doing us a real favour, mate. We're clutching at straws, frankly.'

'Ah, there's a thing,' Alan apologised, setting his tankard down on the table to join them. 'I realised after we'd spoken that I was replacing my old CCTV system on the day Craig died, so I'm afraid it won't be on it.'

'Was the old one not still recording?'

'Regrettably, no. I was up a ladder unscrewing it when his van passed by. I remember turning to wave. Bernard might have something from Station Cottage. I'll ask, shall I? I'm just sorry I can't be more help.'

'Thanks, mate. There probably wasn't anything on it that would have made a difference,' Mil reassured him. 'And we've already got some *seriously* compromising video footage up our sleeves, eh, Phoebe?'

Phoebe looked at him in confusion.

'What's that?' Alan leant forward, all ears, like an eager owl.

'My arse!' Mil cackled. 'I mooned at that one we put up at Hartridge, didn't I, Phoebe?'

'Very high spirited of you.' With a flustered laugh and nod, Alan went to rejoin his friends, several of whom were getting ready to set off for the book group.

'You embarrassed him,' Juno ticked Mil off, then asked jealously, 'Did you really get your bottom out in front of Phoebe?'

'I can show you on the app,' Mil offered, fishing his phone out of his pocket.

'No time!' Phoebe glanced at her watch. 'We must go.'

'Spoilsport,' grumbled Juno, knocking back the rest of her drink.

'You need me to stay over again if Felix is up in town tonight?' Mil offered as Phoebe gathered up her bag.

'I can stay over!' Juno countered, blowing her nose again. 'I think I'm allergic to Kevin Bacon.'

'Felix will be back tonight,' Phoebe assured them quickly, although she was starting to doubt it. But she found being watched over all the time ridiculous, no matter how well meaning.

'In that case, he can join us for last orders when we meet back here to debrief.' Mil collected up their empty glasses along with his beer bottle, whispering, 'Let's get sleuthing, ladies! Find out facts.'

Phoebe gave him a stern look. 'It's a book group, Mil. We'll be talking about the fiction.'

* * *

Juno

'I couldn't get past all those poems and letters,' Juno lamented breathlessly as she and Phoebe made their way across the lane to Inkbury Mill from the pub. 'Gigi insists "dark academia" is all the rage on BookTok. I tried listening to the audiobook last night but dropped off. I'm just hoping some of it has penetrated my subconscious.'

'*Possession* is a great novel,' Phoebe told her, taking one long stride for every two of Juno's. 'Lots of allegories.'

'Nobody talked about the book much last time,' Juno tried to warn her.

At her first meeting, she'd found her hasty speed-read of *White Teeth* largely surplus to requirements. After host Gigi's opening summary of her own thoughts, delivered like a TED talk that required no interruptions, they'd quickly got down to business, namely scandalmongering.

Juno was gambling that few of the villagers gathered in Gigi's top-floor apartment would have read this month's novel apart from their hostess and the newcomer. She was equally certain the centre of attention tonight would not be Byatt or her characters. But perhaps Phoebe knew that too. She looked quietly delighted when it was Penny Fermoy who threw open the door, already half cut.

'*Juno!*' Boyishly louche in chinos and striped shirt, collar up, a Cambridge blue cashmere sweater knotted around her shoulders, Penny had a bottle in each hand, gumshield smile at its most bullet-proof, eyes at their cruellest. 'You brought fresh blood! Phoebe, you're turning into my shadow. People will talk. *Gigi – Dorothy De'Ath's here!*'

Phoebe cast Juno a ghost of a wink.

Uncertain whether to be relieved or anxious, Juno resisted the temptation to comedy wink back as Gigi swooped up, small and vampish in a cape-sleeved top that hinted at varsity don meets sorceress, titian bun tight enough to pull her eyebrows up. 'Welcome, Phoebe! So glad you could make it. No plugging one of your own homespun whodunnits tonight, remember!'

Phoebe shook her hand firmly. '*Possession* always fascinated me.'

'How thrilling to have a populist take!' Gigi said crushingly. 'Let me introduce you to our little thinktank. They're all dying to meet you. Not literally, of course – like poor Craig the postman!' She led Phoebe off into the main reception room.

Glaring at Phoebe's back, Penny murmured to Juno, 'No idea what you see in her. *Super* uptight. Boozy always joked she was Felix's dominatrix, and he should know. Drink? Glasses are on the table over there.'

Juno gratefully accepted a hefty splosh of white in an over-sized glass, telling herself it would help her sore throat and bunged-up nose.

'I always think these evenings would be so much more fun without the homework, don't you?' Penny whispered, almost filling it to the brim.

Whilst Gigi regularly reminded members of the Inkbury Book Group that she was a Doctor of Philosophy, Bad Penny's reinvention as the village's answer to Mariella Frostrup fooled nobody. Famously well-connected, she'd attended far more glitzy publishing launches than she'd read books. Part mascot, part maître d', she had her eye on a bigger goal.

'I only do this gig for Gigi,' she confided in Juno now, then snorted with laughter because she'd mispronounced it 'gidge for giggy'. She repeated it carefully and correctly. '*Gig* for *Gigi*. She's one of the Hartridge Foundation trustees. She's going to help me establish Boozy's cultural legacy. Gallery, arts spaces, sculpture trail, touring exhibitions, that sort of shebang. There'll be festivals galore, exclusive launches, private membership. You must join. It will have an arty vibe with a party tribe.' She stopped, cocking her head and looking up, briefly angelic. 'That's good! *Arty vibe with a party tribe.* I'm going to use that. Do you like that, what's your name again?'

'Juno,' said Juno, feeling crushed.

'Trust me, Juno, Hartridge Court will be *to die for*,' Penny smiled. 'Nothing will stop me making this work. I'm an Aries, so it's a given. Better go into Assembly.'

She weaved towards the main reception room and the book group, wine bottles swinging like a gunslinger.

Following her, suddenly jumpy, Juno quickly assessed the small crowd, grateful to see a host of familiar faces amongst those gathered on sofas, stools and dining chairs. In addition to committee members Gigi, Penny and merry-eyed bookworm Beth Trascott, there were at least a dozen others including punky blonde pub quizzer and caterer Rachel guarding a tray of miniature rarebits, and husband and wife Bernard and Ree who went to everything in the village and had come across from the pub ahead of them to nab the seats closest to the food. All of them were eyeballing Phoebe with interest, as she perched thoughtfully on an upholstered dining chair, book in hand.

Penny was noisily patting the vacant cushion of a three-seat sofa in which she'd rammed a nervous-looking woman in Boden and pearls up against the arm. 'Join us, Juno!'

Juno squeezed herself alongside as Gigi launched into her customary opening spiel: 'Shame, daring and loss, ownership and creativity, let me tell you about *Possession*...'

* * *

Juno loved the fact Inkbury Book Group had been in existence for almost sixty years, propelled through the decades by the excited page-turns of bibliophile villagers, in particularly three generations of one local family.

Established in the 1960s by local school mistress Betty Trascott, it had originally encouraged readers to enjoy gentle romances, warm family sagas and the odd du Maurier for a thrill. Having been spun into a vibrant vicious circle through the nineties and noughties by Betty's university-educated daughter urging members to discuss post-colonial angst, identity politics and their awful husbands, its current patron was a gentler soul. Betty's less subversive, unmarried granddaughter Beth was a passionate bookworm and a dab hand at nurturing new recruits, but Juno could see she was being bulldozed by well-read and bossy Gigi, as were all the group.

Tackling modern classics, with a focus on great storytelling – mostly village tittle tattle and hearsay – Gigi deployed wine, nibbles and ripping literary yarns in her mission to rule the village literary salon. And she had a crack support team of networkers in hospitality.

Tonight's endless supply of Sauvignon Blanc was courtesy of Penny's wine merchant brother who offered group members a discount; professional caterer Rachel had laid on mountains of scrumptious canapes with her business cards served discreetly alongside.

'Top up?' Penny splashed wine in Juno's glass and whispered, 'Look who's one of the swots! *Quelle surprise.*'

Across the room, Phoebe was perched on a dining chair listening intently as Gigi lectured them on Byatt's playful inter-woven timelines. Beside her, the group's materfamilias Beth Trascott loyally made notes for the village newsletter. To her other side, Gigi's small, adoring partner had prayer hands to their mouth, head tilted ecstatically.

Gigi's corvine cape sleeves flapped blackly as she threw her arms out to declare, 'This classic twentieth-century novel is a tour de force, ladies – and Bernard!'

'Bah! What's that?' Bernard woke up with a start on a neighbouring sofa, wife Ree spilling her drink in shock.

'Don't nod off, Bernard, I'm just getting to the good bit,' snapped Gigi.

Juno hoped this meant they'd soon get onto the gossip. Craig's death was bound to be a main topic.

Penny's bony arm jabbed hard into her side as she leaned into her ear with a stage whisper loud enough to reach the highest row at the Albert Hall. 'Awful old bores, the Coles. Used to come with the ghastly Bickerstaffs. Entre nous it was a relief when Norma pegged it. Could talk about a book for hours, that woman. Mind you, so can Gigi.'

'…literary detective novel, love story and clever conceit rolled into one,' Gigi was saying.

Across the room, Phoebe was tapping the spine of her battered copy impatiently against her chin. 'But *why* does it move us, do you think?'

'Questions at the end!'

'I loved Gwenyth Paltrow in the movie,' Penny was confessing in Juno's ear. 'Have you seen it? More wine?'

Juno hadn't sipped any since it was last topped up, but took a hefty swig to make space, sensing a valuable sleuthing opportunity.

'It's delicious,' she whispered back, trying not to mind that Penny was slopping quite a lot of it in her lap. 'French?'

'Yah, my brother lives out there.'

'Mine's in Ibiza. Best holidays ever. Whereabouts is yours based?'

'Provence mostly, although he has an office in Paris with a sweet little flat over it. Great for shopping.'

Juno's ears pricked up. 'Do you ever use it?'

'As often as poss. Love French boutiques, food, men.'

'When were you last there?'

'Fashion week. Took my new squeeze. *Majorly* wet.'

'So many men lack backbone these days,' Juno sympathised.

'The weather was wet, silly!' She snarked with laughter.

'I was in Paris yesterday,' Juno showed off. 'Jolly wet too.'

'Wasn't it just?'

It was hard to tell whether Penny was simply being conversational or had first-hand knowledge, but Juno wasn't taking any chances. Alarm bells ringing, she looked across at Phoebe urgently.

That's when she realised an Inkbury Book Group mutiny was taking place on the opposite side of the room.

Phoebe was defying their host by interrupting her lecture to discuss *Possession*. To everyone's astonishment, Gigi was listening. Then discussing too. Then listening again, and now laughing.

'Gigi's *so* going to shut her down,' Penny breathed.

Juno disagreed. It was obvious both women loved the subject.

Emboldened by Phoebe, bashful Beth Trascott – who had also read and enjoyed the novel – ventured an opinion. Then Gigi's partner seconded it; Ree interjected with a different angle, Phoebe countered and Gigi expanded her point.

'They're bluffing,' Penny sneered.

Again, Juno demurred. It seemed a lot of people in the room had read *Possession*. They were *all* starting to talk about it.

'Have you read it?' Penny whispered to the woman in pearls and Boden to her left.

'Yes, I enjoyed it.'

'You?' She turned to Juno.

Feeling her ego shrink from major to minor, Juno shook her head.

'Should have watched the movie. Don't beat yourself up. Boozy had lots of first editions at Hartridge and never read one. He used to say, "Call me an ignorant ale-swilling pig, Pen baby, but books and wine are just posh cash." God, I miss Boozy.' She topped up Juno's near-full glass again, along with her empty one.

At the mention of Boozy, Juno's detective antennae pricked up once more.

'What was the deal between you two?'

'I was his muse. What's your name again?'

'Juno.'

'Trouble is, Juno, that his vulture family scavenged the art and furniture into storage before his darling body was cold,' Penny sighed, 'but the wine's still in the cellar, the collector's editions in the library. I bet Felix the freeloader and that cow are helping themselves to both.' She glared at Phoebe, whose balletic arms now mirrored Gigi's, both talking animatedly, beckoning others into the chat like Reese Witherspoon and Oprah in a book club dance-off.

'I'm sure they're not,' Juno pacified.

'Boozy promised that place to the public!' she growled angrily. 'It's all in his Letter of Wishes. He loved buying himself things he thought were too pretentious for words. Big houses, fine art, books, wine, *me*.' She laughed silently, head-butting Juno's shoulder. 'He wanted to show us all off after his death, his circus of privilege, with his Bad Penny as ring master!' This time the laugh was louder, shushed by the bookworms across the room.

'You can't take it with you.' Juno offered a placating cliché, her heart softening a little, wondering if there really had been a legacy pact between Penny and the media mogul all along, a sweetly romantic agreement across the social and generational divide.

'I know his dirty little secret,' Penny whispered.

Juno downgraded the sweet romance.

Penny pressed her finger to her lips, giggling. '*Super*-secret.'

Juno realised that Penny wasn't just tipsy, she was fully in her cups slewed.

'In the cellar,' she confided with a playful growl, 'you do *not* want to go down there, trust me.'

'I won't,' Juno reassured her.

'I don't blame you!'

With a muttered 'excuse me', the woman in pearls and Boden extracted herself and bolted across the room to perch on a footstool and join in the conversation about Byatt.

'Think we scared her off.' Penny snorted with laughter, leaning against Juno. Then, tipping the other way and finding nobody there, she nose-dived into the sofa. She let out a low, mournful wail.

Juno patted her shoulder gently, whispering, 'Are you okay?'

'God, I miss being young, don't you?' Penny groaned. 'Boozy made me feel young, but only probably because he was sooo old.'

Juno wanted to argue that they were both still in their prime, but the bookworms across the room were talking in muted earnest voices about chess as an allegory for female oppression, and the moment passed.

'Grab my phone, will you, darling?' Penny demanded, still face-down on the sofa.

Juno located it and inserted it close to where she hoped Penny's hand was. After a brief pause, the screen glowed and a thumb moved around it with remarkable speed before it went dark again.

'Better!' Penny jolted upright. 'Need cheering up! Got my lovely no-strings guy lined up for later.' She dropped her voice, whispering, 'Gorgeous looking. Not from round here.'

Recalling the giant, pirate-like figure in Penny's passenger seat, Juno whispered back, 'Kendall?'

'No, not the Lake District – Portsmouth, I think he said. Just moved to Newborough. Seriously sexy job.' She winked.

'Don't tell me,' Juno returned it knowingly, 'he's hired assassin by day, aficionado of laughter and dancing by night?'

'What are you talking about?' Penny reknotted the sweater around her neck, its bright, cold blue matching her eyes. 'Kain's a rewilding landscape designer. Serious eco credentials. Conserves water, eats only organic, won't drive. Calls me Lady Chatterley and goes like a train.'

'A hydrogen-powered eco-friendly one, I hope?' Juno checked.

Before she could say more, Penny had thrust a bottle of wine into her hand. 'Sod this book talk, it's time to top up and disrupt. Help me out.'

Juno stayed put, watching anxiously as Penny lurched off on a collision course to Phoebe, who was talking animatedly with Beth. Both broke off to look up as Penny splashed wine into their glasses.

'Spoken to your lawyers yet?' Penny demanded loudly as Phoebe angled her knees away from the overspill.

'We're not going anywhere, Penny.'

Penny's angry 'Bollocks!' silenced the bookish talk around them faster than a gunshot in a library.

'Let's not discuss it here,' Phoebe told her quietly.

'Oh, do let's,' Penny hissed, standing up straight and swaying, volume rising. 'You're only living at Hartridge because you were drummed out of town, and Felix is too decent to drop you!' She was haranguing now, her words slurred, ignoring Gigi's attempts to silence her. 'You're a freelancer, I mean loafer, *loader*! You're a freeloader!'

'Touché,' Phoebe said in an undertone, 'with bells on.'

On her other side, Bernard let out an appreciative guffaw. He was winded into silence by Ree's elbow.

Juno watched Penny anxiously, grateful for Phoebe's sangfroid, alarmed how close the wine bottle was swinging to her friend's head as the socialite turned to address the group.

'Did you know Phoebe drove someone to actual suicide? She goaded them into it! Her paper fired her. Everyone in media hates her. She's a death threat target, and she's putting Hartridge and Boozy's legacy at risk. Nobody has a good thing to say about her, *nobody!*'

'Surely you invited more than just nobodies to my memorial service?' Phoebe asked lightly.

Penny looked blank. 'What?'

'You dropped off a fake stiffy in our post box, remember, along with the parish magazine.'

'That's slander!' The wine bottle swung close to Phoebe's head again. 'I've never invited you to anything!'

'Actually, I deliver the parish mags,' explained Beth nervously.

'What are you all talking about?' demanded Gigi, eyes lighting up at the prospect of gossip.

'Something to do with Bad Penny and a fake stiffy,' Bernard reported excitedly, getting another sideswipe from his wife.

Gigi's cranked-up brows found a few more degrees of tilt. 'Have you been playing with that expensive toyboy again, Penny?'

'She's a liar!' Penny fumed, then snarled at Phoebe, 'My lawyers will shred your reputation. See how you like that!'

'I have nothing left to shred, Penny,' Phoebe reminded her,

surprisingly gently, the green eyes full of feeling. 'I think we're in the same boat there.'

'Rot in hell. I bloody *hate* you!' Penny staggered back, turning to glare at Gigi. 'And you are *boring* as *hell*! Some of us have got a *life*. If you'll all excuse me, I've got a hot date later and I need to freshen up.'

She stormed out. Moments later, she stormed back for her handbag then stormed out again.

After a brief pause, she reappeared.

'And Gigi's *my* boring friend, Phoebe, not yours!'

This time, she slammed every door behind her and screamy-roared as she went.

Juno was quietly impressed. Violet Elizabeth Botox had left the building, tantrum echoing.

She sneezed again and blew her nose. She was looking forward to the group's salacious, gossipy take on this.

But to her astonishment, they just started talking about the book again.

Later Juno would reflect that she really should have stopped drinking at that point. Penny's behaviour had been a red flag, after all.

But she'd ended up cosying up to Rachel the caterer on the double piano stool, scoffing her way through the delicious nibbles. Rachel hadn't read the book either, it transpired. She hadn't even read the Wikipedia plot summary. What Rachel did have was plentiful village gossip, including touching anecdotes about Craig Jackman, whose mother Denise – 'salty till you get to know her' – was her best friend, their trio forming the First-Class Minds quiz team. And she knew a great deal about Penny Fermoy – 'earthier than most poshos' – whose parties she had catered for many times, and whose car key she'd hidden in a cool box for her own safety more than once. Rachel also knew a lot about Mil –

combining her surf and turf to describe him as 'salt of the earth' –
who she'd first snogged at a Young Farmers' disco over twenty
years earlier and remained inordinately fond of in a sisterly way.
'Soppier than he looks. Bloody good kisser.'

If Juno had stopped drinking, she might even have realised
that somebody else's life was in danger that night. But in vino,
murder was soon the last thing on her mind.

* * *

Phoebe

'Then Penny flounced out! Three times!' Juno reported excitedly,
eyes not quite focusing. 'Off for an asssnog – arsenig – assigna-
tion with her toyboy! She is *still* just as wild as her It Girl party
years. Amazing.'

'Sounds it!' Mil whistled, uncorking the Remy Martin to top
up her nightcap.

Phoebe wanted to suggest a coffee might be better, but Juno
had already picked it up, swilling it around in the balloon glass
extravagantly.

'Wasn't it amazing, Freddy?'

'It was.' Phoebe humoured her, grateful she seemed to have
drunkenly forgotten precisely what Penny had spouted about
before leaving.

They were lined up on barstools in The Barton Arms,
Europe's 'Final Countdown' on the stereo, a pub tradition when
last orders were called.

Pulling pints of Best into a brace of tankards, Mil complained
that Felix was cutting it fine for their Village Detectives debrief.

'That last train's a slow one,' Phoebe said vaguely. 'Might not
make it here in time.'

She had no way of knowing if he was on it. Her phone had died; it turned out switching off airplane mode drained the battery exponentially. Her own batteries felt much the same, fading fast after using so much brain power. Yet she'd enjoyed tonight's book discussion enormously. So much so that she'd already accepted Gigi's invitation to attend the next book group, honoured to be asked to choose the title. Humbled, she now intended to resuscitate Georgiana Gilmore from her adder bite in *The Library Steps Ripper*.

'I'll take you home if Felix doesn't make it,' Mil repeated his offer, handing the tankard to Alan who was still chinwagging further along the bar with a small clutch of steadfast regulars, and another to Bernard who had joined his friend for a nightcap. 'Albie can finish off here.'

'I think Juno might be the one who needs walking home,' Phoebe murmured as Juno let out a long, loud sigh beside her and started singing along to the 'Final Countdown', doing some vigorous air guitar.

Now her hand slapped on the bar. 'You were wonderful tonight, Freddy!'

Juno's limitless capacity for positivity and largesse never ceased to amaze Phoebe. It worked in inverse proportion to her capacity for alcohol, which was negligible.

'*Vunderbar*! *Merveilleux*! *Magnifique*!'

'Thank you.'

'Felix doesn't deserve you, you know. No wonder he drives you mad. And you are quite right, he's *such* a hothead. I know he's a beautiful-looking man. Beautiful, beautiful, beautiful man, and *so* fun to be with... Where was I?'

Alan and Bernard's gang were watching with interest, Phoebe noticed uncomfortably as Juno picked up her thread again: 'Oh, yes! You're wasted on Felix, Freddy. If you ask me, it was *him* who mucked everything up with Gail *and* he goofed everything up with Seraphine. He wound Otis up too. You're quite right about him not thinking anything through.'

'Yes, quite, but I—'

'*And* I've heard him on the phone to his PA, all those flirty conversations. Bastard!'

'Great you have my back, Juno, but I—'

'And he cost you your house! Your beautiful, beautiful farm with the beautiful meadows and the beautiful beck, although you probably don't want to think about the beck given your beautiful Maud nearly drowned in it. Or was it Amelie?' Her eyes filled with tears. 'Such a frightening thing to happen to them all.'

'Let's not talk about that.'

'Sorry, sensitive subject. Got it. My bad. Tell me, what was all that about Penny and the fake stiffy? Bizarre!'

'Let's not talk about that either.'

'You're right. Moving on. Rachel, who does all Penny's catering – you know Rachel the caterer? Snogged you once, Mil – she says Penny's really gone off the rails since Boozy died. Sad really. Grief can be so disorienting.' Her big grey eyes filled with tears, her heart always quick to empathise, especially when drunk. 'Rachel says Penny's always flouncing out of things – the book group, tennis club, the WI and even church. It's her leitmotif.'

'Her what?' asked Mil.

Phoebe was about to explain when Alan Bickerstaff beat her to it as he returned his empty tankard to the bar: 'A recurring theme.'

'That's it!' Juno concurred. 'Thank you! Penny's a serial flouncer. Flounces over anybody. You know, I think she's seeing Kenneth Ken Doll?'

'The newsreader?' asked Bernard, also returning a tankard. 'Isn't he dead?'

'No!' Juno inhaled with laughter. 'Kenneth is a dodgy dating app guy. Looks like a pirate. Offers late-night no-strings liaisons. Charges for them, too. And his parents wonder why he can't settle down, ha! I need a salt-of-the-earth man. Oh, for an alt-of-the-serf man. Any more brandy, Mil – oops!' Trying to lean dreamily on the bar, she missed, plummeting off her stool.

'Time to go home, Juno!' Phoebe slid quickly off hers to help her up. 'I'll walk you there.'

'I'll walk both you ladies home,' Mil offered, hurrying around the bar.

'We can walk Mrs Sylvian home.' Alan stepped forward courteously. 'It's in our direction, eh, Bernie?'

'Absolutely,' Bernard saluted alongside, 'not much further.'

'That's what I love about this village!' Juno let Mil put a supporting arm around her shoulders, sinking into his side with a sigh. 'You are all so gallant, so generous! Especially you, Mil. You are the best. You're the slut of the turf, I mean slat of the oeuf. If you weren't so young, I'd be quite hopelessly in love with you, you know.'

'Thanks, gorgeous.' He steered her towards the door. 'Let's get you home.'

'No funny business! I'm not like Penny. I still can't believe you and her... D'you know, I think she's seeing Kenneth Ken Doll... She kept filling up my glass tonight, *so* much wine... Oh, I forgot to mention Boozy's dirty little cellar secret, Phoebe!' Juno called over her shoulder as she was propelled through the door.

'Ready when you are, Mrs Sylvian.'

Phoebe smiled gratefully at ageing bald guardsman Bernard, who was standing politely to attention beside her, white-haired Alan a head shorter beside him with his brown brogue heels together. With a pang, she was reminded once again of her father. 'It's Phoebe, and it's really kind of you both to offer but I'd rather just jog straight home on my own, thanks. It's quicker if I cut along Witch's Broom.'

'Wouldn't hear of it this late at night.' Bernard turned to wish their friends farewell, then gestured for her to lead the way to the door. 'There might be undesirables in the church yard or the woods. Teenage thugs or the like.'

'Zombies even...' she cooperated graciously.

'Don't forget the vampires and werewolves.' Alan followed them out with a chuckle.

* * *

Bernard and Alan accompanied Phoebe along Three Bridge Lane, walking far slower than her natural stride, one apologetically creaky-kneed, the other wheezing audibly. If she were alone, she'd run home in less than five minutes; instead, they shuffled along at old man pace, Bernard grumbling good-naturedly that he was waiting for a knee op, while Alan complained between breathless gasps about his high blood pressure. 'Bothersome condition. Forgot to bring my heart pills out tonight.'

When they reached the level crossing, Phoebe gazed longingly up at the warning lights, willing them to flash, signalling the last train from London, which might have Felix in it. But it stayed dark and silent, the station platform deserted.

To their right, Station Cottage's porch glowed, along with an upstairs window behind which Rea Coles was already in bed, reading something deadlier than *Possession*, Bernard told Phoebe. 'She's a big thriller fan, the wife. Loves a crazed stalker with a grudge.'

'That why she married you, Bernie?' Alan chuckled.

'It is!' he joined in until they were both rasping with laughter.

'You go in, Bernard,' Phoebe urged, eager to lose each villager at their respective front doors. 'You two honestly don't have to walk me all the way home.'

'But we must,' Bernard said, leaning hard against his walking stick, still catching his breath from laughing.

'She's right,' Alan croaked. 'I'll take it from here, Bernie.'

'Not with that chest, Alan. Worst I've ever heard it tonight.'

'And what about your knees, old man?'

Phoebe recalled Mil telling her how competitive the two were.

'I'll make sure Alan gets home safe,' she told Bernard with a ghost of a wink.

Bernard looked momentarily peeved before remembering his manners and kissing her gallantly farewell on the cheek, returning the wink with aplomb. 'We did enjoy your input at the book club tonight. You must come out with the dog walkers sometime. Having you and those terriers around might even convince this stubborn bugger to get another dog, eh, Alan?'

'Already ahead of you there, Bernie.' Alan waved him in.

Despite herself, Phoebe felt more invisible threads knitting her tighter into the village, a gossamer safety net woven by these two old timers.

Alan had an old-fashioned torch that he switched on as they ventured beyond the village lights, an owl hooting in Hartridge Woods to their left. Moving at an oxygen-starved crawl, he told her about the school he'd taught in for forty years, along with wife Norma. His wheezing voice cracked with sadness when he talked about her. 'My faulty ticker is down to old age, but hers was from birth. Sadly it meant that we couldn't have children. Each dog we owned was her baby. Our last little chap was everything to her, to both of us.' The effort of saying so much was making his breathing even more laboured.

As they drew level with Bridge Row, now walking at a snail's pace, he paused to glance across at his thatched cottage and sighed, 'Still miss that little face at the window.'

Phoebe wasn't sure if he meant Norma or the dog.

'Please do go in,' she urged. 'I can run the last bit. I need the dopamine fix, frankly.'

'No, no, I'll take you to your door,' he puffed.

'You walk too slowly for me,' Phoebe admitted bluntly, worried going much further would finish him off.

'Well, if we're going to run, I might need my medication,' he joked, then wheezed even more.

She saw him across the lane to his door to make sure he got in safely, dismissing his apologies.

As she walked back up his front garden path, Phoebe heard the railway crossing warning wailing in the distance, half tempted to turn and sprint back the way she'd come in the hope Felix was about to alight on the platform. But she couldn't face the disappointment of him not being there.

Without Alan's torch, it was hard to see. Overhead, the clouds were blotting out the moon, the huge oaks of Hartridge Woods overhanging the lane and making it even blacker. She cursed her phone dying as she started to run into the pitch darkness, moving into the centre of the lane to avoid the potholes and uneven verges.

The owl was still calling in the woods, a lone car audible far ahead on the Old London Road. Behind her she could just make out the sound of the train coming into Inkbury Station.

As she passed the Home Farm entrance, Phoebe heard a car engine starting somewhere ahead of her, then she was almost blinded by headlights blazing on at full beam. The engine revved.

With a squeal of tyres, it started at speed towards her.

Aware that in dark clothing with no reflective gear or torch she'd be almost impossible to spot, Phoebe doubled back towards the farm entrance at speed.

But the car was hurtling towards her way faster than she anticipated, her long shadow shrinking fast.

She let out a shout of alarm, sprinting now.

The lane was narrow here, thickly hedged to her nearside, a deep drainage ditch in front. To her right, Hartridge's high estate walls offered no shelter.

The car was almost on top of her.

Where was the bloody driveway? Where? Here at last!

But as she threw herself left to get off the lane with moments to spare, she realised the car was swerving straight after her, swinging into the farm entrance too, moving crazily fast, split seconds from mowing her down.

With a loud cry of alarm, Phoebe managed to twist away into the hedge and found herself falling though brambles and foliage into the ditch, hitting her head on its muddy bank before splashing into the cold water below, landing hard on her coccyx. Somewhere above her there was a loud, wood-splitting crunch as the car hit a gate post.

For a moment the car seemed to stop on the drive overhead, Roxy Music thudding from its stereo. 'Love is the Drug'. Then, with more squealing of tyres, it reversed back into the lane and on towards the village where the railway crossing was no longer wailing, its barriers back up, the train already on its way west to Dunford.

As Phoebe dragged herself slowly out of the ditch, she saw a phone's flashlight bobbing along the lane, which started swinging round wildly as the figure spotted her and came running over.

'Are you all right? Oh, Christ, Phoebe, it's *you!*'

It was Felix, horrified to find his wife in a ditch on his short jog home.

'I think somebody just tried to run me over,' she told him shakily after he'd helped her out, his arms tight around her.

'Did you see who it was?'

'No, but I'm pretty sure I recognised their taste in music.'

17

JUNO

Juno woke parched and ravenous, her head pounding. Her ankles were unusually warm.

Kevin Bacon was draped across her chest, kneading it with his front paws through her sweatshirt fabric.

She was still fully clothed, she realised.

Tumbling out of bed, she crawled to the bathroom basin to gulp water, then into the sitting room to locate her phone and smartwatch, impressed that she'd somehow drunkenly put both on charge.

It wasn't yet eight, she realised with a relief. Her memory of walking back here with Mil last night was woolly, although she vaguely recalled ranting on about secret sex dungeons then getting increasingly giggly and nervous about inviting him up for a coffee.

Juno crawled to the kitchen for more hydration, pursued by Kevin, who was hungry. Refilling his bowl made her stomach heave.

On the work surfaces overhead, there was no evidence of late-night coffee making, but she did appear to have eaten most of the contents of her fridge. There was just one plate in the sink.

It was all coming back. She remembered dropping her keys a lot in Wheeler's Yard, and Mil taking them to let her into the shop. He'd struggled to herd her through that because she'd wanted to try on the vintage clothes.

She looked down at the sweatshirt. Bright blue and two sizes too tight, it had *The Kids From Fame* printed on it. Further down, her ankles were swathed in brightly rainbow-striped knitted leg warmers.

It seemed she had succeeded in trying on the clothes.

More details of the evening were coming back. Penny pouring her more and more wine at Gigi's, then storming off in a huff. Juno keeping on swigging that wine while everyone talked about a book she hadn't read, and Rachel told her how sad and lonely Bad Penny was. Going to the pub with Phoebe afterwards and only realising she was full-scale drunk when she'd caught herself playing air guitar to 'Final Countdown'. By then it had been too late.

Then, with a groan, she remembered spouting terrible things about Felix in front of a small host of Barton Arms regulars.

She settled on the sofa with a carton of juice and decided she must apologise to Phoebe immediately, and also waste no time updating the Village Detectives on her conversations with Penny and later with Rachel at the book group. This way, she could make it clear her inebriated state was purely the result of immersive detective work.

But when she looked at the WhatsApp group, Juno found an update from Felix, sent last night while she'd been unconscious.

She let out a shriek.

Someone had tried to run over Phoebe, who thought it might have been Penny Fermoy.

Juno read Felix's characteristically pithy summary of what had happened, claiming that the police didn't think it significant enough to send anybody out that night but had promised it would be followed up. He finished with:

> Meanwhile they warned us not to confront
> Penny.

Mil had shared a shocked voice note last night offering whatever help they needed, followed by another this morning telling them that he would call by at Hartridge to charge up their security cameras and talk it over, 'As soon as I've checked Juno's made it through the night.'

Juno quickly replied that she was awake, alive and appalled by what had happened.

> Team breakfast in twenty minutes? I'll bring food.
> Will call for you on the way, Mil.

She needed to urgently establish that she'd done no more than dress up in vintage eighties gear before passing out last night. She also needed to offset all the Sauvignon by eating her own weight in pastries as a priority.

Feeling clammy and faint, she hurriedly showered and changed her clothes, selecting a sombre detective-worthy outfit. She was determined to make up for last night's behaviour. Juno blamed herself for what had happened to Phoebe; she'd sensed Penny's loathing; she should have warned Phoebe, but she'd been too way squiffy.

'You should be on commission,' the deli owner told her when she bulk-bought cinnamon whirls and pain au raisins a few minutes later.

Even hungover and on an urgent mission, Juno sensed a deal to be made, negotiating a 10 per cent discount in exchange for a regular sponsored blog, then photographing her purchases shakily and lopsidedly before hurrying along Witch's Broom to the pub.

'You're keen.' Mil was also fresh from the shower, but considerably less jittery and hyped.

'We have our chief suspect! Penny Fermoy wants Phoebe gone! She tried to murder her last night!'

'You don't think she just didn't see her?' Mil offered a more rational perspective. 'That road's dangerous, and Penny's a bit of a racer. Between you and me' – he lowered his voice – 'she sometimes drives after a drink.'

'Sometimes! Penny marinades in the stuff and points her car at people, Mil! How she's not been breathalysed and banned years ago is beyond me.'

'I think she might have lost her licence for a bit, to be fair, when Boozy was still alive.'

'Well, she'll be behind bars for murder soon.'

'Are you sure?' Mil looked even more doubtful. 'Why kill Craig?'

'She was targeting *Phoebe*. She must have given Craig that parcel to deliver, but it went off too soon. It's obvious when you think about it – poison pens from Bad Penny.'

'Oh yeah,' he nodded, 'when you put it like that...'

'Don't forget Phoebe caught Penny as good as red handed delivering the fake memorial invitation. And Penny told her the trustees would throw out Phoebe and Felix if they were seen to be a threat to Hartridge. Penny's a social media junkie; she knew all about Phoebe being targeted by trolls, *and* she regularly uses her brother's bolthole in Paris! Plus she has all sorts of dodgy contacts from her days partying with oligarchs and rappers, so she's bound to be able to find someone to make a letter bomb.'

'You worked all this out just now?' Mil looked impressed. 'I thought you'd be laid up all day after the amount you shipped last night.'

'*That* was Penny trying to sabotage me because she knew I was onto her!' she explained victoriously, adding for emphasis, 'I'm pretty certain she slipped a Mickey Finn into the Sauvignon to be sure.' She almost believed it.

'Christ, seriously?'

'Good job I'm tough,' she beamed through her cold sweat, hoping he couldn't tell her entire body still felt as though it was being put through a waste disposal unit. 'Now we just have to figure out how to prove it was her.'

Mil looked at her with new-found admiration. 'We'd better act fast. What if she tries to hurt Phoebe again?'

'Exactly!' Juno was secretly thrilled that this put Penny out of the running as a rival for Mil's romantic attention. 'Put some shoes on, we're going round to see her on our way to Hartridge. The Jazz is still at Garage Drum 'n' Brakes so we'll take your bike, shall we?'

'The police said not to go there.'

'They meant *Felix* shouldn't go there, accusing Penny of trying to run down his wife. There's no reason *I* can't pop round as a concerned friend, checking she's okay after her upset last night, is there? We might also bump into the toyboy. Did I tell you I think it's Kenneth Ken Doll?'

'Many times.' He looked amused.

Juno braced herself, knowing she had to ask it. 'Did I embarrass myself last night? Be honest.'

'You were adorable,' he said without hesitation, making Juno flush joyfully. Then he added, 'But you didn't half repeat yourself.'

* * *

The big Italian sports bike roared along Three Bridge Lane, pastries in the back box, Juno clinging onto Mil's wide leather shoulders.

When they drew up outside Hartridge Holt Barn, the big solid wooden gates were shut.

The short journey had added iced bile to Juno's waste disposal nausea. She slithered off the bike and pulled off the helmet to gulp some air while Mil peered over the gate spikes. 'These aren't usually shut. Her car's there. Looks like the driver's door's open.'

'The side gate's not locked.' Juno unlatched it and led the way through, still battling queasiness.

Penny's car was parked at its customary racy angle on the driveway's gravel, its front wing noticeably crumpled. Her ginger cat was lying in the sunlight on top of its roof, tail flicking. It hissed and shot off when Juno crunched closer.

A splash of Cambridge blue by the front tyre caught Juno's eye. 'She's dropped her jumper.'

Except it wasn't just Penny's jumper under the car, she realised as she stooped down to look at it. Penny was lying alongside it, eyes wide open, face lifelessly pale, her body crushed beneath her car's front axle.

Phoebe

'It's our initial belief, upon examining the scene, and with careful consideration, that based upon the amount of alcohol in Ms Fermoy's blood, on balance, she may have been the victim of an unfortunate self-inflicted accident.'

'You can't believe she ran *herself* over?' Phoebe asked DI Mason.

He smiled politely, tramline braces displaying small fragments of the Rich Tea biscuits he'd been slowly nibbling his way through in the Dunford police station interview room. 'I'm telling you that you are free to go, Ms Fredericks.'

'But we both know that's a wildly improbable theory!'

'It seems Ms Fermoy may have just knocked down her pet cat on her driveway.' He checked his notes. 'Damian. The forensic team found a significant amount of ginger fur in the tyre treads. We believe that afterwards she mistakenly put the vehicle in reverse, not park, when she jumped out to check on the injured cat. It then ran over her. For the purposes of clarity, that's the car, not the cat, which ran her over.'

Whilst grateful that the police no longer seemed to suspect she might be implicated in Penny's death, Phoebe didn't buy this explanation. 'At, what, two miles an hour?'

'A heavy blow to the head would suggest it was the tow bar that initially knocked her unconscious, after which the vehicle rolled on top of her, coming to a halt when the front passenger tyre became wedged against her neck and torso, compressing her lungs and ultimately causing death by asphyxia, internal bleeding and spinal compression.'

Phoebe winced. 'That's awful.'

'She's unlikely to have been aware of anything after the initial head injury.'

'And Damian?'

'Is missing. Badly injured animals often crawl somewhere quiet and hidden.'

'The tow bar knocked Penny out, you say?'

'Yes' – he checked his notes – 'a Witter detachable tow bar to be precise. It had tissue fragments and blood on it concurrent with such an impact.'

'Who closed the gates?'

'It's quite possible that Ms Fermoy closed them herself before continuing along the drive. It's a lengthy gravel approach, so that would save her walking back.'

'She was meeting a boyfriend late last night. We think it might be a man called Kain, or Kenneth? Have you contacted him?'

'If he is relevant, I can assure you he is being spoken to.'

'His number must be on her phone. She messaged him from the book group.'

He nodded. Something about his slow, measured blinks told her there was a problem with this.

'Is her phone missing?'

'With respect, Ms Fredericks, I have warned you before about this. Please remember, in essence, who is conducting this investigation, at the end of the day.'

Phoebe nodded, knowing exactly who she trusted to investigate.

* * *

Less than an hour later, the Village Detectives met urgently once again in the Hartridge kitchen.

'Doesn't it seem odd,' Phoebe addressed them, 'that Penny Fermoy dies on her driveway less than a fortnight after Craig the postie is killed on our doorstep, and the police are convinced *both* are self-inflicted?'

'That's all about manipulating crime statistics,' muttered Felix.

'Freddy, you said at first that you thought the police were

right about Craig?' Juno pointed out, still red eyed and jittery from the day's trauma, shredding a tissue in her fingers.

'I said I *wanted* them to be right,' Phoebe explained carefully, 'but now that it seems likely the two deaths are connected, I believe they're copping out.'

'In fairness, they're very short-staffed,' Mil defended, then chuckled. 'Was that a pun, "copping" out?'

'What makes you think the deaths are connected?' Felix looked at her askance, tense and argumentative.

Phoebe wished she could offer more than a lame, 'Gut instinct.'

He let out a dissatisfied sigh.

'I think you're right, Freddy,' Juno rallied, a dependable furnace of support. 'The coincidence does need thinking about.'

'Exactly.' She looked at the three faces in turn. 'Starting with what they had in common? We know Penny's online retail habit made Craig an ally and regular visitor at Hartridge Holt Barn. He delivered lots of parcels and liked watching her opening them.'

'His mother worked for Penny on and off,' Juno offered, extracting a fresh tissue from her pocket.

'They both liked books,' said Mil eagerly.

'Penny didn't read books,' Phoebe dismissed.

They all fell silent.

Juno blew her nose loudly.

'It's not a lot to go on.' Felix said it first, testily unconvinced.

'I *know* they're connected.' Phoebe stood up, frustrated by her lack of evidence and his lack of faith.

'And you're right in the middle of it, Freddy,' Juno fretted, dabbing her eyes.

'Am I, though?'

'The parcel that killed Craig was addressed to you!' The eyes grew wetter.

'We don't know that. The label was destroyed, no tracking for it has been found.'

'What about the funeral and memorial notices?' Felix pointed out impatiently. 'They were.'

'And Penny tried to run over you last night!' Juno gulped.

'Assuming it was her, I'm not sure she even saw me. She was already very drunk at the book group. She'd have been way over the limit, and the road was pitch black. She could have been answering the phone or lighting a cigarette and swerved off the lane whilst doing it.'

Felix shook his head. 'You're forgetting the funeral invitations, the newspaper death notice and OhFeelYa—'

'What if some of that's entirely unrelated?'

'Craig had a garage wall devoted to you,' Felix argued.

'To Dorothy De'Ath,' she countered swiftly.

'Do I know about this?' Juno asked, baffled.

'Eh?' Mil looked equally so.

'The police showed us pictures. I'm sure I told you.' As soon as she said it, Phoebe realised she hadn't.

'Complete with vintage porn stiffies,' Felix laughed hollowly.

Seeing their open mouths, Phoebe explained, 'Craig had fact checked some 1920s erotica mentioned in one of the books, but he was far more pedantic about the steam locomotives,' she added, 'and grammar.'

Juno pulled a sympathetic face.

'Do you have any of the pictures?' asked Mil. Then, when the others looked at him doubtfully, added, 'Might hold some clues?'

'Trust me, they don't,' Phoebe muttered. 'There's probably more useful material on those things.' She pointed at the two little security cameras Mil had brought in to charge up.

'Brilliant thinking!' Juno reached for them.

'There's nothing on those,' Mil scoffed.

'Might there be, though?' Juno looked excited, turning them over. 'They were on Alan's cottage before, weren't they? The micro-cards in these probably have months of comings and goings on the lane.'

'These cameras were taken down just before Craig died, though, remember?' Mil pointed out.

'Still, worth a look.' Juno was ejecting the cards. 'Can I put them in your laptop, Freddy? Eric showed me how to do this with my camera card.'

'Be my guest,' said Phoebe, frustrated that they were getting sidelined, especially when Felix and Mil both started to tell Juno what she was doing wrong:

'That's the HDMI slot.'

'Other way up. That's it.'

'Look for an E drive.'

Unable to take any more, Phoebe stood up and stalked off to let the dogs out.

Standing at the back door, grateful for sunshine and terriers jumping on molehills, she could hear the others still grappling with technology inside.

'Okay – oh, no! Now it says card not detected. It's not working at all.'

'Take it out and breathe on it.'

'Rub it on your sleeve.'

'Still nothing! Hang on, yes! It says it's password protected!'

Phoebe looked down at the back step, picturing Craig there, his eager pink balloon face frozen in shock as he fell backwards.

Instinct had always told her that Craig hadn't made the IED that killed him, no matter how convincingly DI Mason's dogmatic logic and her need to feel safe had tried to sell her closure. Anxiety and guilt had gnawed away inside her since his death, the sense that she would never shake the invisible adversaries from her past, nor the threat she'd put her family under. But what had just happened to Penny had changed that. Phoebe no longer thought the killer might be after her. She felt a different guilt now, a liberating debt of gratitude and burning injustice. One that demanded answers.

In the kitchen, she could hear the micro-card mini drama continuing, Mil's deep voice suggesting, 'I'll call Alan, shall I?'

'Even better, I'll call Eric!' Juno insisted brightly. 'Here we go – hi, Eric, baby! Yes, yes, just having a "computer says no" moment. Can you? It's Phoebe's laptop, but I'm sure she won't mind. Hang on, I'll put the micro data card thing back in. Yes, it's password protected. No, not my camera this time, another one. What's the website I need to type in again? Wait, it's on airplane mode. That's better! Give me the address…'

Phoebe jumped as a pair of warm arms were slipped around her waist, Felix's chin coming to rest on her shoulder, his voice a comforting husk of love and apology. 'You're safe. I won't let anything happen to you.'

He still thought the killer was after her, she realised.

They could hear Juno chattering away on the phone in the kitchen, asking her son: 'Haven't you got some clever AI software that goes through CCTV footage and looks for postal vans?'

'And speeding Audis,' Mil added loudly.

In an instant, it made so much sense, Phoebe felt foolish for not seeing it earlier.

Grabbing Felix's hand, she stalked back inside. 'Forget the sodding camera cards!' she shouted, making Juno and Mil start in surprise and Felix's fingers tighten in hers.

Phoebe realised she might have overdone the dramatic entrance. But now that she had their attention, she demanded, 'What if Penny was the only intended target all along?'

'Who wanted to kill Penny?' Mil asked, flummoxed.

Beside him, Juno told Eric to call her back if he found anything and rang off, pushing the laptop aside. 'Why?'

'We might need convincing.' Felix sat back down at the table, annoyed that she'd interrupted his conquering hero overture.

Phoebe sat opposite, setting out her theory as it came to her. 'The murderer sent Penny the poison pen bomb, but Craig delivered a similar-looking one to her that was addressed to me by mistake, containing health gummies. His scanner was broken and Penny had a lot of packages that day, plus he was too eager to see her unbox all her goodies to double check. Also, he had just got his new electric van that week, both exciting and probably a bit distracting. When he got to me with *her* package – the letter bomb intended for Penny – he was eager to hear all my thoughts on his Dorothy De'Ath revisions, so maybe was not as careful at checking what he was delivering to whom as usual either. If the IED was on a timer, it might have been set to go off once the murderer thought Penny was alone with it. Hence it went off in his hands here.'

'Bit far-fetched.' Juno looked doubtful as well as tearful. 'Especially trusting the post on timing, with all the Royal Mail delays.'

'Poison pens for Penny? Isn't it fitting?'

'I pointed that one out ages ago,' Juno said pettily, blowing her nose. 'Anyway, murderers usually have the same modus operandi, don't they? Poor Penny was killed by being run over, not poison penned.'

'The MO might seem different,' Phoebe elaborated, thinking of her Dorothy De'Ath library ripper, 'but both deaths were at a private home, near a front door, employing a mechanical device, not a conventional murder weapon like a knife, a hammer – gun even – so our killer is hands-off, likes gadgets and cars.'

Mil cleared his throat at this, asking, 'You think they jumped in Penny's Audi while she was checking if she'd knocked down her cat and then drove over her?'

'Possibly. Or they may have already been in the car?'

'Kenneth Ken Doll!' Juno gasped, hands flying to her mouth.

'She told you she was meeting someone that night.' Mil nodded.

Felix had stayed quiet throughout this exchange, fingertips rattling slowly on the table. Now, he asked lightly: 'Meeting who, where, when?'

'Exactly!' Phoebe rattled her nails on the table too, a double-handed Rachmaninoff crescendo to his 'Chopsticks'. 'Penny almost ran me over on Three Bridge Lane not long before midnight, but what had she been doing between book club and then, and where did she go afterwards? Was she alone? Felix didn't see or hear her car when he got off the London train around the same time, and yet she was driving like a lunatic towards the village, and the level-crossing barriers were down.'

'Not a thing.' Felix crossed his arms over his chest, stashing his own tapping fingers tight in his armpits.

'The police put Penny's time of death at between four and six in the morning, possibly later,' said Phoebe, 'but certainly not long before you two found her.' She looked at Juno and Mil. 'What exactly do you remember? Was the car engine still running?'

'No, it was off,' Mil said gruffly, 'no lights on or anything. It was about three quarters of the way up the drive. The driver's door was open.'

'And Penny was squashed underneath!' Juno gulped, covering her mouth again, big grey eyes tearful above her hands.

'Do you remember noticing the tow bar?' Phoebe asked.

Mil shook his head. 'Can't remember Penny ever towing anything. She was no caravanner.'

'This isn't the moment to discuss car accessories, Freddy.'

'What about ginger cat fur? Was there any cat fur under or around the car?'

'The cat was *on* the car!' Juno insisted. 'The police didn't seem to believe me when I told them that. They say it's missing. But I saw it and it looked fine.'

'I didn't see a cat,' Mil admitted.

'It ran off when it spotted your bike helmet.'

'Any sign of trauma, blood, tyre tracks?' Phoebe asked Juno.

'Not that I remember.' She chewed her lip doubtfully.

'We need to go there and take a look.' Phoebe stood up again.

'I can't,' Mil apologised, looking at his watch. 'The pub will be getting busy and Albie doing his nut 'cos it's only him and the part-timers. He keeps complaining I'm becoming one too. Besides, the rugby starts soon.'

'Aren't the police still crawling all over Penny's place?' Felix glanced at his watch too.

'Not any more,' Mil reported. 'When I rode past coming here, it was deserted. There's nobody there.'

'Apart from the cat,' Juno pointed out.

'If it's still alive,' said Mil.

'Damian,' Phoebe said, remembering its name, 'as in Antichrist.'

'As in Damian Lewis,' Mil clarified. 'Came from the same litter as the one you're looking after at Noel Benn's place,' he told Juno. 'Rachel's big ginger mog is the mum. Rachel named them all after celebrity redheads, even the black and white ones. They're all over the village.'

Juno gasped in horror. 'Kevin's *brother* might have been run over? We must go and find him!'

'It's not *Saving Private Ryan*, Juno,' sighed Phoebe, but Juno was already speedily gathering her things.

Mil was strapping on his helmet, flipping up the visor. 'Keep me posted, guys. I'll see what I hear on the grapevine in the pub. Everyone will be talking about it.'

'Poor Penny!' Juno looked weepy again. 'It's too late to save her, but we can save Damian. Can we take the Porsche to your gateway?' she asked Phoebe excitedly.

'It's only got two seats.'

'I'll give Felix a lift on the bike,' offered Mil.

Phoebe said nothing, although she suspected this would involve taking her husband all the way to the pub where he might accidentally have a drink and watch rugby before remembering his detective duties. She was quietly grateful. He was more shaken than he was letting on by Penny's death, and preoccupied by his film's precarious timeline and finances. His tetchy, distracted mood wasn't helping.

She went to shut down her laptop. 'Juno, what on earth has your son done to this?'

'Oh, he said it needed updating! Nothing major. New operating system, I think he said. And he's given you Dorothy De'Ath wallpaper as a thank you. Eric does everything remotely. Amazing.'

'Are all the files there?' Phoebe asked, checking in a panic, amazed to find they were and that her computer was at least twice as fast as it had been before. 'How does he even *do* that?'

'My digital native is getting restless,' Juno joked. 'He's an IT genius, a command prompt alchemist. But I suppose we all think our netizen children are demi-gods, don't we?'

'Say that again?' Felix demanded, suddenly looking animated.

'That we all think our netizen children are demi-gods?' Juno glowed pinkly at her rhetoric.

Putting his hands on his head, Felix nodded slowly, turning

around on the spot, momentarily lost in thought. 'You said as much in Paris, Juno, but I didn't make the connection. We're looking for a Gen Z digital native. OhFeelYa is an algorithm alchemist.'

'Command prompt alchemist,' Juno corrected. 'You're surely not suggesting it's Eric?'

'Well, we know it wasn't Penny,' said Phoebe, telling her husband, 'Go to the pub with Mil, see what the regulars are saying about Penny's death. A few beers might help you see that I'm right about her being the main target.'

'Now that,' Mil agreed inside his helmet, 'is my kind of alchemy.'

18

JUNO

'Here, puss, puss, puss!' Juno peered into another laurel bush. Hartridge Holt Barn had a lot of them, a positive Monty Pythonesque shrubbery. 'Damian! Here, puss!'

On the drive behind her, Phoebe was crouching down examining the gravel. 'There's definitely fur here!'

Juno couldn't bring herself to look. It was her fault the poor cat was probably dead. Why hadn't she spotted it was hurt? They crawled away to die in quiet, secluded spots, didn't they?

She peered behind a rhododendron.

That's where she spotted something lifeless and ginger amongst the ground elder and screamed.

Phoebe sprinted to her side in moments, putting an arm around her.

Eyes squeezed shut, tears eking already, Juno couldn't look, her hands over her heart, chest aching. 'It was still alive when we found Penny. I could have rescued it, taken it to the vet, saved its life.'

'It's a Paddington Bear, Juno.'

Juno opened her eyes. 'Are you sure?'

Lying in the bushes was a cuddly toy. He was missing his duffle coat, hat and wellies, but it was unmistakeably Paddington.

'Damian Lewis might be alive!' Juno cried delightedly.

Picking up the toy, Phoebe examined it closely, carrying it back to the driveway.

'This is the same ginger fluff on the gravel, and I'll bet that's what they found on Penny's car tyres too. It wasn't cat hair at all. It's Paddington's fake fur.'

Juno hurried after her. 'Could Paddington have been lying on the drive when Penny came back? She ran over it, thought it was Damian and jumped out to check.'

'If so, who put it there? And how did it end up in the shrubbery?' Phoebe was examining it thoughtfully. 'Let's keep looking round.'

'Damian! Here, puss, puss.' Juno made her way alongside the house towards the back garden while Phoebe checked through an open-fronted oak-framed car port, one bay of which housed a small, dusty pony trailer.

'Explains the tow bar!' she called back, examining it.

'She probably used it to go to the bottle bank.' Juno moved out of sight alongside the house, finding a row of wheely bins in a wooden lean-to, the glass recycling brim-full. 'Here, puss, puss!'

She heard a sharp slapping sound behind her and spun round.

It came from a side door into the house. There was a cat flap in it that was still swinging.

'Damian!'

Kneeling down, Juno peered through the cat flap.

In the centre of a quarry-tiled floor in what appeared to be a utility room, ginger tom Damian peered back, puffed up to maximum volume.

'I'm a friend,' Juno pleaded.

He backed behind a laundry basket, hissing.

Juno straightened up and looked around her.

Several large terracotta herb pots were playing sentry to the door, mostly full of cigarette butts, although a spindly-looking rosemary was still clinging on to life.

Knowing that no householder was stupid enough to put spare keys under plant pots these days, Juno half-heartedly lifted the nearest one.

There was a key underneath it.

She hurriedly took it to Phoebe, who was still clanking round in the car port. 'I've located Damian and the spare key, Freddy!'

'And look what I found!' Phoebe appeared from behind the pony trailer carrying a wicker hamper. 'It's a pet carrier!' She held it up to reveal a lopsided front grille, its hinges broken.

'Well, Penny did have a cat.'

'Exactly. It was in the trailer, and very recently occupied I'd say. There's fresh treats inside.'

'Maybe she took Damian to the vets?'

'Or somebody caught him and stashed him away in this while they planted a naked Paddington Bear on the drive in the hope that Penny might think it was her dead cat.'

'No!' Juno gasped. 'Who would do that?'

'A murderer? Let's investigate the house.'

'Should we, though? It's trespass.'

'It's cat welfare.' Phoebe plucked the key from her fingers and led the way. 'We have a duty to make sure Damian is okay.'

Juno followed guiltily, crouching down as she walked so that she couldn't be seen from the lane. 'Shouldn't Felix or Mil be here? This could be dangerous.'

'Let them pursue other lines of enquiry. Felix obviously has something on his mind.'

'I honestly don't know why you put up with him sometimes.'

'He's like the most loveable, adoring, delinquent gundog you'll ever meet. Maddening, but unswervingly loyal. Completely irreplaceable.'

'You know, I'm starting to think perhaps I'm more of a cat person after all,' Juno reflected as Phoebe tried the key in the side door. It opened.

Inside, one wall of the utility room was stacked with white goods and cupboards to either side of a Belfast sink. The remaining three walls were layered floor to ceiling with coats and boots, along with ski equipment, a body board, riding gear and even lacrosse and hockey stick. A wonky sign above the door leading into the rest of the converted barn read *Sexy Women Have Messy Houses*.

Once Damian had been coaxed out of hiding with cat food, weaving his way gratefully around their ankles, and his health assessed as optimum, the pair quickly scouted around the house.

'It's huge,' gasped Juno. 'Penny lived here alone?'

'She had a lot of friends to stay, from what I gather. Occasional live-in lovers, though none lasted.'

'There must be clues everywhere!' Juno took in the mountains of correspondence, shopping bags, handbags, newspapers, notebooks and open packages. The walls throughout the barn conversion were covered with poster-sized photos of Penny partying, holidaying, skiing, riding and pouting on endless red carpets, along with professional fashion shoots and magazine covers. None featured Boozy, Juno noticed.

'I had no idea she was so prolific.' She studied a picture of Penny in her twenties wearing a dress made entirely of compact discs. 'I thought she was exaggerating.'

'Penny was a big media star,' Phoebe said, leading the way back through the double-height hall to check another side room.

'An original It Girl before *Made in Chelsea* blew the posh myth. Let's see what else we can find.'

But apart from deducing that Penny had been horrifically untidy, kept almost no food in the house and had enough clothes to change three times a day for a year without wearing the same thing twice, there was no obvious pointer as to who might wish to do her harm, or why.

They found a recent nest of floor cushions, wine bottles, brimming ashtray and open DVD cases in front of a vast flat-screen TV.

'Who watches DVDs any more?' Juno picked one up, turning it over.

'These all have the same label,' Phoebe pointed out, squatting down to look too. 'They've been converted from VHS so must be really old.'

One was still paused in the machine. They played it. A startlingly young, pretty Penny appeared on screen in what was clearly a home movie, laughing with a group of other teenage girls all in bootlace-strapped bias-cut ballgowns. Arms around one another, they posed for the camera before collapsing into giggles, joyfully fresh-faced and carefree.

'She was lonely and depressed and living in the past,' Juno sighed. 'Rachel said as much last night. She never grew up beyond her teenage years.'

Phoebe sat back on her haunches. 'But who would want to kill her?'

'I know I only met her a few times, but I found her quite hard to like.'

'Men always liked her. Felix wouldn't hear a bad word about her.'

'Were they ever—'

'No, I'm certain not. She just seemed to attract male loyalty. Look at Mil. Look at Boozy. He let her live here rent-free.'

'It's got to be a lover who killed her, surely?' Juno gazed around the beautiful home, trashed like a student flat. 'A jealous ex maybe?'

'We need to find out who she was seeing.'

'I still think Kenneth Ken Doll might be "Kain",' Juno reminded her. 'If she threw all her toyboys out of the pram, one might have wanted revenge?' She started to flick through the DVDs. 'Could he feature on one of these?'

'Way too vintage,' said Phoebe. 'But you have a point. A crime of passion may have killed her. And nowadays, most lovers leave a digital footprint.'

Upstairs they found a scuffed pink MacBook in the biggest, messiest bedroom.

'I could get Eric to look at what's on this?' Juno suggested.

'Too risky.' Phoebe started peeking in drawers. 'We're already bending the law way too much being in here.'

'Surprising the police haven't taken this away with them.' Juno tried to turn it on, but the battery was dead and there was no sign of a charger beneath the piles of discarded clothes and shoes. 'Especially if you're right and her phone's missing.'

'I recognise this.' Phoebe picked up a feathery fascinator. 'Penny was wearing it the day I caught her putting things in our post box. Said she was off to the races on a date.' She looked around and located a coral-pink suit, feeling in its pockets. 'Betting slips, members' enclosure badge...'

'Could that date have been with Kenneth Ken Doll?' asked Juno.

'...Memory stick.' Phoebe extracted a thumb drive and studied it with interest.

They both froze as a hoarse voice below shouted, 'Who's there?'

'Shit!' Juno turned to Phoebe in a panic.

Phoebe pressed her finger to her lips and crept to the door to peer out, edging onto the galleried landing to peer down through the glass screen. Juno tiptoed behind her. She caught a waft of Georgio Armani's Sí.

Seeing a figure moving in the hallway below, both women shrank back before they were seen.

At the bottom of the stairs, burgundy haired and red eyed, Denise Jackman was brandishing a lacrosse stick in one hand, a large kitchen knife in the other.

* * *

Phoebe

Phoebe could tell Juno was going to panic. There was a quivering energy, a bunching of muscles, the almost audible pings of tiny hairs springing up. Then came a tiny, squeaky yowling sound in the back of her throat, oddly kitten like.

The woman in the hallway below hadn't spotted them, now stalking into the sitting room, shouting, 'Who's there? I know you're in here somewhere!'

Phoebe pushed Juno back into the bedroom. She was still making strange yowling sounds. 'Shh!'

'She's going to kill us,' Juno breathed. '*She's* the killer. Why didn't we guess?'

'Who is it?' Phoebe breathed back, peering round the door.

'Craig's mum,' Juno whispered. 'I should have suspected something when I overheard her ranting at the beauty salon. Everyone knows Denise is difficult and explosive, even her best friend Rachel says it. The reason Denise has been raging round telling everyone her son was innocent is because she *knew exactly* who made that letter bomb.'

'*She* made it?'

'No, Penny did! Penny was trying to harm you but killed Craig by mistake. Then Denise revenged her son's death by killing Penny. Now she'll kill us for finding out!'

'*Who's up there?*' shouted a voice from the stairs.

'She's heard us!' Juno squeaked. 'That's your fault, Freddy.'

'Shh, you're the one talking.'

'You were the one asking me questions!'

'We need a plan,' Phoebe breathed, glancing round.

'Hide in a wardrobe?' Juno suggested.

'Come out!' warned the voice on the landing. 'I have a knife!'

'You hide,' Phoebe whispered. 'Message Mil and Felix. And record the sound while I talk to her.'

Nodding in terror, Juno dived behind a hanging rail of party dresses.

Phoebe stepped into the middle of the room. 'I'm in here!'

'Who is it?' demanded the rasping voice on the landing, trembling slightly.

'Phoebe, Penny's neighbour from Hartridge Court.'

'I know who you are! The cranky writer. What are you doing here?'

'I came to check on the cat.'

'Up here?' Her face appeared around the door – red-veined and accusing, with just a touch of Jack Nicholson in *The Shining*.

'I was looking for him up here, for Damian. Who are you and why are *you* here?'

'Denise Jackman, I run errands for Penny. *I'm* here to check on the cat.'

'With a knife?'

'Actually, it's an icing spatula.' She held it up and Phoebe realised it was. 'I pulled it off the magnetic wall thing without realising. I thought you might be a burglar. An opportunist, maybe, who heard she was dead and wanted to—' Her face crumpled momentarily. She pulled herself together. 'Take advantage.'

'I promise that's not me.'

'You poking about playing detective, are you?'

'Well, I...'

'I heard that's what you do, you and that gobby fat little woman from Wheeler's Yard who did the last quiz. Well, I promise you won't find anything up here.'

Deep in the wardrobe, Juno sneezed.

'I think I just did.' Phoebe pulled the dresses aside. 'Gotcha!'

Juno shrank back as Denise stepped further into the room, pointing her lacrosse stick accusingly. 'What's she doing in there?'

'Hiding, duh?' Juno snarled.

Phoebe looked at her sharply, surprised by her tone.

'So *have* you found anything suspicious?' demanded Denise, an imposing barrel of a woman in an Iron Maiden T-shirt, with frizzy burgundy hair and a rose tattoo on her forearm. She didn't look like someone to mess with.

Phoebe shook her head, holding tightly on to the USB stick in her pocket.

But Juno had fewer qualms, sniping, 'You pointing that knife looks pretty damned suspicious from here, Denise!'

'Icing spatula, Juno,' Phoebe muttered, hoping she'd calm down.

Instead, Juno marched out of the wardrobe on a mission. 'You murdered Penny after she killed Craig by mistake, didn't you, Denise?'

'You what?' Denise looked confused.

Too late, Phoebe realised that in Juno's imagination, she was standing by the drawing room fire with all the suspects gathered on chintz armchairs.

'Penny wanted Phoebe out of the big house.' Juno folded her arms. 'That's why she had that letter bomb made which she gave to Craig to deliver, but it exploded before he could. It was only intended to maim nastily, but instead it killed him. Last night, you killed Penny to get revenge for your son's death, planting a cuddly toy on the drive knowing she'd mistake it for her cat, then waiting for her to get out of her car to check before jumping in to run over her. Now you're back to dispose of the evidence. Well, we found Paddington Bear and the cat carrier you used to stash Damian out of sight! The police are on their way! The game's over, Denise. Put the knife down.'

'It's an icing spatula.' Phoebe closed her eyes in despair.

Beside her, Denise let out a long, world-weary sigh. 'Are you having a go at me 'cos I called you fat?'

'*Gobby* and fat. And you really can't weaponise words like that any more, Denise. It's cruel.'

'*I've* always been gobby and fat and don't mind saying it!' She gave a cynical laugh.

'That's your choice, Denise. Some of us are genetic victims; I do not identify with those adjectives. Please take them back.'

'Well, you just bloody accused me of being a chuffing murderer!' Denise pointed out, turning to Phoebe. 'Is she for real?'

'Why don't we all go downstairs and have a cup of tea while we wait for the police to arrive?' she suggested.

'Actually, there's no reception up here,' Juno said in an artificially high voice, 'so I didn't call them.'

'That's a relief,' said Denise, 'because I didn't kill poor Pen. But do I know where the teabags are.'

* * *

Downstairs, they sat in Penny's messy kitchen drinking black tea because there was no milk. Damian appeared, mewing plaintively, springing straight onto Denise's lap and head-butting her affectionately.

'I always look after this place when Penny's away,' she explained. 'I've worked for her for years on and off. Can't believe she's gone. First Craig, now her.' She looked momentarily bereft, jowly face forlorn, small eyes wet.

Juno went to fetch her a hunk of kitchen roll, ripping off a sheet for herself to blow her own nose before steering a wide berth around Damian to deliver the rest. 'You know, I definitely have a cat allergy.'

Phoebe signalled her to be quiet as Denise dabbed her eyes and moaned: 'Penny had so much to look forward to; she and Gigi had big plans for the Hartridge cultural hub. Boozy Faulkland really did tell her that's what he wanted. I heard him, more than once. There was a letter too. Penny was going to prove it. I was helping her.'

'You worked for the estate, didn't you?'

'Few years ago now. Before Mr Faulkland passed. I answered emails, kept the website up to date. That's where I met Penny. Nothing I wouldn't do for that woman.'

'When did you last talk to her?' asked Juno.

'A couple of days ago. She'd promised her lawyers would clear Craig's name. She said she knew stuff that would prove he was blameless, and the only justice would be to expose the real targets and make the village safe.'

Phoebe guessed that meant leverage to get her and Felix out of Hartridge. She pulled the USB stick out of her pocket and examined it. 'Do you recognise it, Denise?'

'Can't say I do.'

'Probably just music for the car,' suggested Juno.

'Penny liked CDs,' sighed Denise. 'Roxy Music mostly. Played that to death.' Realising what she'd said, her expression darkened. 'I'm certain what happened to her was no accident,' she told them, her voice cracking, mopping her eyes again. 'Just like my Craig. I don't care what the police say. They were innocent victims. Someone did this to them.'

'I agree,' said Phoebe firmly.

'Her drinking had got so bad again.' Denise shook her head sadly. 'She's been in rehab that many times, and she'd run up debts on all her cards, burned through her trust fund every month. She couldn't help herself; she was like a child. Her family washed their hands of her years ago. She was so desperate for cash, maybe she got involved in something stupid.' Denise got up to fetch a fresh strip of kitchen roll, Damian riding on her shoulder. 'That new boyfriend of hers might know something. Never trusted him, Kevin or Kyle or something.'

'Kain?' asked Juno.

'That's the name. Penny liked how exciting it was, how unpredictable. They never met for long – she'd fetch him from the station, they'd spend a couple of hours together, then he'd push off.'

'Like a gigolo,' Juno whistled, glancing at Phoebe.

Denise sat back down, voice hushed. 'Penny let slip he was some sort of deep cover, military-trained spook, a "sleeper not a keeper", she said. He told everyone he worked in rewilding landscape design, but that was just a cover story apparently.'

'So she *did* fall for it,' Juno sighed. Chin lifting, she squared her shoulders. 'I'll talk to him. Except we never exchanged contacts,' she groaned.

'I suppose you can message him on the dating app,' suggested Phoebe.

'I deleted my profile.' Juno took a deep, martyred breath. 'It's going to have to be Gilbert and Sullivan in the Godlington walled garden.'

'Is that a euphemism?'

'It's an outdoor event,' Juno clarified. 'And it puts me right beside Kenneth Ken Doll.'

Phoebe listened, astonished, as Juno explained that her mother and Kenneth Campbell's father were eager to set them up. 'Mum's only doing it because Dennis wants to curry favour with Eugene Campbell, who is only doing it to try to stop his undomesticated middle-aged bachelor son hanging around like a hyena waiting to inherit. Ken Doll's going through the motions to keep his wealthy parents onside, and now I'm back in the game to go deep undercover on behalf of the Village Detectives.'

'Are you sure about this?'

'There will be a bunch of pensioners there. It's light opera. What could go wrong?'

19

JUNO

'Mum, is the invitation to Gilbert and Sullivan still open? Please say it is!'

'Pusscat, you are *incorrigible!*'

'I can bring your car back when I come. And I'll bring deli treats. Will Kenneth be there with the Campbells?'

'You may have missed the boat there. Last I heard, Pam's friend Spike was laying on a recently divorced niece for him.'

Juno posted a message on the Village Detectives WhatsApp group that evening rounding up everything they knew:

> Bit of a long shot, but we – well, Phoebe really – believe Penny may have been killed by being duped into thinking she'd run over Damian Lewis the cat. The killer hid in the bushes, then when she got out of the car to check, they jumped in the car and reversed over her.

We reconnoitred the house and found a Paddington Bear toy naked in the shrubbery, which we think the killer used as 'bait' on the drive to look like a dead cat. There was also a pet carrier in Penny's pony trailer, which could be where the real cat was kept hidden. And Phoebe found a USB, but it's password protected. (What is it with all these conscientious security measures? It ruins the drama.)

Eric says he'll look at it, but first he's playing a League of Legends qualifying tournament and doesn't want to be disturbed. Meanwhile, his software bots found nothing useful on Alan's old CCTV. There's part of one night missing, but that was weeks ago and probably because the battery went flat.

Eric also checked out Penny's online activity. Her socials are as messy as her house. She drunk posted *a lot*.

He can't find a link between her and OhFeelYa, ditto the 'stiffy' invitations, although the memorial one arrived at the same time as Penny dropped off a parish magazine. (Beth Trascott delivers them to that side of the village, so Penny must have recycled her own as a ruse.)

Denise Jackman – Craig's mum – came to the house when we were there. She has her own keys and did favours for Penny, who she got to know when she worked for Boozy. She confirmed he wrote a Letter of Wishes which stated that Hartridge Court should become a charitable arts centre after his death, but it's gone missing. I've googled and they're not legally binding in the UK anyway.

> The last person to see Penny alive was almost
> certainly her part-time lover 'Kain'. Believed to
> be Kenneth Campbell, a dating app fraudster
> who had multiple pseudonyms, pretends he's a
> spy, lies about his age and charges vulnerable
> women for sex. We believe he was with her that
> night, but for how long? Very possibly our killer.

> I plan to confront him tomorrow in the
> Godlington walled garden, where he'll be
> watching Gilbert and Sullivan. Wish me luck!

Mil was the first to reply with a voice note: 'Not on your own, you won't! I'm coming with you. Albie can cover for me.'

Which Juno found touching, replying with a long row of hug emojis.

She phoned her mother to ask if they could get another ticket for the al fresco performance. 'Mil's super-keen – is it the one with the pirates?'

Judy promised she would reserve another place, and what clever thinking to bring someone dishy along herself now Spike's niece was lined up for Kenneth. 'Always a good idea to show them you're in demand. It's *Patience*, Pusscat.'

'I am very patient.'

'The operetta is called *Patience*. It's about lovesick aesthetes, like the Pre-Raphaelites. Your father was a glorious Bunthorne in the Grosvenor Light Operatic Society when we were first together.' She started singing, '*You must lie upon the daisies and discourse in novel phrases of your complicated state of mind!*'

'I'll try,' Juno promised, although she was starting to feel increasingly nervous about the task ahead. Her complicated state of mind was in knots.

To her further consternation, Felix had posted on the WhatsApp group now, saying that he thought he'd finally worked out exactly who OhFeelYa was, but to prove it he would need to go undercover on a hen weekend in Buxton Crescent Spa.

Wish me luck. I'll let you know if I'm right.

Juno sent a row of shocked emojis, along with a bath, spring, stars and a candle for a spa.

A voice note landed in the group chat from Mil while she was typing:

'Felix, mate, you get the *best* gigs! Want to swap?' he guffawed, which hurt Juno a little if she was honest.

All Phoebe contributed was:

Good luck.

Juno couldn't help feeling a little underwhelmed by this, although she had a shrewd suspicion the Jonathan and Jennifer Hart double act amongst their number must have already pillow talked it all through. She liked to envisage the Sylvians as the glamorous married couple from the eighties TV show *Hart to Hart*, chasing murderers in sportscars then de-briefing naughtily in bed afterwards. Jonathan and Felix both rushed in head first, she recalled.

She called Phoebe straight away. 'Who does he think OhFeelYa is?'

'No idea. He won't say because he's already got it wrong three times. He's being maddeningly secretive. Probably thinks it adds to his mystique. That or he just wants a mini spa break.'

Juno could tell Phoebe was deeply worried, always at her most flippant when hyper-anxious.

'Now tell me' – she was also tellingly keen to change the subject – 'how are you going to tackle Kenneth Ken Doll?'

'What if he really did it?' Juno bleated, harbouring plenty of anxieties of her own.

'At the moment,' Phoebe pointed out drily, 'he's our only suspect.'

* * *

Phoebe

'What a miraculous recovery you've made, Georgiana! We thought that that adder had you gasping your last, darling. Do you remember anything at all about that night?'

'Oh, Dee, it's all a frightful blur. But I do remember a scent. It was jolly distinctive and rather overpowering.'

'Could it have been Molinard Habanita?'

'You know, I think it might.'

Even more racked by insomnia than usual, Phoebe had barely slept, a frenzied moth of a thought flapping around in her head, constantly seeking light in which to see it.

Pulling on her running gear at the first glow of a steely dawn and putting earbuds in to listen to her favourite playlist, she pounded through the woods to the river. The dogs bounded at her heels as she crossed the bridge and on past the church into the village, thinking back over the past few days.

They were missing something obvious; she was certain of it. From what Juno had told her, Kenneth was supremely shady. But he was also so disconnected, so fly-by-night, literally. He seemed to be a strange overgrown man child, just as Penny was a middle-aged bratty teenager, both seeking instant gratification. They'd probably been perfectly suited.

The village was still slumbering. For once she didn't cut along

Witch's Broom but carried on up Church End, passing the archway into Wheeler's Yard where Juno would still be asleep in her little flat.

She turned right to run alongside the village green, past the village's second pub, the historic thatched Golden Balloon where automatic waterers were flooding the hanging baskets, splashing a deluge onto the pavement below. Phoebe crossed over the Dunford road past the war memorial to continue around The Green, letting the terriers race onto it to rough and tumble, yapping shrilly as they examined molehills.

She had no idea what Felix was up to, but that came as nothing new. She just hoped he was safe. Buxton was hundreds of miles away, and yet Phoebe's overwhelming sense remained that they were missing something right under their noses here in Inkbury.

Whistling the terriers to heel, both dogs now muddy-faced and smiling, Phoebe was about to turn left back towards the High Street when she caught sight of the allotments on the opposite side of the lane and ground to a halt.

Hemlock.

Juno had told her there was hemlock in there.

The pen nibs in the letter bomb had been full of it.

Still thinking hard, she ran the last side of The Green then crossed the road again to pound along the silent, dawn-dappled High Street where some of the village's oldest cottages leant against one another at drunken angles.

The package full of pens had been so precisely engineered, so intricate, undoubtedly the work of a skilled expert. It made no sense that this was the same person who had run over Penny, and yet she kept returning to the idea it had to be.

She turned into Three Bridge Lane, so preoccupied that an electric car gliding behind her had to beep for her to get out of the way, its driver waving an exasperated hand and mouthing, 'Get out of the road!'

She waved in apology, pulling out her earphones before unhooking the leads from around her neck to secure the dogs into them, aware that the early birds and commuters were starting to get moving.

Not so the inhabitants of The Barton Arms, which sat sleepily on the bank of the River Dunnett, its white paintwork bathed by golden sunlight as she crossed the famous bridge beside it, still thinking hard. Over the canal, where the moored narrowboats were nose-to-tail prow to stern, dew-kissed and snoozing, then over the silent level crossing, grinding to a halt again on the other side, remembering the night that Penny had almost mown her down. Had it even been Penny at the wheel? They had no proof apart from the car playing Roxy Music. Where had it been going at the time?

Felix had been disembarking from the last train, but the station's small car park was to her right. So if Penny had driven in there, he might not have seen her.

She called him. 'Do you remember who else got off the train the night you fished me out of a ditch on Three Bridge Lane?'

'Funnily enough, not vividly. A few people.'

'Tall, fit guy in his late forties, early fifties? Pirate like?'

'Possibly.'

She could hear faint strains of music in the background, synthesised eighties rock ballads. 'Where are you?'

'Breakfast. It's a juice bar. Do you think Penny's lover came to the village by train then?'

'Or she was dropping him off.' She looked at the station again. Passengers with cars used the side gate to the car park, whereas anyone on foot carried on along the platform to the main exit, which made it quite possible Penny had stopped here without Felix seeing her. But that still didn't explain why they hadn't seen her driving back to Hartridge Holt Barn.

'I'll call you later,' she told Felix, turning away from the car park to run along the lane again.

Crossing the third and smallest bridge over the Hartridge Brook, she glanced across at Bridge Row, the sun rising behind it over the water meadows. Her smile of realisation matched it.

Of course! Alan had a doorbell camera with night vision. He would have footage of that night, taken not long after he'd apologetically wheezed inside, of Penny's car flying past fresh from driving her off the road. And later, perhaps, of it returning.

His curtains were still closed, she noticed, deciding to come back later.

Running on, she couldn't bring herself to look at Hartridge Holt Barn, instead sprinting across the road into the woods, grateful for their shadowy familiarity, the smell of rising sap and loam. Grateful too for her blood still pumping through her veins, loud in her ears, vital and mortal and alive.

She hadn't checked the entrance gate post box in two days, so stayed on the estate's back drive until it intersected with the tree-lined main one, heading up to the Old London Road where the griffons glared down at the early-morning traffic from their high stone pillars.

Inside the box, amongst piles of junk mail, her fingers closed around something horribly hard-edged and familiar.

Phoebe clanged back through the gate to call Felix again. The music was louder, an ambient spa beat of soft bells and synthetic chanting.

'Where are you now?' she asked.

'On a lounger by the mineral pool shielded by *GQ*. You?'

'Front entrance. I got another stiffy.'

'I won't even try and make a joke about that. What does it say?'

'Not opened it yet.'

'Go on.'

She did, wincing. 'It's a wedding invitation. Your wedding invitation.'

'To whom?'

'It says...' She read the names in silent shock.

'Whose wedding?' he repeated.

She read them out. 'Ophelia and Felix invite you to celebrate their union—'

'I knew I was right!' he snarled.

'You said you're at a hen weekend,' she said urgently. '*Whose* hen weekend?'

'Phoebe darling, I know exactly who OhFeelYa is. I'm looking right at her.'

There was a clunk the other end.

'Felix... *Felix*?'

Phoebe dialled DI Mason's direct line.

* * *

Juno

MOTHER LOVES CATCHING HER MAN

I'm going into the field to uncover a killer, followers! We have a chief suspect. One decidedly fishy character has overshadowed this investigation from the start, and later today I am finally going to psyche him out. Fear not, I have back-up. I'm ready for this. So is Kevin.

(Kevin_with_fish_toy.jpeg)

Christ I'm scared. Wish me luck!

Before that, because non-stop excitement comes atcha in Inkbury like a *Die Hard* movie, I have two job interviews. For these, I don't even have to leave the comfort of my own home or indeed wear pants in either the American or British sense. Who knew? Slightly less exciting than tracking down military-trained murderers, I admit, but going commando has more than one meaning.

Juno's plan had been to spend the day mentally preparing for her dangerous mission with deli pastries, a face mask and bubble bath, followed by a lengthy outfit selection then a long, flirtatious briefing with Mil in the pub. This had been scuppered by two job interviews on Zoom.

Moments before the first started, her phone rang. It was Phoebe. Already flapping, in urgent need of the loo and a better webcam angle, Juno pressed 'busy' then muted it to make last-minute preparations and steel her nerve.

The job was 'verbal communications associate' at a mail-order gift company, and the interview was conducted by two managers young enough to be her children. Wearing seventies DJ-style headphones, they read from second screens to corporate-splain for twenty minutes about stakeholder engagement, dynamic team innovation and digital delivery before clicking on a crib sheet and asking her to tell them about herself. Having described her background in comedy, emceeing, blogging and podcasting, Juno asked what exactly the job involved.

'So there's, like, an opportunity to ask questions later?' suggested one of the child interviewers, scrolling their crib sheet fretfully.

'Why not go wild with dynamic team innovation and tell me now.'

'You handle calls and live chat with clients who require support and assistance for complex consumer issues?'

'Sound like a complaints line, only cuddlier.'

'We prefer to call it a customer experience interface? Tell me, Juno, where do you see yourself in five years' time?'

'Ideally, I want to be a private detective. Or your boss.'

She didn't get the job.

Juno made tea and toast and grumbled at Kevin that finding work had been a bubbly, blagging test of charm and chemistry at twenty-five, whereas with double the age and experience, it wasn't nearly as much fun.

Settling back in front of her computer for her second online interview, she picked up her phone to mute it and remembered it already was.

Its screen was striped with notifications. Phoebe had called twice and the Village Detectives WhatsApp group had ten new messages but there was no time to read them because her next Zoom was counting down on her laptop screen.

This interview, for 'co-director of first impressions' at a large Wexshire enterprise college, had more potential, she was certain, already envisaging herself inspiring students and enchanting lecturers.

It lasted less than two minutes with a heavily filtered Head of HR, blonde hair extensions blurring in and out of Golden Gate Bridge behind her. Most of that time was taken up by another corporate mission statement. Then the blonde said: 'The job's front facing, June, so I want to be honest here, I'm not sure you have the personal, people-centred presentation skills for that.'

'But I am a people person!'

'Thing is, Joan, I think you might be better placed in a customer experience interface environment. Less pressure to face front.'

'Is my front face the problem?'

'I'm not sure I like your confrontational attitude.'

'My back chat then?'

'I'm finding your attitude very aggressive, Jane.'

'I'm an all-rounder! I'm quite up and down as well as front and back.'

'Thank you for your time, Jean.' The Zoom meeting ended abruptly.

About to slam her laptop lid down, Juno remembered the password-protected USB stick Phoebe had found in Penny's pocket which she had promised to share with Eric.

The computer's clock told her he would still be competing in League of Legends with professional players worldwide. She slotted it in, opened the website he could use as a portal to her every file and picked up her phone to message a photo of it, with:

> I know you're busy my darling but can you unlock this flash drive for me when you're free?

He sent a thumbs up straight back. He was a legend, like his father.

She owed them both to be front facing, starting by a face-off with Kenneth Ken Doll.

She switched her phone's camera view and took a selfie for her blog. Looking at it, she let out a wail of horror and hurried next door.

'Help me!' she begged her beautician neighbour. 'I look in the mirror, I see could-pass-for-thirties; I look at a photo, I see my mother!'

As usual, the salon was deserted.

'I can squeeze you in for a full make-up makeover masterclass session?'

Juno flopped gratefully into a treatment chair. She'd left her phone in her flat, she realised, but it would have to wait. This was an emergency. If she was going to outwit Kenneth Ken Doll, she needed more front than Blackpool.

An image popped up in her head of its Illuminations and eponymous tower modelled on the Eiffel. She'd not long ago seen a photograph in which it had appeared in the background through a window.

Except now she remembered looking back through a rain-soaked rear windshield at the same scene days earlier. What if the photograph hadn't been taken in Lancashire's seaside mini-Vegas at all? It had been taken in Paris.

'Ohmygod!' she shrieked, making the beautician jump back. 'I think I might just have figured out who OhFeelYa is too!'

By the time Juno marched to the pub with a full face of make-up, she was at her fiercest and feistiest, more convinced than ever that her metier was full-frontal detection.

'Let's get this bastard, Maximilian!' She swung into The Barton Arms like Calamity Jane, Jean, Joan or June through Wild West saloon doors. Then she stopped in surprise.

Phoebe was perched on a bar stool, phone in hand, porcelain pale.

'Thank God you're here, Juno! I think OhFeelYa's kidnapped Felix, and the police don't want to know.'

Phoebe

Phoebe rarely showed fear, less still asked for help, but she abandoned all inhibitions in the face of Juno's bountiful chutz-pah, even welcoming the open-hearted, sweet-scented hug.

'We'll get him back.'

Juno looked different. Very different. But Phoebe was in too much of a wound-up state to work out why.

'This is typical of Felix!' she snarled, harsh because she was scared. 'Swanning off like a bounty hunter without telling anybody what he'd found out. I could kill him.'

'Let's hope Ophelia isn't!' Mil joked, which didn't go down well. 'More likely just kidnapping him to demand a ransom,' he revised quickly, which went down no better.

'What about the police?' demanded Juno. 'Surely they can help?'

'Ha!' Phoebe smarted, looking at Juno again. 'Have you had something done to your face? Botox?'

Not waiting for an answer, she explained that her call to DI Mason had been diverted to the Dunford station front desk, who told her he was out on another case all day. She'd then been put through to Alsop, who cheerfully instructed Phoebe to put the new 'stiffy' in a food bag to preserve it as evidence and then drop it into the station at a time to suit. 'We all think it's ever so quaint, you getting them. We are 100 per cent on this, I can assure you, although poison pen letters are so retro, I'm half tempted to suggest you take it to *Antiques Roadshow*!'

Then Phoebe had blurted her fears for Felix in Buxton, and Alsop had explained there was nothing they could do from Dunford, but if she wanted to take it up with the Derbyshire Constabulary, that was her prerogative.

'Which I did, and they pretty much laughed at me. Felix's phone has been going to voicemail for three hours now.'

'We have to drive up there!' Juno didn't hesitate.

'That's what I said,' Mil insisted, backing her up.

'We'll take the Jazz!' Juno was already hurrying to the door.

'What about Kenneth Ken Doll?' Phoebe hesitated.

'He can wait. Felix needs us. Come on!'

They jumped in the car, engine soon roaring, Britpop blaring. Without warning, Phoebe started to feel the hot glow of her old fire returning, scorching away the panic, melting the frozen fear that trapped her in ice whenever OhFeelYa re-entered her conscious.

Then Juno reversed straight into Mil's Italian motorbike.

'I didn't see it! My false eyelashes hamper my vision.'

'My baby!' He leapt out.

As Juno pulled carefully forward under Mil's boomed instructions, there was a cracking, crunching sound of disintegrating Italian sports bike fender, followed by a heavy clunk of detaching Honda Jazz bumper.

They hurried back inside, where Albie flatly refused to let them take his Defender.

'I'll cable tie the car bumper.' Mil turned to run out again.

'Wait!' Phoebe's phone was letting out a strange ringtone she didn't recognise. 'What is this? What if it's Felix! How do I take this?'

'It's a video call.' Mil looked at the phone screen. 'You know how they work.'

'Only on my laptop!' The glacial throat-pinch of fear was back.

Mil pressed the green circle and the screen changed, the picture flickering, blurring and out of focus. Then a finger wiped the camera lens, which was moving jerkily around showing glimpses of wooden panelling and dim ceiling lights.

'Hello?' said Phoebe. 'Felix?'

'Is that a sauna?' Juno peered over her shoulder to see.

Now a young woman's face was staring at her, mad eyed, weird blue hair like Marge Simpson: 'I'm sorry, I'm *really* sorry! What have I done? It wasn't meant to go this far. It got out of hand! I had no idea how bad it would get.'

'What have you done to him?' Phoebe gasped, dropping the phone in her panic. 'Shit!'

When she picked it up, the screen was showing a settings menu. 'I can't get it back! Oh God, that's *my* face.' She swiped a button in the bottom left of the screen. 'What's it doing?'

'You put a rabbit ear filter on it,' Mil explained.

'Hello?' The woman's face reappeared briefly on screen then vanished again, replaced by Phoebe in a spaceman's helmet.

'Help!' She stabbed a few more buttons, adding floating love hearts and a poo emoji before the call vanished. 'What have I *done*?'

'Here, let me video call Felix back.' Mil took the phone. 'I'll cast it!' Tapping the little screen with the thumb of one hand and picking up a remote control with the other, he turned on the pub's wall-mounted TV. Seconds later, the contents of Phoebe's phone were mirrored on it. The return call was answered straight away.

She let out a cry of relief as Felix appeared on the big screen, larger than life, wearing a towelling robe, an eye-mask pushed up onto his head.

He wiped the lens which was starting to steam up again. 'It's all good! I have OhFeelYa! She's admitted everything. Here she is.'

The phone camera turned to show the young woman, who it turned out had a blue towel wrapped in a turban around her head, cartoon-big eyes red from crying. Someone out of shot had an arm around her.

'I don't even know who that is,' Phoebe admitted, confused.

'I think I do!' whispered Juno reassuringly.

'Introduce yourself,' said Felix's voice.

'It's Leah,' she muttered. 'Leah Lamb.'

'Gail's Leah?' Juno peered closer. The last time she'd seen her, she'd had cropped hair, glasses and bad acne.

'I knew it!' Juno air punched beside her.

A dark-haired figure leaned into shot now. 'She's really sorry, Phoebe. I had no idea, flower! Like Leah says, it got completely out of hand.'

'Gail!'

'She'd stopped it all. She promised it had stopped. But then me telling her I'm getting married has triggered it again.'

'Why did she target me?' Phoebe asked, trying to process that Gail's daughter was OhFeelYa, and no doubt OhManiacNymph too. 'Why me?'

'She hated it when I was so upset about our friendship ending.'

'You called my mum Victoria Sponger!' Leah pushed back into shot, both their heads now on screen, the manga-eyed, pixie-faced similarity obvious. 'Every week Mum would just cry and cry after she read your column. Like she cried and cried when you stopped being friends. Like she cried and cried that time we were staying over at your place after your Bonfire Night party, and she got dead drunk and after you'd gone to bed she took her bra off and told Felix she loved him and, and he said she was beautiful and sexy, but that he would never cheat on—'

'Always was oversensitive, you know that!' Gail butted in. 'Me and Leah are the same that way. We overreact. You *saw* that?' she whispered aside.

'I was *ten*, Mum!' she hissed back. 'For years afterwards, I thought that you would marry Felix if Phoebe and the twins were out of the—'

'I was very, *very* hurt about Victoria Sponger,' Gail told the camera, budging her daughter out of shot. 'That was dead mean of you, Phoebe.'

'I wrote you a letter to apologise for that,' Phoebe said numbly, still trying to take it in that little Leah – with whom she and the girls had baked fairy cakes and watched *Toy Story* – was OhFeelYa who had ended her career.

'Life's not a Jane Austen book!' Leah jeered, edging back in. 'I saw that letter in the mail pile and brought it back. *Too long; didn't read.* You weren't big enough to come round in person, so that's your bad.'

'Phoebe wrote to me?' Gail turned to her daughter in shock.

'Ages ago. After the Bath University open day, remember?'

'You never said!'

'You never look at your post! Only sad acts like her bother with it.'

Phoebe felt another painful truth land. 'Is that why you sent me the fake funeral notice, the memorial and wedding invitations?'

'You're so analogue, snail mail's the only way to get your attention. You're not even on Facebook any more and I thought all Karens are on Facebook.'

'Is it any surprise given what you did last time?' Phoebe fumed. 'I lost my professional reputation because of you.'

'I didn't realise that would happen!' The cartoon-big eyes widened again, defensive this time. 'OhFeelYa and OhManiac-Nymph got *way* more traction than I expected. It went viral so fast. Not gonna lie, it's what I now do in fashion.'

'She's an algorithm alchemist!' Gail boasted.

'But why start it all up again? Why resurrect OhFeelYa after so long?'

'That's my bad!' Gail dived in quickly, but Leah leant across her, blinking at the camera.

'Mum told me she wanted to make things up with you, maybe even invite you to the wedding, and I started to panic you'd realise what I'd done before. I was going to bring OhManiac-Nymph back from the dead, try to make it better, but when I went on X as OhFeelYa to test the vibe, Felix wound me right up. It's his fault.'

'You tagged me into a death threat against my wife!' said Felix's voice out of shot.

'She's a filthy temper.' Gail tried to get in camera shot.

'I was A/B temperature testing dark feed clickbait engagement!' Leah protested, leaning closer to the lens. 'You *completely* overreacted.'

'She's been dead stressed out at work,' Gail butted in again, talking over her daughter's shoulder. 'Always flying about – London one week, Paris or Tokyo the next. The pressure's unreal. Burning out young makes people behave irrationally – look at Winona Ryder shoplifting or Britney Spears shaving off her hair – and Leah still is just a—'

'Shut *up*, Mum! I knew what I was doing. Phoebe doesn't deserve your forgiveness, and he's still a high-key jackass. He triggered me.'

'Did you send the letter bomb too?' Phoebe demanded.

'What letter bomb? No way! Ow, Mum! Stop it!' The blue towelling turban started unravelling as Gail began poking at her daughter with a wooden sauna ladle.

'You little idiot! They could have you arrested for this!'

'I didn't send any bomb! Ow! Stop hitting me with that.'

The phone screen was steaming up again.

It was turned to face Felix, who wiped it, head bobbing as he moved away from the shouting match, wiping his perspiring face with his towelling arm, a sudden blast of light bleaching out the screen for a moment as he left the sauna and walked through somewhere bright with flashes of glass and foliage.

'There's an outside possibility we could have her prosecuted for malicious communication' – he spoke on screen like a documentary maker – 'but given how stretched the police are, I think we'll leave it to Gail to dole out home justice, don't you? Keep it private.'

Phoebe glanced behind her, where a dozen village pub regulars were gazing at her husband on the big screen, Inkbury's answer to *The Equalizer* in a bathrobe.

'Yes, I think that's best,' she agreed, then asked Felix when he'd be home.

'When the trains deliver me. We need a car.'

'So do I,' groaned Juno.

'Me too,' muttered Mil.

'We could get a blue Volkswagen van and paint The Mystery Machine on the side?' Juno suggested brightly.

The others pretended she hadn't said this, although there was a whoop from one of the regulars.

Mil hastily stopped the call casting, addressing the phone screen admiringly. 'Felix, mate, how did you work out she was OhFeelYa?'

'Something Juno said about dismissing suspects being just as important as gathering them got me thinking. She said sometimes it's only when you've taken the brightest gems out of the jewellery box that you see one you've overlooked.'

'I said that?' Juno looked pleased, then gasped. 'That's from Freddy's book!'

'You also told me you thought OhFeelYa was from our kids' generation, using slang like Karen. I fixed on Seraphine as a result, especially with the Paris connection. But later you were talking about how brilliant Eric is, and you called him an "online alchemist" or something. That's when I remembered Gail saying the same to boast that Leah had been doing Dior's digital PR. As soon as that landed, it all started adding up.'

'And I *knew* I'd seen a picture of Paris somewhere,' Juno said breathlessly, 'but it wasn't until today that I realised where. It was on Gail's phone. Leah had shared a picture of the wedding dress with the Eiffel Tower behind it, only I mistook it for Blackpool.'

'Leah flies back and forth all the time. Her mum tells her everything, so that's how she knew we'd visited Dallowbeck then gone to Paris. She confessed everything as soon as I confronted them.'

'Impressive, mate.' Mil air punched. 'The Village Detectives have one in the bag!'

'Just a killer to ensnare now,' muttered Phoebe, catching her husband's eye on screen as Mil handed her phone back.

'Be careful,' Felix warned. 'I'll be home as fast as I can.'

'We'd better get going!' Juno squeaked, looking at her watch.

'I'll get the cable ties,' said Mil.

'To restrain Kenneth Ken Doll if he gets violent?'

'They're to reattach your car bumper, Juno.'

20

JUNO

'Pusscat! Over here! It's about to begin.'

Juno gratefully closed in on her mother, resplendent in rasp-berry Lagenlook linen, hair now dyed lime green, beckoning her towards a vacant fold-out fishing chair like an eager aubergine.

'Where's Mil?' demanded Judy as Dennis – oddly regatta themed in striped blazer, cream trousers and boating cap – supplied a plastic champagne flute brimming with Kir Royale, accompanied by multiple noisy air kisses. 'Are you two an item now? We all know how much you fancy him.'

A deep voice sniggered in Juno's ear.

'He's around and about.'

Mil had insisted on standing at the back of the audience, wearing an earpiece he'd borrowed from Bernard who, along with Alan, Juno was starting to suspect were the village's real hired assassins by day and aficionados of laughter and dancing by night, or at least retired ones. Her own corresponding earpiece was attached to a lumpy radio set hidden in a money belt under her dress, now poking out like a hernia. To talk back, she had to remember to mutter into her chest where the wire housing the microphone was threaded up through her bra.

This hadn't been her plan at all.

'Agent Millionaire here, do you hear me, over?' The gruff voice spoke into her ear again.

'Um...'

'Quick, Pusscat, load your plate before it starts. There's smoked trout and spring onion quiche, pork and apricot sausage rolls, truffled duck pate en croute and wagyu sushi beefcake.'

'I repeat, do you hear me, over?'

'Which would you like, darling?'

'Yes!'

It was very difficult listening to two conversations at once.

She pushed her earpiece in more firmly as Mil said, 'Have you located Kenneth Ken Doll, repeat, have you located Kenneth Ken Doll, over.'

'Yes! Hello!' she said to the Campbells, who were in fold-out chairs beyond her mother and Dennis, hunky Kenneth Ken Doll furthest away, brooding murderously beside a rabbity, middle-aged brunette in a tea dress, who was fanning herself with the programme.

'I've put you and Mil next to Pam and Spike, Pusscat,' Judy stage whispered. 'They're dying to know how the case is going, although Pam's just taken Spike off for a precautionary comfort break. Have you brought my car back?'

'Yes, freshly valeted! There's just a slight issue with the rear bumper...'

'What issue?'

'Shall we do Mil a plate of food and a Kir Royale?' She chair-hopped closer to the picnic and also closer to Kenneth.

'Where *is* Mil again, Pusscat?'

She looked round. 'Behind the delphiniums, I think.'

'Do not reveal my whereabouts,' Mil demanded in her ear. 'Two sausage rolls and the beefcake for me. Have you engaged the target? Over.'

The overture was already striking up on stage. There was no sign of Pam and Spike. Juno was still five seats away from Kenneth. With a sinking heart, she realised this was a long game. And she was going to have to sit through light operetta while she waited.

'What *is* this shitshow we're watching?' Mil demanded in her ear. 'I thought you said it was Gilbert O'Sullivan on tour?'

Just as the overture had tooted and timpani-rolled into a crescendo, Juno's phone started ringing loudly with 'I Wanna Be Adored' and she hastened to silence it, embarrassed, glancing down at the screen, where Eric's photograph was beaming hot geekily at her before she hurriedly swiped it away.

'Turn that thing off, *Pusscat!*' Judy hissed beside her.

'I have to call him back!' she whispered, looking around for the quickest route out of earshot.

'Not *now*.' The matriarchal order was absolute.

Putting it on mute, she pocketed it in frustration, glancing along the row to Kenneth Ken Doll, who was already on picnic seconds, pirate side-burned cheeks bulging. He looked back dispassionately. Were they the eyes of a killer?

On stage, a host of buxom young actresses had draped themselves decoratively to start singing 'Twenty Love-Sick Maidens We'.

There was still no sign of Pam and Spike.

'This is my kind of show!' Mil exclaimed in her ear.

* * *

Phoebe

High with relief that OhFeelYa had been unveiled, Phoebe set out early to meet Felix's train, terriers obediently on leads so she could call in on Alan in Bridge Row first, without upsetting him with the sight of them loose near the road.

To be certain that she was never the killer's intended target was so liberating, she felt like high fiving him on the doorstep, beaming widely.

He looked taken aback by such vivacity. 'What an unexpected treat.'

'I brought your SOS wristband back.' She proffered it. 'Thank you so much. We've now found the person who was trolling me. They're not dangerous.'

'Oh, that is good news!' He stooped to greet the dogs.

'I do have another small favour to ask.'

'Of course, come in!'

She followed him into the kitchen, grateful for its time capsule reminder of her parents' era before warm pine and colourful tiles were subsumed by uniform grey and granite, the only modern touch the little Echo Show screen, which was telling them it was a cloud-free twenty-one degrees outside. Perfect weather for outdoor opera. She hoped Juno was okay. A worried pulse ticked in her temple at the danger she might be putting herself in, grateful that Mil was there as back-up.

'Would you be able to share your doorbell footage from the night Penny Fermoy died?' she asked Alan.

'Of course!' He snapped his shiny brown heels together and nodded his head gallantly. 'Let me make you a drink first. Tea, coffee, something stronger?'

'Coffee would be lovely. Strong, yes.'

'Only way to take it. Can I offer your dogs some treats? We have a few left from... well, we have a few.'

The terriers wagged themselves all over as he reached a Bonio tin down from a shelf to share them out. 'I do like Jack Russells very much. Need to keep them on leads, mind you. Incorrigible wanderlust, terriers.'

'Do you mind me asking, what happened to your dog?'

Alan looked up, his thick white eyebrows angling wistfully. 'I found him dead in the garden, poor boy, lying in his favourite spot.'

He looked so stricken with sadness, she regretted asking it.

'It's terribly kind of you to help me,' she said, eager to move on.

'Not a jot, my dear.' Busying himself making coffee, Alan explained that the computer and hard drive on which he stored footage from his security cameras was in his garden workshop. 'My Wizard of Oz HQ, Norma called it. She disliked gadgetry in the house, and I'm still in the habit of keeping it out there. I've now got that smart screen' – he pointed to the Alexa sitting discreetly beside an old-fashioned set of kitchen scales laden with cast-iron weights, now offering a feta traybake recipe – 'but the business end is in my "man cave", I think you youngsters call it. Would you like a tour?'

'Honoured.' Smelling the coffee, she felt a familiar twinge reminding her that she'd reached her caffeine limit two cups ago. 'Would you mind if I just...'

'You know where it is.'

In Alan's downstairs loo, Phoebe took comfort in the framed *Private Eye* covers and the familiar spines of cartoon books.

She looked up at the diving helmet, trying to work out what was missing.

* * *

Juno

Watching Gilbert and Sullivan with Mil's commentary on an earpiece was, Juno reflected, rather like an excitable, live-action version of Gogglebox. His delighted surprise was infectious. He loved it, booming with laughter and humming along to the catchy choruses.

By contrast, Kenneth Ken Doll only had eyes for the picnic, now on his third round of venison scotch eggs and blue cheese galette, switching seats with his parents so that he could get closer to the folding table. This had advantageously moved him two seats closer to Juno.

'Can I swap places with you and Dennis?' she whispered to her mother.

'No,' Judy hushed back.

'Check out that Dragoon kit!' Mil exclaimed in her ear as the lovesick maidens' military suitors marched on in red dress uniform with plumed pith helmets.

Juno's phone vibrated against her hip. Using a paper napkin as cover, she slipped it from her pocket and quickly checked it. Eric had messaged a link to a file on his cloud drive:

> This was on the USB. Matches with the missing night from the other micro-cards you shared. Look at 01.22 a.m.

Napkin aloft, Juno discreetly clicked it, finding it was just more CCTV footage of passing cars and moths. She was still trying to find the time slot when her mother leant closer urgently. 'Swap chairs with me, Pusscat. I need to have a girl-talk with Pam.'

She looked up. Pam was returning, stooping low as she made her way through the picnickers to creep back to her seat, whispering apologies. Spike wasn't with her.

Hastily sharing Eric's message and link with the Village Detectives WhatsApp group, Juno obligingly switched seats.

Now just Dennis separated her from Kenneth.

* * *

Phoebe

Alan's workshop stretched along the entire rear boundary of his pretty waterside garden, discreetly shielded by hedging. It was effectively three large timber sheds linked together like train carriages. Phoebe found this pleasantly fitting, given two of the three were devoted to his model railway hobby. In the first shed, he showed off a vast 1:76 scale table-top landscape on which multiple trains raced around hills, across viaducts and through tunnels, into perfect little towns and past rural request halts. It was a life's work. No wonder Alan had two cameras trained outside and one inside.

In the second of his coupled-together workshops, a smaller table housed a more modest steam-engine set up in a different scale, alongside which were multiple shelves of neatly ordered spares, boxes, books and tools. Beyond these was a run of wooden work benches, on top of which sat several industrial-looking tools including a laser cutter and a 3D printer.

The third 'carriage' was an Aladdin's cave of retro and modern tech, boxy old monitors lined up alongside modern flat-screen ones, more storage shelves neatly packed with keyboards, drives, cables and other computer parts.

'Here we go.' Alan sat down in front of one of the more

modern computers, vanquishing a train screensaver with a twitch of a mouse, then logging on.

'Take a seat, Phoebe.' He plucked wire-rimmed reading glasses out of his breast pocket and propped them on his nose. 'Let's see. That would be overnight on the... Ah, yes, here we go.'

He didn't need telling the date or time, Phoebe realised, settling on an old fabric office chair while the terriers snorted and sniffed around the skirting boards.

'There's you and me,' said Alan, playing it at double speed so they walked like comedy characters, crossing the road and wiggling up to the door in red-eye close-up, Alan puffing and blowing, before Phoebe jogged off at a Benny Hill glamour model clip. There followed a lull during which insects danced white in front of the little camera and then, 'And... is this Miss Fermoy's car?'

Phoebe watched the big silver hatchback race past. 'Yes! That's after she almost ran me over.'

'Let's see when she comes back.' He fast-forwarded more cars coming and going along the Three Bridge Lane, then paused on one.

'This looks like it. It was half an hour later. There you go. Do you need to see anything else?'

There was something not right, Phoebe realised, but she couldn't work out what. 'Hang on, yes, sorry. Did she have a passenger either way?'

Sighing patiently, he switched it on again and replayed the clip. 'It would seem so.'

In the first clip, Penny was clearly alone. In the second, there were two people in the car.

She and Alan peered closer at it, but the car interior was too dark to make out more than two shadowy profiles.

'I do hope that helps.' He closed the program.

'Have the police seen this?' Phoebe asked.

'They haven't requested it.' He logged off, the train screen-saver kicking back in. 'Although I've complained enough times about traffic speeding along the lane, her nibs from Hartridge Holt Barn chief amongst the perpetrators, alas. I heard that they think Miss Fermoy's death was accidental though?'

'They do, but I don't. Would you mind playing the rest of that night's footage through at speed until it gets light?'

The sigh was a little less patient this time. 'Of course. If you'll forgive me, I must answer a call of nature, but you are most welcome to look at it while I'm gone.' He reopened the computer window, clicking so that it was playing at double speed.

Left alone, Phoebe watched it intently. In her pocket, her phone rang with Felix's custom ringtone, Peggy Lee's 'Fever', probably to say his train was running later.

She started to fumble for it when something on screen made her reach for the mouse instead, clicking to rewind and rewatch it.

* * *

Juno

In Godlington's walled garden, cynical pretender and poet Bunthorne was prancing around the temporary rostrum stage, tossing his wig as he lamented pretentious aesthetics.

Mil was chuckling in Juno's ear. 'Bonkers, this is!'

Beside her, Dennis, who had indulged in one too many glasses of Kir Royale during the picnic, was nodding off, champagne flute lowering in his slackening fingers.

Juno leant closer. 'Dennis?'

Saying a silent apology in her head, it took her the barest of nudges to ensure its contents spilled in his lap.

'Blast!' He jolted awake, looking down to see a deep pink stain spreading through the cream twill. 'Drat!'

The audience nearby hushed him.

'What's that?' Mil was alert in Juno's ear.

As she'd hoped, Dennis muttered hasty apologies and crept hurriedly off towards the main house to go up to the apartment and change.

Pretending to be engrossed watching winsome heroine Patience being swept about prettily onstage, rebuffing Bunthorne, Juno niftily moved up a chair.

Then, as Patience took romantic advice from a woman in a massive feathered hat, Juno leaned across to Kenneth, who was loading his plate with cheeses.

'Hi, Kendall.'

'It's Kenneth,' he growled, his mouth full of French bread.

In her ear, Mil was breathing encouragement. 'Go, girl! Stay calm!'

'Not Kain either?'

He finally looked at her, dark eyed and sullen, then glanced across at his parents and back to her. 'Nope.'

'Not a hitman sleeper spy and sleeper-arounder?' This didn't sound right, so she hurried on in an undertone. 'Tell me, Kenneth, did you meet up with Penny Fermoy the night she died?'

He turned to her, narrow eyed. 'This a joke?'

Around them, the audience let out a ripple of laughter as Patience swooned at the sight of her drop-dead-gorgeous child-hood sweetheart, a dead ringer for Brian May circa 1975.

'Don't pretend you don't know she's dead,' she told Kenneth,

who was still squinting at her, one eye now closed, as though
looking through a rifle sight.

His lip curled into a sneer. 'You're lying.'

'She died two nights ago.'

The plate dropped from his hand. 'You're lying!'

'You were there.'

'Not Penny!'

'Shh!' hissed the audience around them.

Juno side-eyed Kenneth, biding her time while Patience and
young Brian May flirted then agreed he was too perfect for her to
love.

Beside her, Kenneth was shaking his head, eyes wild, big
shoulders hunched.

Juno cut herself a wedge of Manchego for strength, carefully
setting the cheese knife out of his reach. Was he trying to work
out how to escape now he knew they were onto him, she
wondered? He had the dangerous air of a rhino about to charge.

'What's happening?' demanded Mil in her earpiece.

'I think Ken Doll might bolt,' she muttered into her hidden
chest mic.

'I meant in the opera,' said Mil, as Bunthorne stomped back
onstage with the twenty lovesick maidens in tow. 'Never mind.
On standby, over!'

Kenneth was staring at her wide-eyed now, asking in an
undertone, 'How did she die?'

'Don't pretend you don't know that,' she whispered back.

To her astonishment, tears were welling in his murderous
pirate eyes. 'She was my best bloody client.'

There was more disgruntled shushing nearby.

Juno edged her chair closer, whispering, 'When did you last
see her?'

'Two nights ago.'

That tallied up with Penny messaging him from the book club, Juno realised.

'She picked me up off the last train from Newborough.'

So Penny had almost mowed Phoebe down as she'd raced to the station to collect him.

Juno recalled the nest of cushions and converted home movies by the TV in Penny's barn conversion, imagining her watching her younger self while she waited.

'Why so late?'

'I have a security surveillance job. Top secret.' His eye flicked nervously towards his parents.

'Where?' Juno pressed.

'Asda,' he muttered. There was an ironic insouciance to the way he said it that made her heart quicken, the hired assassin myth still hanging on by a thread.

'And how long did you stay?'

'Until the first train.'

'What happened that night?' Juno was forced to turn away as Dennis noisily air-kissed her other side, almost swallowing her earpiece as he reclaimed the seat beside her, now wearing crimson trousers that matched those of the Dragoons rejoining the maidens onstage.

'What have I missed?' he whispered.

'Sex, mostly.' Kenneth leaned in urgently on Juno's other side to answer her question. 'She took a bit of warming up, mind you.'

'Really?' Dennis leaned across her too.

They were all shushed again.

Juno waited until Dennis was distracted by the lovesick maidens, who all seemed to fancy Bunthorne like mad, dancing around buying raffle tickets for the chance to win him in marriage.

'Go on,' she hissed at Kenneth.

'She'd had too much to drink,' he told her. 'We'd had a row in the station car park because she was way over the limit. It's not the first time. I'm banned, but I still drove the car back to hers.'

'And reversed over her!'

A few more shushes made them break away briefly.

'No!' Kenneth leaned back in. 'We got in the pool, fooled around, listened to old rock.'

'Wouldn't it have been easier to drown Penny in there?' Juno stared at his handsome, murderous pirate face, longing to understand.

'Why would I want to kill her? I told you she was my best client.'

'She really *paid* you for sex?'

'I'm good,' he said indignantly. 'Keep myself clean and fit; give pleasure, no bullshit. Never disappoint. You women all love a man's man.'

'Actually, I don't,' said a voice behind him, and the rabbity brunette joined in the conversation. 'I prefer someone more fluid and emotionally intelligent.'

'Me too,' murmured a voice beyond her.

'Rubbish, he's gorgeous,' said another. 'I wouldn't say no.'

Looking around, Juno realised the audience nearby had stopped shushing and were now listening in avidly, including Dennis, and Kenneth's open-mouthed parents. Ignoring winsome Patience springing onstage to announce that she would sacrifice herself to imperfect love by marrying Bunthorne after all, they were enthralled by hunky gigolo Kenneth. Here was a romantic mercenary with mojo far sexier than any floppy-haired poet or uniformed Dragoon.

'I was more than a paid service to Penny though!' Kenneth defended. 'She said she was training me up to bring in from the wild; she took me to Paris and the races; she bought me designer clothes and accessories.'

'It's like *Pygmalion*,' gasped an onlooker.

His handsome face looked sad, staring at the stage again, where the Dragoons and their maidens had coupled up, singing and waltzing adoringly. 'I loved her.'

Juno took a moment to absorb this, tears threatening as she watched the character who looked like Brian May sauntering back on stage with a poetry book, and the maidens hastily dumping their soldiers to crowd round him singing: '*Who is this whose manly face bears sorrow's interesting trace?*'

Looking up from his book, Brian May wailed, '*I am a broken-hearted troubadour!*'

In Juno's ear, Mil's gruff voice boomed, 'What do they see in that prat?'

Juno turned to Penny's broken-hearted beau, whose passport and tuxedo were always packed, scuba gear at the ready, her own heart softening. 'I had no idea you were so close.'

He gave her a knowing look. 'She didn't feel the same way about me. Mostly, she called me late at night for sex. You ladies often call at that hour, I find. Or swipe right.'

She cleared her throat, recalling her own late-night dating app flirtation with him. 'What time exactly did you leave last time?'

'I always catch the first train to Newborough, quarter to six. Penny drove. She had a kinky thing for goodbye kisses, so we left early.' His downturned smile suggested reclining seats and privacy glass kinkiness.

'Do we know this girlfriend?' Kenneth's mother demanded disapprovingly.

'She sounds rather fun,' a deep voice chuckled beyond her.

'She's dead, Eugene. Keep up.'

Juno jumped as her earphone spluttered into life again. 'Millionaire here! *Urgent*. Meet me in the laburnum tunnel, repeat, meet me in the laburnum tunnel. I have fresh intel! Bring the beefcake.'

'You're coming with me.' Juno reached out and grabbed Kenneth's hand, surprised by how compliantly he came.

Behind them, she heard her mother call across to the Campbells, 'Always was impulsive in love and romance, my Pusscat. Especially since *Bridgerton*!'

21

PHOEBE

Watching Alan's doorbell-cam footage over again, Phoebe knew something didn't add up, although logic refused to supply the answer. She'd reviewed it three times and still couldn't spot what was bothering her unconscious mind about the two separate journeys Penny Fermoy had made to Inkbury railway station in the hours before her death. Apart from the fact that using a car for such a short journey was a wasteful carbon load, and using it whilst drunk was unconscionable, she was certain something obvious was eluding her.

She sat back to stretch. The terriers had curled together in a yin and yang nap at the far end of the room where a large window overlooked the brook.

She stood up and paced around, wondering where Alan was, fingers wriggling for distraction. She examined the museum of computers and the shelves of old and new tech, picking up bygone calculators and CB radios, pagers and watches including the SOS bracelet. She examined a chunky mobile phone that looked prehistoric, turning it over before realising it wasn't so old after all. She'd signed a little screen like this with the wrong end of a pen enough times.

A fresh thought striking, she put the device back and hurriedly sat down to rewatch the videos once again. This time, she spotted the difference.

'Sorry about that!' Alan finally reappeared, out of breath but less vexed. 'At my age, one's rather a slave to the old bladder! Found anything useful?'

'Yes.' Too excited to stop to think, she pulled her chair closer to the computer desk to replay what she'd just seen.

When Penny had first driven to the station at close to midnight, it had been so dark that – even with Alan's high-res night-vision bell-cam – it was hard to see small details. 'But if I freeze here – look – the car's tow bar is clearly visible. And here it is coming back, still there. Now let me fast forward to a journey she makes to the train station a few hours later... and...'

'It's missing,' Alan observed.

'Exactly! It was detachable, so anybody with the right key could remove it. They're often stolen as a result. You can buy master-sets on eBay.'

'Goodness, can you?'

'At some point between Penny bringing her lover Kain back from the station and dropping him off there again, the tow bar of her car was removed. I believe whoever did that killed her.'

'How?'

'When Penny returned from dropping Kain back at the station, they were lying in wait. They'd placed a cuddly toy on the drive near to where they were hiding, knowing Penny would probably mistake it for her cat and stop in a panic to look. When she did, they stepped out behind her and hit her over the head with the tow bar, knocking her out. They then reattached the tow bar to the car, which they reversed over her to make it look like an accident.'

'Goodness, how ingenious.'

'Over complicated.' Phoebe wrinkled her nose. 'Then again, so was the poison pen bomb that killed Craig the postman.'

'You think the same person did both?'

'Certain of it, although they were only ever targeting Penny, and I'm not convinced that they set out to kill on either occasion, simply inflict maximum pain. That's why the cuddly toy was there. They wanted Penny to think she'd run over her own cat, hiding the real one in a pet carrier in the pony trailer instead. Whoever it is wasn't cruel enough to actually kill an innocent creature.'

'Well, that is thoughtful.'

'Of course the obvious suspect is Kain, her mystery lover. He's a liar with a shady past.'

'And was it him, do you think?'

'We both know it wasn't, Alan.' She looked up at him.

'You surely don't suspect...' His white eyebrows shot up and he wheezed in shock, stepping back against his crammed shelves of gadgetry. '...me?'

'Why would I? A man who could barely walk from the pub to his cottage is hardly going to dash half a mile across the fields to detach a neighbour's tow bar and clunk her over the head with it, is he?'

'Precisely.'

'But that's the thing about over-engineering things. The killer put almost as much thought into their alibis and scapegoats as they did their crimes both times. Hamming up the angina for my benefit walking home, knowing Bernard would compete for attention. Doctoring CCTV footage to remove anything incriminating, changing over your whole system even.'

Phoebe turned back to the computer. 'Have you wiped the rear garden and workshop camera history stored on this yet, or will that show your movements the night Penny died?'

She knew, even as she clicked the mouse to search for the footage, that Alan wouldn't deny it. But she wasn't prepared for the speed or dexterity of his reaction.

Two thick ratchet straps were clinched around her chest and arms, tightened in split seconds to tether her firmly onto the office chair. She shouted for help, her first instinct to kick out.

Then she heard the stickily sharp sound of duct tape unrolling.

Tethering the tape end to the chair's base pole, Alan spun Phoebe deftly round to tape her legs together, their wild flailing reduced to violent jerks and shakes which tipped the chair over, cracking her head against a desk leg. She let out an involuntary cry of pain, followed by even louder shouts for help before they were muffled by another strip of tape.

'I must apologise for being a bit rough,' said Alan breathlessly, backing rapidly away, 'but you've left me no choice.'

Phoebe stared up at him, furious and terrified. Then she looked desperately round for the terriers, who should be barking and biting.

Spotting two lifeless little shapes still lying against the skirting boards, she let out a wail of horror in her throat.

* * *

Juno

Mil was waiting in the flower tunnel that lay beyond the archway at the rear of the walled garden. It dripped exotically with yellow flower clusters like pendant lanterns.

'Message from Felix on the WhatsApp,' he reported urgently, holding up his phone. 'He's just watched the video link you shared. Here – you look! Where's the beefcake?'

'I brought him.' She indicated Kenneth Ken Doll over her shoulder.

'The sushi one your mum made,' Mil groaned. 'I'm famished. No matter. Can you tell me what is going on in this?' He showed his phone to her.

Juno watched it. 'Eric sent this to me. It was on Penny's flash drive. It's just more of Alan's CCTV. Hang on... what are these two doing?'

On the footage, a car flew past the cottage, then a few moments later it reversed back into shot and stopped, a familiar-looking silver hatchback. A tall figure got out of the passenger's side, looking down at something on the lane, then they started to wave their arms at the driver still inside the car, pacing around to the door to wrench it open.

The driver almost fell out. It was recognisably Penny, apparently very drunk. Staggering around to the other side of the car to look at what the passenger was pointing at, she bent double again, turning away.

'Is she laughing?'

'Yes,' said a deep voice. 'Nervous giggles. Let's call it female hysteria.'

Kenneth was looking at the video.

'Is that you?' asked Juno, pointing at the tall figure on screen who had stepped back, throwing their arms up as Penny reeled around briefly, then vanished from sight.

When she reappeared, she was holding something that she threw over the garden hedge.

'What *was* that?' asked Mil.

'Roll it back to before the car goes past,' ordered Kenneth.

Juno did.

This time they all saw two small, bright spots of light gleaming across the lane. An animal was on the opposite verge, a fox or a muntjac maybe. It started purposefully across the road. A split second later, Penny's car passed through the shot like a bullet. Afterwards there were no gleaming eyes.

'You murdered Penny because she ran over a fox?' Juno asked Kenneth.

'How many times? I didn't kill her!'

They could hear the Gilbert and Sullivan first act coming to its close inside the walled garden, the cast all singing noisily on top of one another.

'And that wasn't a fox,' added Kenneth. 'It was a little dog.'

Juno looked at it again, tears welling, but the screen started flashing as another app took it over. In her pocket, her own phone was vibrating like mad too.

'It's the SOS wristband!' Mil realised. 'Phoebe's triggered the SOS band.'

* * *

Phoebe

Lying on a carpet-tiled floor, taped to an office chair, Phoebe realised she'd played this one very badly.

It seemed Alan felt he had too, although that was no great comfort. 'You made me panic. I hadn't planned this contingency very far through; I'd only got up to dosing the dog treats with melatonin. Your little chaps are perfectly fine, by the way. Just having a good sleep. Quite safe.'

She blinked an angry thank you, craning to see her dogs snoring obliviously against the skirting.

'You're right that I couldn't possibly kill Penny's cat, although I confess, I dislike the creatures. Norma insisted on having one years ago, kept leaving dead birds in my slippers. For some reason they love me. Damian Lewis was unusually keen on rubbing himself against my ankles whenever I went to Hartridge Holt Barn to complain about her nibs speeding on the lane. I had to make sure he was safely out of the way.'

Phoebe groaned. She should have recognised the old-fashioned cat carrier she'd found in Penny's pony trailer. It was missing from the top of the bookshelf in Alan's downstairs loo.

'You found the thumb drive, I take it?' he was saying. 'Foolish of me to give Penny that. I thought it might prick her conscience.'

Phoebe tried to say that she hadn't seen what was on it, but it just came out as incoherent moans.

'I'll be more careful this time.' He crossed to the computer and started clicking the mouse. 'Let's start by switching all the CCTV cameras off, shall we? Now we'll wipe and format the data cards... Then we can factory reset the hard drive. Technology is wonderfully obedient, unlike dogs.' He right clicked a few more times, let out a satisfied 'ta da' and turned to look at the sleeping terriers indulgently. 'The vet gave me the melatonin tip, but I was rather forgetful about it I'm afraid to say. That's why I blame myself for what happened. Poor little chap. Quite the saddest of deaths. Never saw the car coming. I'm sure he felt no pain, at least.'

Phoebe realised he must be talking about his wife's dog.

'He was also getting a bit old and deaf, poor boy. Aren't we all? He'd crossed that road thousands of times.' Alan drew up the other office chair and perched on it, adopting a hands together storytelling pose. 'He'd often ask to be let out in the middle of the night, whining and scraping until I came down. I kept reinforcing the garden fence, but he could escape alongside the brook when the water was low. He'd sometimes take himself off for a moonlit walk, always the same route. I used to imagine Norma's ghost was restless, but the vet thought he just had a spot of doggy dementia.'

Phoebe wriggled her fingers behind her, quietly testing what she could move.

'You must understand it's not the accident I was angry about so much, it's what that woman did afterwards. When I found him in the morning, he looked like he was asleep on the lawn. There was a spot he liked to lie in the sun, and that's where he was. It was only when I got closer that I saw...' He closed his eyes, looking as though he was praying.

Phoebe felt the hard edge of the ratchet strap lever and gripped onto it.

Alan stood up and walked to the window, beneath which the terriers were now snoring audibly. He stooped to pat them, then straightened up, looking out through the glass. 'I buried him up there by the willow bower. It's where Norma liked to sit and watch the brook, where her ashes are scattered. Never floods up there. They can watch it together. That's rather lovely, don't you think?'

Phoebe nodded, her one free hand working at a ratchet lever feverishly, desperate to break free and half-nelson him.

Alan turned back to face the room, frowning at his computer screen. 'When I found him, I knew something terrible had happened to him to be injured that badly. I thought maybe his death wouldn't be in vain if I could prove how dangerously people speed along the lane. But it was so much worse when I tracked down the camera footage. Penny Fermoy laughing and throwing his body over the garden hedge like rubbish.' His anger made him breathless, wheezing for a moment.

Appalled, Phoebe made sympathetic noises which turned into a low groan as the ratchet slipped from her grip.

'I confronted Penny,' Alan said with a determined sniff. 'I told her I knew what she'd done. And you know, she didn't even remember?' His voice suddenly hardened. 'We've never got on. Stuck up and vain, that woman. Norma liked her more, but my wife liked everyone. Did you ever meet Norma?'

Phoebe shook her head, eyes conveying regret, fingers fiddling furiously for the ratchet strap mechanism behind her. It was back in her palm now, cool and solid.

'Yes, I heard you're stand-offish. Clever, though.'

He walked to his shelves, carefully rearranging the things she'd moved. 'Norma wouldn't have approved of me making my little device for Penny. But I did enjoy planning it all. And as you've just discovered, I did it so meticulously, right down to ensuring Craig's scanner wouldn't work.'

Phoebe made a shocked recognition noise, and he nodded intently, picking up the clunky device she'd mistaken for an old phone. 'Zebra Symbol TC75, standard issue Royal Mail equipment which, like detachable tow bar keys, are readily available on popular internet auction sites. But you worked that out, clever girl.'

Tugging at the ratchet hinge, Phoebe knew she wouldn't be strapped to an office chair if she had.

'I'd warned Penny that I would write to the police, send them video evidence of her nibs drunken driving. She just sneered that her lawyers would shut me down with one well-worded letter. That's when I decided to wipe the smile off her face with a well-penned package.'

Phoebe winced.

'I did it for Norma. Pen nibs was my little joke.' He gazed out to the garden again, to the spot his wife's ashes were scattered. 'We used to refer to Penny Fermoy as "her nibs". "Her nibs up at the big house" when she was at Hartridge Court, then "her nibs up the road". The device was quite a challenge. Over-engineered again, of course. I only meant to make the woman suffer, not kill her, and certainly not poor Craig.

'He called in here on his round the day he died. I lied about that, sorry. I'd sent myself a tracked package, a rare Farish Inter-city Swallow model engine. Craig loved to see parcels opened, and he was quite obsessed with N gauge trains. It was natural to invite him in to examine it. While he was distracted, I switched his scanner for one I'd disabled.'

Phoebe nodded in appreciation, feeling the first ratchet release behind her.

'Stroke of luck he had that new van. He wanted to show it off to me. I'd been planning to say the parcel I'd made for Penny had been delivered here in error, but there was no need. I simply popped it in the back of his van while he was guiding me round.'

Phoebe rolled her eyes appreciatively, working on the second ratchet, more adept at it now.

'Except human error is so unpredictable, isn't it? So fallible.' Without warning, he stooped down and ripped off her mouth tape. 'Stop trying to loosen the ratchet straps. I can hear the clicks.'

'Understood,' she said quickly, lips stinging furiously.

'Craig's human error cost him his life,' Alan sighed. 'He delivered my special parcel to you. I feel very bad about that. Very bad indeed.' He sat back down dejectedly. 'He was a lovely lad. A true modelling enthusiast. Rare these days.'

Phoebe had no doubt of Alan's regret, but the fact her legs were taped to an office chair was preoccupying her more, as was coughing furiously to mask the sound of the second ratchet snapping free.

Alan was too busy talking to notice. 'I might have left it there, but it troubled me terribly that Craig had died so unnecessarily. And you and your little crew got involved, which bothered me even more. You had no clue, all lathered up about internet stalkers. Just so pointless when that woman was to blame for everything, don't you see?'

'So you decided to kill her?' Phoebe slipped her engagement ring around her finger so the diamond was facing inside, its snaggy setting sharp enough to start ripping quietly at the duct tape.

'Not kill,' he corrected. 'I'd already planned it out; I was simply waiting for the opportunity to present itself. That landed in my lap when your friend Juno let slip in the pub that Penny was meeting her lover. He always came on the last train and left on the first. I couldn't wait to get home. You're right that you were my alibi; I confess I puffed a little more than usual walking back with you, and yes, I knew Bernard would ham along to get more sympathy. Very am dram, but you fell for it. You were charmingly kind.'

'My pleasure.' Phoebe felt her ring cut through the duct bands around her legs, but she couldn't reach her ankles.

'I saw her car go to the station and return, then I grabbed what tools and equipment I needed and made my way to Hartridge Holt Barn across the fields. The cat always sat on top of the bonnet of Penny's car when the engine was cooling, so he was straightforward enough to scoop into a carrier and put in the pony trailer. While Penny and her chap were occupied in the swimming pool, I removed her tow bar with a duplicate key.

'I came home and took a nap. They have an unusual but

timetabled relationship, so I'd set an alarm for 5 a.m., not that I needed it; ruddy prostate always gets me up around then. I got back to the barn just as they were setting off, stayed out of sight.

'As soon as they were gone, I put a toy bear on the driveway fashioned to look like a dead cat, then hid. When she came back, Penny drove straight over it. Didn't even notice. I panicked. I never meant to hit her so hard, but she was almost inside the house by the time I caught up with her.

'Closing the gates was a schoolboy error, but it was getting light and I was worried somebody would see. A passing runner, for example.' He gave her a wry look. 'I needed to move her into position behind the car in a wheelbarrow, then put the tow hook back on. She was unconscious but still very much alive, you must understand. I didn't mean to drive over her at all, just move the car back a bit, but I'm not good with automatics. Dropping Paddington was sloppy, too. Then I found the ruddy cat had escaped. What can I say? I'm a fogeyish amateur.'

He stepped closer, reaching down and tugging at the ratchet straps. 'Now what did I tell you about loosening these? There we go. That's better.'

Phoebe was once again trussed against the chair back.

'Still, third time lucky, they say. I hope it won't be too awful for you, my dear, but you'll understand why I can't possibly let you go now. The good news is that I have saved up lots of sleeping pills, which rather numbs the senses. They'll be taking effect right now. And I have the weights from Norma's kitchen scales. I gather death by drowning would be rather apt given your social media furore. And this time, I *do* mean death.'

* * *

Juno

'Faster!' Mil urged as Juno swerved the Jazz through Inkbury, its rear bumper clattering behind them like Just Married cans.

'I told you those cable ties wouldn't hold it,' she complained.

'You need to replace that,' said a voice in the back, where Kenneth Ken Doll was stooping to prevent his handsome head hitting the car's roof.

'Why did you even come?' Mil demanded jealously.

'I want to finish off Penny's killer!' Kenneth declared furiously.

'We just need to save Phoebe!' Juno wailed, careering into Three Bridge Lane. Ahead, orange lights were giving way to flashing red ones.

'The railway crossing!' Mil groaned.

'Drive faster!' urged Kenneth, whooping. 'Penny would have loved this!'

Juno slammed on the brakes just in time, the barriers already wobbling down as the incoming train trundled to a halt at Platform 2.

She knew from experience that when a train was in the station, it always took forever for the barriers to rise again.

'We can run over the walkway!' Mil threw himself out, sprinting through the gateway onto Platform 1.

Juno clambered out to hurry after him as fast as she was able. She could hear police sirens in the distance.

'Can you release the child locks?' wailed Kenneth, still trapped in the back of the Jazz.

But Juno had no time to spare. Mil was already leaping his way down the westbound platform steps two at a time as she panted up the eastbound ones.

But ahead of them both, springing from the incoming London train like a greyhound from a trap, was Felix.

Forced to take a breather on the top of the footbridge, already getting a stitch, Juno watched in wonder as Felix hurtled along Three Bridge Lane in the direction of Bridge Row.

The police sirens were louder now, racing along the Old London Road.

Then Juno realised the sirens were carrying on past the Inkbury turn and wailing away towards Newborough.

Below her, Mil was sprinting along the lane in Felix's wake as though he had a rugby ball under one arm and a touch-down in his sights.

Please let us not be too late, she prayed, clutching her cramping side and breaking into a run.

* * *

Phoebe

Phoebe resurfaced, gasping for air, then plunged under again, arms frantically flailing, trying to grasp something solid.

The brook was deep in places and fast flowing, its bed less uniform than the river to which it was a tributary, gouged deep in the chalk, its sides knotted with goat willow roots.

Phoebe swallowed a bellyful of rushing water as reeds wound around her wrists like stays. For a moment, she felt like giving up. It was no good; she was losing this battle.

Then she spluttered up again, desperately gulping air.

Underwater once more, sound muffled, impossible to see beyond the thick green reeds and churned-up mud and dirt from tussling on the riverbank. She tried to kick further downstream, but her ankles were still strung with duct tape, some of which had caught around a tree root. This was hopeless. Pointless.

Then, through the blur, she saw a shape, a body. She heard

the roar of effort deep in her chest as she kicked towards it, reaching out for it, ignoring the arms trying to fight her as she wrapped hers firmly around it and pulled it up with her, a super-human effort, bursting out through the surface.

'Phoebe! Baby! Christ! You're okay? You're okay!'

'Felix!' She hugged him then let go, pushing him away, looking round frantically. 'Help me! He's in here somewhere.'

'Who?'

'Alan! He's taken a load of pills and weighed himself down. I was trapped in his workshop. By the time I broke free and got out here, he must have gone under. Help me look! We can't let him drown, we just can't!'

They plunged back underwater, side by side.

A huge splash upstream made them both resurface.

But it was Mil, wading towards them, waist deep. 'It's okay! I'll get you guys out. I got this. I'll – agh!' He disappeared with a loud sploosh as the stream bed dropped away steeply.

'Look for a body!' Felix ordered when he reemerged.

They all disappeared again, working their way along the stream like bog snorkellers.

Phoebe spluttered up first, choking now, her lungs punched to nothing from inhaling so much water and silt.

'What are you doing?' Juno's voice shouted from the lane bridge.

'Looking for Alan!'

'He's just up there! I can see him from here. Leaning against that tree. Is he... dead?'

Together, they waded another fifty yards downstream, Juno jogging breathlessly down from the bridge and along the bank beside them.

Behind a thick curtain of weeping willow, Alan was propped

up against its rough bark, a tankard of beer alongside him, along with an empty pill bottle and his well-polished brown shoes neatly placed together. He appeared to have lost consciousness whilst in the middle of taking his socks off.

'He's still breathing!' Mil reported, pulling a soggy phone from his pocket. 'Damn, this is crocked. Call an ambulance, Juno.'

In the pockets of Alan's waxed jacket were the heaviest weights from his wife's kitchen scales, along with her long-nosed photograph and a leather dog lead.

'I think he's just asleep.' Felix checked his breathing and pulse. 'Deeply asleep.'

'He must have taken all the sleeping pills and then dropped off before he could wade in,' Phoebe realised, reaching down to pull his socks up for him.

'Ambulance, please!' Juno got through to the emergency services.

As she did so, a great screeching of tyres from the bridge made them all turn in time to see an orange Honda Jazz flying through the hedge and plunge bonnet-first into the brook.

'Bloody prat,' Mil groaned.

He and Felix turned to splash their way towards it, but the driver was already climbing out, bellowing: '*Where is he*? I'm going to kill him!'

The sound of police sirens was fast approaching from the direction of the village, Phoebe realised with relief.

'Who *is* that?' she asked Juno, watching as Mil and Felix barred a giant, long-haired Aquaman lookalike in black leather and denim.

'Kenneth Ken Doll,' Juno sighed. 'Now I know he's quite angry, but you have to admit, he is *gorgeous* looking.'

'Seriously?'

'It's okay, I've gone off him.' Juno shrugged, admiring Mil rugby tackling him to the ground.

Phoebe sat down beside sleeping Alan, weak legged with exhaustion, shock starting to kick in.

'There is a willow grows aslant a brook,' she quoted, wiping away an unwelcome tear. 'That shows his hoar leaves in the glassy stream.'

'Ophelia's no more.' Juno sat beside her, a warm arm wrapping round her shoulders.

Phoebe leant into the embrace, immeasurably grateful for its support, and for friendship. 'Nor are poor Craig and Penny.'

They both watched the bubbling water, lime-green reeds writhing just beneath the surface.

'In a funny way, I suppose you could say Craig looked out for Inkbury's misfits like Penny,' Juno reflected, glancing over her shoulder at Alan. 'He always made time to talk to the loners and oddballs.'

Phoebe recognised the description.

'You know, I think I might get more involved in village life,' she told Juno. 'You're quite right; I should get out more.'

'I am *so* pleased! You'll meet lots of villagers at my housewarming party. They're all dying to get to know you, the mysterious novelist from the big house. You'll wow them all.'

Phoebe managed a smile, although she wasn't sure she was ready for full-scale wowing just yet, just a quiet return to being sociable. 'Gigi's asked me to host the next book group discussion. She even suggested I choose the title for discussion.'

'Just as long as it's not Virginia Woolf,' Juno sighed. Then she watched her face closely. 'Oh, no, Phoebe, you're not really suggesting...'

'I thought George Eliot.'

'Phew!'

'*Mill on the Floss.*'

'I don't know that one.'

'Trust me, it's very good.'

There was a pause.

'Does anyone drown in it, Freddy?'

'You'll have to read it to find out.'

22

JUNO

MOTHER LOVES HOUSEWARMING PARTIES!

Tonight's the night I throw open my doors! I adore hosting parties, so this will be the first of many, I guarantee.

My fellow Village Detectives are all coming, natch, along with a bunch of new friends from the village. Also Mum and Dennis and some of the Godlington set, including Pam and the Campbells. Pam's friend Spike can't join us because of the lack of an accessible loo, which is a shame, although Pam says it's no biggie because it was getting kind of intense between them, and she's a free spirit. I admire that. #BeMorePam.

I think I may have invited too many people for one small flat, so I'm going to let people mingle in the shop as well, which Mil says my landlord Noel would probably be cool about because he had lots of parties there, although we've no way of knowing for certain because he's incommunicado in the Shetland Isles. That's the official line at least... I asked Mil what the chances are of the shop being available to lease as a going concern and he's promised he'll ask next time Noel gets in touch. I must stop letting myself get excited about the idea, but can't help imagining my gorgeous vintage bric-a-brac boutique and, just maybe, the detective agency office upstairs…

This flat is lovely, but I absolutely must find my dream doer-upper soon. Let's face it, I'm going to be a grandmother in just a few weeks. Eek! And I know Eric's being super evasive about how involved he'll be in his child's life, but I've got my heart set on having the perfect little nursery room ready just in case. It's frustrating that Phoebe's been dragging her heels finding out if the derelict lock cottage might be available from the Hartridge Estate. Instead, she suggested Alan's place will probably come up for sale soon, but who wants to live in a murderer's house?

I secretly feel a bit sorry for Alan, who was way more murderous than I think he ever intended to be. I'm very proud we worked out it was him though, even if Phoebe keeps insisting that we were lousy at it, and it's absolutely the last time the Village Detectives do anything. She's wrong, of course. I can't wait for our next case. I'll talk her round.

I am just a tad concerned that Phoebe might get a bit irritated by the fact there's a lot of Village Detectives merch in my flat, all ordered before she got so sniffy about my 'VD' logo. Hopefully she won't spot the coasters, cushions and mugs. The shower curtain's trickier to hide, but I'll try hooking it over the rail. Then there's the duvet set…

One thing I am determined to put an end to is dodgy dating apps. I joined one last week and its first suggestion was Kenneth, now calling himself Kalvin. He's still advertising himself as a hired assassin in scuba gear. Shame he didn't use that to dive into Hartridge Brook rather than Mum's car.

There's still a bit of hoo-ha about that, given he's unlicensed and uninsured. For now, the couple at Garage Drum 'n' Brakes have the Jazz and have promised to see what they can do. They've also promised to help me liberate my Mini. I've invited them to my party tonight too.

I love this village. Everyone is *so* friendly, welcoming and generous. The Barton Arms is a pub full of pals, the deli serves the world's most moreish pastries, and I have family on my doorstep, plus a bloody marvellous best mate living in the kitchen of the nearest stately home.

We could just do without anybody being murdered here for a while.

And certainly not at tonight's party…

ACKNOWLEDGEMENTS

I'm indebted to the brilliant Boldwood Books team, who are amongst the most talented and enthusiastic people I know in the business. Publishing director par excellence Isobel Akenhead steers my criminal capers with passion, infectious laughter and terrific insight. Magnificent managing editor Hayley Russell, production stars Ben Wilson and Leila Mauger, marketing gurus Claire Fenby-Warren and Marcela Torres, and sales dynamos Nia Beynon and Isabelle Flynn, are all a credit to this ground-breaking, award-winning, game-changing publisher. CEO Amanda Ridout remains my industry hero and a true champion of commercial fiction. Thank you all; I continue to count myself immensely lucky to be a 'Boldie'.

Gratitude also to my wonderful, collaborative, patient and oh-so-talented cover designer Rachel Lawston and to eagle-eyed copy ed Cecily.

Huge, heartfelt thanks to all the brilliant team at Curtis Brown, especially my powerhouse literary agent and sounding board, Sheila Crowley.

Limitless hugs as always to my family and friends, many of whom I listed excitedly and extensively in the first book of this series, and all of whom I love beyond words, so I'll write no more of them here because I'd far rather tell you in person (but probably not on social media because I'm hopeless at it, as you know).

The greatest whoop as always goes out to all of you who have read *The Poison Pen Letters*. Whether you read one book a year or one a week, I'm so grateful you made this one mine. To all those who have enjoyed my other novels and keep coming back for more, your loyalty means so much. To every one kind enough to review and recommend The Village Detectives, I can't thank you enough; it makes a world of difference. Phoebe and Juno – and I – can't wait to tackle their next case...

ABOUT THE AUTHOR

Fiona Walker is the million copy bestselling author of joyously funny romantic comedies. She has grown up alongside her readers, from nineties London party-animal to dog-walking country mum, and her knack for story-telling remains as compelling as ever. Fiona lives in Shakespeare Country with her partner, their two daughters and a menagerie of horses, dogs and other animals.

Sign up to Fiona Walker's mailing list for news, competitions and updates on future books.

Visit Fiona's Website: www.fionawalker.com
Follow Fiona on social media:

facebook.com/fionawalkeruk

x.com/fionawalkeruk

instagram.com/fionawalkeruk

pinterest.com/fionawalkerauthor

ALSO BY FIONA WALKER

Village Detectives Series

The Art of Murder

The Poison Pen Letters

Poison
& Pens

POISON & PENS IS THE HOME OF
COZY MYSTERIES SO POUR YOURSELF
A CUP OF TEA & GET SLEUTHING!

DISCOVER PAGE—TURNING NOVELS FROM
YOUR FAVOURITE AUTHORS &
MEET NEW FRIENDS

JOIN OUR
FACEBOOK GROUP

BIT.LYPOISONANDPENSFB

SIGN UP TO OUR
NEWSLETTER

BIT.LY/POISONANDPENSNEWS

Boldwood

Boldwood Books is an award-winning fiction publishing company seeking out the best stories from around the world.

Find out more at www.boldwoodbooks.com

Join our reader community for brilliant books, competitions and offers!

Follow us
@BoldwoodBooks
@TheBoldBookClub

Sign up to our weekly deals newsletter

https://bit.ly/BoldwoodBNewsletter